HEARTLAND

a novel

HEARTLAND

DAVID WILTSE

ST. MARTIN'S PRESS ✽ NEW YORK

Wil

This is a work of fiction.
All characters and events portrayed in this novel
are either fictitious or are used fictitiously.

HEARTLAND. Copyright © 2001 by David Wiltse. All rights reserved.
Printed in the United States of America. No part of this book may
be used or reproduced in any manner whatsoever without written
permission except in the case of brief quotations embodied in
critical articles or reviews. For information, address St. Martin's
Press, 175 Fifth Avenue, New York, N.Y. 10010.

www.stmartins.com

BOOK DESIGN BY ELLEN CIPRIANO

LIBRARY OF CONGRESS CATALOGING-IN-PUBLICATION DATA
Wiltse, David.
    Heartland: a novel/David Wiltse.—1st ed.
        p. cm.
    ISBN 0-312-26957-9
        1. Secret service—Fiction.   2. Conspiracies—Fiction.
        3. Nebraska—Fiction.   I. Title.

PS3573.I478 H43 2001
813'.54—dc21   00-045966

First Edition: March 2001

10 9 8 7 6 5 4 3 2 1

The creative imagination is a happy wanderer that ends up leagues and dreams away from where it started, but it always needs a point from which to begin. In this case that beginning was with Billy Mimnaugh—that wild colonial boy—and the girl with Bette Davis eyes—a very tame wild woman. And also with Gib and Kathy and Naomi and Jane and Pat and Harry and Jim and Dave and Lipp, and the whole class of 1958. And, of course, my hometown, which I have now, for the second time, unjustly maligned in print.

HEARTLAND

CHAPTER ONE

Minneapolis

S ome people trail squalor behind them," Walter Matuzak was saying, eyeing the building with disgust. A massive, burly man, he
had the sensibilities of a Dutch housewife, a strange fastidious-
ness, Billy thought, in a man who used his bulk like a battering ram
even in casual conversation.

"Like a tail," Matuzak continued, rapping on the basement door,
"swish, swish, everything was okay, these assholes walk by and fucking
chaos. Like one of those dogs, what do you call them, setters? Tail
sticking out there like it's on a wire, swish, bang, knock everything out
of place."

He had a certain point, thought Billy Tree, although he questioned

1

the dog analogy. How else to explain a hovel like this in a town as clean and spread-out as Minneapolis? Billy saw movement behind a curtain, a suspicious eye peering past cloth that had once been white and now looked as if it were used to polish shoes.

"He's in there, wondering what kind of monster is banging on his door," Billy said.

"I know the asshole's in there," Matuzak said, hitting the door with the side of his fist. "I can smell him."

It was their fifth on-site investigation of the day with two more to go before calling it quits and Matuzak, never a patient man, was just one more aggravation away from fuming. The President's impending visit had the city aswarm with law enforcement people like an anthill disturbed by a careless boot.

"Who is it?" a voice asked from the other side of the door.

"Federal agents, Mr. Posner," Billy said hastily to forestall Matuzak's angry growl. The time to frighten a subject was after you were inside, not while he could still bolt out the back way. "We just want to ask you a few questions."

"Are you the IRS?"

"No, sir, nothing like that. We're Secret Service. You're not in any trouble. This won't take but a few minutes."

"Just a second."

"Probably went to tidy up," Matuzak said. "Do the vacuum, a little light dusting."

"Mustn't judge a man by his housekeeping, Walter."

"Man chooses to live in an outhouse, tells you something about his character, doesn't it?"

"Or the state of his bowels. Maybe he can't help it."

"Oh, please. No sociology. What do you want to bet the inside is covered with grime you'd have to chip off with a chisel?"

"What do you suppose D.O.Y. stands for?" Billy asked, changing the subject, holding the copy of Posner's letter. Matuzak took the plastic-covered letter between finger and thumb as if it were contaminated. It was signed "A. Posner, D.O.Y."

"Dork of the Year," Matuzak offered.

"Digital Yank Off."

"Dickweed Or Yams," Matuzak said, pounding the door again.

"That's probably it. Why didn't I think of it?"

The door opened and a pasty face peered at them through blood-shot eyes. Billy edged in front of Matuzak and showed his badge.

"A. Posner?"

The man blinked like a mole, blinded by the sun.

"Are you A. Posner, sir? I'm agent Billy Tree of the United States Secret Service."

The man continued to stare at them as if stupefied.

"You want to let us in?" Matuzak growled.

Billy smiled at the man, engulfing him in a warmth that was as sudden as it was insincere. "Won't take a minute."

The man responded by smiling back, revealing as bad a set of teeth as Billy had ever seen, a mouth overcrowded with canines that wrestled and overstepped one another like a snarl of barbed wire. Billy felt a momentary surge of sympathy for the man, forced to go through life like that in the land of orthodontia. Not hard to imagine the cruelty of his childhood.

Posner stepped back, admitting the agents.

Matuzak muttered under his breath, "Charming Billy." Under his breath or not, it was clearly audible. Posner turned, temporarily puzzled, thinking he had been addressed.

"I don't have to talk to you, do I?" Posner asked, deferentially. Billy detected the slight foreign accent, which would account for the teeth.

Matuzak stepped closer to the man, almost toe-to-toe. He was half a head taller and twice his size. "What's the problem?"

"No, I was just . . . no problem." The man smiled again. Billy noticed Matuzak wince at the sight of his teeth.

The room offered no signs of dementia, which was what agents looked for first. No pictures of the President used for a dartboard—it was surprising how often they saw that. No swastikas on the wall, no instruments of torture. The room was grubby, the walls stained with watermarks, the furnishings cheap and sparse, but the place had its own sense of order. An amazing number of the angry letter writers lived in a litter of pizza boxes and overflowing ashtrays.

Matuzak had moved behind Posner. He ran a finger across a tabletop as if he wore a white glove and held it up behind the man's back, disgustedly and triumphantly, for Billy to see. Posner had failed Walter's test of character.

"We thought we might have a chat about this," Billy said, holding out the copy of the letter Posner had written.

"Did the President read it?" Posner asked, pride of authorship lighting his face.

"No, *we* read it," said Matuzak. He continued to search the room, his nose aloft, as if seeking the source of an unsavory smell.

"It's a federal offense to threaten the President of the United States, Mr. Posner," Billy said. He moved toward a collapsible card table that served Posner as a writing desk. The computer atop it looked as if it had been recovered from the dump.

"Threaten? I didn't really threat . . ."

Matuzak took the letter from Billy and waggled it in front of Posner's face like a preacher with proof of sin.

" 'Maximum retribution,' " Matuzak quoted. "You're offering the President of the United States 'maximum retribution,' Dickweed. What is that if not a threat?"

"I can explain all this," Posner said, sounding as if he might burst into tears. Matuzak's impression of barely suppressed fury often had that effect. Billy did not think he'd ever seen Matuzak really dangerously angry, but he did a wonderful imitation.

"That would be very good if you explained it, Mr. Posner," Billy said. "We don't want to trouble you any more than necessary, so if you could just help us to understand . . ."

Billy glanced at the computer screen. Posner was on the Web, some news group talking about infrastructures. Every malcontent in the country seemed to live on the Internet.

Posner was nodding his head vigorously, eager to oblige.

Matuzak lowered his face to Posner's level, moving as slowly as a derrick easing down a heavy load.

"That would be real nice, Dickweed, if you would help us to understand."

"I can show you in my bedroom?"

"You want to take me to your bedroom, then?" Matuzak growled with exaggerated patience as if speaking to a half-wit.

"I can show you in here," Posner said, preceding Matuzak into a narrow hallway leading toward the bedroom and the bathroom.

"You like yams, do you?" Matuzak asked, following him.

"Yams?"

Billy heard Posner's baffled reply from the hallway.

"You eat a lot of yams, Dickweed?"

With the two of them out of the room, Billy looked more carefully at the computer screen. Politics. The kind of feverish polemic favored by the extremist fringe, everything, even the phrasing seeming slightly askew. . . . Billy saw the words "Defenders of Yisrael." D.O.Y.?

Posner stood in the hallway again.

"Could you come in, please?" Posner sounded slightly distressed, looked embarrassed. He withdrew into the bedroom and Billy stepped into the hallway.

The floor was cracked linoleum, crumbling with age. Just before he reached the bedroom door Billy heard a gurgling sound as if the toilet plumbing were having problems.

Matuzak was dancing next to the bed, his toes gliding just inches off the floor. It did not seem possible, a grown man off the ground with no visible means of support, no ropes, no strings. It flashed through Billy's mind that Matuzak and Posner, who stood on the bed just behind Matuzak now, were in collusion in some secretly con-trived conjurer's act of levitation. It took Billy a moment to notice the big man's purple face, the eyes popping, the mouth open and emitting the gasps of strangulation that Billy had thought was plumbing, another moment to process the filament-thin piano wire running through a metal ring secured on the ceiling, the loop around Matuzak's neck, the crimson line across the agent's throat where the wire had already sunk deep beneath the flesh with the force of Matuzak's weight and bit deeper still with each spastic contortion of the dying man, threatening to decapitate him before it suffocated him. Matuzak's hands clawed desperately at the wire, the skin of his throat was torn and bleeding from the action of his own frenzied fingernails, and his elbows flapped as if attempting to fly, to elevate, to lift himself above the weight of his body that was killing him.

Behind the agent's body, like a puppeteer with his dying mario-nette, stood Posner. He smiled, his teeth looking now like a shark's mouth, as he pointed Matuzak's service automatic at the heart of Billy Tree.

Billy took a step backward for balance, as if the grotesquerie of Walter dancing by the neck had jolted his equilibrium. He was stunned, but not yet fearful, not at that point. But as he recoiled his foot caught in a crack of the linoleum and he fell. His right elbow broke the fall and the force of it left his arm temporarily paralyzed and useless. Posner leaned around Walter's jigging bulk, aiming the automatic at Billy, jerking it and jerking it. Unfamiliar with weapons, Posner had neglected to remove the safety, and clawed at it now, trying to fire the gun. Lying on the floor, Billy struggled to make his disabled right arm behave his will and retrieve his own weapon from the shoulder holster. His arm flopped on his chest like a grounded fish, a useless, pointless, defenseless thing. Posner finally found the safety, removed it, and aimed again at Billy.

The room seemed to be filled with noise, solid with it, as if they moved and breathed in a medium of sound. Matuzak gasped and choked and gargled his final breaths, Posner howled like an animal and Billy added his own frantic keenings to the mix. He knew then, as his numbed fingers flapped ineffectually against the lapel of his jacket, seeming miles away from his weapon, that he was going to be killed.

"No, no!" he said at first, as if Posner could be forestalled by a simple command, then his nerve broke, he held up his left hand to catch the bullet, and he pleaded for his life. "Please, don't! Please! Don't!"

The first shot struck Billy in the right femur, shattering the bone. Billy felt no pain, just an enormous blow, as if he had been hit with a sledgehammer. He was completely stunned for a moment, unable to think, feeling he had been pole-axed in the head in addition to the leg, and he watched Posner aim again, leveling at his chest, but was unable to react, unable to move, caught in the glue of slow-motion dreaming. Posner was going to kill him in a fog, in time-arrested movement, and Billy was going to die with cinematic surreality, tumbling languidly into death as a stunned ox in an abattoir sinks to its knees.

But Matuzak's moving body nudged Posner's arm as he fired again. The bullet struck the floor beside Billy's head with a deafening roar, as if it had been detonated inside his eardrum. Shards of linoleum and underlying wood splintered into the side of Billy's face, and these he felt. The pain of the splinters awoke him, snapped him from the stupor inflicted by the blow to his leg, and Billy was suddenly overcome with fear. Posner aimed once more.

"Oh, please, mister," he said, reverting in an instant to a terrified child. "Please, no!"

And then Billy felt himself let go, felt his sphincter fail, felt the hot, watery putrefaction spill forth from his body.

Posner fired again, hitting Billy in the chest.

"Oh, God, mister, please. No more. No more."

Billy begging, pleading, sniveling like a child, waiting for the shot, praying for his life as if Avi Posner was the Virgin herself and not a half-mad fanatic with the teeth of a beast and Matuzak's Smith & Wesson.

He was going to die now, he knew. There was no hope of crawling away, no way to avoid the bullets. Posner would kill him piecemeal, pumping badly aimed shots into him until one of them found a lethal target. He could see Posner's arm extended past the screen of Matuzak's body, half of Posner's head peering round, taking aim; he saw Posner's teeth, lips peeled back as he howled his murderous delight.

Without his knowing it, Billy's arm regained its ability to move. Without feeling it he grabbed his weapon from its holster under his left arm. Walter twisted violently, swinging abruptly in front of Posner, blocking his aim.

Billy fired at the part of Posner he could see, then fired again and again, the bullets slapping into Matuzak's bulk with the thump of a bat against a bag of wheat. The agent's body recoiled, swinging backward into Posner, then slowly forward, twisting at the same time. Billy caught a full glimpse of Posner, teeth still bared but his eyes now puzzled. Billy emptied the clip, firing through Matuzak to where he thought Posner's trunk must be.

When the clip was empty Billy put down the gun, waiting to be killed. Matuzak's backward sway was arrested and suddenly the agent's body vaulted forward, arms flying to the side with the momentum, like a scarecrow sprung to life, animated by the devil. Posner collapsed to the floor beneath Matuzak, his T-shirt speckled with red eruptions. Matuzak's body swung back again, then fell atop Posner as the added gravity of the arc snapped the wire.

For a moment Billy felt nothing, thought nothing, saw nothing but an ant walking upside down on the ceiling. Then the pain and the horror slammed into him simultaneously and he began to scream.

*　　*　　*

It was not the noise of the shooting that Billy remembered most about the Incident, not the holes blown in his body, not the dancing toes of Walter Matuzak doing the ballet in midair—giving a new meaning to "light-footed"—not even the teeth of his assassin, though he remembered all that, woke up sweating from dreams of all that. Nor was it the pain. Oddly, even at the time, even when the bullets ripped into him, it was not the pain that troubled him most. The thing about his murder that most haunted Billy was his loss of dignity. At least loss of dignity was one way to put it. As if his futile posturing effort to stop the nurse from removing his pants, flailing to keep her hands from his belt, actually stabbing himself to prevent the scissors from slicing his trouser leg, were all in defense of dignity. Modest, the emergency room workers said indulgently, commenting, in the way they had, as if he weren't consciously there, as if he were just a collection of wounds and not a half-crazed man trying weakly to keep his pants on so no one could see what was in there. And Billy vainly pushing away the nurse until two of the larger orderlies held him gently but persuasively by the shoulders, pressing him down onto the gurney while the others struggled to save his life, dignity and modesty be damned.

As if he had any dignity left at that point. As if he hadn't squandered it all lying on the floor while Posner shot him again and again.

It wasn't really his murder, of course, even though Billy thought of it in those terms at first. He just wished it had been.

He didn't care about the men, the men could get fucked, the lot of them, but his problem with the nurses was they knew, they all knew. He was certain it ran through the hospital, the word on Billy Tree, virulent as the new TB, spread by that first emergency room attendant, the one who cut off his pants and found his dishonor tracked down his leg, stinking, runny, disgraceful.

He couldn't face them, the many women of the ward who fed him, cleaned him, nurtured him like a baby, first battled to keep him alive and then to make him strong and whole, couldn't meet their eyes when they tended him with their unflagging, impersonal good spirits. And this from Billy Tree who had spent his life talking to the girls. A flirt, some said; a charmer, according to others, putting a better face on it. Kissed by the blarney, they would have said in the old days. Full of shit, said the enemies. Charming Billy. And he couldn't look at the ladies, knowing they knew what they knew.

We don't back down!" Uncle Sean roaring in his face, a full grown man tossing it like a dare at the eight-year-old Billy. "The Irish don't back away from a fight. We don't need to be starting them, mind, but we never back away. Famous for it." Sean, face red as a boil, looking always just this side of exploding from so much blood pounding away in his cheeks and nose, pale tufts of hair sprouting from his flaming ears like stands of wild prairie grass.

"Famous for it." Then looking round for agreement and the others chiming in on cue.

"Tough as old shoe leather, the Irish."

"A proud people."

"You never show them your back unless they're lying on theirs, Billy." This from Uncle Tim Wittrock, about as Irish as the rooster they were eating for dinner, and not a great deal bigger. "Timmy bites them on the kneecaps," the others said, announcing it with pride. A real scrapper, Tim. Hard-nosed and feisty, German-American by genealogy, Irish by marriage. An honorary Mick. If it was an honor, Billy thought.

Irish coming out the ears when the family got together, everyone outdoing himself in his Irishness as if every reunion was Saint Pat's Day in school and you'd get a pinch—or an unanswerable shot in the arm from the other boys—if you were caught not wearing green. Gaelic bonhomie and assertiveness slopping over as if it were the holiday of the great snake charmer Patrick himself and they'd already passed round the first fifth of whiskey and the second six-pack—though the sauce only amplified the feelings, it didn't initiate them. The intermarried Swedes and Germans straining to find some drop of wayward Celtic blood as others elsewhere might lay claim to "one thirty-second Cherokee," a badge of exotica and merit, as if it mattered, as if anyone gave a damn—which a lot of them seemed to, the older ones, although Billy was never sure how much was pride and how much bluster and how much simple habit.

"You never back down, boy!" Sean again, with Billy's father, Lord James, nodding agreement and brandishing his fist in the background.

"Listen to your uncle," says Lord Jimmy Tree, drunk as a lord again—hence the nickname, the man himself being about as noble as the morning after, checking the discarded cans for just a taste of the rabid dog that bit him.

Sean, encouraged, egged on by the others, growing more and more belligerent, leaning ever closer as if the young Billy were not only deaf but resisting.

"You never back down. You never give up." Face so aflame Billy thought to see the prairie grass in his ears ignite.

"Never say 'uncle,' never give the bastards an inch!" This from another kinsman, what matter who, they all of them took the party line at times like this. Tough as nails, we are. Tough as stone, tough as an old steer, tough as death itself. Our clan is like your snapping turtle, boy, once he gets his grip on you, you have to cut his head off to get free.

"It's what made us what we are!" Sean again. Every time, every meeting, every get-together.

And just what the fuck are we? Billy yearned to ask in later years, but by then the damage was done. He was one of them. Tough as tough. Never a quitter in all the world. Have to cut his head off first, you would.

They made a fuss of him, of course, declared him a hero even as he was on the surgeon's table, issued a medal while he was still woozy from anesthetic, rushed the District Director over to pin it on his chest before he could speak straight, half drooling his denials of heroism. There was even some talk of the President himself coming by, though nothing came of that.

A day later the Deputy Director came to call, a singular honor that called for a photo op as the Director, a whey-faced politician, reattached the medal to Billy's hospital smock as if for the first time.

"Was Walter alive when I shot him?" Billy asked, finding control of his tongue at last.

"Walter?"

An aide whispered in the Director's ear.

"Agent Matuzak." The Director nodded, having lost the gist of the question. "A hero."

"Was he alive or dead when I shot him? I think he moved of his own accord just before I shot."

"We prefer to assume he was dead," said the Director.

"Did I kill him, or not?"

"We prefer to assume he was dead. . . . We in the Service are immensely proud of the valor you have displayed in defense of the President of the United States . . ."

"I killed my partner to save my ass," Billy said.

"An agent died in defense of his partner. It is just this sort of heroic action . . ."

"I shit myself," Billy interrupted.

The Deputy Director looked at his watch. "Does this man need medication?"

Three days later, still in his hospital bed, the tubes still filling and draining him as if he were artificial life maintained in a chemical retort, Billy resigned from the Secret Service.

He was patched, seamed, and hemmed, flushed with antibiotics, pumped with drugs and painkillers, and still he failed to thrive. Finally they put him in a private ambulance and sent Billy Tree home, happy to do it, claiming it was the gift of a grateful nation, but Billy knew they were glad to see the last of him after his weeks in the hospital, his subversive murmurings causing unrest among his visitors.

They called it home. "Sending you home, Billy. Back to your people, loving arms, bosom of the family, good for the body, good for the soul." But Billy didn't call it home; Falls City, Nebraska, was simply were he grew up, a scratch on the Great Plains with a population of a mere five thousand people, and at that still the largest town for fifty miles or more in any direction through the corn and wheat and soybeans. He had left it without a backward glance; it hadn't been home for years. The Service had filled that space for him for a decade and a half, whatever government-provided accommodation he found himself in, whatever city needed to be screened for malcontents, radicals, and psychos serving well enough for Billy Tree as a temporary base, a place to hang his hat and take his women and ply his curious trade.

Best to get this incident behind you, the government shrink had counseled. It seems very large to you right now—holes in his body, a rip in the seam of his soul, two dead men, a friend betrayed, a code dishonored; yes, it seems large, Billy thought—but given time, given the placid, familiar surroundings of home, you'll gain a new perspective, blah-blah. After the second visit, Billy threw the shrink out. The priest he wouldn't admit in the first place. What did he need with a confessor when he was telling every passing stranger what he had done? Billy needed no urging to unburden himself, he couldn't shut up, his sense of guilt spilling from him as if he were the Ancient Mariner, bent on talking forever. The burden grew no lighter.

He had no wife so they dumped Billy on poor Kath, as if she had nothing to do besides tend to the wandering boy. What with all the experience of her sometimes husband, the on-again-off-again, now-you-see-him, now-you-don't Stuart Sime, maybe they were right. Peripatetic Stu, gone for a year or two, and Kath would take him back, sober him up and pat his head and make a place for him in her bed as if she had no calendar, no memory, not a grudging bone in her body. Maybe she was the one to take in Billy after all. Saint Kath, beautiful, forgiving little sister.

So they wrapped him up and shipped him home to Falls City like a Christmas gift. The relatives were overjoyed and they came aswarming in the first few days to see what the government had sent.

"A hero. A natural hero, bless his soul," said Uncle Sean, "and didn't I always tell you he had the stuff?"

"I had the stuffing shot out of me," Billy said, but no one attended him. They stopped listening the moment they saw the medal. Sean had found it somehow and brandished it over his head as if it were his own.

"We're so proud of you," said the aunts. The men could not bring themselves to that kind of sentimentality, so they showed their pride by clapping him on the shoulder, waving clenched fists and upright thumbs in front of his nose. Several of them winked, hoping to transmit all of their emotion in the blink of an eye. And then, the confrontation over, they proceeded to discuss him as if he wasn't there.

"I shit myself and shot my partner," Billy said, but they took the disclaimer as further proof of heroism.

When they filed out, each stopping with a word for Kath as if she were the widow and they just leaving from a wake, they confided that

Billy was not quite himself, implying that it was perhaps Kath's fault, that she had somehow failed to notice this dip in his mood. He seemed a little low, a little down, a little off his feed.

"He needs a bit of time," she told them, and they nodded sagely at the recognized wisdom of this. Time was a grand healer, after all, famous for its medicinal uses. They should have realized that Kath was on the job. Good as her mother, sweet Annie Keefe, martyr and angel, wife to Lord James. They were a little ashamed for having doubted her. As they drove home together, the men talked of his valor, hinting, after the first gush, that it was nothing more than they themselves would have done in similar circumstances. The women ignored the posturings as they had long since learned to do and voiced concerns about his spirits and the men told them not to worry, Kath was on the case and Billy was as resilient as he was brave. He was one of them, after all. Not an ounce of quit in any of them. The women agreed this was all true and continued to worry in silence.

"There's no point in talking to them like that," Kath said. "They don't want to hear what you think you did wrong. They want a hero. It makes them feel better about themselves. Best just to shut up about it."

"What I *think* I did wrong?"

"You're alive, aren't you, Bill? How wrong could it have been?"

"I'm not quite sure how to quantify it for you. How deep is the ocean, how high is the sky?"

"The man was killing you, Billy. You did what you did, and who can blame you for any of it? What else could you do?"

"Well, let's see. With one perfectly aimed shot I could have severed the wire that was holding Walter up, and when he was out of the way . . ."

"There's a load of crap, Billy. Even you can smell it."

"It's all crapola, Kath. Don't think I don't know that. The shame, the guilt, the whole macho code of courage, it's all crap, I've realized that for years. You don't measure a man by how he does in a fight. That's just Uncle Sean and the others demonstrating how big their balls are, like a herd of bulls at an auction, I know that. It's just shit stacked to the ceiling."

"So why are you acting like such an idiot about it if you don't believe in it?"

"I said it's crap, Kath. I never said I didn't believe in it."

CHAPTER TWO

Falls City, Nebraska

The cherry red truck crept along the main street of Falls City like a mobile danger signal. Thom Cohan was reminded of certain venomous reptiles and amphibians that broadcast their peril with similar bright colors, but he was caught on the sidewalk, there was no place to quietly disappear and he was too proud to be seen obviously avoiding the confrontation that he was certain would come. If he started running from vermin, when would he stop?

The town shopping street was never filled except on parade days and the truck slid into a parking spot a few paces in front of Cohan like a serpent finding its hole. Sandy Metzger stood up in the bed of the pickup, grinning already, his countenance a pudding of fiery spots, his head swathed in a blue bandanna like a pirate.

"Why it's Thhhom!" he called, accentuating the silent "h" in Cohan's name. "What a piece of luck."

Cohan took a few more steps, hoping briefly to walk away from the trouble, but he quickly realized that trouble would only pursue him down the street. He turned and faced young Sandy Metzger. Having any of the Metzgers behind his back made him uneasy.

"Hello, Sandy."

"Well, hello, Thhhom. How's it hanging?"

Sandy dropped from the bed of the truck with the resilient knees of a fifteen-year-old and hurried in front of Cohan. He was not tall, but bulky and firm as a barrel with the hard muscles of a laborer supplemented by weight training. Steroids, too, Cohan speculated, eroding the little brain and boosting the testosterone to lethal levels. If he continued to grow, he would be as big as his father who sat in the driver's seat, regarding Cohan as dispassionately as if he were something helpless cornered by a cat.

"How the hell are you, Dr. Cohen?" Sandy extended his hand, his face fairly ripped apart with a false smile.

"Co-*han*." Cohan ignored Sandy's hand.

"How's your ass, teach?"

"Now why would you be interested in my ass, Sandy?" Cohan asked.

The boy's smile vanished and he put his hands on his hips, shifting his weight from foot to foot. The analogy with a serpent was complete, Cohan thought. He looks just like a cobra about to strike, right down to the little eyes and the puffed-out hooded neck.

"Ask him he's still a Hebrew," said Curtis Metzger. One massive bare-sleeved arm rode outside the open window at all times, as if he were holding the door closed with it. A skull with a WWII German helmet was picked out in blue and red ink on his bicep.

"You still a Hebrew?" Sandy asked.

Cohan was of Irish descent, long since completely Americanized, but he refused to play their game. Denial gave them legitimacy, he thought. Faced with half-witted bigots, he would not deny being Jewish or African-American or Asian or any other thing they felt they had the right to despise.

"Are you returning to high school in September?" Cohan asked.

"You going to let me back in?"

Cohan heard the surprise and hope in Sandy's voice. Maybe the boy wasn't as completely lost as Cohan had thought.

"Fuck high school," said Curtis Metzger from the truck, speaking without emphasis as if merely stating a known fact.

The boy may not be lost, but the father is, Cohan thought.

"Not your best idea," said Cohan.

"No, that ain't my best idea." Metzger emerged from the truck and moved his huge frame to the sidewalk. "You want to know my best idea, you dingleberry Jew?"

Cohan didn't trust himself to answer. Anger rippled beneath the surface of this enormous man like something wild caged beneath his skin, and the occasional placidity of his manner did nothing to conceal it. Hatred without overt passion seemed to Cohan to be the most dangerous of all.

Metzger moved to stand toe-to-toe with Cohan. The smaller man involuntarily took a step backward, cursing himself for it. There seemed to be no one else on the street, no one to witness yet another act of intimidation by the Metzgers. Sandy took a position at Cohan's side, grinning widely again.

"My best idea would be to get rid of all the Hebrews, principal Cohen. Starting right about where I'm standing."

"Co-*han*."

"Goldberg," Metzger said, as if correcting his pronunciation.

"You might want to shift some of your focus to your son's education, Mr. Metzger."

"I might want to shift some of my focus to you."

"Shit your focus on him," Sandy contributed.

"Wouldn't need to worry about his education if you hadn't kicked him out of school, Cohen."

"I suspended him. He was a disruptive influence. He can get back in for the new term. He knows that. You know that. It was a necessary disciplinary action."

"You saying he needs discipline?"

"All children do," said Cohan.

Metzger pulled a leather work glove from his belt and tugged it on. "Stand up here," he ordered.

Sandy winced.

"I said stand up here, damn it," Metzger said.

"What are you doing?" Cohan asked.

Metzger lifted his gloved fist as slow as a sledgehammer. Cohan grabbed the man's arm.

"For God's sake . . ."

Metzger shrugged him off. "You want some, too? You got to get in line."

"No, Pappa," Sandy said.

"I said *stand*." Metzger brought his fist down against Sandy's temple. The boy crumpled, grasping at the parking meter to keep himself from falling all the way to the ground. The bandanna sagged over one eye.

"You monster," Cohan choked.

"There's your discipline."

Cohan tried to help Sandy to his feet but the boy shrugged him off and rose of his own accord, one hand still on the parking meter to steady himself, pushing at the bandanna with the other. His eyes teared and his nose was running but he glared at Cohan with contempt.

"Don't need nothing from you."

Cohan turned again to Metzger, who casually drew the glove from his hand and tucked it back in his belt. "Are you out of your mind? This boy is a minor. That's child abuse."

"He can't take that, he ain't got much chance in life."

"I could report you to the police."

"You could shit, too."

"You can't do this to people. To a child."

"What do *you* know?" Metzger asked.

"Yeah, what do *you* know?" Sandy added. "Shit storm's coming. Where you going to hide, Thhhom?"

"Consider yourself reported," Cohan said. He stepped around Metzger and couldn't quite conceal his relief when the big man did not try to stop him.

"Better find a hidey-hole," Sandy said.

Cohan walked a few yards and turned into the first doorway, as if that had been his destination all along. He found himself in a quasi-pharmacy that sold more perfume, greeting cards, and last-minute gifts than medicine. For a moment he looked blankly around the shop, trying to control his breathing, then stared vacantly at the rack of birthday messages that seemed to mock him with their intimations of jocular goodwill. It appeared at that moment a world singularly lacking in goodwill. Cohan's limbs continued to tremble for several minutes.

Metzger's cherry red pickup pulled to the curb and Joan Blanchard came out of the house and sat on the top porch step. A large splinter from the porch prodded her in the thigh but she refused to move, accepting it as punishment for giving Duane Blanchard any time at all, even from a distance. She should have waited in the house for Duane to release their son from his weekend visit and not have to look at him at all—and not give him the satisfaction of being looked at.

The truck was designed by the manufacturer to evoke nostalgia, formed with a modern version of the plump, caressable, pampered curves of the early 1950s, and Duane stood with his hand along the fender as if it were a woman's hip. Yet *another* woman's hip. As if Metzger's truck were one more conquest and he wanted Joan to admire him for it like all the others. Duane held the curious belief that every- thing he did was to be applauded, and he stood there every time, proud of himself, looking for approval as much after disasters as victories, dropping his battle scars or his latest infidelity on the doorstep with equal triumph, like a cat with a dead bird.

"Hey, Mom," Will called, waving and rising from the bed of the pickup, his face lighted with spontaneous happiness. Joan thrilled to see him like that, still glad to see his mother, still able to forget, if only for a time, the masculine demands of taciturnity. In another moment he would slide back into his teenaged sullenness, but at least Joan glimpsed briefly the little boy she loved. It was warming to know that the essential Will was still somewhere within that gangle of adolescent limbs. She lifted her hand in return.

Will turned and exchanged an elaborate handshake with Sandy Metzger. As if they were in a secret society, Joan thought. Or street kids, here, surrounded for five hundred miles by farmland. Ghetto boys among the corn and soybeans. Will wore his jeans as low on his hips as he could push them without resorting to suspenders, but she could see that they were still too short. Something more he needed, something more to buy for a boy growing like a weed. She noticed a darkening welt on Sandy's face and winced with realization of how it got there. Curtis Metzger was little more than a dark bulk within the cab, but she had seen as much of him as she ever cared to.

Will vaulted to the ground and waved negligently at his father as he started for the house. Duane grabbed his arm and Joan felt herself freeze. How often had he done it to her, just like that? Let her think she was past him, safe for the moment, free, then the last-second clutch at her arm, demonstrating his control. She would go when he allowed her to go, and not before. Duane never let anything pass freely, not his wife, not his child, not a perceived challenge, not a final word. There was a fear in her heart that one time Duane would fail to release their son entirely, that he would keep him by his side, cleave to him in defiance of the courts and the law—and then disappear. Vanish like all the other noncustodial parents in the country, kidnaping their own children, leaving frantic mothers to grieve and search in vain. . . . Not that Duane was likely ever to flee from trouble. He loved it too much to avoid it.

Duane pulled Will to him and spoke softly. Joan watched the happiness drain from her son's face. When Duane was finished, he shoved Will away, opening his hand and holding the pose as if he had just flicked something unpleasant from his fingers. The gesture was so disdainful that Joan thought of killing her ex-husband. It was not the first time. She rose and put her hand on Will's shoulder as he passed but he shrugged her off.

"He wants you to go talk to him," Will muttered.

"If he wants to talk, he can come to me," Joan said.

"He says he can't. Restraining order." Will hurried into the house. Joan turned to follow.

"I hear Billy's back in town," Duane said, raising his voice just enough to carry the distance. Saying just enough to stop her.

"Who?"

"Oh, who. Like you didn't know."

"Who?"

"Who do you think?"

"I don't need riddles, Duane."

"Billy Tree," said Duane.

Joan knew, of course. News spread like contagion in Falls City. In a town in which a citizen's vacation to the Grand Canyon merited an article in the local paper and the population was marginally decreased every year by the permanent exodus of 80 percent of the high school graduates, the return of the native was the information equivalent of a bumper crop. Everyone knew about it. And Billy Tree was not just any native son, either, hadn't been before he left and certainly wasn't now when he came back, the conquering hero, bedecked with medals and presidential bunting.

Joan let Duane talk on, giving him the pleasure of thinking he had known first. It did not do to allow Duane to see that she was interested, not in anything, certainly not in any man.

"Got himself shot up, but I guess he'll live. . . . Could have used some more shooting, apparently." Curtis Metzger's guffaw sounded from the cab. After a moment, Sandy joined in uncertainly.

"Why'd he come back here?"

"Well, I don't know, Joan. Thought I'd leave it to you to find that out. Might want you to nurse him."

"Good-bye, Duane."

Joan entered her house. With perfect timing, Duane had his last word before she was out of earshot.

"He's at his sister's," he said.

Will was at the refrigerator. Always hungry, always thirsty, devouring things as if they were what ailed him and he ate them for revenge, Joan thought.

"I asked you to stop hanging around with Sandy Metzger," she said, trying to keep her voice calm. She didn't want to fight with him as soon as he returned, but it seemed inevitable. It was as if he carried the smell of his father on his body after a visit and it took days for it to wear off.

Will shrugged. "Dad goes to visit Mr. Metzger. Sandy's there. He's not so bad."

"Does he still have the swastikas on his wall?"

"He doesn't mean anything by it."

"It's impossible to not mean anything by a swastika. It *screams* meaning."

"Not to Sandy," Will said. He took an armload of food and sat in front of the television.

"I'm going to school," she said.

"School doesn't start until next week."

"For you. For us, it starts now. When I come back, I want to talk about you and the Metzgers and your father."

"You going to see old principal Thhhom Cohan there?"

"What does that tone of voice mean?"

"Nothing."

"I mean apart from the obvious disrespect intended. What do you have against Principal Cohan?"

"Nothing."

"He's a good educator and a good man."

"Okay, if you say so."

"Who says otherwise? . . . Has your dad been bad-mouthing him again?"

"Well, is it true?"

"What?"

"What Dad says about you and him."

Joan felt herself color. If there was any way to defeat Duane's innuendos, she had never discovered it. Each new knowing smirk, each raised eyebrow had its intended effect upon her, and the further off the mark they were, the more difficult to squelch. Not that the suggestion of a relationship between her and Thom Cohan was that far off the mark.

"I don't know if it's true, but coming from your father the chances are that it's not. What does he say?"

"I don't want to talk about it," Will said.

"Then why did you bring it up?"

Will busied himself with food. So young, she thought. So confused. And why not? Who wasn't, these days?

"You better tell him to watch out, is all," Will said.

"What does that mean?"

"Sandy says if he reports any of that child abuse junk, he's going to clean his clock."

"Sandy sounds like his father, which is not a compliment. I want you to stay away from those people."

"They're Dad's friends, I can't do anything about it."

"Of course you can."

"What am I supposed to do? Say, 'Oh, Dad, don't take me over there, my momma says they're bad people.'"

"Something like that might do it," she said, knowing it would only delight Duane to thwart her wishes. "Never mind. I'll talk to your father about it."

As she left the house, Will spoke to her again. How like his father, she thought. Knowing just how to arrest her, giving her just enough to catch her attention, and usually at the wrong time.

"Seriously, Mom. You better warn Mr. Cohan. Sandy isn't kidding."

"Sandy Metzger is an idiot."

"Yeah. So? You told me yourself they're dangerous."

"He's just talking," Joan said. "Just sounding tough for his father."

"I know. . . . But his father wasn't around."

Joan hesitated for a moment outside her house. Her normal route to the high school was a fifteen-minute walk. If she went left instead of right, just for variety, it would take her another five minutes—and lead her past Kath Tree's house. It had been a long time since she had taken the alternate route. She turned left—just for variety. As she walked she thought of Duane Blanchard as a younger man, corn dust in his hair, wheat chaff on his clothes, smelling always of dry grain and the silo where he worked . . . but what a good-looking man. They had married for passion, hers as well as his. Hers had died first in bed, victim of too little consideration, too little patience, too little affection to precede his own gratification; and then it had died again in the rest of her life, victim of insensitivity, selfishness, too many other women too many times. . . . When she came in view of Kath Tree's house she stopped thinking entirely and concentrated on walking. She made herself pass the house without a glance. She took this route only for variety, she told herself, just a change in routine. When the house was well behind her, she realized that she had not been breathing properly, either.

CHAPTER THREE

He squatted in the field of milo that abutted the high school
playing field, the stalks rustling when he moved and the
bearded heads of seeds that topped them rattling softly like
dry sand underfoot. The heat was always the worst just before school
when football practice started, when the humidity was so high that
sweat would not evaporate into the still, sodden air. You felt like you
were carrying fifty pounds of soaking jersey as well as all that padding.
Slamming into a blocking dummy made an audible squish. He hated
football practice.

From his position in the field, the picture window of the school
library was at eye level, no more than sixty yards away across the play-

ing field. He sighted an imaginary rifle at the window, using his thumbs to aim, and went slowly down the row of teachers. He could take any one of them, anytime he wanted. The only one moving was Cohan, but not rapidly enough to be a problem. His pattern was regular and predictable, moving from one side, pausing in the middle, moving to the other side, pausing again, addressing always the ones directly in front of him with all that bogus eye contact, all that false sincerity. Holding his thumbs in line on Cohan, he slowly pulled his forefinger in the practiced finger squeeze. "Bang," he said softly.

It would be easy. It would be like shooting tin cans from the bridge over the Muddy River. Easier. He shot Cohan again, then squeezed his finger several more times, imagining the delayed reaction, the others rising to their feet in alarm, then the panic, the screaming, the chaos of running bodies. Shooting deliberately he could take down six, seven, maybe even ten before they had all figured out what had happened and had sense enough to get below the window. Teachers were not very smart people. Then he would turn and go back the way he had come, crouching below the level of the milo stalks. It would work, why wouldn't it work? Nothing could stop him from doing it, he knew that. And who was going to catch him? The police? Not in this town. The sheriff? That was good for a laugh. No one could stop him, no one could catch him. It was an excellent plan.

He lay in the dirt for a few minutes more, practicing his shots, going through it thoroughly this time, carefully miming working the bolt on the rifle before each shot. Six, he could take out at least six, if he wanted to.

Satisfied at last that he had done what preparation was needed, he turned and walked quickly but carefully out of the field. If it rained before he came again with the rifle, the prints would be gone. If not, he would walk the same row and deal with them on the way out. There would be plenty of time before the teachers organized themselves enough to call for help, plenty of time before the law arrived.

Perched on a chair, elbows on knees, face in hands, peering down from his second-story bedroom window like a gargoyle, Billy Tree watched the street life of Falls City unfold below him. Like a *cowardly* gargoyle, he thought, forced to glower from inside the building, more frightened than frightening. But he was there early, not to miss a thing in the teeming activity of the town. No paperboy, no pickup truck, no spotted dog passed unnoted by Billy Tree, gargoyle and observer. And in between passages he could always watch the squirrels chase each other through the branches of the oak tree across the street. Once, a dog, a lapsed spaniel, had barked at those same squirrels. It was a full life, thought Billy.

The highlight of his day approached and Billy Gargoyle leaned precipitously forward, hands upon the sill. Huford Peck shambled into view along Harlan Street, working his way south along the highway that intersected the town. He would make several circuits of the town before nightfall, covering most of the streets in an unvarying pattern whose logic and intricacies were understood only by himself, stopping only to pick up items of interest that had fallen on the roadside or sidewalk and stuffing them into a plastic shopping bag before moving on. Huford had made the same circuit when Billy was a boy. Where he slept, where he kept the treasures he found, how he survived had all been mysteries to the young Billy. He had once seen a woman emerge from her kitchen and hand Huford half of a cooked chicken. The chicken had gone into bag along with the bottle caps, lost coins, pretty pebbles, or whatever it was Huford collected. He had paused long enough to say thank you, though. Young Billy had noted that. Huford could talk, he just preferred not to.

Billy leaned out the window as Huford passed in front of his house.

"How's it going, Huford?"

Huford looked up, startled to hear a voice from the sky. Or perhaps accustomed to it, Billy thought, perhaps expecting further instructions from space. It took the man a moment to locate the source of the sound. Billy waved and Huford took a step backward, amazed to see a gargoyle move.

"Thought you was dead," said Huford.

"I am."

"Oh."

"How's the work coming?"

"Good." Huford put the plastic bag behind him, protectively.

"Nice to see you again," said Billy.

Huford squinted for a moment in concentration, as if Billy radiated a bright light, then continued on his eternal rounds, eyes to the ground, lips moving silently, feet shuffling in a sustainable stride that would take him miles and miles each day. And where does he get his boots? Billy wondered. Who provides him with his shirts and coveralls and hat? . . . Well, the hat was no puzzle. Half the men in Falls City sported a stiff-billed cap advertising a tractor or a seed company. The other half sported Stetsons. I ought to get a cap for myself, thought Billy. Help me blend in, the Harlan Street Gargoyle, chapeau provided courtesy of DeKalb Seed.

He heard Kath behind him, home to feed the cloistered brother asquat the windowsill, the toad in the upstairs room, Billy Tree, local eccentric and hermit and failed tough guy, pal and god-figure to Huford Peck. Bologna sandwich on white with mayo and mustard for the gargoyle. Pickles added if she thought to ask first.

"She come yet?" Kath asked. Billy did not turn to face her.

"Who?"

"Who are you sitting there hoping to see? . . . Joanie Blanchard."

"Never heard of her."

"Three days running," said Kath. "I never saw her come this way in ten years, suddenly she's going by on her way to the high school, back home for lunch, back to school, back home."

"It's a busy street."

"Yeah, about three pedestrians a day. Huford Peck and Joan Blanchard . . ."

"Who's the third?"

"I was allowing for random chance," said Kath.

"Haven't seen him, yet."

Kath put a plate on his bed, then stood behind her brother, her hands on his shoulders. She felt him tense at her touch, then slowly relax under the gentle kneading of her fingers.

"You could come downstairs and eat like a human," she said, her voice as tender as her fingers.

"Not ready for that yet," he said.

"There's just me down there," said Kath. "Nobody would be looking at you, you wouldn't have to face anybody."

"Like you don't count?"

"Oh, Billy. Nobody cares what you think you did or didn't do. Nobody's judging you. You're just not that important to most people."

"Ouch. You just gouged my ego."

"And I love you and I've put up with you all my life, haven't I?"

"Ah, but you're a well-known saint, Kath."

"To be honest, Billy, I'm more concerned with whether or not you put the toilet seat down than I am with what happened—except that it practically killed you and turned you into a basket case."

"Apart from that, though?"

"Ah, Bill," she said with a sigh. "I hate to see you hurting yourself. If it was somebody else doing it to you, I could defend you, but how do I protect you from yourself?"

He took her hands and held them on his chest and leaned back against her. "You're the best, Kath."

"Yeah, right."

"I mean it. The absolute best."

"Right. Something in me brings out the suffering in men, Billy, and you know it. They indulge themselves around me."

"That's balls."

"What do they call it? Enabler, right? I'm the best enabler."

She tried to pull her hands away but he held them tightly.

"Lord James was a drunken shit," Billy said. "That wasn't your fault."

"You're not going to blame it on Mom."

"I'm going to blame it on *him*. He didn't need any enabling, he did it all by himself. And old Peripatetic Stu is also a drunken shit."

"You going to tell me he isn't my problem?"

"He's your problem, Kath. He's not your responsibility."

"And you?"

"I'm not a drunken shit. I don't drink much at all."

"Is that an improvement, with you locked up in your room, not fit for human companionship, me waiting on you like a maid?"

"It's no improvement. A drunken shit can always sober up. There's no hope for a plain shit."

She rested her cheek atop his head. "You're not a shit, Billy, you're just hurting. So are they."

"Don't lump me with them. I want a category all to myself. 'Ace coward and whiner' would do."

"I heard you again last night."

"Sorry."

"No, no. It worries me that you're suffering, is all."

"They're just nightmares, Kath. Nothing to be afraid of. . . . Nothing for *you* to be afraid of. Bad enough they scare me out of my wits, they shouldn't scare you, too. I'm just sorry I wake you up."

"I don't sleep much anyway . . . I never know whether to come in and comfort you or if that would hurt your pride."

"I don't have any pride left. What do I care if you see me sniveling in my bed?"

"You're full of pride, Billy. That's the problem. . . . Will you please come down and have lunch with me? There's nothing wrong with you physically that a little exercise wouldn't cure."

He patted her hand, then pressed it to his lips.

"Can't do it, Kath."

"Let me know if you get tired of bologna," she said brusquely. "I just bought some headcheese."

Too late he called after her, asking for a pickle.

As Kath's footstep receded down the stairs, Billy inched his chair closer to the window. He leaned his head against the edge of the frame, looking as far to the south as possible without leaving the safety of his room. Now here's a gargoyle with a lively interest, he thought. Maybe Quasimodo is more like it—somebody ugly hanging from the side of the building, at any rate. And lusting after the village maid below.

"Do you see her?" Kath called from downstairs.

"Who?"

"Ha!"

He could hardly miss her. Joan Blanchard was the only person on the street. Head up, striding purposefully, she passed Billy's window without a glance. Each leg seemed to catch the sun as it moved forward, glowing like a new cartridge shell beneath the Bermuda shorts.

"Why don't you call her?"

Billy was startled by his sister's voice. Kath had ascended the stairs and come up behind him while he was raptly watching Joan Blanchard walk.

"Call her?"

"I have a phone you could use."

"Why would I call her, Kath?"

"Why do you suppose she's suddenly taken to walking past your window in shorts?"

"She's got to exercise those legs somewhere. They can't look that good all on their own." Joan turned the corner and was gone. Billy felt diminished.

"She wants you to contact her. What does she need to do, wave semaphores?"

"Not ready for the direct eyeballing, yet, Kath."

"You look fine. Just skinny."

"Handsome as ever, no doubt, but what if she looks a little deeper? What if she sees beneath my glamorous exterior?"

"Considering who she married, I don't imagine she cares. And that's it, Bill. That's more self-pity than I care to put up with. One way or another, you're sticking your nose outside this house."

"In time, Kath. Got to give me time."

"Balls," she said. He heard her footfall stomping down each step, trying to crash through the wood.

CHAPTER FOUR

Pat Kunkel filled the doorway, all bulk, weapons, and clothes. He wore long sleeves all year-round, even in the oppressive heat of late August, and sweat stains mottled his uniform like birthmarks. His gun belt and pistol sagged on one hip, the handcuffs, radio, and baton on the other, and his stomach lopped over his trousers in front, giving him the appearance of being a fatter man than he was. But fat or lean, he was an imposing figure. Without his smile, he would be frightening, Kath thought, but she knew him far too well to feel anything in his presence other than gratitude and a recurring embarrassment. How many times had he stood on her porch like this, smiling sheepishly, one massive arm effortlessly supporting her drunken husband, Peripatetic Stu, as Billy called him. And earlier, when he was on the local police force before becoming sheriff, performing the same function with her father, Lord James, in his final years as carouser. But always with patience, understanding, and a sympathetic tilt of the eyebrows that said boys will be boys—even though her men seemed to be more boyish than most.

"How are you, Kath?"

He bent his head and hunched slightly in the doorway, as if ashamed of his height.

"Good, Pat. And yourself?"

"Oh, fine, can't complain." He hesitated and his smile grew crooked as if to apologize for what he was about to say. "You're looking awful pretty."

The cherished ritual dance began, a formal little gavotte, very dainty and charming and ultimately as impersonal as its form was elaborate.

"Oh, stop."

"Nope, no you do."

"That's how you keep getting elected, isn't it? You flatter every woman in the county."

Kunkel looked at his feet, his shoulders bouncing with a self-conscious chuckle. Kath could predict his coming denial.

"Naw, now."

"Sure, that's how you do, Pat Kunkel. A shameless flatterer. . . . It's a nice quality."

"You know what my dad used to say about your mom? He called her Annie Keefe, the prettiest girl in town. Any town."

He had told her many times, but Kath saw no reason to remind him. "Really?"

"Yep. True."

"How sweet . . . but I don't imagine your mother liked hearing it."

"Oh, he just meant it in a—what do you call it?—in an aesthetic way."

"How nice."

"You know what?"

"What?"

And here was the best part, where he twirled his partner, then dipped her to the floor in choreographed imitation of intimacy.

"You look just like your mother."

Kath slapped him playfully on the arm. "You're shameless."

Kunkel chuckled again, studying the floor. The dance was over, they had learned no further steps and each was abruptly left with the awkwardness of normal motion.

"You want me to go up and see him, then?"

"Why don't you?"

He moved toward the stairs, never having looked directly at her after the first fleeting glance of greeting. What a sweet, shy man, thought Kath as he lumbered up the steps, his equipment nearly hitting the walls of the stairwell. Most men used compliments like a wedge, standing poised behind them, all edge and anticipation of a crack in the surface. In Kunkel's case, they seemed to spill out of him as the result of an excess of kindness; there was plenty for all and he asked nothing in return. She wondered if he was the same considerate, bashful person around men. And if so, how strange a choice of professions. Kunkel was the reason Billy had gone into law enforcement, never so much a hero or mentor as just a good example. She wondered if she should still be grateful for his influence. Wouldn't Charming Billy Tree be a more nearly whole man today if he were selling ad space or real estate or anything else where the worst he would see in a day was an angry customer?

Pat Kunkel, too big for his clothes, shirt buttoned at cuffs and neck, stood over Billy, mouth agape. Gawking, he was, thought Billy; and so big he induced claustrophobia just by his presence.

"Pat, me boy."

"Christ you're thin, Billy. You ever eat anything?"

"I gnaw on my spleen now and again. Been on a diet yourself, I'd say."

Kunkel tugged at his shirt, pulling it away from his stomach as if it would somehow find extra room for his bulk. "Shirt's shrunk, I think. I sweat so damned much."

"You ever consider short sleeves? That's where they cut them off at the elbow?"

Kunkel shrugged. "I'm in the car all day, it's air-conditioned. Or I'm in the office, it's air-conditioned. . . . You ever think of using anything in here? Like a fan, maybe?" He flapped a hand in front of his face. "It's what-do-you-call-it?"

"Hot?"

"Stifling. You need some ventilation."

"I got my own personal ventilation, Pat. Got the assorted holes in my body."

"Yeah, I heard. Hurts, don't it?"

"Now that you mention it, I did notice some discomfort. You ever been shot, Pat, me boyo?"

Kunkel pointed to a spot on his back as if Billy might see it through the shirt.

"Sneaked up behind you, did he?"

"Naw, hell, I turned and ran soon as I saw he had a gun. Didn't even know I'd been shot until I got to the car. Saw my blood and nearly fainted." Kunkel looked at the floor and chuckled self-consciously in the same manner as when complimenting Kath. "Scared the living shit out of me, Billy, that's the truth. Here I am, hot-footing it towards my car—ain't never been fast, but I want to tell you, I was *moving*. I heard the shot and I'm thinking, Whooo, Lord, he missed me that time, just get me to the car and I'm out of here, I'm out of this damned business. This is Richardson County, it's not Kansas City, nobody's supposed to be shooting at me."

"Did you shoot back a'tall, a'tall?"

"Naw. He sobered up a little bit, came out to see if I was all right. It scared him as much as it did me. This was Jimmy Boudreau, out past your uncle Timmy Wittrock, there? He was just drunk and pissed off about something, you know. Jimmy's not so bad when he's sober."

"I notice you stayed in the profession."

"Well, I figure, who can do it any better? Besides, if Jimmy's tearing things up out there I send a deputy now." Kunkel looked around the room, noticing his surroundings for the first time. French wallpaper covered the walls, the lamp shade was adorned with ruffles. "This your old room?"

"Like it?"

"Kind of froufrou, isn't it?"

"There's a term I don't hear often enough. Kath's old room. Mine is reserved for Stu, should he ever return."

"They don't still sleep together, then?"

"Bit nosy, aren't you, Pat?"

Kunkel chuckled. "It's the job, Billy. The sheriff's got to know everything." He looked around the room again, tugging at his shirt, hoping he might have missed an air conditioner on the first pass. Billy sat in the only chair; the only other option was the bed.

"Let's take a ride," Kunkel said.

"I don't go out."

"Crap."

Kunkel took Billy's arm and lifted him to his feet, then propelled him out the door.

"I don't want to go outside, Pat. Seriously."

They stood at the head of the stairs.

"You start to tussle with me here and we'll both fall and I'll land on top of you," said Kunkel.

"Did Kath put you up to this?"

"One step at a time," said the sheriff. With an arm around Billy's waist and a knee in his backside, he eased him onto the first step, and then the next.

"I'll walk, I'll walk," Billy said.

"That's what they all say." Kunkel maneuvered Billy down the rest of the stairs atop his knee.

"I'm not an invalid."

"I thought you must be, else why not get out of the house and come see your old friends?"

"Have a nice talk," said Kath, smiling from the kitchen.

Billy pointed a finger at her but could manage only "You . . ." before he was hopped out the door like a kangaroo with a prod on its tail.

Kunkel eased himself into the car, daintily pushing gun and baton to the side like a woman adjusting her dress, then squirming for a moment before coming to rest.

"You look like a man with piles, Sheriff."

"Matter of fact. It's the pressure of this damned job. I'm lucky I don't have to carry an inner tube with me. Well, you know what it's like."

When he turned on the ignition, the air conditioner roared to life at its highest setting. Billy rode with a steady wind of cold air at his ankles and in his face. They drove south on Harlan Street, stopping at each of the three red lights, to the edge of town, a five-minute trip.

"You were in law enforcement," Kunkel continued. "You know the pressure. Everybody's waiting for you to make a mistake. You got a crime, they expect you to solve it yesterday, like you're Sherlock Holmes. And even if you know who did it, you can't arrest them without proof, and these days how you going to get proof? You can't even stop their cars without reasonable grounds. How about you know the prick did it? How come that's not reasonable?"

" 'Tis a daunting challenge, for sure."

Kunkel cocked his head as if he had not heard right, blinking at Billy before continuing.

"You used to be able to slap them around a little. Use a rolled-up newspaper, it didn't leave any marks. Hell, they expected it, they knew how things were. Now you breathe in their face and they scream abuse. And if it's a minority? Christ, they use your balls for shish kebab."

" 'Tis ungrateful shites they are and all."

"I never understood why you do that." Kunkel blinked again, as if his lack of comprehension were a matter of vision.

"Do what?"

"Talk like that. Why do you do that accent?"

"I'm Irish."

"Yeah? I'm German but you don't hear me talking like a Kraut."

"You can get over being German."

"Uh-huh."

"But if you're Irish, lad, you're Irish forever, and dat's the trute of it. . . ."

"Gets kind of annoying."

"Irony is not always appreciated."

Kunkel nodded politely as if grateful for the instruction. He turned the cruiser back north on Stone Street, running parallel to the previous traverse. The town was laid out on a grid, twenty blocks long, fifteen wide, give or take a few lanes biting into the surrounding cornfields, and Kunkel could drive past every house, business, and outbuilding in half an hour. Drivers and pedestrians alike nodded cursorily at the sheriff's car with the casual gesture of greeting to someone seen so frequently as to be scarcely noted. Kunkel was so much of a local feature that his recognition value had fallen below the level of an actual wave. It was only when they noticed Billy that their heads turned and their hands rose uncertainly, doubtful of what they saw. Most faces were of British, German, or central European stock, giving the people a look of sameness that Billy had not seen for years. There was a comfort to the homogeneity but a certain uneasiness, too, as if he had misplaced something and could not remember what or where. I've become a cosmopolitan, he thought with self-mockery.

"What minorities are you talking about, Pat? Everyone I see looks like you."

"Handsome folk, aren't they?"

"If you don't care how they look."

"This is a culturally diverse country now, Billy, didn't you know? Don't you watch television? We got minorities, all right."

They waited for the streetlight by the county courthouse, which sat in the town square, the proximate center of the municipality.

"Where do you have them hidden?"

"They drift in from the cities. You'd be surprised. Lots of Hispanics at the new grain elevator, bikers from all over hell, some homeboys from Kansas City and Omaha. Got an Oriental family couple years ago."

"Asian."

"Got that, too. The place has changed since you left, Billy."

"Looks very much the same to me. I must have driven up and down this stretch a hundred times every weekend. Don't know what I expected to find."

"Nookie, I imagine. That's what I was after at that age. That and a little excitement."

"As if either one was going to fall off a passing truck."

"We got a bit more excitement than we used to," Kunkel said. He drove the east-west streets, shuttling slowly back and forth across the weave of the town, his head bobbing in automatic recognition of the citizenry.

"I can see that," Billy scoffed. "Don't know how you manage to sleep nights."

"The problem is, you can't see it. Most of it happens after dark and I'm too old to stay up for it. . . . Tell me what your reaction to Falls City is after all this time, Billy. I'm interested."

Billy pushed the air vent so it directed more of its blast toward the driver. The word 'chilblains' crossed his mind although he wasn't certain what it meant.

"My first reaction is there's no place to hide."

Kunkel laughed. "You're right about that. Not enough trees in the whole town to build a house, flat as the sole of your shoe. I remember as a kid being amazed that my parents always seemed to know where I went and what I did before I even got home. Of course kids think if they're hunkered down in a car that means no one knows where they are. 'A hive of glass, where nothing unobserved can pass.' Didn't know I had the soul of a poet, did you?"

"I was just realizing that when I was out parked with a girl, you probably knew about it."

Kunkel laughed. "I knew where everybody was. Your favorite parking spot with what's her name was just past the bridge over the Little Nemaha."

"I thought I was so clever."

"You can only see that spot from about five miles in any direction."

"At night?"

"You used to make the mistake of driving with your headlights on," Kunkel said. "I'd just sit in the dark and watch where everyone went."

"You were awfully young to be a dirty old man," said Billy.

"You got to start early if you want to be any good. Besides, I was just doing my job, protecting the youth of the town—from each other."

"Actually, that wasn't what I meant by no place to hide," said Billy, "but it explains a lot."

"What did you mean?"

"I was speaking professionally. No very good places for a would-be assassin to hide. A relatively easy place to secure."

Kunkel chuckled humorlessly. "That's what you think."

"I mean for a few hours, to defend one man. My job was very selective." Billy pointed to the water tower that rose four stories high at the north end of town, far and away the loftiest structure in sight. The name of the town was emblazoned on the side of the holding tank in letters ten feet high. "The only good spot for a sniper would be the water tower, and how would you get down?"

"Did you ever meet the President, Billy? I used to look for you on television. Thought I might see you running alongside the car or something."

"Never got the assignment, but I ran with the Vice President for a few months. Mostly I did what they call pre-event security. Checked out people and places before the President arrived."

"Like a scout?"

"Something like that."

"Did you like the work?"

Billy watched an elderly woman calling to her recalcitrant dog. A mother with an infant on one arm unloaded groceries with the other. A farmer drove past in a pickup, his cap pushed back, revealing a strip of ghostly white skin above the tan. During the transit of the town Billy had seen no one out of place, no one concealing a weapon under a suit coat, no madmen, no fanatics, no killers.

"I liked the job, yeah. Didn't meet very many entirely stable people, but I liked it . . . I'm not sure why."

"Same reason I like my job," Kunkel said. "Even on the bad days, even when you spent that last hour hip deep in the worst mess people can make out of their lives, you know you do it better than anybody else can. That's why I like it, anyway."

"Not me, Pat. I always knew I could be replaced in a minute. . . . I don't mean I wasn't good at it, just not irreplaceable."

"What did you like about it then?"

"The people, I guess. I liked talking to all the people, even the crazy ones, I liked trying to read them, trying to figure out what they really wanted. A lot of them, the letter writers, just wanted somebody to pay attention to them. And some of them wanted to get caught."

"That right?"

"You must see some of that, too. A criminal who's just so bad at his work you know he wants you to catch him."

Kunkel laughed. "I don't get that many volunteers for jail; but I got my share of crazies to deal with. You ought to give this a try, Billy. Right up your alley."

"Where does Huford sleep?" Billy asked.

"Speaking of crazies, you mean? In the old power plant. You remember that, down there just past the rail yard? You used to hear that thing thrumming away in the background, got too close it made your fillings shake."

"Not sure I remember it."

"Well, Huford does. It's empty, nothing in there but those old diesel generators. We're hooked up to the grid these days. It's just a big old cavernous building; he's got his blankets and treasures in there, not hurting anything. Why the interest?"

"I was just realizing we have a lot in common. I might have to join him someday."

Kunkel turned east on Fourteenth Street. When they passed the high school, he asked, "You call Joanie Blanchard yet?"

"Why would I call Joan? She's married, isn't she?"

"Divorced. Kath didn't tell you?"

"I didn't ask."

The sheriff grinned slyly. "Yeahhh. You probably didn't notice her walking past your house four times a day, either."

"How do you know about that?"

"I told you I know everything. You just took the full tour of the town with me. I do that twice a day, once or twice a night. How much do you think I miss?"

"I hate when you know things."

The city street became Highway 159 and they were in the countryside without transition between the last of the houses and cultivated land.

"So why don't you call her?"

"You and my sister have been coordinating efforts, it seems. Why should I call her?"

"What kind of question is that? Did that guy shoot your pecker off?"

"Well, I haven't looked, to tell the truth."

"I doubt that he did. He'd need a scope to find it."

"Ouch, you really know how to hurt the poorly endowed, Patrick."

"Of course you'd have to deal with Duane Blanchard if you ever actually got together. You might not be up to that. Last guy who dated his wife Duane went after with a roll of nickels in his fist or something. He used to box Golden Gloves, you know. He not only beat the shit out of him, must have scared him half to death, too, because the guy wouldn't press charges."

"I take it Duane doesn't believe in divorce."

"Not as far as he and Joanie are concerned. She's got a restraining order slapped on him. He's not supposed to come within one hundred feet of her, but there's no limit to how close he can come to anybody foolish enough to take her out, of course. . . . Something like that might frighten off an Irishman like yourself. I can see that."

"He's still doing that? I remember when we were kids he was pounding on every guy in school, one after the other."

"How'd he do with you?"

"I bit him on the kneecap after he beat me into the ground."

"You did a little better than that, as I remember."

"What do you do, watch the sparrow fall, too?"

"I've had my eye on you for a long time, Billy." Kunkel sighed.

Billy glanced at the sheriff and saw the weariness in his face to match the tone of his voice. It occurred to Billy for the first time that Pat Kunkel was no longer young.

"Why, Pat? Why me?"

"Because you were interested in my work. And the only one who was."

They were approaching the Missouri River, where the flat land around Falls City gave way to deepening corrugations and hills billowed away from the great water as if the river itself had been stone-skipped across a still liquid earth and the resulting ripples had been frozen into geology. By the time they reached Falls City the waves of land had diminished to mere wrinkles in the landscape, but closer to the Missouri the hills rose and fell in swells. They were in a trough when Billy first heard the drone of machinery, insistent as the sea, and saw a man-made cloud above the crest of the approaching hill.

When they topped the rise, the giant grain elevator filled the landscape, as startling and out of place as a section of the Great Wall of China on the Nebraska plain. It rode upon the sea of waving green like a battleship, ten stories high, a quarter of a mile long, interconnected cylinder upon cylinder of concrete silos. The diesel trucks and railway cars sitting on the adjacent spur track were as dwarfed as tugboats and tenders tossing in the wake of a leviathan.

"My God," Billy exclaimed.

"That's new since you left, huh?"

"I've never seen one that big."

"They got them bigger, I guess, but this'll do. They truck in wheat and corn from the smaller elevators within about a hundred-mile radius, then send it out on the train to the mills."

Billy looked up at the cloud that hung ominously over the elevator.

"Grain dust," Kunkel said. "It goes away with a good breeze. We're in an inversion right now, according to the televison."

"You mean it moves? It looks like it's glued up there."

Kunkel waggled a finger at the roadside. As they drew closer to the building, the foliage became first speckled, then solid gray under a steady precipitation of dust. Billy thought it looked as if the entire landscape had been tested for fingerprints.

"A little rain, a little wind, and it's gone," Kunkel said. "It's never really quiet, either. Even if they turn all the machinery off you can hear it kind of groaning and creaking. You got ten million bushels of grain in there. It never really settles, it just keeps slipping around itself. Kind of alive."

"That's creepy."

"You don't want to fall into one of them silos, I know that much. Might as well be in quicksand, it'll suck you right down. The more you wiggle, the quicker it goes. But they say you'd only go down so far 'cause once you stop struggling the grains will sift down around you, kind of holding you up. They pour more grain on top and you could have a whole horse just floating halfway down in grain, stay in there forever, never go all the way up, never go all the way down. . . . The horse would be dead, of course."

"You've got a ghoulish side to you, Pat. Not only handsome and witty, but a bit macabre, as well. What a guy."

"I sort of like the place," Kunkel said. He needed to raise his voice as they approached the entry drive. The rumble of engines and the whine of machinery was interrupted by a whooshing hiss as grain swept down a pipe into a waiting rail car. More dust filtered up to join the hanging cloud. "It's like having our own private mountain range. Close your eyes and that sounds like a whole bunch of skiers going downhill, doesn't it?"

"A whole *bunch* of skiers."

"Besides, it's kind of like looking at the kitchen tables of the whole country, before they do. Think of all the bread and cornflakes in there. Sort of makes me proud . . . not that I've got anything to do with it, really."

"It's part of your county, Pat...."

With a sudden oath, Kunkel accelerated hard and switched on both lights and siren. He swerved into the entry to the elevator complex, slewing sideways across the driveway, his eyes fixed in the distance. An aging Chevrolet Impala the color of a wilted carrot approached from the direction of Kansas City, chopped and crouched low on its springs as if preparing to pounce. In a countryside where high clearance on dirt roads and furrowed ground was prized, if not essential, the chopped Chevy could not have been more out of place. It slowed as it approached the entry to the elevator site and four young black men peered curiously at the squad car as if flashing colored lights were a novelty to them. The driver's scalp was shaven, one of the passengers wore a blue bandanna on his head, another a woolen watch cap, and the fourth a homemade chapeau of cut-off panty hose, the severed end tied off and bobbing above him in a jaunty knot.

"Gangbangers," Billy said. The carrot car growled and shot forward, heading toward Falls City.

"You got it," said Kunkel. As the squad car jumped in pursuit, he pulled the shotgun from its clips beneath the dashboard. "I may need you to back me up, here, Billy."

"Get on your radio."

"Too late for that."

Ahead of them, the Impala was slowing and pulling onto the shoulder of the road.

"Just hold that shotgun where they can see it. When I get to their car, I want you to stand by my left front bumper and let them have a good look at the shotgun. Don't go anywhere else, just stand there and make yourself visible."

"Pat, this isn't the way ..."

"May not be the Secret Service way, but it works for me." He pulled his car off the road, staying well behind the others.

"I have a thing about guns," Billy said as Kunkel stepped out of the car and adjusted his belt before starting forward. It hit him like a bolt as he said it for he had not realized until just then that it was true.

"I'm counting on you, Billy."

"*Don't* count on me, goddamit. I don't want to be counted on."

But the sheriff had already covered half the distance to the other car. Billy saw the effects of tension on his old friend as the man who previously had moved in a bear-like shuffle, almost comically heavy and awkward, now bore himself with the taut expectation of an athlete. Pat Kunkel was suddenly Sheriff Kunkel and a man to be wary of. I wouldn't want to mess with him, Billy thought.

The shotgun rested heavily on his knees and Billy could feel a fine film of oil where his fingers touched the barrel. The metal had picked up the chill of the surrounding air in the car and was icy cold. Billy jerked his hand away, trembling. The tremor spread and in an instant his whole body was shaking.

He clenched his teeth and clasped his arms across his chest against a cold that came from within.

"Jesus," he muttered. "Just don't shit yourself."

As Kunkel reached the other car, Billy heard his own chuttering breathing coming in spasming gasps, like those of a freezing man. Like Avi Posner's demonic laughter. He saw Posner's crocodile teeth grinning on the inside of the windshield.

"Oh, ya evil shite," said Billy. His brogue boomed loud in the closed car and he laughed at hearing himself. He got out of the car and took up his position by the left front fender.

Kunkel was bent over, his hands resting on the Impala's window, and he was talking fast to the occupants of the car. Billy could make out no individual words but the tone was unmistakable. The sheriff was stern, admonitory, and brooking no argument. From where he stood Billy could see only the back of the men's heads.

With a rhetorical flourish, Kunkel swept his arm toward Billy and then stopped, abruptly, puzzled. The faces of the black men turned toward Billy and one of them broke into a smile.

Enraged, Kunkel took one step back from the car and put his hand on the butt of his pistol.

"Ahh, fuck no, Pat," Billy said. He felt his insides liquefy. Posner's laughter grunted in the rumble of the car's idling engine.

The Impala accelerated suddenly and pulled away, barely missing Kunkel's feet, and raced back onto the highway with a roar of power unexpected in such an aging vehicle.

Kunkel stalked back to Billy. "What the hell was that? Where was the gun? You were supposed to let them see the gun!"

"I had a little moment with your windshield," Billy said.

"I don't know what that means. How frightening do you think you are, standing there without a weapon?"

"Scared the hell out of myself."

"You think this is funny? Those weren't tourists who got lost, you know. Those are KC gangbangers, probably got enough guns and drugs in that car to start a war."

"I thought you were going to drag them out and go at them with a rolled-up newspaper."

"Why didn't you bring the goddamned shotgun? I was counting on you."

"Don't, I said don't. I told you. I don't want anyone counting on me."

"Now you tell me."

"I told you before."

"I thought you were a goddamned hero lawman, Billy."

"Aw, no, Patrick me lad. 'Tis a bit of a sniveler you got on your hands now, don't you know."

"And cut the Irish shit, too."

As they approached Falls City, the Impala shot past them in the opposite direction, heading toward Kansas City. The passenger with the panty-hose chapeau thrust his middle finger in the air.

Kunkel shook his head wearily. "Too proud to make a U-turn when I told them. It's always attitude with those people, got to show the Man. Act like a bunch of teenagers."

"I think they are teenagers."

"Teenagers with guns and drugs and attitude and racial contempt."

"Unlike our good selves," said Billy.

"The Secret Service really broadened your outlook, didn't it? How nice for you."

"I had some black partners. It helps."

"What did you mean you had an incident with the windshield, anyway?"

Billy hesitated. "A visit from an old acquaintance."

"I don't know what you're talking about."

"I hope you never do. What did you say to those guys in the car?"

"I told them to get the hell out of Dodge or my partner would blast them with the shotgun."

"Did they mention their civil rights?"

"I didn't notice an ACLU lawyer in there with them. Did you?"

"You knew they were coming, didn't you, Pat?"

They were back at the town square. Kunkel led Billy to the front booth of the Chat 'n Nibble Café, where they had a view of the courthouse.

Kunkel grinned sheepishly. "You're not as dumb as you act. How'd you know?"

"I rode with you for an hour and you never had your radio on. That Impala had a high-gain antenna and a phone antenna, and I'm willing to bet they had a scanner, too. If you had talked to your dispatcher, they would have picked up your conversation and known where you were."

"Maybe I was just on my break and didn't want anybody to know where I was."

"Yeah, maybe, but you grin and get all bashful when you lie. Did you know that, Pat?"

Kunkel looked at the tabletop and laughed. "Caught me. Good thing I'm a cop and not a criminal."

"So what was going on?"

"A drug run, I'm pretty sure. Route 159 doesn't lead anywhere those boys'd be wanting to go except here."

"Who are they delivering to? Four of them like that, they looked more like a war party."

"That's the thing. I don't know."

"I can't believe you have a drug problem in Falls City."

Billy looked at the human-size Statue of Liberty standing on the square. A United States flag hung limply from its pole on another end of the quadrangle.

"You've spent too much time running next to the Vice President's car, Billy. There isn't a town in the country without a drug problem, I don't care how big. People want 'em, people use 'em, people buy 'em." The sheriff looked at the other patrons of the café and then took in the view through the window. "There's nobody in here or out there I could swear wasn't using a little something now and again. Pot at a party, a little coke for the special occasion, ecstasy for the big date, LSD in the punch bowl for revenge, speed for the big job—that's a favorite at harvest time. We got people sniffing glue and chewing mushrooms and you name it. It's not like when I was a kid; nobody condemns it anymore. Oh, they disapprove of the dealers and nobody likes a junkie, but when it comes to their own personal use, that's different. I remember when people would walk out of a party in outrage because someone was snorting a line. Now they just wait their turn."

"It can't be that bad *here*."

"What's so special about here except our good selves? I've got three deputies and the reason I go around with my radio off is because I don't trust that any one of them isn't part of the problem. The truth is, the only person in town who I know for sure isn't part of it is you, and that's because you just got here."

"The answer would be no, Pat."

"I haven't asked it yet. Daytime visits by those boys are unusual. I just got lucky today. For obvious reasons they prefer to come at night. Problem is—this goes no further, right?"

"I hate making promises before I know what it is."

Kunkel drew his hand over his face and shook his head as if to throw off his weariness. Billy saw the features of the younger man beneath the accretion of age and remembered the big cop he had once idolized, the man with the uniform and the broad shoulders who brought his father home after a night of drinking, smiling at his mother, winking broadly at the boy, Billy, as if there was nothing to this business to take seriously. It had been a tenuous initial connection but it had made Billy aware of Pat Kunkel, and Kunkel aware of him, and the friendship had grown despite Lord James.

Kunkel leaned forward intently. "If this gets out, it could hurt me, Billy."

Billy shrugged. "Okay, a provisional promise. I'll keep it to myself unless there's a good reason not to."

"What kind of promise is that?"

"If you tell me there's a bomb planted in the courthouse I can't promise I'm not going to tell everybody."

"Why would I tell you not to tell somebody that?"

"Hell, I don't know, Pat. Why would you take an hour of your valuable time and drive me around town—unless of course you're going to ask me to help you in some way."

Kunkel looked over his shoulder, then turned back to Billy. "You always were prickly. You just like being different, don't you?"

"Different from who?"

"See, there it is . . . Okay, here's the thing. If this gets out, I'm dead, but . . . I've lost my night vision. I don't trust myself on the highway at night. Somebody hits me with his high beams and I can't see for shit. Things just kind of jump out of the dark at me; it scares the hell out of me. . . . There, you got my ass in your hand. The voters find out I'm impaired and I'll never get elected again."

"Thank you for your ass, and a fine big butt it is, but I'm not going to work for you, Pat. That is what this is leading up to, isn't it?"

"You wouldn't have to be a deputy or anything. Just let me use your brain once in a while. You're a trained observer. People will talk to you who won't talk to me."

"I doubt that."

"Oh, come on, you're Charming Bill Tree. I know the women will talk to you at least."

Kunkel's face darkened as Curt Metzger's cherry red pickup cruised slowly past the square. Metzger glanced in his direction and raised his hand in a taunting wave.

"Kath tells me the principal is trying to charge him with child abuse," said Billy. "If you're asking me to join a posse to arrest Curt Metzger, count me out."

"Thom Cohan's a nice guy, but, Christ, Billy, sometimes you got to look the other way. I'm not saying Curtis should go around whopping his son upside the head, but have you had a look at Sandy Metzger lately? He's big as a car. Course Curt's big as a truck, but still, I don't call that child abuse. Plus Sandy is one mean piece of work, going to be as big a pain in the ass as his father. Cohan's just breeding a scab on his nose, if you ask me, fucking around with the Metzgers."

"I remember as a kid I always wanted to bash Metzger with something heavy from behind, then run like crazy."

"That's about the only way to tackle him, all right. I hope I never have to take him in."

"But he wasn't much of a football player. You'd think with all that bulk."

"Too slow. Slow and stupid and mean. . . . What say, Bill, will you give me a hand?"

Billy swept spilled sugar into a pile in front of his coffee cup, then forced himself to look Kunkel in the face. "I can't do it, Pat. You saw that today. Sometime somebody's going to pull a gun and you're going to look around and I'm not going to be standing by the fender, I'm going to be running across the field like a striped-assed ape. And you're going to end up with another hole in you."

Kunkel stared at him for a long time before speaking. "I thought you were better than that, Bill."

"I did too, for a while."

Kunkel dropped money on the table and walked out of the café. Billy looked out the window for a long time, trying to determine whether the face in the glass that brayed mockingly at him was that of Avi Posner or his uncle Sean.

CHAPTER FIVE

The constant strain of being pleasant to her colleagues made Joan yearn for her lunch breaks, when she could leave without explanation and with full cordiality and be alone on her walks to and from her home. It was not that she didn't like most of them well enough, in small doses, it was that she couldn't take *all* of them in concert all day long and still maintain the smiling, cheerful countenance they expected from her—that she had *led* them to expect from her. She realized she had only herself to blame for a reputation as happy peacemaker, but that did little to quell the desire to snap at one or another of the more annoying ones at times, to inform them brusquely that she was no longer interested in their emotional turmoil, their petty feuds, their points of view—if she ever had been. Things would get better once the students returned to school; she got along with the kids with no hypocrisy called for. In the meantime, she needed her walks. Was everybody else like her, she wondered, acting nice all the time and feeling crisply antisocial within? Or was she the only curmudgeon in disguise?

By the time she reached Seventeenth Street she was aware that the truck was behind her without turning to look. She didn't need to see their faces to sense their presence, Duane smirking suggestively, Curt Metzger staring at her with that frightening, unreadable scowl. It had become more frequent lately, this curiously restrained automotive stalking, the bright red truck trailing the legal five hundred feet behind her, following her home, waiting somewhere, then slipping onto her trail again as she returned to the high school after her lunch. It made her want to scream with frustration but she refused to give up the pleasure of her walks, refused to let Duane win. If she turned and yelled at him, if she even glanced back at the truck, Duane would revel in her capitulation, her rage, her despair at being haunted. All it meant to him was that he still had power over her. Sometimes she thought that was all he had ever wanted, to own her and control her.

Lately Duane had become even more obsessive, if that was possible. In the beginning he had popped up only occasionally, making random visits, as if he had stumbled across her path by coincidence, but this was the third time he had followed her home in as many days.

She walked to her house on Chase Street, striding purposefully, telling herself to forget about her pursuers, to enjoy the beauty of the late-summer day, to clear her mind, to think of *anything* else, and never to give him the satisfaction of looking back. She reached the safety of her house exhausted by the effort. When she peeked from behind a curtain to watch the truck pass, there was nothing there. Joan sank into a chair. Had she imagined the whole thing? If so, she was haunting herself and no further assist from Duane was needed. He had won.

A five-minute walk from Joan's house, Kath was in her kitchen when she heard the old wood of the porch sag under someone's weight. There was no need to hurry to the door. Any of her friends would enter without knocking, voicing a premonitory hello as they leaned in, then continue to call a greeting as they roamed through the house until they found her.

This time there was no hello, and Kath heard the steps moving heavily toward the kitchen.

"Who is it?" she called. She was greeted with silence, which gave her just a second's fright before the footsteps stopped outside the kitchen.

"Who is it?" she asked again. "Billy?"

The thought of Stuart, her husband, flashed through her mind and she half-expected to see him lean around the door frame, grinning with boyish guilt, expecting forgiveness, but at the same time she knew it was not his tread. She dried her hands and moved toward the door leading to the dining room, still holding the towel.

Duane Blanchard stepped into the doorway.

"Hello, Kath."

Kath stepped back, startled.

"Didn't mean to scare you." His mocking smile suggested he meant to do just that.

"You didn't scare me," Kath said.

"People never admit when they're scared. You ever notice that, Kath?"

"What did you want?"

Blanchard leaned against the door frame as casually as if this were his own home, but to Kath it seemed that he was blocking the exit.

"It's a social call," Blanchard said.

Kath tilted her head to one side.

"I didn't know we were such good friends."

"That's only 'cause you don't like me. You never have. Why is that?"

"I'm kind of busy now, Duane."

"I'm just on my lunch hour myself. If we had more time you'd explain why you don't like me, though, wouldn't you?"

"I would need some considerable time."

"A lot of your friends do, did you know that?" His grin insinuated even more than his words. "A lot of your friends. You'd be surprised."

"I certainly would. Now if you'll excuse me . . ."

Blanchard took a step toward her.

"I came to see old Charming Billy, heard he was home and full of holes. Thought I'd pay my respects."

"He's not here," she said, immediately regretting the admission.

"I know. He's driving around with the sheriff. There's a pair for you, law and order everywhere you look."

"They'll both be here any second," Kath said. She did not know why she felt threatened by Blanchard's presence. His insinuations were nothing new.

"Ooooweee, wouldn't that be scary...but since he's not here, maybe I'll just deal with you. I wanted Billy to give a message to my wife."

"Why don't you do it?"

"Hey, I'm not allowed to talk to her. Didn't you know that? Sure you did."

He leaned closer to her and Kath forced herself not to step back. His eyelids were rimed with grain dust.

"Everybody knows all about me and Joanie, don't they? . . . Or they think they do."

"Why would I give a message to Joan? I seldom see her."

Blanchard laughed. "Oh, Kath. Do you really think I don't know she's taking to walking past here every day? That's why I thought Billy might want to give her my message. Since they're seeing so much of each other."

Kath turned at a sound behind her. Curt Metzger stepped through the screen door of the backyard entrance and stood there, his bulk filling the space. Kath felt herself blanch.

"Hello, sweetmeat."

"Leave," she said, when she could control her voice.

Metzger winked at her, unsmiling.

She turned to Blanchard. "Please leave now." She heard her voice breaking.

"Why, sure, Kath. I'm a working man, anyway. I got to get back to the elevator. Just wanted to give you the message."

"What is it?"

"Tell Billy to tell my wife . . . No, I tell you what. Just tell old Billy that I was here. Tell him Curt and I came by to see him and hope we'll find him next time."

"You're not coming again," Kath said.

Metzger barked a laugh. Duane paused in the doorway and grinned.

"Oh, sure, Kath. You know you want us to."

When the men were gone Kath locked her doors in daylight for the first time in her memory and then sat at the kitchen table and wept.

I t wasn't Duane. He wouldn't hurt me, I know that. He's just full of himself."

"He's happy enough to hurt other people," Billy said.

Kath shook her head, insistent. "It wasn't Duane who scared me."

"Metzger, then. What did he say?"

"Nothing. He called me 'sweetmeat.'"

"You were terrified when I got home."

"It's not what he said . . . we . . . I have a history with Curtis Metzger."

Billy waited, knowing he would not like what she told him next.

Five years ago, a Halloween party for the town children in the old armory, the vast space darkened for ghostly effect, Kath costumed, foolishly perhaps, as a belly dancer, and serving punch, supervising the haunted house, helping out. Metzger was there with his ten-year-old son, but just one parent among many, Kath scarcely aware of him. She stepped into a storeroom to replenish the house of horrors' naked eyeballs with more peeled grapes and suddenly Metzger was in the room with her, the door closed, his massive bulk blocking the exit. He had muttered something and they had spoken, briefly, Kath unaware of the meaning of the words, only the intent of his presence in the pitch-black room. He pressed her against the wall, stacked boxes of crepe paper tumbling at their feet; groped at the naked flesh of her midriff, ran his hands up and down her bare arms, moaning as if any uncovered skin were an excitement too strong to resist. Even in her panic she blamed herself for dressing too provocatively, as if it were in any way her fault, as if men she had known all her life would be unable to control themselves in her presence. His breath was ripe with alcohol and he fumbled at her with a curious tentativeness for an intended rape. She was pinned by his weight against the wall. He could do with her whatever he wanted, but his fingers trailed over the top of her neckline, trembling, and he leaned his face into the hollow of her neck, mumbling and kissing. She heard the word "sweet" repeatedly and realized that in his own deluded way he was attempting to seduce her, not force her.

She spoke his name softly, hoping to calm him. "Curt," she said. "Curtis . . . Not like this."

"Oh, Kath," he moaned, pressing his pelvis against her. She felt his hardness pushing at the bare skin of her belly and the metallic rasp of his open fly.

"Kath, Kath." Gasping, rocking against her. He grabbed her hand and put it on himself and almost simultaneously exploded, wetting her stomach and her hand. As he cried out and spasmed, she instinctively put her free hand on his back and held him.

He leaned against her, but now limply, needing support in his temporary weakness. Reflexively, Kath patted his shoulder. He seemed so harmless now, even ridiculous in his incontinency, as desperate, intemperate, and hasty as a teenager. After a moment he straightened and stepped away and Kath heard the quick grate of his zipper being closed.

The incident seemed over; she expected him to open the door and leave. She was already thinking she would use the crepe paper to clean herself when his fingers closed around her throat. Lifting as he squeezed, he held her at arm's length, choking, speechless, scrabbling with her toes to find the floor.

"You bitch." No anger in his voice, just deep contempt. "I ought to kill you. I really should."

And for a moment Kath thought he would. Sightless in the dark, her eyes saw flashes of color, her throat closed by the incredible strength of his hand. His thumb and fingers dug into the sides of her neck with such force that they seemed to meet in the middle. Without leverage she couldn't kick him and her own hand pawed ineffectually against the sleeve of his work shirt.

"You keep quiet, you hear me? I ever hear about this, you're dead, sweetmeat." She could not even nod to indicate agreement. "I figure I owe you one. I'll catch you again."

He released her and she tumbled atop the boxes. Minutes later, when she had cleaned herself and found the strength to walk, she stepped out of the closet and nearly collided with Sheriff Kunkel, his Darth Vader mask doing nothing to disguise his badge, uniform, and gun. For a moment she melted against him as if she might faint, but she would not allow herself to start crying for fear she might never stop.

"Why didn't you tell Pat?" Billy asked.

Kath looked at him as if he had missed the whole point of the story. "Because I believed Curtis would kill me. I still believe it. I've never told anyone until now. Who could I talk to in this town and be absolutely certain he'd never hear about it?"

"You could have told me."

"You were in Denver or Dallas or someplace, and what good would it do, anyway? I can't prove anything, the bruise on my neck went away . . ."

"You wouldn't have to prove it to me."

"And what were you going to do about it? Come storming into town like a posse to save my honor? If you shot him you'd go to jail, and if you didn't have a gun he'd tear you to pieces."

For a moment Billy was silent and brother and sister looked away from each other. Each felt that in some way he or she had failed the other. At last he said, "Do you have an empty coffee can around the house?"

After politely asking permission, Billy filled the coffee can from a neighbor child's sandbox. At home he rummaged through his brother-in-law's bureau and selected a pair of black, midcalf socks. He pulled on them to test the elasticity, then placed one sock inside the other and filled the inner one with sand. He tied a knot just above the bulk of the sand and another at the very tip of the sock, thus forming a grip where he could hold the homemade sap.

Slipped into his front pocket it made a pronounced bulge.

"'Twill make me a very popular fella," he said to himself.

CHAPTER SIX

ill Blanchard leaned against the door of Sandy's room, breathing heavily, his arms burning with the pain of lifting weights, and watched Sandy hoist twice the iron that had done him in. Sandy pumped like a machine, his eyes on his muscles the whole time as if he expected to see them grow with every repetition.

"You kind of a pussy, ain't you?"

"I don't do this all day, every day," Will said defensively.

Sandy switched the weight to his other arm and glanced at Will. "I do other things."

"What?"

Sandy smiled slyly and his eyes grew smaller. Sweat poured from him in the closed bedroom, but he seemed not to notice. "I make plans," he said.

Will was grateful for conversation of any kind. He felt no obligation to keep working out if he was talking. There were few options at Sandy's house. He either pumped iron in Sandy's bedroom, or watched Sandy do it. Various bottles and pills occupied one entire shelf along with protein bars and food additives. Will ate the bars but declined the mysterious pills and drinks when Sandy offered. Sandy was never specific about what they were, and Will suspected that he probably had no clear idea himself.

"What kind of plans?"

"I'm going to be bigger than that asshole." He nodded his head toward the adjoining room. Will could hear the voices of Curt Metzger and his father barking and laughing on the other side of the door. Asshole was Sandy's only name for his father; Will had never heard him call him anything else.

"Bigger and better. I'm going to do everything better than the old asshole." Sandy ran the fingers of his free hand over his bulging biceps as he continued to curl the weight up and down. It was a loving stroke, almost erotic. "Asshole's always talking about how he's going to do something. You know what?"

Sandy lapsed into silence again and Will thought he was lost in a reverie of his own body.

"I realized he ain't going to do nothing. He's just going to talk, sit in there and drink beer and jack his jaw with your dad about how they're going to raise all kinds of hell, but he ain't ever going to do squat."

Sandy stood and pulled weights with either hand into his armpits, like a bellboy with very heavy suitcases.

"He's too old. I ain't too old. Lots of things need doing, you know? Lots of things need someone with the balls to do them, but you get past a certain age and you lose your balls. Old asshole's lost his balls."

Will paid little attention when Sandy went into one of his rants. He doubted that Sandy had much understanding of what he was saying, either. Their fathers were in the other room, jacking their jaws, and Sandy was in here, exercising his, along with the rest of his body; it was hard to see the difference. Will was naturally inclined to side with Sandy, if only because they were the same age, but most of the time he spoke in code, alluding to dark forces and a vision of the world that was unfamiliar to

Will. He let his eyes wander to the poster on the wall opposite the bed, the poster that Sandy would see first thing when he woke up and last before he slept. A huge swastika, smaller representations of the Imperial German eagle, the iron cross, a helmet, hands raised in the Hitler salute, all set against a background of warplanes, tanks, and soldiers marching as if from out of Armageddon. Will was still not certain what his mother objected to. He saw the swastika all the time, all over the place, in movies, on television, on book jackets. No one said they should stop making movies and documentaries about the Nazis. How many times had he seen Hitler, arm lifted to cheering throngs, the twisted cross on his armband, on the dais, on the flag in the background? What was the big deal if Sandy had it on his wall? It was just another symbol to his generation, no matter what it might mean to his parents, no more apt to inspire someone his age to action than a poster of Jimi Hendrix or the Grateful Dead. They were all from a different time, and who cared anymore, anyway?

"I can give you something to get you going."

Will realized he had been drifting. "What?"

"You want something to get you going? I got something."

"What?"

"You just pop it when you need to do some reps, you know?"

Sandy rummaged through a drawer and came out with a handful of pills and tablets.

"Where'd you get it?"

Sandy smiled cunningly and his eyes all but disappeared, which made him look even more devious, Will thought. The Metzgers were not good at clever.

"It's not hard."

Will studied the varied pills, tempted to try something, anything, if only it were being offered by someone more trustworthy than Sandy. For all he knew, it would shrink his brain and eyeballs and make him sweat all the time, like another Metzger.

"I guess I better not," he said, reluctantly.

"You really are a pussy, ain't you?" Sandy popped two pills into the back of his throat and swallowed without water, then laughed to show his fearlessness.

Stupid pills, thought Will, and he's overdosed on them.

"Big things," Sandy said. He returned to his weights. "I'm going to do big things. And then, poof! I'm out of here."

CHAPTER SEVEN

T he house was dark so he worked with a flashlight held in his mouth. He selected the sneakers from among the mix of shoes and boots and sporting footwear on the floor of the closet. The sneakers were last year's fashion choice, high-topped, thick-soled, autographed by one of the top ten or twenty basketball players in the NBA, and treaded with a trademark design all but guaranteed to propel the wearer faster and higher than heretofore humanly possible.

The .22 rifle was in the hall closet, the shells on the shelf. He loaded the gun, carefully counting the shells because he planned to recover the casings later. He wrapped the rifle in an afghan blanket of pink and gray squares that was used to hide the rip in the sofa. He would use the blanket to lie on and then as a drag to cover his tracks in the field of milo. On the back of an envelope from the mortgage company he wrote his brief message in pencil, then signed it with a swastika.

For a long moment he stood in the living room, thinking carefully if there was anything else he needed to do, trying to imagine what others would look for when they came to the house. Confident that he had done all that was required he left the house and got the bike where it rested against the side of the building. Steering with one hand and holding the blanket-wrapped rifle in the other, he walked to the road.

The town slept in the way only small towns could slumber, completely, without paranoia, without defense. There were no lights visible for several blocks in either direction, not even the ghostly flickers of televisions or computer screens, and no cars moved on the roads. Far to the east he thought he could make out a brightness in the sky where the earth curved out of sight. It would be the cloud of dust hovering over the elevator, reflecting the light of the moon. Just outside of town, past the shadow of the water tower on the northern horizon, the tips of the corn plants would be shining with silver from the same moonshine, field on field of glowing treasure.

He took a final look around at the town in its last repose of innocence. After tomorrow no one would sleep well again.

The teachers were gathered in the library again, making their final preparations before school started the following week. It was as hot as it had been all month, and they had the window open, which was perfect for the sniper. No glass for the bullets to shatter. Shattering glass would make people flinch, make them aware of the problem right away. With the window open, he could get off a number of shots before anyone knew what hit them, so to speak. There would be no panic for a much longer time, the targets would hold still and cooperate.

He smoothed the blanket on the dirt, spreading it so that his upper torso would not touch the soil at all. Dirty pants were never hard to explain, but a grimy shirt required some lying, and he wanted to do as little lying as possible. Not that anyone was going to notice his appearance when there was so much chaos going on, but why take unnecessary chances?

When everything was to his liking, he took his position on his stomach, propping himself on his elbows, easing the rifle to his cheek. Sweat ran into his eyes and the figures in the schoolroom swam fuzzily in his vision. He wiped his eyes on his sleeve and realigned the rifle. He selected his first target.

Joan Blanchard lifted her leg from the wooden chair and felt it cool immediately on exposure to the air. They were sweltering in the room and perspiration stuck her skin to the wood and her limb came away with a noise like that of a Band-Aid pulled from a wound. The teacher beside her, Sharon Shattuck, glanced at Joan and smiled. Joan was glad she had worn her shorts, a luxury of comfort that would be denied her once school started, but she hated the way her thighs looked when she sat down. Nicely shaped when she stood, they seemed to double in size when pressed against a chair. She crossed her ankle over her knee and let evaporation do its work.

Principal Cohan was pacing in front of them, talking, cajoling, joking, probably raising the temperature in the room with his amazing energy. So much enthusiasm for education. She remembered when they had that much enthusiasm for each other. He had worn down her resistance with just such energy, focusing on her as if she were the only thing that mattered to him at all. An interest that intense was very seductive. And dangerous, for he had pursued her recklessly, in school, in public when he should have assiduously avoided her. Never overtly enough to be unmistakable—he was not a fool for all of his excess—but obviously enough to give the gossips something to latch on to. Joan was already and perennially a target for gossips; it needed no further attentions from Cohan to set tongues wagging.

He was an attractive man and at moments like this, with his eyes glowing with eagerness, she wondered that she had managed to resist him as long as she did—although she had to admit that resistance was easier in the face of such persistence, because she knew he would not go away at the first rebuff. She had waited long enough, but not too long. It was the sort of relational calculus Joan had made many times in her life, but seldom since her marriage to Duane and even less often since their divorce. Duane was always around her still, like an intimidating cloud, court order or not. In the end Duane had destroyed her relationship with Thom Cohan, too, although not as dramatically as he had with others. There were no threats that she knew of, no blows; just a gradual diminution of interest on Cohan's part, a turning in upon himself. Something serious and dark had come to influence him, and Joan assumed it was Duane's tightly coiled, rawboned looming presence.

Or it could simply be that she'd lost her appeal, she realized. She looked at her thighs, pressed against the chair. They looked absolutely enormous from this angle. And she had to be sitting in the front row so everybody could see them. Which meant that Thom could see them, she thought. Had she put herself in front to be closer to him? Or to catch the breeze through window?

Cohan stopped speaking abruptly and turned his head, then slapped his shoulder as if he had been stung. He turned to face the window, annoyed at whatever was behind him, then took a sudden step backward toward the teachers. His head lurched back as if loose on his neck. He turned again, arms flailing, grabbing for something that wasn't there, then toppled into the lap of Sharon Shattuck, the teacher next to Joan. The pap, pap, pap in the distance was lost beneath the sudden clamor of voices saying the principal had fainted.

Sharon Shattuck had made an effort to catch him, but now she threw her hands into the air, waving at the same wasp that stung Cohan. Joan managed to turn Cohan's head and then Sharon collapsed atop her, pinning her against the principal. Someone pinched her in the thigh. Sharon convulsed on top of her and began to gurgle.

Joan struggled free, annoyed, and tried to get to her feet as she heard the screams for the first time. The room was solid with the noise of people in fear. Panicked voices were yelling at her to get down, then someone grabbed her ankle and pulled her. She was aware that the pinch in her thigh would not go away even as she toppled into the mass of bodies on the floor.

CHAPTER EIGHT

P at Kunkel's voice on the telephone strained for control. It was a tone Billy had heard many times during emergencies, when trained men were trying not to panic.

"We got a lot of people down. Cohan's dead, one of the teachers pretty close. I could really use a trained eye over here, Billy."

"What happened?"

"Looks like a sniper."

"Shooting?" Avi Posner's beastly teeth bared themselves in the wallpaper over Billy's bed.

". . . Got a problem? . . . Billy?"

Was it a problem that he saw Posner pointing Walter's service automatic at him again? Was it a matter of concern that the air had become acrid with the stench of gunpowder? Billy decided it was.

"Quick as you can," Kunkel continued in his ear. "I want you to tell me what you see before the state police trample all over it. There's quite a mess."

Billy heard the sheriff's ominous tones emerging from Posner's dragon mouth amid the seriated fleurs-de-lis upon the wall. Quite a mess, said the dragon's mouth. We know what that means, don't we, Billy boy? We know all about messes.

"You there, Billy?" Kunkel asked.

Was he there? Was Billy Tree, the volunteer hero, the man who was prepared to take a bullet to shield the President, there at all anymore? Or was he still in Minneapolis, writhing on the floor, cringing and crying and shitting his pants in terror.

"I don't think I can be much good to you, Pat," he said. Posner grinned, pleased, and bobbed and weaved behind Matuzak's corpse.

"I just want you to look, Billy. Give me a hand. I don't want to screw it up."

I don't want to look, thought Billy. I've seen it, I know what it looks like, it looks like blood and splintered bone and torn flesh, and mucus and body sera and things you've never seen come out of a person, and never should have to see again. It looks like everything fearful you can imagine and it will fill your dreams forever after.

"Can't help you, Pat."

"Judas Priest, Billy. Just take a look."

I'll look at Avi Posner instead, Billy thought. I'll watch him doing the two-step with poor, levitating Walter, dancing over my hero's grave and smiling at me like a crocodile. I've got him right here on the walls of my head. Why should I bother with your fresh mess, Sheriff?

Kunkel made no attempt to hide the contempt in his voice. "The sniper's not here anymore, Billy. There aren't any guns. There's nothing to be afraid of."

Oh, Patrick, do you think I have so little imagination that I limit my fear to guns?

"Joanie Blanchard got shot, too," Kunkel added.

*   *   *

Billy asked for strips of cardboard and they were cut for him from a discarded packing crate in the school Dumpster. Moving one strip in front of them while kneeling on the other, Billy and Kunkel crawled the length of the milo row, carefully keeping their own footprints out of the forensic site. Billy paused with every transfer of cardboard, carefully eyeing the row parallel to his own, where the sniper had come and gone.

"Why would he bother to drag this row so carefully?" Billy speculated.

"So we wouldn't know where he was," said Kunkel.

"Leaving one row smooth and all the rest natural? He might as well have put up an arrow saying 'I went here.'"

"So why?"

"He didn't want us to see his footprints, I guess, but..." Billy stopped, holding up a hand and freezing, as if they were traversing a minefield. "He made a misstep."

Kunkel crawled forward, squeezing next to Billy, and looked at the angular print that had slipped outside the row, evading the drag that smoothed everything else. Beside the chevron mark of the sole was part of the first letter of the manufacturer's name. The entire imprint took up no more than a square inch of soil nestled next to a plant stalk, but it read as legibly as a signature.

"Not much," said Kunkel.

"But maybe enough," said Billy. "It looks like the heel print of a sneaker. It was important to him to hide it; it's probably important to us."

They marked the fragment of a footprint with triangular yellow plastic flags stuck on wires, moved carefully around it, and advanced down the row.

"That's his only mistake on this side," Billy said. "One step one inch down the row."

"It's why you're here, Billy. My boys or the state assholes would have stepped right on it."

Billy stopped again at the end of the row where the sniper had lain. The impression was deeper there and the drag less effective.

"You'll want a camera here, Pat." He pointed with a lanciform leaf from the milo stalk as a stylus. A faint quilted imprint was visible in the dirt at the very edge of where the Afghan blanket had been.

Billy looked toward the school, back to the depression where the gunman had steadied himself for the shots. The weight of the gun and the sniper's upper torso had rested on the points of both elbows, and the dents in the soil remained.

"He was lying on something, then he used it to drag his way back out of the field and cover his tracks," Billy said. "He had a weight of some kind on that drag to get it deep enough to do any good, probably the gun, maybe something else, because it did a pretty effective job. Except right here."

"Wasn't as thorough as he thought," said Kunkel. "Must have been in a hurry. Well, he'd have to be, wouldn't he?"

"In a hurry, maybe, but not in a panic."

"How do you know?"

"He took the time to pick up his shell casings."

They traversed the field again, shuttling forward on their cardboard through the row on the other side of the sniper's alley, but found nothing. Back at the road Billy walked carefully through the ditch that adjoined the field, his face to the ground, his feet never moving until he had probed the next step with eyes and hands. The ditch was choked with weeds but bare soil showed through along the top rim, where the ground had folded downward from the field.

Kunkel stopped and stretched his back. "I've done so damned little of this kind of thing. I feel useless."

"You're doing fine," Billy said, paying little attention to him.

"Mostly I just talk to people. Everybody will tell you whatever they don't want you to know, give 'em time. But you got to know who to talk to, first. . . . You got eyes like an Indian all of a sudden?"

Billy stopped at the sight of a cylindrical depression in the top of the bank, a few yards away from the sniper's chosen row. Parting the weeds carefully, he found another, thinner hole in the soil two inches away. He marked the site with more yellow flags and stood on the road.

"How'd you know that was there?"

"He had to be able to get away quickly and he wouldn't risk parking his car where anyone could see it."

"What is it?" Kunkel asked, leaning closer.

"My guess is it's from the handlebar of a bicycle. The smaller hole would be from the handbrake."

"The sniper came on a bike?"

"He came on a bike. And if we assume he got off the bike and went forward to enter the field rather than walking back the way he had already come, then he came from that direction." Billy pointed north.

Kunkel was suddenly furious. "You're telling me it was a kid? Bullshit! A kid crawled in there and shot those people? No, oh, no. It wasn't any of my kids, goddamn it!"

Billy did not reply. He had never seen the sheriff so angry.

"You didn't see those teachers in there. I did. He picked them off like he was taking target practice, like he was shooting tin cans off the bridge. No kid would do that. Maybe in your world, but not in mine."

"It's the same world," Billy said softly.

"No, it's not. No kid from Falls City would do that."

"Drugs?"

Kunkel kicked at the road. "The bastards! The bastards!" He hurled a handful of yellow markers in the direction of the squad car. "I'm going to get 'em, Billy! I swear to God."

"Easy, Pat."

"These are my kids! I watched over every one of them, just like I watched over you. They're my family, this whole town is my family. You don't know what it's like. You go from city to city, you probably never see the same face twice. I live with these people, I know everything about them. They're not angels but nobody here would do this thing. Nobody."

Billy nodded. He kept his voice low and calm. "Let's get the guy with the gun, Pat. Maybe you're right. Maybe he isn't from here." Or maybe he's still somewhere in the field, Billy thought. Maybe he has us in his sights right now.

Billy squatted abruptly in the ditch. His back felt so exposed his flesh pimpled into goose bumps in anticipation of the bullet. He pretended to look for evidence until he was certain he had enough control to walk to the car without breaking into a sprint.

"What are you looking for now?" Kunkel asked.

"Just being thorough." Billy's eyes continued to work even though his brain was fighting panic. A depression in the weeds caught his attention.

"Somebody else was here," he announced.

"What?"

Billy riffled the weeds to one side, following the signs in the earth. "Here's the sneaker mark, or the toe of it, at least. It's fairly deep, probably because he was dismounting from the bike, or else he was sprinting, eager to get out of sight. At any rate, it's just the toe. . . . I don't see any other marks—from the shooter."

"What else do you see? I don't see shit there."

"You got to get down closer, Pat, but don't. You'll just mess up the area. Right here there's another shoe print."

"How can you see through those weeds?"

"I can just see the edges of it, where his sole bit into the slope. He was bigger than the shooter—at least his shoe was."

"Could have been anyone who ever walked in that ditch, couldn't it?"

"Anyone who walked here *after* the shooting."

"How do you know it was after?"

"Because the second print—it looks like a work boot without much tread left on the sole—is on top of the shooter's sneaker."

The sheriff stared dumbly at the small patch of weeds under Billy's hands. "You mean we got a witness?" he asked finally.

"Could be," Billy said. He rose and brushed his hands against his pants before stepping out of the ditch onto the road. He looked slowly in all directions. They were so exposed. So vulnerable. They might have a witness. They might have another shooter. They might have two rifles trained on them right now from anywhere in the fields on either side of the car. Billy hurried to the car, forcing himself to keep from breaking into a dead run.

The smell of the hospital struck Billy two steps outside the door and he paused, staying back as Kunkel advanced into the building.

"What now?"

Billy exhaled repeatedly through his mouth, puffing out his lips.

"I was in a hospital for a long time. They all smell the same."

"This another windshield thing?"

"I'm all right."

"You're blowing like a fish."

Billy tried to grin. "Having a little moment here, Patrick, boyo."

Kunkel made no attempt to hide his annoyance. "You have a lot of moments. Christ's sake. Want me to wheel you in?"

"Just let me dissolve, I'll seep under the door."

"Work to be done here, Bill. I can't hold your hand."

"I'll manage this part. You go find the shooter."

"I hate to think you're right about who did it."

"Go ask him." And let me struggle with my demons on my own, Billy thought. It's hard enough without witnesses.

Kunkel turned back toward the car. "And breathe through your nose. You'll scare the patients."

Or end up one myself again, Billy thought.

Joan awoke from the anesthetic with an insistent pulse of nausea and the sight of Billy Tree standing beside her bed. I must look great, she thought before she vomited onto the floor.

Billy rang for the nurse, then busied himself looking out the window while Joan finished throwing up and wiping her face on the sheet. When he looked at her again her skin was ashen with a tinge of green.

She slumped back against her pillow as if exhausted.

"And how are you?" she said.

Billy laughed. "Ah, Joanie," he said. "What a girl."

"Took you long enough to show up."

"Been a bit under the weather myself. Thought I'd better wait until we were on even terms."

She smiled thinly and closed her eyes. "Stand back," she said and retched again over the side of the bed.

CHAPTER NINE

U nable to sleep, Billy gargoyled at first light, watching forms and colors in the street and yard reclaim themselves from the night. Avi Posner might dance and leer on the wallpaper behind him as he had through the dark hours, but outside the window Billy saw only the quick scampering of squirrels, heard the challenge and enticement of birdsong. A flock of crows had selected his block in which to roost and they responded to the shock of sunlight with the horror of a flock of vampires glimpsing their nemesis, cawing in anger, alarm, and defiance.

They called and squalled and dared each other through the passing of a pickup truck but fell into silence as if pausing to take a collective breath on the arrival of the sheriff's squad car, cruising slowly toward the south. Billy watched the car creep along the asphalt of Harlan Street, going too slowly even for the tires to whine. Pat Kunkel was at the wheel, his head patrolling patiently from side to side like a slow-moving gear, mechanical and thorough—but he did not look up, did not note Billy in the second-story window, the frightened goblin of Harlan. Billy lifted his hand, then let it fall, realizing he was unseen. Easy to tell that Pat was not trained by the Secret Service. Snipers always took the heights for a better field of fire; agents started searching for them from the top down.

I can't sleep and he doesn't seem to need to, Billy thought. Or is he battling his own demons? Has the shooting at the high school unnerved him? It was hard to imagine Pat unnerved by anything; he was a man as much in control of himself as he was of his county. Maybe he was not idly patrolling even now, but looking for the shooter, as if the rifleman would be as oriented to daybreak as the birds, emerging from his hole with the first rays, shooter as early worm.

Within the house the telephone rang, muted by closed doors, and Billy heard Kath's tread upon the floor. He could imagine her voice, blurry with sleep, edged with annoyance at being awakened at this hour. And then a sound from outside, a low rumble from the north like distant thunder, but more insistent, and on the move. Craning his head out the window, Billy saw a figure hurrying on the sidewalk, his arms flapping at his sides like the wings of a fledgling bird, instinctual but useless.

"Huford," Billy called.

The man kept coming, his mouth wide open, his arms flailing in an attempt for more speed. His ever-present plastic bag slapped against his leg. Terrified, Billy thought.

"Huford." Louder this time. And then again, louder still to penetrate the panic. "Hey, Huford! What's the matter?"

Huford slowed in his mad scramble, head swiveling to find the source of the voice.

"What's the matter?"

Huford clasped both arms across his chest to protect his plastic bag.

"They want it," Huford said.

"Who?"

"Them." Huford looked to the north, where the thunder increased.

"I don't think anybody wants your stuff," Billy said. "You want some breakfast? . . . Come on in, I'll make us some eggs."

Huford stared at Billy, baffled by the offer.

"They want what I know," Huford said. "They want my shiny."

"What's your shiny?"

Huford shook his head violently. "I found it, it's mine."

"Finders keepers. I don't think they want your shiny. I'll make the eggs into a sandwich for you if you'd prefer. You can take it with you."

The thunder closed on them and broke down into the individual roar of engines and the first biker came into Billy's view.

Huford gasped and dashed away, arms again trying for flight. Even in his fright he did not vary his route. Scared out of what wits he has, Billy thought.

And then the bikers were abreast of Billy, their rumble hiccoughing as they geared down to cut speed now that the highway had reduced itself to Harlan Street; law-abiding outlaws, staying within the limits. Billy counted eight of them, living stereotypes in their motley of chain and leather, Hell's Angels or a passable copy, part of the American chamber of horrors for the past fifty years, like the Klan, a threat more from the past than today, the evil of their legend far greater than their deeds. Some of our quasi-official American boogeymen, Billy thought. An acceptable masquerade.

Their motorcycles gleamed in the early sun as it struck them almost head-on and their engines coughed and choked, indignant at being reduced to such temperate pace. Billy watched them pass and squinting into the sun he saw Huford in the distance, scurrying away from the bikes with his peculiar clipped-wing stride.

"Joan called."

Kath stood in the doorway.

"Joan?"

"Who? Who?" she mocked. "Joan Blanchard. Ever heard of her?"

"Oh, that Joan."

"They're releasing her from the hospital. She wondered if you could give her a ride. . . . Take my car, I'll walk to work, but you're going to have to buy one soon."

"Am I going somewhere?"

"You have to help them, Billy."

"By noon this place will have so many cops and state police they won't be able to fit me in with a crowbar. I've already seen a television truck come to town. That must be a first."

"Pat needs you."

"How is Pat going to explain a civilian walking around, poking his nose into things?"

"He's helped us often enough in the past. How can you turn him down?"

"I'd do him more harm than good."

Kath glared at him.

"When did Joan want me to get her?"

"Oh, you can find the time to help *her*."

"Time is not what I lack, Kath."

"Billy, they're saying a kid might have done this. One of the high school students. That isn't true, is it?"

"I don't know, Kath."

She shook her head. "Not here. Not one of our boys."

"Well . . ." He stopped, not knowing what comfort to offer. Had anyone yet figured out a reassuring response in a nation where a generation of youths had taken to guns as their predecessors had to hockey sticks and ball bats? It seemed to be anybody's boys, anywhere, city or suburb, killing teachers and students as though they were animated villains in a video game. What comfort was there to offer the community that would never trust its children again?

"You have to help," she repeated.

Billy looked for refuge in silence but found none there.

"When we were growing up, who did you look up to, Billy? Who were your models of how to be?"

"It sure as hell wasn't Lord Jimmy Tree, was it? . . . I guess I looked up to Uncle Sean and Uncle Tim Wittrock and that whole bloodthirsty bunch. And wasn't that as big a mistake as you ever need to make?"

"I looked up to two people," Kath said. "I modeled myself after our mother—and you, Billy. My big brother who always did everything with such grace and humor and always did the right thing."

"And wasn't that as big a mistake as you ever need to make?"

"I begin to wonder," she said.

* * *

Joan was wheeled to the hospital entrance and used crutches to get to the car. As she settled heavily into the passenger seat and clumsily hauled in her bandaged leg, her face turned ashen and Billy wondered if she was going to throw up again.

Her lips barely moved as she said, "Got some pain."

"They'll give you something," he said.

"They did."

With her head against the headrest, her eyes closed, and the color washed from her face, her cheekbones seemed to press against her skin with painful prominence. Billy noticed the permanent smile lines beginning to form at the corners of her mouth, the tiny wrinkles at her eyes. She was no longer eighteen, he realized. She was thirty-eight and, for the moment, looking older. And quite beautiful, Billy thought.

"You staring at me?" she asked, her eyes still closed.

"What?"

"Are you checking me out in this vulnerable position?"

"No."

"Feels like it."

"Just admiring you."

The corner of her mouth twitched. "Why do men always say 'what?' even though they heard you the first time?"

"What?"

She opened her eyes and the blood flowed back into her face.

"Cute," she said.

"I was thinking the same thing."

"Oh, please. I look like I just got out of the hospital."

"On you it looks good."

"Careful, my stomach is still queasy," she said. She waggled her fingers to indicate he should drive.

After a moment of silence she lifted her fingers again, as if her mouth were somehow connected. "Who did it? Who shot us?"

"I don't know."

"The hospital staff says it was a student."

"We don't know that."

He glanced at her. Her eyes were still closed.

"What's going on?"

He could not tell if she was asking about her situation or the whole country.

"Don't know, Joan."

"Will you tell me?"

"If I find out."

"You will."

And what was the source of such confidence? he wondered. What had Billy Tree done lately to make her think he'd solve anything at all?

Billy slowed as a television truck raced by with the arrogance of an ambulance.

"They must have heard you were released. You got out just in time."

"They're going after me?" Joan asked.

"They'll want to talk to you."

"Why? I don't know anything."

"That won't stop them. If nothing else, they'll want to know how it feels to get shot."

"Get me home," she groaned.

He drove carefully, one eye on her, wincing in sympathy as she reacted to every bump in the road. When they approached her house she drew a shuddering breath.

"You all right?"

Suddenly she was crying silently, tears running down her cheek.

"Have you got a pill?" he asked.

"Sharon Shattuck was the sweetest person I ever met," she said.

He took her hand.

"I know. Several others said the same thing."

"Why would anyone want to kill Sharon? She didn't have an enemy in the world."

"Why would anyone want to kill the principal?"

Joan was silent.

"Who would want to shoot you, for that matter?"

She wiped her eyes with the back of her hand and looked at him for a moment.

"Right," she said at last, sounding unconvinced.

When she hesitated at the porch steps with her crutches, Billy lifted her into his arms and carried her into the house.

"Like a feather," he said.

"Charming Billy."

He held her in his arms longer than absolutely necessary and turned his face to hers. They were only inches apart.

"Not now," she said, turning away.

"I wasn't going to."

"You were thinking about it."

"If you condemn me for my thoughts, I haven't got a chance."

"I wasn't condemning you. I didn't have a toothbrush at the hospital, I've got a hole in my leg, and my son may be in the house. . . . Will!"

Billy eased her back onto her crutches and she hobbled toward her son's bedroom.

"I can wait while you brush your teeth," said Billy.

She called "Will" again in his room, as if to flush him out from hiding under the bed or in the closet.

"He's not here," she said, worried.

"He's a teenage boy, isn't he? He'll be home for the next meal."

Joan shook her head. "He wasn't in his bed last night."

"Maybe he made it."

"Made his bed? Please. See if there's a note on the kitchen table."

"Nothing. . . . Is there a girlfriend?"

"Where is my son?"

"Come on, he's a kid . . ."

"People are being shot! Where is my son?"

"When did you last see him?"

"He came to the hospital on his bike last night. I expected him again this morning before I checked out."

"Who does he run around with? We'll call his friends."

"Lately it's been Sandy Metzger. . . . What is it?"

"Probably nothing."

"Billy, please, you should see your face."

"Pat Kunkel called me just before I came to get you. . . . He can't find Sandy Metzger."

"Why is the sheriff looking for Sandy Metzger?"

"Why don't I drive around a little bit? It's a small town, I'll find him."

"Do you know what he looks like?"

"No."

"Then how do you expect to find him? Billy, what are you not telling me?"

"Nothing. He's what, fifteen? Nobody was home so he spent the night with a friend, not necessarily the Metzger kid, he could be anywhere. He'll turn up."

"What about the Metzger kid? I know something is going on. Tell me. . . . Do they think Sandy shot us?"

"Could Will be with his father?"

"Not legally. But, yes, I wouldn't put it past Duane to take him, just to drive me crazy. . . . Sandy? Is it Sandy Metzger? Where's Will!"

"Nobody's saying it's Sandy, Joan. Calm down. I'm sure your boy is fine. I'll check with Duane."

"He'd be at work right now. . . . Billy, you know Duane is very dangerous, don't you?"

"That's how I remember him."

"I don't mean high school dangerous. In his rages—sometimes I think he wants to kill me."

"Considering that someone just shot you, that's a very interesting statement."

As if borne down by the weight of possibility, Joan toppled onto the sofa. She heaved her wounded leg up and lay back, her face in her hands. A deep groan seeped through her fingers.

"Are you hurting again? What can I get for you?"

"Find my son."

"Will you be all right alone?"

"Find my son!"

"Unless you want your thirty seconds of television time, don't go to the door when the crew shows up."

"You think they'll come here?"

"Oh, they'll come. Just don't answer the door. They don't have time enough to waste on anyone they can't find easily."

When Billy stepped onto the porch a deputy sheriff was waiting, leaning against his squad car. A lean young man with black hair and a prominent Adam's apple, he straightened as Billy approached.

"Mr. Tree? I'm Bert Lapolla. Sheriff wants to see you," he said, using the sheriff's title as if it were his name, with the same exaggerated deference some confer on an athletic coach. "Your sister said I might find you here . . . but I didn't want to interrupt anything."

"Interrupt what?"

"Well, I didn't know . . . I saw you carry Mrs. Blanchard in from the car."

I should have known, thought Billy. I'm about as inconspicuous as a mouse on a dinner plate. At least during the day.

"Is that a smirk, Deputy?"

The deputy's Adam's apple jerked in his throat. He looked like a heron struggling ambitiously to swallow too large a fish.

"Sir?"

"Mrs. Blanchard and I are old friends."

"I figured that."

Billy spoke in his Irish accent. "Not a gobshite, are you, lad?"

Lapolla looked at Billy, puzzled.

"Never mind," Billy said. "Do you know Mrs. Blanchard's son, Will?"

"Sure do."

"Have you seen him around anywhere today?"

"No, sir, I don't think I have."

"If you do, tell him to go home, will you? His mother's worried."

Billy glanced around Joan's house and yard for a bicycle. As he walked toward the garage, the deputy started after him, uncertain what to do.

"Mr. Tree? Sir? Sheriff asked me to get you?"

"In a minute."

Billy opened the garage and looked for the bike. This was not the city, kids did not store their expensive Italian racers in the house, or remove the tires when they chained them on the street. Will's bike would be outside or on the porch or in the garage. If it was gone, then Will was gone with it. In another year, when he was old enough to drive, it would be a different matter, but now it was his only reliable transportation and, as Billy remembered it, any self-respecting fifteen-year-old would be too proud to walk anywhere.

Billy followed the deputy to Curtis Metzger's house and added his car to a string parked on the street. A town police car was pulled into the driveway and a state police cruiser was parked very close behind, as if the two had engaged in a race to get the preferred spot first. Billy saw the local police chief talking with a state police officer on the cement slab and cinder-block step that served as a porch. The state trooper had his hand on the doorknob as if he could barely restrain himself from going in. The chief glanced at Billy, then quickly away, caught in the act. He said something to the state cop but the cop did not turn to look at Billy.

"Where's Pat?" Billy asked the deputy.

"Sheriff went to the elevator to fetch Curt Metzger from work. He says to wait. We have a warrant, but Sheriff wants Mr. Metzger to be here when they enter the house."

"As a courtesy?"

"Well, you don't want to get Mr. Metzger mad if you can avoid it."

"Why didn't he send you to get him?"

"He could have. I could certainly do that. . . . Only, it's . . . Mr. Metzger sometimes needs kind of special handling. Sheriff gets along with people real well."

Billy nodded agreement. Pat Kunkel probably didn't offend even the petty crooks he worked over with his rolled-up newspapers. His popularity extended beyond his county, too. Billy noted the trooper at the door and several more lounging by their cars. The state outranked the sheriff and could do pretty much as they wished in these circumstances—they were waiting out of respect for Pat.

"Pat probably wants to keep Metzger away from the TV people, too," Billy said.

"TV people?"

"Haven't you seen the truck? I would have thought they made a beeline for the sheriff's office."

"I've been patrolling," said Lapolla. He gave Billy a sidelong glance and tugged at his belt. "You're an expert, huh?"

"Expert?"

"At this kind of thing."

"What kind of thing is that?"

Lapolla included the house and troopers with a gesture. "You know. Assassination."

"Is that what this is?"

"Isn't it?"

"I don't know yet," said Billy. "Maybe."

"Sheriff said you're the best there is at this."

Billy was unable to control a burst of laughter.

"Pat has a fondness for overstatement."

Lapolla looked at Billy shyly. "I heard about you."

Billy saw his throat jerk as if the fish were still alive.

"Yeah? What did you hear?"

"Just about your problem there. Getting shot and . . . you know. I would have been scared, too," the deputy confided.

"You would, huh?"

"Sheriff says . . ." The deputy stopped himself, reconsidering whether to repeat what the sheriff said.

"What does Sheriff say?"

"Well . . . you know . . . just." The fish threatened to leap back into the deputy's mouth.

"Why don't you see if you can find a bike around here, Deputy? Would you mind doing that?"

"A bike?"

"Bicycle. Sandy Metzger's bicycle."

"You want me to find it."

"Either that or tell me what the sheriff said."

"I'll take a look." The deputy hurried off as if released from a leg trap.

Billy surveyed the assorted representatives of law enforcement, all of them studiously ignoring him, all of them, Billy knew, also noting his every move. Either they didn't know who he was and were wondering what he was doing there—or they did know who he was and were wondering what he was doing there. Billy assumed the latter because no one had approached him and warned him off. The likelihood of his being unrecognized by any cop within Richardson County was practically nil by now. News travels fast in a community where there is little of it, and shameful news faster still.

They were stern men with minds and moral codes in some ways as stiff and creaking as their leather belts and creased uniform trousers. They lived in a world of gun oil and rapid judgments and Billy knew the syndrome all too well. It was a profession that called for immediate, *correct* action above all else. Like fighter pilots, he thought, constantly rationalizing why the latest crash could not possibly have happened to them. There was always something more *he* could have done that the other man had not. Some way the other man could have avoided the flameout or dodged the bullet as *he* would have done in that situation. Self-doubt meant hesitation, which meant mistakes, which could be lethal. They might make light of Billy's behavior in his presence as Pat had done, but that was little more than a form of courtesy, like not mentioning the spinach caught in his teeth; it was not absolution.

And how many of you would have been scared, too, he wondered. How many of you would have dissolved and regressed to a child and begged for mercy while shitting yourself and fired through your partner's body to save yourself? It was not those who would have done the same that Billy cared about. It was those who would not. How many of the truly brave were present and regarding him with contempt? He heard Posner cackle an answer. All of them, Billy boy. Everyone but you.

Which made Lapolla's sympathetic admission surprising, Billy realized. Pat had picked a very soft man for deputy. Lapolla trotted up to him now, shaking his head.

"Can't find a bike."

"Okay. Thanks."

Lapolla stood beside him, a little winded from the trot. And also exaggerating it a bit to emphasize his labors, Billy thought.

"Looked everywhere," the deputy said.

Billy felt as if he were expected to pat him on the head and say "good boy."

"I don't want you to get the wrong impression about what Sheriff said," the deputy continued. "It was just, you know, nice."

" 'Nice'?" Billy wondered what that all-purpose word could mean in these circumstances.

"He likes you," Lapolla said.

The two men looked away for a moment, both embarrassed by an admission of male affection, even one, in Lapolla's case, that did not involve him.

Billy broke the silence by asking, "Do you get a lot of bikers going through here, Bert?"

"Bikers?"

"Not the kind I just had you looking for. Motorcycle bikers. Hell's Angels, that kind of thing."

"Sometimes, I guess," Lapolla said vaguely. "Not all that much."

"You had some this morning."

"Yeah? I missed them, I guess. I was patrolling. Were they causing any trouble?"

Billy wondered where Kunkel sent his deputy to patrol if he didn't notice anything Billy could see out of his own bedroom window. Certainly no place where acuity might be required. He must be the deputy in charge of cornfields.

"They seemed to be scaring the daylights out of Huford, but that's all I was aware of."

Lapolla shrugged. "Well, Huford. It doesn't take too much to get him going."

"Really? I would have thought he lived pretty much in his own world."

"Sure, I guess. But you can't go much by Huford."

"He's a citizen, though, right?"

"Who, Huford? I suppose."

"The bikers had him really wound up."

"Sheriff told us to leave the bikers alone if they weren't causing any trouble. He doesn't want any ethnic problems."

"Ethnic problems? What ethnic group do bikers belong to?"

"Whatever they call that," the deputy said. "Sheriff knows how to handle these groups. He doesn't want us to hassle any of them."

Billy tried to imagine the deputy hassling eight leather-clad, tattoo-covered biking outlaws. It took a considerable stretch of the imagination. Kunkel was probably wise in telling his deputies to leave them alone. If they were all like Lapolla, they'd be eaten alive.

"You could ask Sheriff about it yourself," Lapolla added as another Richardson County patrol car eased to a stop.

The sheriff's vehicle came to rest in front of the driveway, blocking the autos belonging to the chief of police and the state trooper. A bluntly effective way to assert his primacy, Billy noted. Kunkel got out first, leaning briefly against the car roof and studying the group. He looked to Billy like a Secret Service agent checking to make sure things were safe before allowing the passenger to step out. An older, portly agent, to be sure. One who felt very much in charge of the situation and his audience, as well as his passenger. But as Kunkel continued to survey the scene, his image took on a new cast. A grin, small yet visible to everyone, lit up his face. He became a man pleased with his accomplishment; the angler who had brought in the biggest fish but was compelled by modesty not to crow about it.

As much a whale as a shark, Metzger emerged slowly, as if moving his huge bulk were a feat requiring considerable negotiation between seat and door frame. And Pat brought him in his car, Billy thought, instead of letting Metzger drive himself. Keeping control of him at every stage along the way. Very good police work, considering that Metzger was not under arrest. And there was no doubt that Metzger took some considerable controlling. As he rose to his full height he seemed to dwarf the car, making his emergence a kind of circus trick.

None of the troopers actually sucked in his breath on seeing Metzger for the first time, but there was a feeling in the air as if they all had done just that. Curtis Metzger had always required some getting used to, Billy recalled. And after twenty years' absence, Metzger seemed to have grown even more massive.

He stood on the curb, glowering at the uniforms. Kunkel moved to his side.

"Why don't you open the house up now, Curtis?" said the sheriff.

Metzger continued his slow tracking of the police until his gaze came to rest on Billy Tree.

"Hello, asshole," Metzger said.

"You remember me, then," Billy said.

"I remember you're an asshole."

Billy grinned. "And after all these years, too. It touches a man's heart, it does."

Metzger blinked at him.

"Why don't you open up for us now, Curtis?"

Metzger pointed at Billy.

"Best watch your ass."

"Ah, Curt, me lad, sure, I thought you'd be doing that for me then."

Metzger blinked again.

Billy's accent was as thick as he could make it. "Great asshole watcher that you are."

Metzger looked at Kunkel, who was shaking his head, trying to get Billy to stop.

"What's that shit?"

"Begorra, 'tis me ethnic self bubbling right up. Irrepressible, don't you know, dem Irish."

"I never thought you were funny," Metzger said.

"Really? I always thought you were."

Metzger took a step toward Billy. Kunkel grabbed at his arm.

"In fact, everybody did. We used to sit around laughing at you, Curt. Except the girls, of course. They felt sorry for you," Billy taunted.

Kunkel planted himself directly in front of Metzger.

"That's enough, Billy."

"Just warming up, Pat."

"In front of a dozen cops," Metzger snarled. "I want to hear your mouth when we're alone."

"I can hardly wait. I got a few choice things to whisper to you, too."

"Billy, for Christ's sake. We got a procedure to deal with here. Let's just get that out of the way." Kunkel raised his voice. "You all know Billy Tree, don't you? He's going to be giving me another eye here."

Oh, great, Billy thought. Tell the staters they don't have enough sense to handle it themselves.

Kunkel continued, making it worse. "The Secret Service has been interviewing all kinds of assassins to find out what they're about, what makes them do it. So Billy's an expert on this kind of thing."

"Not really," Billy muttered. "The interviewing was a different department."

"You still in the Secret Service?" asked one of the state troopers. "Or is that secret?"

The others laughed cruelly. They all knew the answer to that question.

"We about through with the introductions?" Billy asked.

The impatient trooper on the doorstep twisted the doorknob aggressively. "You want to let us in here, Jerkoff? Or do we kick the door in?"

Metzger swung his baleful stare from Billy to the trooper.

"I ain't afraid of that fucking badge."

"Hey, hey, hey!" the sheriff yelled. "Mr. Metzger's been good enough to cooperate with us, let's all show a little mutual respect. Curtis, for shit's sake, open the door."

"Getting a little tired of the sideshow with your man and asshole here," said the trooper.

Billy noted that he was the asshole.

"That's not a nickname I'd care to have stick," Billy said, grinning. "It's just for my close friends."

"Get used to it," said another trooper under his breath. And that takes care of any lingering doubts about my reputation, Billy thought. Billy Tree, Irish asshole and coward.

"Could we just get on with it, please?" Kunkel asked. He held the insistent trooper in his gaze for a moment. "Or should we wait for the camera crews to find us, Meisner?"

Meisner, the trooper, swallowed his first response. "Where are they now?"

"At the high school, taking pictures of each other. I, for one, don't want to have to talk to them until I have something to say. How about you?"

"I'm not holding things up." He threw his hands in the air in a display of innocence.

Metzger strode to the door. The police chief stepped off of the cement slab, but Meisner gave way only half a step, just room enough for Metzger to insert his key. The two of them crowded ludicrously on the little stoop like penguins on the last unmelted block of ice.

Matuzak would have done that, Billy thought. Locked horns and not given an inch. And where is Matuzak now? Posner asked. Billy glimpsed his murderous demon in a reflection in the dark sunglasses of the closest trooper, grinning like a tiger.

In the living room, Meisner was pulling on latex gloves. "He doesn't touch anything," Meisner said. He didn't bother to look at Billy.

"Not even a souvenir?" Billy said.

"Just as well if he doesn't talk, either."

Kunkel stood in front of Billy, effectively walling him off from the room with his bulk.

"What the hell do you think you're doing with Metzger?" Kunkel hissed.

"Just old friends."

"Christ, Billy."

"What did you have to do to get me in here?"

"I spoke to my colleagues *reasonably*. Why don't you try it for the next few minutes?"

"I hear you've been saying nice things about me," Billy said. "Better watch that."

"What are you talking about now?"

Lapolla hovered uncertainly behind Kunkel.

"Sheriff? . . . You'll want to look."

Billy crowded into Sandy's bedroom along with five officers. Their uniforms and leather made them seem like sudden animations of the soldiers on the poster that dominated the room like a burst of light. Storm troopers on the march on the wall, state troopers in the bedroom. But the soldiers in the poster, marching out of hell and into worse while lightning flashed around them, left no doubt about their murderous intentions. All the troopers in the room wore latex gloves the pale white color of skimmed milk, giving them a faintly effeminate appearance, dandies from the royal court from the wrist down. It was not an observation Billy shared with the others.

One of the troopers held an empty .22 caliber cartridge shell between thumb and finger. He sniffed it and passed it to the man next to him, who also sniffed. The man nodded, as if in concurrence with some unspoken opinion, then offered the shell to Meisner.

"Where?" Billy asked.

The trooper looked to Meisner, who was taking a turn smelling the shell. A roomful of perfume testers, Billy thought, surprised there was any odor left.

Meisner inhaled deeply, then nodded with grim satisfaction.

"Where'd you find it?" Meisner asked as if the question had just occurred to him from nowhere.

The trooper indicated a rack of CDs where two disks had already been removed. He pulled two handfuls from the rack and revealed three more empty shells, each standing on end like a miniature trophy. Billy watched the others indulge in an orgy of sniffing and surveyed the rest of the bedroom for a moment before easing past them to kneel at the floor of the closet. Amid a stew of shoes and boots jumbled together on the dusty floor were a pair of expensive sneakers sitting upright and together within a ring of darker wood that outlined them. Billy poked gently at one of the sneakers with his little finger, nudging it far enough to one side so that he could see the darker outline.

"What the hell's he doing?" Meisner demanded.

Kunkel stepped toward the closet, as if positioning his body defensively in front of Billy.

"Don't touch things, Billy."

"These would be the shoes to match our prints, I'd guess," Billy said. "Size ten."

"Don't fuck with them," Meisner said. "You're tampering with evidence."

"Oh, I don't think you'll find much real evidence," Billy said. "See this ring in the wood? Just water dissolving some of the dust. The shoes have been washed."

"Let *us* determine if the shoes have been washed."

Billy stood. He spoke to Kunkel. "I've seen enough. I'll be in the other room."

Metzger sat in a huge overstuffed chair, much worn by use, obviously his favorite perch, and glared at the officers milling through his house. When he saw Billy, he fastened on him.

Ignoring Metzger was like pretending not to see a bear in the room, so Billy smiled broadly and winked as he fingered a pink and gray afghan quilt on the back of the sofa.

"So, how's life, Curt? Everything going the way you hoped?"

"I hear somebody shot the shit out of you."

"Well, he did, you know. Like I was a dartboard."

Billy knelt behind the sofa and saw a fine dusting of earth that had fallen from the afghan.

"Not a great housekeeper, are you, Curtis? Not one for white gloves."

"He should have shot you in the mouth."

"Your son has some interesting posters on his wall."

"He's got his beliefs. I heard he did shoot your balls off, though. If you ever had any in the first place."

"I got the regulation issue to start with. Unlike you and yours, I didn't take steroids to shrivel them up."

"You want to try them out?"

"I already heard about them, Curt, lad. From what I understand, they'd be kind of hard to find. The shrunken ones are always premature."

"What's that supposed to mean?"

Kunkel came in at the sound of their voices. Billy pointed to the Afghan while continuing to smile at Metzger. Another state trooper came out of Metzger's bedroom holding a fistful of papers covered with large-size print and freehand drawings of an insignia that was a twisted cross, but not quite a swastika.

"What's this shit?" the trooper demanded. "Are you some kind of Nazi?"

"I'm a free, white American male no thanks to you government assholes. I got nothing to hide."

"He's got his beliefs," Billy said.

"Fucking A."

Kunkel sighed heavily. "Billy, will you shut up?"

"Did your son ever talk about wanting to be famous, Curt?"

"What?"

"Did he want people to talk about him?"

"What the fuck for?"

"I don't know, Curt. So he'd get a good table in a restaurant?"

"I don't have to talk to you."

"Just talk to *me*, Curt," Kunkel said. "Did Sandy ever talk about wanting to be famous?"

Metzger shrugged. Conversations with his son took the form of command and response. There was little in the way of character revelation.

"Not to me."

"Did he ever seem suicidal?" Billy asked.

Metzger looked to Kunkel for guidance.

"Did he seem like he wanted to kill himself?" Kunkel repeated.

"You nuts?"

"How about Sandy? Is he nuts?"

"He ain't the one who's nuts," Metzger said darkly. "Some people fucking around with the wrong people, they're nuts, they're the ones out of their fucking minds."

"What did he say? . . . I've seen enough, Pat. I'll leave the rest to the experts."

"You're going already?"

"I think it's pretty clear, isn't it? Unless you want me to go sniff some shells in there."

"I'll talk to you later, then."

"Where does Duane Blanchard live?"

"You got a warrant for Duane?" Metzger asked.

"Just a social call. We're old pals."

Metzger grinned with satisfaction. "Oh, yeah. Duane's going to bust your ass you go out to his place."

"That's why I thought I'd do it now, while he's still at work. Don't tell him though, okay, Curt? . . . Where's he live, Pat?"

"This sounds like a bad idea, Billy."

"My specialty."

Kunkel shook his head. "What are you going to do out there?"

"Joan's kid is missing."

"Kid's a pussy," said Metzger.

"Is that a regular confusion you have, Curtis? You get young boys mixed up with pussies? That would explain your premature problem."

"What the fuck are you talking about? What's he talking about?"

"Billy, will you stop goading him?"

"Tell me where to go and I'm gone."

"You're supposed to be helping me, not confusing things. . . . He lives at the old Bedwell farm. You know where that is?"

"Yeah. He's farming?"

"The Gibson brothers are working the land, Duane's just got the farmhouse and the old feedlot. He's got some chickens and some pigs."

"Got a boar out there'll eat your asshole for you," Metzger volunteered.

"Well, thanks, Curtis. If I want my asshole eaten and you're not around, I know where to go."

As Metzger heaved himself out of his chair, Meisner entered from Sandy's bedroom holding a .22 rifle in his gloved hands.

"Under the mattress in the kid's room." he said.

Another trooper came from the kitchen, waving an envelope triumphantly. " 'Try this for big, asshole,' " he quoted. The trooper held the note so everyone could see the swastika. "Stuck on the refrigerator with a magnet."

CHAPTER TEN

⟨⟨⟨⟨⟨⟨—

The two television trucks were outside the high school as Kunkel had said, their lights and cameras and cables spilling onto the street, making passage a one-way squeeze. Neighbors of the high school were being interviewed with the building in the background, as if their proximity to the school would give them insight into who would want to kill teachers, and why. They were lined up, waiting their turn before the cameras. Later, an editor in the city would rate their performances for emotional content before airing the most distraught. A citizen offering a dispassionate assessment was destined for the cutting-room floor. Billy avoided the temptation to rubberneck at the spectacle as he drove slowly past. He found it obscene and refused to watch it on television; there was no reason to gawk in person. Half a block away from the cameras an aide was hurrying toward the trucks, tugging an overweight priest by the arm to give his fifteen seconds of theological salve. Father Emro, Irish on his mother's side and thus a favorite of the uncles. Billy was surprised to see the cleric looking so good after twenty years, although the bloom in his cheek could have been the flush of booze or the strain of exertion.

As he left the camera trucks behind the unaccustomed hubbub faded and the habitual quiet of Falls City reasserted itself with the drowsy warmth of a thick blanket. It was the first time he had been alone and unmonitored in the place of his youth, he realized, and without Pat beside him to guide or distract, he found that the familiar yet long-forgotten sights and shapes and colors began to reassert themselves in a new way. He passed a house on Fulton whose faded Victorian facade of filigree and wrought iron had somehow convinced him and his friends that it was haunted. It seemed no less haunted now.

On McLean Street he slowed at a small park and remembered vividly an afternoon when he had sat on the swing and read a book by Joseph Altschuler, a vivid tale of a boy stolen by Indians, the sort of adventure story that was the staple of his youth. How much had that influenced his future choice of jobs? he wondered. Could an innocent preference for action stories lead to a shoot-out with a crazed Sabra in Minneapolis?

A block farther on he saw a tree, just a tree, with branches low enough to the ground to inspire a child to climb. Billy could not even remember what his relationship to the tree had been, whether he had woven it into fantasies or if it was some Druidical response, but he felt his throat thicken with emotion.

All at once every yard and every building seemed to come alive with memories and he drove past the sidewalks he had walked on years ago in what seemed like slow motion, as if passing through a thick and viscous medium of nostalgia.

On Harlan Street he turned right and headed for the highway and the section corner half a mile from town where the grids of the geometric county roads intersected. As Billy drove, the corn on either side of the road swayed gently in a mild breeze, giving the fields a sense of heaving life, as if the ground itself were breathing. He remembered the long-forgotten feeling of moving through a landscape whose topography was altered by every puff of wind. In corn and wheat country, it was not the hills or rivers that delineated the land, but the grain itself, the solid blanket of plant life that ceaselessly shifted and sighed. Occasionally, like a propitious alignment of planets, the sun and wind would coordinate in such a way that an entire field would cease to respond to the breeze in a moving wave and rise up all together, holding its long green leaves in concert like a mirror to the light and the field would flash for an instant like a burst of illumination from a nearby star, a miniature nova in a field of grain. Then, with a self-congratulatory sough of collapsing leaves, the light would blink out and the restless emerald carpet would resettle itself upon the land.

Billy sought a wider spot at the margin of the road and pulled to a halt. He stood beside his car and watched the verdant fields waving and winking their luminous eye. The earth itself seemed playful, coyly greeting him and welcoming him back. The long green leaves sawed and scraped against each other, producing a music of stress and relief. He had forgotten so much about his native land, he realized, the good as well as the bad, and he let the memories flood back on him now, the quiet sounds of an earth that was never really silent, the smell of the dirt, even the heat of sun on his neck. For it was a very different sun in the country than in the city, the one inescapable reality of the plains, the sine qua non of farm country. In such flat, crop-dependent land it was easy to understand why the Aztecs, other maize growers far to the south, had worshiped the sun. Indeed, it was difficult to understand why anyone would ever do otherwise. There could be no more natural, generous, ever-present, or searingly cruel god than the sun.

Something about the past, or some selective and romanticized sense of the past overwhelmed him and he found himself on the verge of tears. Everything around him, every sight and sound he had experienced while driving through the town and out into the country attacked him with nostalgic impact and he felt completely defenseless. He did not know if he was weeping for this demanding, beautiful landscape, the repressed, unsophisticated, taciturn people who inhabited it, or a lost image of his innocent youth that seemed to dwell here, suddenly hovering and haunting every wind-shaped contour, every faded, crumbling barn, every rust-covered and abandoned piece of machinery. But he knew that a large part of him was still here, and it was in conflict with another part of him that had chosen to leave and stay away for twenty years.

He shook his head vigorously, reluctant to wipe at the tears that clouded his vision for fear that acknowledging them would only induce more. His mind screamed at him, chiding him for his complete capitulation to cheap sentiment. You don't belong here, Billy, he told himself. You never did. Why did you concoct your phony Irish lilt from imitation brogues in old movies in Falls City, Nebraska, where the accent is as flat as the land, if not to say that you were a visitor only, a curious tourist among the Germans and Bohemians and their dust- and mud-covered way of life? . . . That is what his head told him. His heart was giving him a more disquieting message.

As he approached the Bedwell farm, the pavement stopped and the roads turned to dirt. After a hard rain they would be little more than grooved ruts, no place for a passenger car, and an inexperienced driver would find himself sloughing and spinning in mud to his axle, trying to follow the tracks of big-wheeled tractors and pickups. In summer, as now, a car would send a rooster tail of dust pluming behind him. Billy was now in pure farm country, onto the local roads where directions were no longer given in terms of left and right, but by the compass points, as if everyone had a permanent concept of north embedded in his mental gyroscope, and woe betide those without it. Billy realized that he had long since lost his ability to orient himself without reference to a map or a street sign. When he was younger he could close his eyes, twirl around, and still point unerringly north. Now, on a cloudy day or starless night, he would be lost; his Nebraska survival skills were gone.

He remembered the Bedwell farm, and the Bedwell girl, a sweet, bespectacled girl with pigtailed dark hair and a serious mien, even as a preteen. During his first year in high school Billy had worked for several weeks on an adjoining farm, gouging recalcitrant scrub oak stumps from the ground with ax, metal levers, and tractor in a small stretch of doomed land bordering a creek that the farmer hoped to convert to tillable field. Bare-chested and sweating, though hardly a man at fourteen, he must have presented an interesting spectacle to a curious ten-year-old because she stopped by the fence for several days to watch him work. He did not remember her first name, if he had ever known it, but she was shy and studious and he realized that in some innocent way he was a titillating spectacle to her. On the fourth day she brought him an ice-cold Pepsi and Billy could feel the distinctive bottle in his hand twenty-four years later, thinner, less bulbous than a Coke, with curved grooves making a slow spiral on the glass. It seemed the most delicious, most nearly perfect drink he had ever had, and he drained it in two long drafts. The Bedwell girl had smiled, in her serious way, to see his pleasure at her gift and Billy had winked at her. And carried her in his mind ever since, it seems. He wondered where she was now that Duane Blanchard was living in the farmhouse.

The front door was locked, as was the back. Billy pulled his car next to the house, climbed onto the roof, and found a second-story window open. Duane's bedroom was a fetid mess, smelling of unwashed sheets and stale beer and dried sweat. It was not a place to linger long and Billy had no interest in Duane except for any recent contact he may have had with his son. A quick look told him all he cared to know about Duane's current domestic arrangements. Too many of the loners, the angry letter writers, the crackpots, and the cranks that Billy had investigated over the years lived just like this, like animals nesting in a den, nosing aside the detritus just enough to have a smooth place to sleep.

Another upstairs bedroom had been slept in, although how recently he didn't know. It was sparsely furnished and the bed was a cot with a pillow and a light blanket. A monastic cell where no occupant had left any telltale marks behind other than the imprint of his head on the pillow, no bobby pins or barrettes, no stray socks, no combs, no loose change in the cracks of the floorboards. If Will had spent the night there, it had not been in much comfort. Not that a fifteen-year-old boy would necessarily notice, he thought.

Billy looked out of the bedroom window at the feedlot that started only a few yards beyond the back door. A handful of chickens wandered the lot in their ceaseless quest for food, pecking at the dusty ground. A large sow and several smaller pigs sought the meager shade offered by the barn. Billy saw no bicycle. In the corner of his eye something flashed far to his right. He moved to another window and looked past the feedlot to a line of trees bordering a stream that cut through the property like an unhealed wound. As the wind rearranged the boughs of the scrub oaks he saw the flash again when sunlight struck something reflective in the copse of wood and leaf.

In a small ground-floor room that had probably served the farmer as an office, Billy found the same racist, white-supremacist material that had offended the trooper in Metzger's house. A few pamphlets were on a folding card table, a copy of a well-known racist novel in paperback was lying facedown on the floor beside the table. He recognized the twisted insignia on the cover of one of the pamphlets, the same quasi-swastika he had seen in Metzger's house.

There were no posters, no framed photos of dour men in hooded bedsheets, no Aryan banners, no real indication that Duane took the material any more seriously than soft-core pornography, a source of mild titillation, but still Billy was chilled by the resemblance to Avi Posner's room. Men infected with murderous hate did not necessarily wear indications emblazoned on their foreheads. A truer test of the depth of their conviction might be the casualness with which they treated it, as if virulent hatred were simply an accepted fact of their lives.

Next to the pamphlets were a pair of black driving gloves. Rather than lying flat, they sat upright, holding their own shape. Billy lifted one and was immediately aware of the unusual weight. Duane's hands were bigger than his own and his fingers slid in easily. The leather covered his hand to the second knuckle, leaving the tips of the digits free for delicate manipulation. The weight of the glove was entirely over the first two knuckles, the hitting part of the fist. He flexed his hand and felt the weight shift with it, bending and straightening with just a hint of resistance. Lead tape, he guessed. Pliable and heavy. Heavier still to the person being hit. He smacked his gloved fist into his open palm and immediately wished he had not. There was no effect on the gloved hand. Foam rubber encased the fingers, protecting them from the lead and the concussion of a blow. But Billy's open palm felt as if it had been struck by a baseball bat. They were not brass knuckles, but just as effective. Duane could pound a man senseless wearing those gloves, then handle a pencil to write a note. Billy dropped the glove back to the desktop with a dull thud.

A .22 rifle and a .12 gauge shotgun rested against the wall in the closet—nothing the least bit remarkable about that in rural Nebraska. Duane's truck would probably contain another rifle and a search might turn up a handgun as well. The same could probably be said of most of the farmers in the county and half of the homeowners in its towns, too. It was a land where men hunted with neither qualm of conscience nor public opinion to deter them, and they knew and understood firearms as both utilitarian objects and works of aesthetic beauty. It was not uncommon for a man to buy an extra weapon just because he liked the look and heft of it, just as someone in the suburbs might purchase an extra car with three already in the driveway. They were not gun-happy, or NRA fanatics, Billy knew, just men who had known guns from their youth and took them as a natural part of existence. Billy had been that way himself, had yammered and cajoled until Uncle Sean made him a gift of his first .22 at the age of ten—Lord Jimmy Tree being understood to be too drunk to handle a firearm, even if only to bestow a birthday present. Unlike the ever-growing number of city dwellers who ran home at the first slight to grab their pistol and fire at their enemies, it would not occur to these men raised with weapons to turn them on each other. . . . Natural heirs of the culture of the Old West, they did not live by it. Until now, Billy reflected soberly. It had obviously occurred to someone to do just that at the high school.

Feeling a little silly after having sneered at the troopers, Billy sniffed the barrel of the .22. It did not smell of gunpowder; it did not smell freshly cleaned and oiled. It smelled as if it had rested in place for months, unused. Disappointed but not surprised, Billy leaned the weapon against the wall where he had found it.

In the kitchen, hanging on a peg just beside the back door were several rings of keys. One was marked "housekeys" in fading pencil on a yellow tag and it held three copies of the same key, obviously something Duane did not want to lose. Billy slipped one of the spares into his pocket and left the house.

The chickens hurried toward him, expecting food as he crossed the feedlot. Two of the smaller pigs approached him, too, making hopeful snorts. Some of the chickens turned their attention to the pigs, following them closely, expecting their hooves to stir up insects.

Billy gave the sow a wide berth even though the pigs looked large enough for her to have stopped defending them. She cast a bleary eye on him, but otherwise did not move from her bed of dust.

The massive barn door slid reluctantly on rusting rollers and Billy was assailed by the scent of enclosed rage as a shaft of light penetrated the gloom of the building. In a pen in a corner, close to the door, stood a huge boar, its black body almost invisible in the darkness so that its tiny, baleful eyes seemed to float above straight white legs. With a grunt it launched itself across the pen and rammed into the wooden slats next to Billy. Billy leaped back instinctively as the pen creaked from the blow. The bottom two slats had been reinforced with metal bars, but it still looked dangerously flimsy. Two hundred and fifty pounds of furious animal could do a lot of damage over time.

The boar backed into the middle of the pen, trembling angrily, debating whether to charge again. There were scars on its head and snout and as Billy's eyes adjusted to the gloom of the barn he could make out a few drops of blood oozing from a reopened wound. This was a determined as well as dangerous animal.

During his years in the city, Billy had been amused by the spate of pig-loving in recent years. They starred in their own movies and people had taken to strolling the streets with miniature varieties on a leash. He had wondered if any of them knew what a mean-spirited beast a full-grown boar could be. They were kept penned up because of a hair-trigger ferocity that undoubtedly served their wild cousins well, but made them a menace around other animals. Except for the tusks, they were the same animal that men used to hunt, cautiously and in numbers, on horseback. Only a fool followed a wild boar into a thicket on foot. At times they ate their own young. Billy had heard of a case where a boar at breeding time had attacked and killed a human toddler. He had seen one practically disembowel a particularly stupid dog. And if hungry enough they would eat anything, including human flesh. He had always taken care not to rouse a suckling sow, or a boar under any circumstances.

Billy backed away from the pen, his eye still on the boar. When he got far enough away, the hog seemed to relax somewhat and Billy took that as the minimum safe distance and allowed himself to examine the barn itself.

The Gibson brothers kept some of their machinery in the barn for convenience and it appeared well cared for. The lubricating nipples by the axles were topped with fresh grease and there was no rust anywhere. A bicycle stood next to a harrow. Not exactly hidden, but certainly out of sight to the casual visitor. One would have to be looking for it to find it.

The boar grunted at him as Billy kept his respectful distance and stepped into the feedlot once more. He walked through the chickens, disappointing them all over again, to the edge of the feedlot from which he could see the scar of trees snaking its way through the fields. Something flashed again. It seemed unlike the Gibsons to leave any machinery out in the open—and why in the trees?—they were better farmers than that. Billy climbed to the top rail of the feedlot fence for a better look but still could discern no shape among the leaves to account for the blinking flash.

He dropped on the other side of the fence and started through the field, a nearly useless triangle of land between the creek and the road that the Gibsons had sewn with alfalfa. It would make sweet hay for some livestock eventually, but not here. Grass was one of the few things pigs did not eat.

Halfway to the tree line, Billy saw the trail of dust rising above the corn like a low-lying contrail. Someone was coming, and fast. That took a little longer than expected, Billy thought. Metzger must have had some trouble getting to a phone to alert Duane. Probably because half a dozen cops were trying to get him to tell them where his son was.

Billy jogged back toward the farmhouse. He made it as far as the barn before Curtis Metzger stepped into the feedlot.

"Well, well, hello, shitstick," Metzger said.

"You do know how to sweet talk a guy."

Billy backed toward the barn until he felt the incline of the entryway. He kept his eyes on Metzger.

"I don't see all your cop friends here." The big man walked slowly toward Billy, occasionally kicking out at one of the fowl skittering around his feet. The birds squawked and jumped and hurried off, then folded back in again around his passage. He never really came close to making contact, Billy noted, doubting that it was from any humane instincts on Metzger's part. He was just slow. He had been slow as a football player, too. Huge, but lumbering, requiring several steps to get up to speed and then too many to slow and turn. Billy doubted that the intervening years had improved his reflexes.

"My cop friends have forsaken me, Curt. 'They flee from me who sometime did me seek.'"

"Whatever you think that means." Metzger slowed even further as he got closer. The more slowly he moved, the more menacing he became, Billy thought.

"So what brings you out to Sunnybrook Farm, Curtis? I was expecting Duane."

"Duane's busy. He asked me to take care of it. I said I'd be happy to."

"Take care of what, now?"

"Kicking your ass."

"Ah, well, nice of you to think of me, but you needn't have bothered."

"What are you doing out here?"

"Waiting for you, as it turns out. What are you doing here? What's so interesting about this place that you have to scurry out here to protect?"

Metzger stopped and cocked his head to the side.

"What are you and Duane hiding out here?" Billy continued.

Metzger cocked his head even farther so that he appeared to be viewing Billy out of only one eye, like a bird studying a worm. A slow smile creased his face.

"You ain't going to find out, that's for sure."

Billy stepped into the gloom of the barn, feeling backward with his left hand, his eyes still fixed on Metzger.

Metzger followed, then paused just inside the door where the ground was hard as asphalt, pounded down by the passage of men and machines and animals. "I'm going to beat the shit out of you."

"What will my cop friends say?"

"They won't say shit. I'm within my rights. You're trespassing."

"I believe you have the right to beat the shit out of me only if I'm trespassing on *your* property, Curt."

"You wish."

"Then I guess I could beat the shit out of you because you're trespassing, too."

"Well, let's see how that works out."

Billy stepped back until he felt the slats of the pen behind him. The boar grunted ominously.

Metzger took another step forward. He was three paces away from Billy.

"Now, Curtis, I'm going to warn you one time. If you try to hurt me, I'm going to break your nose and maybe your jaw and throw you to the hogs."

Metzger laughed. "What you going to do that with?"

Billy pulled the homemade sap from his pocket. It looked like nothing more than a darker shape in the gloom.

"What's that supposed to be?"

"It's a sock, Curt. Sort of like the one you beat off in."

"I'm not like you, I don't need to beat off. If I get horny, I just fuck your sister."

"I've been meaning to talk to you about that. That's why I brought the sock, as a matter of fact."

"You're going to need a whole lot more than a sock, asshole."

"No, actually, this will do fine."

"I heard you turned chickenshit."

"Indeed, I did, boyo. Folded like a wet noodle. Just like your dick. Or so the girls tell me."

Billy watched the thoughts pass over Metzger's face in waves. The big man wanted to attack, but he thought better of it, waiting for his eyes to adjust to the darkness. Restraint was not easy for him, however, and the effort at self-control registered as a grimace. Wait all you need to, Billy thought. He wanted Metzger to be able to see when he charged, because he wanted him to know where he was going. A matador has that cape for a reason, Billy thought. He needs to know exactly where the bull is heading. In some ways a blind bull would be more dangerous at close range than a seeing one. It might get lucky with a lunge. A bull that could be focused, however, would be predictable.

"I told them they were wrong," Metzger said. "You couldn't *turn* chickenshit, because you were always chickenshit in the first place."

"I'm afraid of many things, Curtis. Some days I'm even afraid of my wallpaper. But I don't want you to act on misinformation. I'm not now, and never have been, afraid of you. I'm not carrying this sock because I'm afraid of you. I brought it along to punish you."

"You shit too."

"But I'm not shitting now, boyo. I'm going to bust you up for what you did to my sister."

Metzger charged, but hopelessly slowly. Billy stepped to the side and hit him in the face with the sap. The big man took a step backward, his mouth open, blood already spurting from his nose, and sat down heavily. For a moment he seemed not to know where he was, then he reached for his face, his fingers trailing through the blood.

"That would be from the broken nose," Billy said. He repositioned himself so that his back was against the slats of the pen again. The boar shuffled excitedly behind him. "How's the jaw? Okay? Not broken? Well, nobody's perfect."

Metzger shifted his focus from himself to Billy, who leaned against the pen with studied casualness.

"Funny thing about this sock deal, Curt. Tremendous concussive power, but it leaves no marks of its own. Didn't even break the skin."

Metzger got slowly to his feet and spat the blood that had run into his mouth.

"You're dead," he said.

"I know that feeling. . . . Now, Curt, I want you to understand that the broken nose is from me. Just for old time's sake. The next one is from my sister."

"I got something for your sister."

"Yeah, but it doesn't work, does it?"

Metzger tested his teeth with his thumb. It was a poor attempt at distraction, and when he charged again, Billy was ready. He broke to the opposite side this time and smashed the sap against the back of Metzger's head just as the big man collided with the pen. The slats hit him at waist level and his momentum, with an added impetus from Billy's blow, carried him over the side of the pen in an awkward flip. He landed on his back, his breath exploding.

Billy heard the boar grunt, heard Metzger's scream, but did not look back.

He was all the way to the section corner before the adrenaline released him and he began to shake. Sweat broke out on his forehead and in his armpits and his chest quivered when he breathed. If it wasn't fear, it seemed a convincing simulation. Sunlight flashed off his windshield as he turned south to go to town and Billy squinted and saw Posner in the glass, smiling jaggedly. He seemed rather pleased with himself.

CHAPTER ELEVEN

Joan lay on the sofa where Billy had left her, hobbled once to the bathroom, then returned to the sofa, waiting for his return. Bed would have been more comfortable, but she had never felt right lying on the bed with her clothes on and undressing seemed like an impossibly difficult chore. Besides, she needed to be ready to move when called about her son—although who might call or where she might be needed was not at all clear. Never mind how she would get there with her leg the way it was and her car a stick shift. Still, although only a few steps removed from the bedroom, the sofa was closer to the action if there should be any. She did not really think that anything had happened to Will, her reaction on not finding him at home had been as much a release of the tension of the events as genuine concern about her son.

This was not a town in which bad things happened to fifteen-year-old boys. The fact that something terrible had just happened to adults seemed so unreal that it had not yet changed her view of Falls City and the lazy, sleepy security of the place. It was impossible to imagine that anyone would ever wish ill to gentle, harmless Sharon Shattuck, much less hate her enough to kill her. She was such a good soul; Joan regretted never taking the trouble to get to know her better, but she was not drawn to good souls. Something in her nature sought friends who walked a bit outside the lines. She was attracted to the rebels and the engagingly quirky, always had been. In Falls City it didn't require much to qualify as a rebel. Voting as a Democrat would do it. Talking loud in a hushed room would also serve. She had a bit of a reputation as a wild woman, herself, although what she had ever actually done to warrant such repute—as opposed to what she talked about doing—she did not know. It was more the glint in her eye and a willingness to speak to strangers. Or flirting with inappropriate men. And a fat lot of good that trait has done for me, she thought ruefully. A self-proclaimed wild woman who has never done anything braver than to divorce an abusive husband. Now pushing forty, lying on her sofa with a hole in her leg and yearning for nothing more than stability.

Thom Cohan was not harmless the way Sharon Shattuck was, of course. He lived too much by principle for that to be the case. Anyone who believed in things enough to stand up for them offered a certain impediment to the freedom of others. A man who would not yield could be a man in someone else's way—but that still made no case for killing.

Her own shooting troubled her less than the other two although she knew that should not be so. She assumed she must be in denial but for the moment it seemed an acceptable condition. It was far less frightening than following the train of thought that originated with the assumption that the bullet that struck her had actually been intended for her. Whoever meant to kill her, to kill *her* and not some random victim, was still out there. She did not know which assumption was worse, that murderous rage had popped up spontaneously like some quantum phenomenon with a rifle, or that she and Thom had been targeted. Any way she twisted it, she could not include Sharon Shattuck in a homicidal design. She could put Thom and herself together, however. The pieces dovetailed all too convincingly. If he had actually known that Thom Cohan had slept with her, Duane was probably crazy enough to do something about it. But their actual liaisons had been very discreet and cautious, and the affair had ended some time ago. Still, Duane savored his vengeance cold as well as steaming hot and liked to administer punishments for imagined grievances again and again.

A car pulled into her driveway and moments later she heard a single knock on the back door before the door opened.

"You decent?" Billy called, stepping into the house.

"Well, I'm dressed anyway. I never thought there was anything indecent about being naked in your own home, though."

Billy rounded the corner from the kitchen and stood at the foot of the sofa.

"That depends whether or not you're having tea with the vicar, I suppose," he said. "Not that you have a vicar around here."

"No, I've never had a vicar. How about you?"

"Not when sober, at least. I'm sure I'd remember."

She lay on the sofa, her head propped against the armrest on one end, her naked feet atop the other. He lightly touched her bare foot, a gesture that struck her as surprisingly and shockingly intimate.

"Oh!"

"What?"

She shook her head, astounded that she had felt the touch all the way through her body.

Billy placed his palm on the top of her foot. His hand was warm and dry.

"How you feeling?"

"I'm surprised it doesn't hurt more," said Joan. "The anesthetic was worse than anything."

"You were lucky. It just hit the flesh of your thigh."

Joan craned her head to look at her legs. She still wore the shorts she had on when she was shot. It had been more than a day since she had shaved her legs and she knew they would feel like sandpaper.

"You couldn't miss those thighs," she said disgustedly.

"You have great legs. Beautiful legs."

"Fat," she said, but pleased that he disagreed.

Billy smiled at her. "Beautiful. And you know it."

He looks like he's going to try to jump my bones as I lie here, she thought. Under the circumstances, she wouldn't let him, of course, but it would be nice if he tried. At least she thought she wouldn't let him.

"What color is Will's bike?" he asked, unexpectedly.

She had to think for a moment before recalling the color and make.

Billy nodded. "It's in Duane's barn. The bed in the guest room was slept in."

"That son of a bitch. He heard I was in the hospital and snatched my son."

"Looks like it."

"He's not allowed. It's not his weekend."

"Do you think he might have taken him to work with him? He's not on the farm, I don't think."

"He could have. The bastard. I'll have Pat Kunkel get Will back and throw Duane's ass in jail."

"Pat's a little busy right now," Billy said. "Why not just call Duane and have him bring Will home?"

Joan laughed unpleasantly. "Have Duane voluntarily do something I ask him to do? Fat chance. He knows this will drive me crazy."

"What does he want?"

"What he always wants, to manipulate me, to make me jump through hoops for him. He wants me to make him feel powerful, the sick son of a bitch."

"I'll get your son back."

"No."

"No?" He lifted his hand from her foot and gestured consternation with both hands. He did not return his hand to her foot.

She shook her head. "Not Duane, Billy. Let Pat do it, he seems to be able to deal with him."

"You question my social skills?"

"Is that what you call them?" She lifted the foot of her uninjured leg, bouncing it entreatingly on the sofa's armrest. Billy seemed not to notice.

"Duane is dangerous," she continued.

"You keep telling me that."

"Because he is. He beat Scott Falter nearly senseless."

"I heard. Why?"

Joan was silent. "No good reason," she said finally.

Billy enclosed her foot in his hand and she gasped again. His hand was so warm. He held it for a moment, then slowly, firmly pulled his hand toward her toes, stretching the muscles. Joan closed her eyes and groaned with pleasure.

"Feel good?"

She groaned again in response. He continued to massage her foot with long, slow pulls. After a moment he ran a finger between each of her toes in turn.

"Jesus," she said. "Who knew?"

"You've never had a foot rub?"

"Is that what this is? I thought it was some sort of out-of-body experience."

"So we have a first," he said.

"Never, ever, ever stop."

He ran his fingernails along the top of her foot from ankle to the very end of her toes. Joan shivered with pleasure. Billy watched her reaction closely.

"It's almost too intense—but it's not," he said. "Just takes a little courage."

"All this is in my *foot*?" And just what could he do with the rest of me? she wondered.

"I can't believe you've never had anyone do this," he said.

She opened her eyes and saw him smiling at her, pleased with himself. He likes giving pleasure, she thought. How unusual in a man.

"Who would do it? Duane wouldn't demean himself."

"It's not all that exotic."

"It is if you've never had it. Do you know what the word 'massage' means to most men? Three digs at your shoulders then they grab your boobs . . . don't stop, don't stop."

"Why did Duane beat up Scott Falter?"

Joan hesitated. Billy released her foot.

"You are a cruel, unsubtle bastard," she said. "You're torturing me for information."

"I could hit you with a rolled-up newspaper if you prefer," he said.

"Maybe later."

He put his hand on her foot again and slowly moved his thumb along the sole. Joan sighed, closed her eyes again, and told him about Scott Falter.

Scott was a pharmacist from Auburn, a town of a few thousand souls thirty miles away. Short, barrel-chested, prematurely balding, he seemed in many ways an unlikely suitor. Only a few inches over five feet herself, Joan had never dated a man shorter than she was. Leaning down to kiss him felt odd and when they embraced standing up his face fit into the hollow of her neck. She was accustomed to pressing her head against a man's shoulder. Although the disparity in their heights did not seem to bother Scott—he had seldom known it otherwise—she had taken to wearing flats whenever they were together in deference to his ego. Or what she assumed was his ego, acknowledging to herself that so many years with Duane may have given her a twisted sense of just how vulnerable a thing the male psyche really was. Scott was not glib, not obviously bright—although she assumed a pharmacy degree required some degree of intelligence—not funny, not sexy, not "hot." He possessed none of the charm or outlaw appeal that Joan usually responded to. He was stable, stolid, a little boring. But he was ardent. He had reaffirmed Joan's belief in the power of ardor in romantic transactions.

"He sent flowers, a Valentine's card, birthday card—all before we even had a date," she said.

"You like flowers?"

"I love them. And I loved that he *sent* them, not on any special occasion, just because he thought of it. And he called just to talk. I mean, I know it was all to a purpose, but not an *immediate* purpose. It wasn't like a man saying nice things while he works on your bra strap. It was like he was just there, in the near distance, smiling, waving. Not pushing in any aggressive way. I mean I had told him I didn't think it was a good idea to go out together, so when he sent flowers or a Valentine, it wasn't as if he immediately followed it with a request for a date. It was as if he sent them just because he liked me."

"Joanie, you've never lacked for men who like you."

"Thanks for the assumption, I guess, but you don't really know what I've done for the past twenty years, do you?"

"You're right."

"Believe me, having a man who just genuinely seems to like you, for your own self, without getting anything out of it—that is *very* seductive. Especially when you've got nothing more . . . intimate in your life. Which I didn't."

"So you went out with him."

"I didn't particularly like him. I mean, I never *dis*liked him, I just wasn't attracted. Not to *him*. But to the rest of it, the wooing, the courtship, yes. It was very . . . sweet. And so unexpected. He showered me with attention, but from a distance so I never felt threatened or smothered. As a man you can't imagine how good it makes you feel to get flowers delivered to your door, or to your office in the high school, for no particular reason. Just because somebody cares about you."

"So you went out with him. Can't blame you for that. It sounds like I'd go out with him, too."

"I don't need to justify going out with anyone. I'm single."

"I know."

"You give great foot, Billy, but that doesn't give you the right to judge my life."

"I wasn't, I don't. I'm just trying to find out what happened between Scott Falter and Duane."

"Why? It's over."

"You keep telling me how dangerous Duane is. Maybe I should know more about him."

Joan considered her words carefully. "Duane is dangerous to anyone he thinks is involved with me. If you're not involved with me, just stay out of his way and you should be fine."

"I am involved with you, Joan. You're a friend. You could use some help."

"I'll get Will back on my own, don't worry about it. And we were friends twenty years ago, Billy. That doesn't have to mean anything now."

"But it obviously does. I'm here, aren't I?"

Joan gently removed her foot from his grasp. "We *were* just friends, weren't we? I don't think my memory's that bad yet. We were part of the same group, that's all."

"That's all."

"You never dated anyone for very long, as I remember. . . . And certainly not me."

"Duane saw to it that nobody else dated you. . . . I guess he still does. But you're right, we never dated, we never went out . . . but there was a . . . moment."

Joan looked at him silently. She was not going to help.

"You've probably forgotten it," he offered, waiting for her to join him in reminiscence. She continued to look at him, her face now expressionless. "A New Year's Eve? Our senior year?"

"I was always drunk on New Year's Eve. I don't remember much about them," she said.

Billy smiled sadly. "Well, I'm glad I do. It's sustained me through the years, that brief memory."

She laughed explosively. "Bullshit!"

A grin lit his face. "In times of sorrow, I had but to think of holding you in my arms, twenty years earlier."

She kicked at him playfully. "Ah, Charming Billy. You were always so full of it. No one could believe you from one sentence to the next."

"Just my way of masking sincerity, telling the truth. Is it my fault no one takes me seriously?"

"Yes."

"Ah, you're a hard case, you are, lass," he said in his brogue. "A man could get a chill from ya, he could, sure now."

"I don't remember the Irish accent from high school, though."

"It's a little refinement I added recently. Charms the lads as well as the ladies."

"You could always make me laugh, Billy."

"And you could always make me poor heart beat faster, sure you could. Even if you can't remember it at all, at all."

"Oh, I remember it. We were all in Denise Schatz's basement. The stroke of midnight and for some reason I was alone for a second. I don't know where Duane was, probably outside fighting somebody. All the couples are kissing and suddenly here comes the great Billy Tree, walking straight at me. Homing in on me like we belonged together. It was like a soldier getting off the train and going for his girl."

"I couldn't believe Duane wasn't there. I figured I had to act fast."

"You didn't kiss me like you were thinking about Duane."

"Not during the actual kiss, no. That would have put me off a bit."

"Kisses, plural, as I remember."

"I may have got carried away."

"Or maybe I did. . . . It was a memorable moment, Billy," she said softly.

"Yes."

"I put a lot of store by kisses in those days. I thought you could tell something about the person by them."

"It takes a good deal of kissing to learn otherwise," he said.

"I'm not sure how you can tell anything about a person anymore."

"Behavior over time."

"Maybe, but I doubt it. People can always act one way and think another. In fact most of us do, most of the time. . . . What are you staring at?"

"I can't believe how lovely you are, Joanie."

"Oh, Billy don't say things like that to me. Not while I'm wounded. It's not fair."

"I don't play fair, I don't fight fair. Never saw the point."

"You and Duane have that much in common, at least."

"Have you noticed how he keeps coming into our conversation, no matter what we're talking about?"

"If you're going to say nice things to me, you'd better keep him in mind."

"Right you are. Excellent way to sober me right up when I'm about to be overcome by sentiment."

"He gave Scott one warning. I can't promise he'll do the same with you."

"He told Scott to stop seeing you?"

"Not that politely you can bet, but I don't think he did anything physical the first time. He just popped up in front of Scott, out of nowhere, making him feel *very* vulnerable, I'm sure. He loves surprises, most of all when you think you're safe. Anyway, he scared Scott enough for him to start carrying a gun in his car. He didn't scare him enough to stop seeing me. I wish he had."

"What happened?"

"Oh, Duane did what he does. He waited long enough for Scott to let his guard down, we went out a few times, never even saw Duane, never saw his car, never saw him lurking in the shadows—but I'm sure he was there somewhere. Then one night Scott brought me home, walked out to his car—and there was Duane. Scott went for his gun and Duane proceeded to beat him half to death. He was wearing his gloves—he has these gloves, black gloves, they're like the kind racing drivers wear, but they've been stiffened or hardened or something, I don't know what, but he never seems to hurt his hands, no matter how much he pounds on people. I could see their faces in the streetlight, but his hands were too dark, it was like he was hitting Scott with nothing at all."

"He did it in front of you?"

"Oh, sure. That was the whole point. It's me he's trying to scare as much as anybody stupid enough to spend time with me. . . . I called the police, but they came much too late to help Scott. The police were afraid of Duane, they *are* afraid of him. Fortunately Pat Kunkel showed up. He pulled Duane off of Scott or he might still be beating on him."

"Was he arrested?"

"Pat doesn't necessarily arrest people. He just moves them away from trouble. He got Duane out of here while the police got an ambulance for Scott. Nothing was ever done because Scott went for his gun before Duane touched him. Self-defense."

"Sounds a bit beyond that."

"Scott never pressed the matter. I guess he'd had enough. Of Duane. Of me. Maybe he thought Duane would kill him next time. Maybe he was right."

"And how did you react to it?"

"Oh, it worked. I got the point."

"I mean with Scott. Did you ever see him again?"

Joan looked at Billy as if he were crazed.

"And put him in further danger? Of course not. I haven't seen or heard from him since. . . . What, do you think I should have?"

"I don't know. If I'd suffered that kind of abuse because of a woman . . . would I want her to write me off?"

"I didn't write him off. I was trying to keep him alive."

"Did you tell him that?"

"I didn't need to. What are you getting at?"

"Somebody shot you, Joan. That usually requires a serious grievance."

"You think it was Scott Falter because I didn't send him a get-well card? Get serious. If he was going to shoot anybody, it would be Duane."

"You would think."

"It makes no sense."

"I've spent fifteen years dealing with people who picked the wrong person as the source of their grievance. These things don't always take a straight line. People get very twisted."

"If you're after twisted, go after Duane. . . . But don't, Billy. Really, I mean it. Stay away from him. He probably knows you're here right now. Don't make it any worse."

"Ah, you know me, Joan. Never the man for trouble, haven't the stomach for it, at all, at all. I'm more the kiss-the-girls-and-make-them-cry kind of boy."

She looked at his lean face for a long time without speaking. The prominent cheekbones, the dark brown eyes, the sensuous mouth were the same as she remembered them from their youth. Billy had always looked like a handsome cross between a Sioux and an Irishman, but something had been taken away over time. For all the flirting, winking, and dodging, it was a serious face and it seemed to Joan that somewhere over the years it had lost not only the baby fat but the true merriment that once danced behind those eyes. She still saw devilment there, but little joy.

"I don't think you're any kind of boy anymore," she said sadly. "I'm afraid you've become a man."

And that can only mean more trouble, she thought.

He seemed to read her mind. "Not me, Joanie. Nothing to worry about with me. I've become a coward. It suits me."

After he left her he drove to the florist's shop in the town's single hotel. He paid cash for a bouquet to be sent to Joan Blanchard but when they asked if he cared to include a card, he just smiled.

"Ah, that would be giving it away now, wouldn't it?" he said with a touch of the brogue.

The young clerk was certain the man was some kind of foreigner, he had such a funny way of talking.

CHAPTER TWELVE

W hat could you have been thinking?" Kath demanded when he told her what he had done to Curtis Metzger.

"I thought you'd be pleased."

"Pleased? You've made an awful enemy, Billy."

"We weren't real close to begin with."

"Do you think he's going to let it go at this? Do you think Curt Metzger is just going to say 'well, okay, I tried to rape his sister and he broke my nose, so I guess we're even?' He's not going to leave it there. He's going to come after you."

"What did you want me to do?"

"I didn't want you to do anything! Did I ask you to do anything?"

"Did you honestly think I wouldn't do anything after you told me that story? You're terrified if he's even in the same room."

"And how do you think I feel now? What if he decides to come after me instead of you?"

"I had to do something, Kath. I couldn't just let it go."

"Why not? *I* did. *I'm* the one it happened to. . . . Couldn't you at least have done something more creative?"

"I thought the boar was a good touch."

"Couldn't you have made him pay without letting him know it came from me and you, at least? Did it have to be a beating? You men are so stupid."

Billy felt that he could not very convincingly argue the point.

The sheriff's department was located in the town's former armory, an architectural anachronism left over from the Depression that had been converted to offices by the installation of walls built from cinder block and a cheap, fake lauan paneling that gave an oddly Oriental atmosphere to the municipal business. Windowless, airless, lighted by a fluorescent ceiling fixture that resembled an inverted feed trough for chickens, Kunkel's office was as much a cell as the one two doors farther down the narrow corridor where the prisoners were housed. Bars instead of walls were just a formality and might have been an improvement over concrete and lauan, Billy thought. They might at least give the illusion of openness.

Kunkel sat in an old-fashioned wooden swivel chair behind the dreary universal government-issue olive drab metal desk. The sheriff was never truly still, even when at rest, turning, jiggling, shifting his weight. It could have been an ongoing process to accommodate his sore back, Billy reflected, or it could as easily have been a way to deal with the claustrophobia imposed by the office.

"One pisser of a day," Kunkel said. "You ever have to deal with these television people, Billy?"

"A few times. Persistent, aren't they?"

Kunkel shook his head back and forth as if he had just been given a stunning blow and was trying to clear the dancing lights from his vision.

"They just keep coming at you, no matter what you tell them."

"Like being swarmed by gnats," Billy said.

"Except you can't swat them. Once they got that camera on you, you know you got to be real careful or they're going to be showing you with your foot in your mouth, again, and again, and again."

"You don't want to be one of their highlights, that's for sure. . . . And yet?"

Kunkel waited, one eyebrow arched.

"Come on, Pat. Admit it. There's more to it . . ."

Kunkel laughed. "Ah, shit. You're good, Billy."

"You kind of liked it, didn't you?"

Kunkel continued to laugh silently, his shoulders shaking. He pointed a finger at Billy, a proud teacher with his student.

"You got those people, you got the cameras and the tape recorders and the note takers—you wanted to keep talking, didn't you, Pat?"

"They did seem kind of interested in what I had to say."

"It's intoxicating to have people really pay attention, isn't it?"

"You didn't used to be this smart, did you?"

"It was hard to let them go, wasn't't? A letdown when they turned off those lights and that little red eye on the camera went out. . . . I used to wonder how they got all those people to talk to them, right after some disaster, people in a state of shock, some asshole sticks a mike in front of them and asks them how they feel—I never knew why they bothered to answer them . . ."

"Until they were asking *you* questions," Kunkel said knowingly. "You got it right, Bill. It was kind of fun. I was sorry I couldn't really tell them anything. They would have held me up by my ankles and shook me to get the change out of my pockets if I'd let them."

"Well, they'll be here tomorrow, too, I imagine."

"I expect. Meanwhile, like I don't have enough to do already, I get this complaint from Curtis Metzger. Seems you whopped him from behind and sicced that half-crazed boar of Duane's on him."

"I whopped him from the front, too. In the interest of a balanced attack."

"Sounds like you're proud of your work."

"If you're going to do a thing, do it well."

"What put your mind to it, exactly?"

Billy told him of Metzger's abortive rape of his sister.

"Kath should have come to me," Kunkel said when Billy finished.

"She didn't think she could tell anyone about it, Pat."

"What the hell am I here for?"

The sheriff threw a bent paper clip into the wastebasket in frustration, then reached for another from his desk.

"People have got to learn to have more faith in law enforcement," he continued. "I would have handled it a lot more discreetly than you did. . . . You did a fine job, though, Billy, I must say. Curtis was howling all the way to the hospital. The hog just missed the family jewels."

"It sounds like they're paste anyway."

"He *will* be mildly pissed at you, I suspect. You'd better give him a wide berth for a while."

"As far as I'm concerned, the business is finished."

"I'll have a word with him, you understand, but there's only so much I can do. . . . I do worry about your health, Billy."

"I've been concerned for a long time myself."

"You may have just put it in jeopardy."

"That's what my sister seems to think."

"I'd have to say you were downright reckless, tackling a man as big and stupid and mean as Curt Metzger and just bunging him up a little. I have to wonder what made you take a chance like that? You trying to prove something?"

"Just a little primitive justice, is all."

"Uh, huh. Well, I'm supposed to be providing the justice around here. You sure you weren't fighting some demon of your own, sticking your neck out like this?"

"It didn't impress him."

"Who? Curtis?"

"The demon."

"Uh, huh. Well, I'll leave that to you and your shrink. . . . Listen Billy, I would like to keep you around and in working order. I need your help seriously now with this shooting, you know that. Those reporters will be dogging my every move, but they don't know you. You could move around, do some things for me, if you would . . . but I got to tell you, you might be better advised to leave town again for a time."

"Curtis won't be sneaking up on me for quite a while yet, I don't imagine."

"Hard as it is to believe, Curtis has his friends."

"Duane."

"A different breed of cat altogether, our Duane. Maybe I'll have a little preemptive talk with him, too. . . . Not that I think he's necessarily inclined to fight Metzger's battles for him, but Duane never needs much of an excuse. . . . I think I can keep him away from you, though. . . . Unless you're showing an interest in his woman."

"Joan doesn't think of herself as his woman."

"Well, Joanie . . . Joanie's kind of a wild one, you know."

"No, I didn't know."

"Now, don't get feisty."

"Sure, now, I wouldn't be after doing such a ting, at all, at all."

"Don't get all weird, either. I just mean Joanie's got kind of a history of . . ."

"Of what, Pat? Put a name to it."

"I don't actually know what's going on, you understand. But she . . . shit, she'll talk to anybody. I mean men no woman in her right mind would be talking to. And there's something about her—hell, face it, she's damned attractive and she gives the impression of . . ."

"Being friendly?"

"Okay, Bill. I can see you don't want to hear anything against her. And it's not against her anyway, not really. It's not that she ever does anything—she just seems . . . possible. You know?"

"Possible."

"I'm being polite, here . . . I *like* Joanie, don't get me wrong."

"I don't think I'm getting you wrong, Pat. I think you're getting *her* wrong. I think maybe Duane is whispering in your ear."

"I wouldn't let Duane close enough to whisper in my ear. The stupid son of a bitch is crazy enough to bite it off. . . . Look, Billy, all I'm saying is those two have been loving and fighting each other for twenty years. You don't want to get in the middle of a cat fight."

"She thinks he's stolen her son."

"First of all, he can't *steal* Will, the boy is his own son. He might have him with him at the moment, I don't know. She was in the hospital, it's not that unreasonable to take care of your son when the mother can't, now is it?"

"Are you going to get him back for her?"

"When I got time, Billy. We're a little busy right now."

"I'll get her son for her."

"Well, now, I don't want you to do that. That will only cause trouble. . . . What is all this, anyway? You and Joan never had anything going on in high school, did you?"

"No."

"You been in touch with her all the time you were gone? You have one of those E-mail affairs?"

"No. I haven't spoken to her since I left."

"You been pining for her all this time?"

"No. Can't say I've even thought much about her until I got back."

"So what's the deal? Why are you . . . what's going on that's got you so riled up?"

"Sure, 'tis me Irish blood."

"Let me tell you something, Billy. You were a Secret Service agent, and I know you were a good one—don't give me that guff about how you failed, because Kath and your uncles kept everybody posted through the years about all your medals and commendations and shit. I know you were damned good at what you did. But the sheriff of Richardson County isn't just a peace officer, he's an *administrator*. I have to *administer* this whole county, that means all the people in it, to keep them friendly and peaceable and under control. And the best way to do that is not always the obvious and easy way. Sometimes it makes more sense to just separate two drunks who are fighting than throwing them both in jail. They'll be a lot more grateful to you in the morning, too. You see what I'm saying?"

"The gist seems to be 'sit down and shut up and mind your own business.' That about it?"

Kunkel grinned. "You're a pisser, Billy. Yeah, that's about it. I'll get Joanie's boy back to her, you help me find Sandy Metzger."

"You think they're together?"

"I've got no reason the think that. From all I see, Sandy was doing the shooting all on his own. I would think he ran off on his own."

"You don't want Sandy Metzger, Pat."

"I don't?"

"Not if you're looking for the shooter. I don't think Sandy did the shooting."

Kunkel leaned back in his chair and put his feet up on the desk in an elaborate display of making himself comfortable.

"I assume this will take a while," he said when he was settled. "Because it seems to me we have the cartridges, the gun, the shoes, the blanket, the note, all found in his room or his house. Plus we have one fled perpetrator. I don't know what that adds up to in Washington, but here it looks pretty cut-and-dried."

"And maybe one of the dumbest perps you've ever had, wouldn't you say?"

"The boy's a Metzger, what do you expect? He's always talking about how he's going to do something big someday. How he's going to be bigger and badder than his old man. He's on steroids, too, I wouldn't be surprised. Maybe something else as well, we'll know more about that when the lab checks in about some of that stuff in his room. He's also some sort of Fascist-Nazi, whatever that crap Curtis believes in is called. Not to mention being kicked out of school by Thom Cohan, who he subsequently shot three times. Motive, mind-set, opportunity, enough physical evidence to convict a lawyer. You found bike tracks in the ditch, Sandy's bike is missing ... I'd say that's enough to arrest him, wouldn't you?"

"Arrest him, no. I wouldn't do that, Pat. Those newspeople will have him fixed as the killer as soon as you do, whether he is or not. I think he's not. But in any case, if they have any justification for reporting that it was a kid shooting his teachers, you think you've got the press here now? You'll have them crawling in and out of your nose. They won't be able to get enough of it. Find Sandy and talk to him, sure. But don't arrest him—if you find him."

"We'll find him. Where can he hide around here? Wait, there was something else I wanted to ask you. What was it?" He scratched his head in parody of a man remembering. "Oh, yeah. Why in hell do you think he didn't do it?"

"The shooter we first learned about, the one who crawled through the field of milo and fired the shots while lying on a blanket, was a careful man. He was careful enough to get into that field and back out again without anyone seeing him. He was careful enough to pick up his shell casings. He was careful enough to lie on a blanket so he wouldn't leave any telltale impression in the dirt, and he was careful enough to go to considerable trouble to cover his drags by dragging them clean when he walked backwards out of that field. Right?"

"But not so careful he didn't leave a footprint."

"One footprint, right. Or more accurately, one heel print. Let's start with that. You're walking backwards, dragging a blanket between two rows of milo not much farther apart than shoulder width. The milo plants are spaced how far apart from each other, two feet, three? Your whole purpose is to cover your footprints, so you have to be conscious of where you're walking, right? But somehow he manages to step off the track, between two plants, and leave a perfect impression of his heel. How did he step back onto the track without hitting a plant, leaving just that one print? If he did hit a plant, he'd know he was off track, right? He was walking backwards, he could *see* the print he'd just left, couldn't he?"

"He made a mistake. He had to be in a hurry, he'd just shot people."

"It's like walking on a tightrope, going backwards, between rows like that. You'd know if you stepped off, Pat."

"The fact is, he left a print."

"The fact is, a print was left."

Kunkel put his feet on the floor and threw another paper clip into the wastebasket. "Meaning?"

"Meaning I think the shooter left the print deliberately."

"Then why would he go to the trouble to cover his tracks?"

"Because the print he left for us to find was not his. He didn't want us to know anything about himself, but he did want us to find a print from Sandy Metzger's sneaker. I think he carried the shoe with him and pressed it into the ground while erasing all the imprints of his own shoes."

Kunkel shifted restlessly in his chair. "And I think he made a misstep and didn't notice or didn't have the time to go back and fix it. This is not a mental giant we're dealing with here, Billy."

"So Sandy goes to the trouble of covering his tracks, picking up his shells—how many casings did you find in his room, by the way?"

"Four."

"And how many shots were fired into the school? Three into Cohan, one into Sharon Shattuck, one into Joan—so five at least, right? Did you find any more bullets in the schoolroom?"

"Not yet."

"He fired five times, picked up four shells. Where's the fifth?"

"Does it matter?"

"I don't know. What do you suppose he did with the other one? . . . So Sandy shoots five times, hits five targets, picks up his shells, then he hightails it home, washes his sneakers but doesn't dry them quite well enough, takes those shells he so carefully saved and hides them where a blind man could find them, stacked up like trophies, and then hides the murder weapon. Where does he hide it? Under his mattress? Under his *mattress*?! Please. Why not paste a sign over his door saying 'Look in here for all the clues you need'?"

"Billy, sit down. You're getting red in the face. Look, you've been dealing with fairly clever criminals, right? People who are planning to kill the President or the Vice President or the first lady or whoever. Maybe those are smart people, I don't know. I guess they must be. I guess they must be difficult to find and hard to catch and that's why you need all the brains of the Secret Service to get them, but in Falls City—I say this with no disparagement to my fellow citizens—but around here the crimes are not big and the goofs who do them are not bright. They leave clues whatever they do. Remember Dicky Dorr? He broke into the Stucker place, stole some stuff, put it into one of their pillowcases, and walked straight home through the backyards with his loot." Kunkel paused like a good comedian. "It was the middle of a snowstorm. He left his tracks in six inches of fresh snow. All I had to do was walk over there. He had put the pillowcase on his own pillow. It was monogrammed with the initials 'K. S.' "

"Maybe we should be looking for Dickie Dorr in this case."

"I think we got his spiritual cousin in Sandy Metzger."

"But, Pat, the shooter was trying to *hide* his tracks. Why bother to do that and then leave the blanket and shells and weapon and shoes—plus a goddamned note—in his own house? Why go home and drop them off, wash his shoes, leave them behind, then jump on his bike and disappear, for that matter? If you're leaving town, why not go right away? Why not just jump on that bike and ride like hell?"

"He went home to hide the gun."

"Using 'hide' in the same sense that you hide an Easter egg. It was meant to be found."

"What about the note?"

"Do we know who wrote it?"

"Of course we know who wrote it. Sandy wrote it to his father and signed it with a swastika."

"It was written to 'asshole,' whoever that might be. It seems to be the nickname of a lot of people these days, myself included."

"It was what he called his father behind his back. The only thing he called him. Everybody knows that."

"Metzger's group doesn't use a swastika, by the way. It's something that resembles it, but it's different."

Kunkel shrugged. "So?"

"So, another inconsistency, is all."

Sheriff Kunkel fought to retain his patience and the struggle played out on his face like a series of small, suppressed pains.

"Come on, Billy. You're stretching pretty far. It's obvious Sandy wrote the note."

"In fact, nobody wrote it, did they, Pat? It was printed, in block letters. That's awfully hard to trace, it's not like writing in cursive. Anybody could have printed it."

"I'll have to take your word for it. I'm no expert on handwriting."

"Well, notes are something I do know about. Typewritten notes, computer printed notes, handwritten notes, block-printed notes, notes with letters cut out of magazines—it's hard to threaten the President without some kind of note. And block letters are as hard to pin on anybody as anything, harder than a typewriter, harder than a printer."

"See, Billy, you're thinking too big again. This is not a threat to the President. It was a note from Sandy to his father. Why else would he put it on the refrigerator? Who else would see it there?"

"How about a houseful of cops?"

Kunkel heaved himself to his feet. It took him a second to stretch his back completely, an action accompanied with tics and grimaces that did little to mask his annoyance. "Where are you going with this?"

"You wanted me to advise you, right? Well, so, I'm advising you."

"I'm listening, Billy. Don't misunderstand me, I'm grateful for your thoughts—but I haven't heard any advice yet. What are you telling me?"

"Keep looking for Sandy, but don't stop looking for somebody else, too."

"And who would that be?"

"Whoever wanted to kill Thom Cohan or Sharon Shattuck or Joan Blanchard. Or all three."

Kunkel sighed, making no effort to disguise his weariness. "Someone other than Sandy Metzger, you mean?"

"Someone who thought Sandy Metzger would be a very convenient scapegoat. . . . Look, Pat, I'm not saying that this case has to fit a pattern—but it's so far outside of it that it doesn't make sense. In half of the shootings at schools like this that we've studied, the killers want to get killed, either by the police or by their own hand. Our shooter obviously didn't want to get killed or he wouldn't have run away, and, according to his father at least, he wasn't suicidal, either. Most of them want to be famous, but how are you going to be famous if no one knows you did it?"

"How about being real pissed off. Do any of them do it just to kill somebody?"

"Believe it or not, they never seem to do it to kill somebody specific. They do it to create a situation where they are the center of attention."

"Is that what Lee Harvey Oswald was doing? Was he following a pattern?"

Oswald, of course, was the bête noir of the Secret Service, the embodiment of their ultimate disgrace.

"Oswald was different," Billy said quietly.

"So, maybe Sandy is different, too. You don't mind if I pick him up and find out, do you?"

"If you can find him."

"That's the second time you said that. Why won't I be able to find him?"

"I think it's very likely that he's dead," Billy said. "Or soon will be."

CHAPTER THIRTEEN

⁓≈≋≋≈⁓

The access to Route 73 had been changed a decade earlier and a spur that once was part of the highway had became a county road. Several small businesses, including the motel, still lined the old highway like jeweled accessories on a vestigial limb. Business had not been hurt substantially because there was little drop-in trade from the highway in the first place except at the gasoline service stations. On his way out of town, Billy stopped at a drive-in restaurant, a relic from the 1950s where it was easy enough to imagine a waitress on roller skates wheeling her way to a 1958 Thunderbird—except that the parking lot was gravel and the only other customer was in a pickup truck.

Billy had worked there as carhop himself for a brief period during high school and he wondered if he had ever looked as fresh-faced, open, and guileless as the boy who loped toward him, order pad in hand. There was none of the strut, none of the self-importance, none of the simulated inner-city attitude that seemed to afflict most of the teenagers portrayed by the media. This boy wore no baggy clothes, no earrings, no tattoos visible on the skin exposed by his white T-shirt. He looked like an athlete in a community where there was neither opprobrium nor excessive praise attached to sports. The rest of the nation was looking at its teenagers with a jaundiced, cynical eye while running them through metal detectors and drug tests; this was the kind of kid, on the surface at least, of whom it was very difficult to imagine any serious misbehavior. . . . And yet how many adults had been quick to assume it was a teenager who had taken the shots at the high school?

In his rearview mirror he saw a sheriff's car creeping slowly past like a shark in an aquarium, heading north. Lapolla or one of the other deputies, Billy thought, off to patrol the cornfields or wherever Pat sent them to keep them out of trouble. At that moment the setting sun appeared in his mirror and Billy squinted and looked away.

He ordered a corn dog, a treat from his youth when he had come here with a date, trying to ply her with sweets and fats, or after the date, to exchange lies with his friends. He remembered Joanie from that time, leaning from a car window, smiling, waving to the group that seemed to gather around her wherever she went. My, how she had sparkled in those days, he thought. Friendly, outgoing, pretty as a girl ever needed to be, but with an edge to her, a kind of knowing humor that made her even more attractive. She seemed able to say with a glance that she understood all about a boy and what he was up to, she wasn't about to be fooled by his tomfoolery, and yet she liked him anyway and didn't mind a bit of teasing. It was quite a bit to say in a glance, but it made the twinkle in her eye seem to extend to the whole of her being so that she glinted in the light like a jewel in the grass. She still had that quality, Billy thought, even with a bullet hole in her leg. Was that the trait that the sheriff called "possible"? The subsequent twenty years in Falls City had not dulled her luster, but Billy was surprised that she was still in town. She had seemed destined for the bigger world, for a more glamorous setting. So few of his contemporaries had escaped the gravity of their hometown. Many had drifted off to neighboring communities or resettled in carbon copies of Falls City in Kansas, Iowa, Missouri, other small and shrinking towns stuck somewhere between then and now. What was the tug that kept them in Falls City—or at least a Falls City of the mind—that he had broken free of so early and easily?

The corn dog was a hot dog on a wooden skewer breaded with cornmeal. The concoction seemed to have been injected with lard rather than just fried in it and the partially cooked cornmeal was about as edible as the skewer. After two bites Billy gave up. Either he no longer had the stomach he once had, or his taste for animal fats had altered considerably. He summoned the carhop with a flash of his lights.

"How's everything?" the boy asked.

"Fine . . . in its own way."

Billy placed a twenty-dollar bill on the tray that attached to his window and door. "Keep the change," he said. "You got a second?"

The boy glanced at the shack with the wooden awning that housed the kitchen and its vats of boiling fat and shrugged his shoulders.

"Sure."

"You heard about the shooting at the high school, didn't you?"

"Oh, yeah. I haven't heard about anything else. It's awful, isn't it?"

"Who do you think did it?"

The boy was taken aback by the question.

"I don't know. The TV's saying it was a kid, but . . ." He shrugged his shoulders again.

"Do you think it could be anybody you know?"

"No." The answer was quick and emphatic. "No."

"How about Will Blanchard?"

"Will? No way! . . . Are you saying he did it?"

"Absolutely not. How about Sandy Metzger?"

This time the boy hesitated, then shook his head. "No. Sandy's a little weird. . . . Are you with the televison people?"

"No. I used to live here. I'm just curious."

"Sandy's weird, but he's not crazy. . . . Oh, you're Billy Tree, I bet."

"Not too many people who used to live here ever come back once they leave, is that it?"

The boy laughed. "I guess not. You're working with the sheriff, huh?"

"Not really."

"Oh. I heard you were."

You and everyone else in town, Bill thought. There were no secrets here, he reminded himself. He had to remember that.

"Not really," he repeated, wondering why he bothered to deny it when everyone had concluded it was so. "What do you mean when you say Sandy Metzger is weird."

"I didn't mean anything by it. He's not weird like Huford Peck or anything. Nothing like that. He's just a little . . . different with some of his thinking. I shouldn't be saying anything. Sandy's fine."

"Do you like him? Personally?"

"Sandy? I don't know him very well."

Billy considered the likelihood of that in a town this size.

"Who doesn't like him? . . . Is he a popular kid? Do others make fun of him? Does he have any serious enemies?"

The boy shifted uncomfortably, rearranging some of the gravel with his toe. His loyalties were being tested for the change of a twenty-dollar bill.

"Does anybody hate him?" Billy continued. "Does he hate anybody?"

The boy shook his head, his eyes focused in the distance, as if considering the matter profoundly.

"I don't know anybody who hates anybody," he said sincerely.

Billy was stunned by the simplicity of the answer. He had forgotten what it was like to live in a world where such a statement was credible. Ethnic hatred, racial hatred, political hatred, religious hatred, the free-floating, unfocused hatred of the streets—for two decades he had been immersed in it. In his professional life, where thoughts of assassination permeated the atmosphere like a communal nightmare, in the newspapers, on the television, in the very innards of every city he had ever served in, hatred, its outbursts, its control, its placation were facts of daily life. At times hatred seemed not only to be concentrated in the big cities, but the very reason for the accumulation of vast numbers of people in a small space in the first place, as if true, murderous malice were too diffuse in the countryside to be effective. It needed to be compressed and subjected to the constant irritant of other people before it could precipitate in pure form out of the indiscriminate mist of human emotions.

The boy noticed Billy's reaction, and misread it. He felt he had to clarify. "Nobody really gets all that steamed up," he said. "Some fights, maybe. A punch in the mouth. Nothing all that serious."

"Well, somebody did," Billy said. "Somebody got murderously steamed up." He felt immediately clumsy and cruel for thrusting reality into the face of an innocent. Was it better to leave him believing in a childhood world where emotion never got so out of hand that it couldn't be relieved by the thwack of helmet and shoulder pads? On balance, probably not, Billy decided. When he pulled away from the drive-in he was tempted to tell the boy to watch his back.

The town of Auburn was a half-hour ride away. Billy remembered when it had seemed as distant as a foreign land. He had conducted a postal flirtation with a girl from Auburn while in high school—a one-sided correspondence, for the most part, the ardor of his early pubescence leaving the poor girl baffled, and, apparently, with nothing to say. That was before he was old enough to drive. By the time he had access to a car and its backseat, communication by mail seemed as quaint as a covered wagon and a trip to Auburn absurdly unnecessary. There were plenty of local girls happy enough to join him in the car, even a few willing to make the long-distance trip to the backseat.

He had not thought of the girl from Auburn since his passion succumbed to one empty mailbox too many. Had he really been such a romantic, he wondered, to write to a girl he met once at a ball game cheering for the opposing team—which automatically made her exotic, even foreign, not to say an enemy, since relationships with all neighboring towns were colored by athletic rivalry. Apparently he had, although he could no longer remember anything whatever about the girl. And he was not sure he knew very much about the boy anymore, either. He was still around, at least in Falls City, because Billy could feel him tugging at his memory and his sentiments, pulling on the easy strings. But did he really know him anymore, did he know what he wanted, what he was capable of, what he thought about the world? The misguided epistolary romance had surprised Billy when he recalled it, and it was hard to identify with the innocent belief in romance that must have inspired it. He was far too savvy now, too experienced in the untrustworthiness of the heart to put his emotions in an envelope and send them off with faith and the lick of a postage stamp. A writer of billets-doux at fourteen, hunter of letter writers at thirty-four, a . . . what, at thirty-eight? Cynic? Coward? Ex–Secret Service agent, ex-husband, ex-hero, ex-romantic, ex–letter writer, ex-athlete, ex–small-town boy, ex–big-city man, ex, ex, ex. Or was he still all of those things, all at the same time? He couldn't decide if he had a foot in all camps or a foot in none, and if in none, what was he walking on? He imagined himself like the cartoon character who has run off the cliff into empty space and doesn't know it yet, his feet pedaling and making purchase on thin air—until he looks down.

"Don't look down, boyo," he said aloud. He knew what waited at the bottom of the chasm, mouth open, laughing, teeth as jagged at the rocks.

Did any of those cartoon characters ever make it to the other side of the gulf by running on air, he wondered. Or were they all doomed by the recognition of gravity? Not that it mattered for the cartoon characters, they were never really hurt. Smashed wafer thin by the fall, they were up and at it again in the next scene, full-bodied and none the worse, nor the wiser, for the experience. Billy was not that resilient. He wasn't sure he'd survive another fall. He wasn't entirely convinced that he had survived the last one.

The falling sun followed him in his mirror all the way to Auburn, burning with a beautiful scarlet that tempted him to look at the same time that it blinded. The brilliant glow was probably man-made, a result of the light filtering through the cloud of dust from the grain elevator, but it was no less beautiful because of the human influence. The shimmering green of the corn was man-made too, genetically altered, hybridized, after decades of research no more than a distant cousin to nature's maize. There was nothing all that natural about nature anymore, not in farm country. Only the weather was beyond control.

Scott Falter was still in his pharmacy when Billy arrived and although the shop was closed, he opened the door for him. Billy tried to imagine a shopkeeper in Manhattan unlocking for a strange face after hours.

"I'm Billy Tree, from Falls City," Billy said, and realized that he was, indeed, from Falls City. He had not identified himself that way in two decades. In Nebraska, it was good enough for an entrée.

"I'm closed," Falter said, even as he stepped aside to admit Billy.

"This is a social call, sort of. I'm a friend of Joan Blanchard's."

Falter lifted one arm defensively as if to ward off a blow, or a memory.

"I have nothing to do with her," Falter said. "That's all over."

"I know. This is . . . you heard there was a shooting at the high school in Falls City?"

"I've heard of nothing else. . . . My, God, was Joanie shot?"

"She's fine. She's fine. In a few days she'll be as good as new. She was hit in the leg, but there's no permanent damage."

"My God. Fucking kids. What do we have to do, look behind every bush now? Do you know how many teenagers I have in here every day?" He waved his hand at a soda fountain that looked as if it were preserved from the 1950s. Not retro, not recreated. Just still there. "And every one of them has a .22 at home. Or worse."

"Was it a .22? I didn't hear that on the news."

"Wasn't it? . . . Who are you?"

Curious that it had taken him this long to ask, thought Billy. "Just a friend of hers. Trying to figure out why anyone would want to shoot her."

"How is she?"

Billy watched as Falter's face softened with concern. Whatever the man had once felt for her had not been entirely beaten out of him.

"She's all right. Really."

"If she needs any medication or anything . . . well, I guess she's got that."

"She's all set. But I'll tell her you're concerned . . . if you want me to."

Falter hesitated. He wrapped his arms across his chest. His forearms looked like those of a linebacker and although he was shaped like a barrel, as Joan had said, it was all hard, firm muscle. Duane must be very good to have done such a number on this man with just his fists, Billy thought.

Falter's pride and concern overcame his fear and he broke his contemplative silence.

"Sure, tell her I'm concerned. . . . And say hi, too, would you?"

"I will."

"You know about the deal with me and Duane, I suppose."

Billy nodded.

"I figured you did when you asked if I wanted to say hello. . . . What kind of friend are you?"

"Just a friend friend."

Falter studied Billy openly and skeptically. "Um-hum. . . . Well, it's possible, I suppose. You haven't know her long, I take it."

"With an interruption. We went to school together. I just came back to town."

Falter moved his head up and down as if that explained something.

"Just an old acquaintance?"

"Should we be forgot and never brought to mind?"

"I can think of some I'd as soon forget. So did Joan send you to see me, or what?"

There was a low rumble from outside the store, like a monster clearing its throat. Falter did not hear or was not interested.

"She thought you might want to know how she was."

"So why didn't she call me?"

"What makes you think I couldn't just be her friend?"

Falter grinned ruefully. "Well, you look straight to me. Why would you *want* to be just her friend?"

"I could be married."

"Are you?"

"No," Billy said.

"I didn't think so. So why just a friend?"

"I have an old war wound that limits me?"

"If you say so. It wouldn't be fear of Duane Blanchard, would it? . . . Nothing wrong with that. I might even call it prudent."

"I take it you don't believe a man and woman can just be friends," Billy said.

"Only women believe that," Falter said. "I don't know how she was back in your school days but Joan is a very . . . attractive girl. Woman."

"If you like them pretty."

"I don't mean just pretty. Although there aren't many really pretty girls in real life, have you noticed that?"

"Um," offered Billy.

"You see them on television, but how many pretty ones do you ever actually meet?"

Billy considered the question for a moment. It seemed a matter of definitions and standards, but Falter was not interested in an answer.

"Well, I can tell you, in my life, practically none. Joanie is. But there's something else about her. I don't know what to call it, a quality. . . ."

Billy nearly offered the word "possible," but bit it back.

The pharmacist had been sitting opposite Billy at one of the three Formica tables that supplemented the soda fountain. Now he moved to sit on the fountain counter itself so that he looked down at his interviewer. Billy assumed that a man that short took the high ground whenever possible. It was his shop, he could sit wherever he liked.

"Joanie's *alive*," Falter said, pleased to have found the proper concept. "She's just more *alive* than most people. I don't know how else to put it. She's got more 'juice' than other girls. Women. I could not believe my luck when she finally agreed to go out with me. It was like winning the lottery. I had to ask myself, why me?"

"You bought a ticket."

"Hum? Yes, well, sure, I did step up, that's true. I chased her, no question about it. Nobody else was. I don't know why. I *didn't* know why. I found out."

Falter swung his legs back and forth over the edge of the counter like a child.

"Did you think about suing Duane Blanchard?"

Falter spun one of the counter stool seats with his foot. It creaked as it twirled. "I thought about all kinds of things. Suing was fairly low on the list. . . . You know, the kind of fantasies you have when you want revenge. Kneecapping, that sort of thing. Still not a bad idea, come to think of it. Do you know anybody in Chicago?" It took Falter a long moment before he smiled to let it be understood he was just joking. Billy noted that the leg-swinging had stopped.

"I was told it was just self-defense," he continued. "That I'd have no chance of getting a conviction."

"A lawyer told you this?"

"It seemed better all around just to let it go," he said vaguely.

"How so?"

With a giant push of his arms, Falter propelled himself off the counter several feet through the air. He landed like a gymnast trying to hold his finish and looked down at his feet for a moment. Billy wondered if he did this often and was trying to hit some predetermined mark on the floor. How to amuse yourself when working late and alone.

"How'd you do?" Billy asked.

Falter laughed sheepishly.

"Short of the record," he said.

"Maybe it was the wind."

Falter continued to laugh like a man amused by his own idiosyncrasies, then stopped abruptly.

"I was about to go home," he said, an unsubtle hint.

"Do you often work this late?"

He shrugged. "Sometimes. People come late, they need something, if I know them I let them in. They wouldn't be bothering me after-hours if it wasn't important."

It wasn't until the low rumble moved past the shop and into the distance that Billy was aware he'd been hearing it all along.

"You didn't know me," Billy said.

"You looked harmless."

"It's come to that, has it? What would me uncle Sean say to such a ting?"

"You lost me."

"Well, I'm elusive, I am. You ever run into Duane Blanchard since the beating?"

"I wouldn't call it a beating. It wasn't that bad. I can take care of myself pretty good."

"You ever see him again?"

"Joan didn't send you. What's the deal?"

"I'm just trying to figure who might want to shoot her."

"Haven't they got enough cops doing that?"

"They have a few."

"Kids are crazy these days. Who knows why they do something like this? He'd have to be out of his mind in the first place. He could have been shooting at anybody."

"That's what the cops think."

"Maybe you ought to let them do the thinking."

"Is Duane Blanchard crazy enough to shoot his wife?"

Falter crossed his store and rearranged tubes of sunscreen lotion in a cardboard display. When he spoke he seemed to choose each word carefully, weighing it briefly before offering it.

"He didn't kill me. I guess that means he's not completely crazy."

Falter opened the front door and stood beside it like a host seeing out his guest.

Billy paused in front of the shorter man.

"Anything you want me to say to Joan?"

Falter looked out on Auburn's main street for a moment. If he was seeking inspiration for a pithy response, he didn't find it. He shook his head.

" 'Hi' will do. Joanie made her choice."

"You don't think she chose to get shot."

Falter had to tip his head back to look Billy in the eye. It was the first time he had truly done so during the entire interview.

"She chose Duane," he said bitterly.

"I don't think so. It's not a choice."

"They say sometimes a prisoner comes to love his cell," Falter said. He was already closing the door on Billy's back.

CHAPTER FOURTEEN

B illy drove until he was out of sight of the pharmacy, studying his rearview mirror for headlights to see if he was being followed. He made two right turns and returned to the rear entrance of the pharmacy, parking where he could just see the alley behind the shop but was not visible himself from the pharmacy. Old-fashioned streetlights with oblong bulbs looking like giant lemons atop fluted columns of dull green lined the main shopping street like some early Edisonian display of the miracle of electric lighting, but where Billy sat, one street removed, the pretense of serious illumination was dropped and long shadows covered him from the fading light.

A pair of headlights showed briefly in his mirror as a car two blocks away started to turn onto Billy's street and then abruptly changed its mind and swung away. Billy was alone on his street and in the darkness and free to contemplate his experience with Scott Falter.

Why had Falter put up with that interview without ever once asking if Billy was a cop? Most people would have. A stranger was asking probing and personal questions. Did Falter's lack of curiosity about his questioner betoken an unusual openness in nature? A spotless conscience? Or did he know who Billy was to begin with? Had he been told to expect Billy's arrival? Was that why he was working late? Or was the shop open so that Falter could deal with whoever was trying to keep his motorcycle quiet. Since when did bikers value silence and discretion? The roar when the cycle started behind the pharmacy was unavoidable—the machines were not designed to be mute—but after that the rider had all but crept away until he was far removed from the pharmacy. But there were no stealth motorcycles, that defeated the demands of the ego the machines were made to flatter, and this had been a big American hog, built for noise. So was the biker trying to keep quiet so Billy wouldn't hear him? Or Falter? Had Billy's arrival interrupted something? Prevented something? Or was it all meaningless coincidence? Billy's training had taught him to distrust coincidence. Patterns meant something, the skill lay in the interpretation.

He heard a cycle engine again, no longer moving at a crawl, but growling into town, perfectly comfortable with its own racket, as brazen as a lion roaring its way across the veldt. The single beam of the headlight turned the corner and for a few seconds it was pointed directly at Billy as it pulled off the main street and headed toward him. Because of the light, Billy could not make out the rider until the cycle turned into the alley behind the pharmacy, and then there was little to see. A large shape, a helmet, the suggestion of leather shining in reflection from the headlight off the buildings.

The cycle was parked out of his view, but he could still hear it. The rider had left the engine running this time. Was he in a hurry now? Or more concerned about being observed? Sounds traveled well on the summer night air and Billy could hear a screen door slam shut. The biker revved his engine. Defiance? Just high spirits? The motorcycle wheeled out of the alley and turned away from Billy, back toward the main street, then negotiated the corner and was gone.

Billy drove parallel to the biker for two blocks before joining the main street and heading out of town, back toward Falls City. He caught a glimpse of headlights on the street he had just abandoned and for a second had the eerie feeling that someone was shadowing him from a distance just as he was following the cyclist. But when the street became the highway no headlights appeared in his mirror and Billy returned his attention to the man in front of him. He let the cycle gain in distance—it would not be hard to keep a single taillight in sight, and he did not want to make the biker nervous.

As he drove, Billy closed his right eye, accustoming it to darkness. A quarter moon was partially obscured by scudding clouds and it blinked at the earth in celestial flirtation. They reached the road sign announcing Verdon, a hamlet of a few hundred that lay off the highway in its entirety, making no pretense of connection with the wider world that drove by, offering no comforts, no service, not even buildings, nothing whatever to mark its presence on the landscape but the standard black and white rectangle quoting the size of the population. The land began to buckle slightly here, eleven miles from Falls City, and occasionally the motorcycle's taillight would vanish momentarily within a slight dip in the road.

Billy checked his mirror and saw only a pair of headlights far in the distance, not close enough to be a factor. He flicked on his turn signal. If the biker was keeping track of his presence, he would expect Billy to disappear soon, and when the biker vanished into the next dip, he did. Billy switched off his headlights and turn signal and opened the eye that had been closed. With his night vision already functioning in his right eye he could see well enough to follow the road without headlights, but he would be invisible to the rider in front. At this distance the biker might occasionally catch a glimpse of moonlight off the windshield, but he would have to be watching for it, and even then it would be difficult to distinguish it from a random flash of reflected moonlight from the surrounding cornfields.

The lights behind him kept their steady distance, but they were far back. Billy doubted that from that far away even the reflectors on his taillights could be seen. He had effectively stepped out of the visible world and now traveled in a cocoon of space and darkness.

The motorcycle was slowing and Billy matched its speed, keeping his distance. A glance in the mirror showed that the vehicle behind him was coming on unchecked, narrowing the gap. Its headlights were altered by the haze of heat still rising from the asphalt so they seemed to dance separately, unattached. His rear reflectors would be visible to the car behind him soon. If the driver did not react, Billy would tap his brakes, sending a flash of Morse to indicate his presence. Stealth would be pointless if he were rear-ended by a passerby.

The motorcycle turned off the road and Billy could see its light jouncing along a rutted surface as it followed a path parallel to a small river. Billy braked once as he crossed a bridge and then turned carefully onto the path the biker had taken. Stray moonbeams broke through the clouds and their light reflected brightly off the river, bathing Billy's car in illumination. He would be visible now if the cyclist looked back, headlights or no. He was driving as much by feel as vision on a path never intended for the suspension of a passenger car and he did not know where he was going or what was waiting for him.

What am I supposed to be doing, he wondered. I have no idea what's going on, if anything at all, and I'm diving in nose first just because of the thrill of the chase. He stopped the car, cut the engine, rolled down the window, and listened. The taillight of the motorcycle had blinked out, whether because of a sharp turn in the patch or because the rider had turned off his lights, it was impossible to say. He could be waiting ahead in the darkness, as masked by the night as Billy had thought himself to be moments before. There was no human sound coming from the direction the biker had taken, but he heard clearly the ripple and splash of the river and the rustle of surrounding vegetation in the breeze. A cornfield lay on his left, close enough for him to touch the stalks, but soybeans carpeted the field on the other side of the river, hugging the ground and affording Billy a clear view of the highway from which he had come. The headlights of the car that had been so far in the distance were approaching quickly now, and as he watched he saw them separate slightly as the two motorcycles deviated a little in their tandem course. They were decelerating abruptly, preparing for the turn after the bridge. He had been followed all the way from Auburn, he realized; they had seen him drive without lights, watched him trail the other cyclist. And had waited until now, when there was no way out, to approach.

Billy crawled through the open window so the light would not flash on when he opened the door. The longer they thought he was still in the car, the better. Using the shelter of his vehicle, he darted into the cornfield, catching a glimpse of at least four headlights as they emerged abruptly from the path that the original biker had taken. The night was suddenly alive with the roar of cycles. He had stumbled into a nest of bikers, or been lured in, more likely, and now they were swarming out of the nest like vengeful hornets.

The corn was over his head so he could not be seen as he raced across the field, but it was impossible to run dead straight and his shoulders hit individual plants, leaving a wake of aberrant quivers and crackling noises to those observant enough to notice. He counted on the fact that his own unsubtle noises would be lost to the bikers under the rumble of their engines. They were revving their motors in threat gestures, like mountain gorillas pounding their chests, hoping to accomplish with display what they feared to try with violence. They would get over that, he knew. Taking courage from each other, they would approach the car soon enough, convince themselves he was not lying on the floor with a shotgun trained on the first face to appear, and begin to search for him in earnest.

And if they found him, what then? That would depend on what he had stumbled into. If they were just a band of merry bikers, out for a nocturnal get-together in somebody's cornfield, then maybe all he had to fear was some intimidation and humiliation. I'm up for some of that, he thought. Humiliation is so much my dish that I'm serving it up for myself, scooting through the local flora like a clumsy rabbit. What did another helping of degradation amount to, what could the bikers put him through worse than what he was doing for himself? . . . But. If it had really been an ambush. . . . If they had enticed him, lured him, followed and ensnared him—but why? Why him? And why bother? It was not as if Billy were hard to find. What could it possibly be about? It made no sense, but that was not relevant at this point. Paranoia was easy to come by when running through a cornfield at night with the sound of cycles rolling like so many crazed kettle drummers all around him.

He heard the change in pitch and saw flashes of light clipping the tops of the corn plants; he did not need to look back to know that the conference was over and they were coming into the field after him.

Billy threw himself facedown in the dirt. His chance for escape lay in concealment, not speed. There was no way he could outrun a motorcycle, not even in a cornfield, and if he was erect and moving, their lights would pick him up. If he was going to run like a rabbit, he should freeze like one, too. Predators sought motion. Lying flat, he would be visible only if one of the cycles came directly down his row.

Billy rubbed dirt on his face to reduce the shine, then slowly rolled onto his back so he could see them as they came. Hearing them was no problem.

One cycle advanced three rows to his right, another four rows to his left. They came deliberately, working with surprising discipline, scanning the rows to either side. When they were nearly abreast of him, Billy closed his eyes to remove another source of reflection. The difficulty with freezing like a rabbit was that his heart threatened to leap from his chest. It seemed to be shaking his body with every beat like a heart attack victim being galvanized by a defibrillator. Billy would be more respectful of rabbits in the future.

The lights passed over him and the roar of the engines diminished. Billy watched the cycles recede. He estimated that he was closer to the far end of the field where the motorcycles were heading than he was to his car. Not that the car would do him any good now, anyway. He had left the key in it, the engine running. It had bought him time by contributing to the deception that he was still in the auto, but it had cost him the car. The key would be in the pocket of one of the cyclists by now and the car, for all he knew, could be in the river.

Billy rose and ran after the motorcycles, safe from their headlights now. He watched as the lights stopped moving, then abruptly turned to make another pass through the field. He flung himself onto the ground again just before the beams swept his row. They were closer together now, closing the net. If he had been smart he would have gone into one of the rows they had already swept, but he wasn't smart, he was half-panicked and shit scared and without a plan.

The cycles were only two rows away on either side of him this pass. Billy lay petrified, his eyes squeezed shut, willing himself to sink into the earth completely. Christ, I've been here before, he thought. It was the same position he had lain in, the same fear he had felt, the same desire to sink through the earth as when Posner was killing him.

When they passed he rose and ran again, darting into the row that one of the cycles had just driven through. He counted on seeing their beams when they turned again—he could not look back as he ran without stumbling into the corn.

Suddenly there were lights in front of him. He dived and turned and saw lights behind him as well. The ones from the rear started another pass while the ones that stood on the edge of the field that he had been trying so desperately to reach remained in place. They were casting continuous light, there would be no time when he could rise and run in darkness, and they had tightened the search area even further—a cycle filled the row on either side of him now.

He would be seen, he was no rabbit, he was a man in a cornfield, a huge lump in the dirt, and the spilled light from both cycles would illuminate him as if he were standing on a stage.

Billy tried frantically to think, to remember what he had been taught in the Agency's classes on self-defense, what he had done in the past when in danger, but Posner kept dancing in his brain, distracting him with mocking laughter. There was a weapon, there was always a weapon of some sort available, his instructors had said, an ashtray, a chair, a pencil—and best of all your service automatic, nestled cozily in your armpit or on your waist or ankle. But he had no service automatic now and the instructors had never mentioned a cornfield. Secret Service agents had no experience of corn or wheat or milo . . . but Billy had. Kneeling, he tugged at the nearest corn plant. The roots came up grudgingly with clumps of dirt clinging to them, adding weight. The stalk itself, swollen with stored moisture, was stiff and surprisingly heavy. Billy had dueled with such makeshift weapons as a youth, hacking at a playmate as with a broadsword and he knew the painful, shocking blow they could deliver. Especially if they took you by surprise.

As the cycles approached Billy stood and swung his makeshift weapon at the biker to his right. The clotted roots caught the man in the face and he went down with a yell, pulling the bike atop himself, its wheels spinning uselessly. The second cyclist stopped abreast of Billy and hesitated briefly. He had been occupied with thoughts of the hunt, not the capture, and did not know what to do when suddenly confronted with a prey alive and swinging.

The stalk had bent at the middle from the impact on the first cyclist and hung in Billy's hand, as useless as a broken spear. He flung the remnants at the hesitating biker and rushed him, sidestepping slightly so he could come in from an angle and use the weight of the motorcycle against him. Billy hit the biker like the football player he had once been, his forearms parallel in front of him and braced for the contact. The second biker was still astride his cycle and unable to maneuver either himself or the bike at such close quarters. Billy's thrust hit him just below the shoulder and knocked him off balance. He clung to the cycle for support, tipping the heavy machine off its own center of gravity. Billy completed the maneuver with a push against the bike's fuel tank.

The biker cried "Hey!," sounding more indignant than angry, and then collapsed as his machine fell against his leg. Chains on the biker's jacket clanged metallically against the cycle.

The first biker was struggling to pull himself from under his bike, and Billy chose that machine because it was already in gear. He had never ridden a motorcycle in his life, didn't know the first thing about one, but if the wheels were already engaged with the engine, all he should have to do was point it.

He yanked the cycle up by the handlebars and it was already moving as he leaped onto the seat. The motorcycle seemed to have a mind of its own and like a headstrong horse it took Billy across the rows instead of through them, bumping with each new row, the cornstalks slapping him on the head and body, threatening to knock him off the machine. He managed to turn its head into a row and found himself going toward a darkness where his beam was the only light to be seen. He was going in the wrong direction, back toward the river, but he decided it might not be the wrong direction after all. The bikers were behind him, where he wanted them, and when without a plan, one strategy seems as good as another.

It took the bikers a moment to comprehend what had happened but the lone light bouncing away from them was all they really needed to know, and in a few seconds they were after him, their engines roaring with outrage at his escape from their net.

Billy heard them coming after him with a concerted growl that rose above the sound of his own engine. They knew what they were doing, they would be coming a great deal faster than he was fleeing and this time he was showing a light to lead them on. Billy glanced at the unfamiliar controls, hoping to find a switch to douse his lights but just keeping the machine heading between the corn rows and at a speed he could manage was task enough. They would catch him before he reached the river, or they wouldn't. It was just a question of speed now and stealth could be forgotten.

Billy saw colored lights twisting in the sky above the corn just before he became aware of the cycle coming up fast on his left side. Another nudged him from behind, knocking him off balance. Billy burst from the vegetation within a few feet of his car, hit the rutted path already out of control and teetered toward the river. He had the presence of mind to pull his legs up just before he and the motorcycle parted company and plunged in parallel toward the water.

He stayed under the surface as long as his lungs would permit, pulling hard in the direction the river wanted to take him. When his head broke into the air for his first gasping breath, he was already on the other side of the bridge.

Colored lights continued to spin through the sky and he realized that an emergency vehicle, ambulance or police car, was parked on the bridge, obscured from his sight by the concrete span. Billy ducked under again and swam as hard as his clothes would allow. When he reemerged he could see a sheriff's car on the bridge. There was no sign of the bikers and a flashlight beam probed the surface of the water where he had plunged in.

Billy let the sluggish current propel him away, floating on his back, while watching the activity by the bridge. He felt a little like Huck Finn watching his own funeral as the flashlight beam was replaced by the high-powered spotlight on the sheriff's car, tracing swinging arcs across the water. Searching for Billy Tree, incautious cyclist, fallen hero, flaming coward, all-around fool.

The river deposited him on a sandbar and left him there, rippling around his knees before moving on downstream. Billy stood, sinking immediately to midcalf in the saturated mix of silt and sand. The bridge was just out of sight around a slight turn in the river, but he could still hear the sound of voices, then the crackle of static on a two-way radio, surprisingly loud considering the distance.

Billy stood a minute longer, aware that he was sinking deeper at a nearly imperceptible rate, but with his attention focused on the sounds from the bridge, as if he expected to hear his own eulogy. And what would that sound like? he wondered. It would require even more hypocrisy than the average clergyman had at his command—which was going some—to make him sound like anything other than anidiot, jibbering with fear, running from a bunch of amateur tough guys that he would have faced down and shamed with his courage only a year ago.

The crackle of static stopped and the engines of the six cycles came alive. He heard them rev, heard them bump across the rutted path, hit the highway, and accelerate into the distance and saw it all as clearly in his mind as if he stood atop the squad car watching them go. The colored lights continued to flash in the sky, going nowhere.

Forced to leave his shoes behind in the sucking muck, Billy extricated himself from the sandbar and swam to the shore. By his estimate, he was the length of three cornfields from the Falls City town line, and from there only a few hundred yards from home—if Kath would still let him call it home after he had abandoned her car to the mercies of the bikers. The dirt was not uncomfortable under his stockinged feet and he was invisible to all but himself as long as he was in the cornfields. If only he could contrive to stay that way for the next several years, he thought. Getting to town would take about an hour, he figured, but it would be the easy part. Negotiating the town streets about the time the sun came up would be the shameful half of the journey. He might have stopped dripping by then, but there was no way he could look like anything other than a drowned rat. Maybe he would meet Huford Peck on his morning rounds and they could walk to Billy's house together, the two local half-wits, both scared into panic by men on motorcycles. And they weren't even after my "shiny," Billy thought. It was unlikely that Billy even possessed a shiny, whatever it might be. Billy had initiated his own disaster, after all. He wasn't just being picked on, a likely target for a bit of harassing fun, as Huford was. *Billy* had followed the *biker*. Whatever had compelled him, whatever idiotic impulse had led him by his nose, was now forgotten.

After a time Billy became aware of the colored lights of the sheriff's car moving slowly parallel to his path, heading back into town. Lapolla or some other hapless deputy had finally given up the search. Or gone back to town for the cannon. Wasn't that the procedure? To fire a cannon over the water to raise the drowned corpse? Not that the Little Nemaha was anything like the Mississippi. If a cannon was required on the Mississippi, a shotgun would do to raise Billy's bloated body from the Little Nemaha. Not that there was any reason to compare himself to Huckleberry Finn, Billy thought. Whatever else Huck may or may not have had, he had guts.

CHAPTER FIFTEEN

As he had feared, the sun *was* up by the time he reached the town limits. He wasn't even going to be granted the privilege of sneaking into town in the dark. Nor do I deserve it, he thought.

He felt eyes upon him every step of the way. People rose early in farm country, and, as Billy had already learned, they saw everything. And now they saw *him*, but what they might make of him, a sodden, shoeless man stepping out of the corn and onto the pavement, making his way purposefully down the town streets at the crack of dawn, was anybody's guess. The town was already traumatized, half-paralyzed with the fear that one of their children had turned killer. Maybe it was time for other manifestations of disaster, toads falling from the skies and strange men emerging from the fields.

A sheriff's car was parked in front of Kath's house behind Kath's car, mysteriously transported from the river. Lapolla is probably telling my sister that I've drowned, thought Billy. And in I'll walk, like Lucille Ball's Lucy after one of her comically complicated days with "some 'splainin' to do."

But it was not Lapolla. Pat Kunkel sat behind the wheel, his head back, asleep—yet not asleep. He opened one eye as Billy approached, squishing slightly, then closed it again as if he had only seen exactly what he expected.

"If I could just have a minute of your time," Kunkel said, eyes still closed, but a grin now twitching at his lips.

Billy found a newspaper already spread across the passenger seat. Kunkel held a thermos of coffee on his lap and he poured some into a Styrofoam cup for Billy.

"So, what was that? Mr. Toad's wild ride?" Kunkel asked.

"I was thinking more Mark Twain."

"It was good for a laugh, whatever it was." Kunkel proved his point by laughing.

"Good for the self-esteem, too," said Billy. "I feel top of the world right now."

"You look it."

"How come you're not dragging the river?"

"Do people really do that? I don't think you could drown in the Little Nemaha if you tied cinder blocks to your ears."

"You were searching for my body long enough."

"Hell, I knew you weren't in there, Billy. I saw your face first time your head popped up. I just acted concerned so those yahoos would give up on chasing you. The rest of the time we were fishing out the bike you rode into the river." Kunkel laughed again. "Wish you could have seen yourself. I gave you a six for style points."

"A source of innocent merr-i-ment, of innocent merr-i-ment."

"If you say so."

"Gilbert and Sullivan, actually."

"Those boys didn't think it was so innocent. They wanted to charge you with assault on two of them, theft of a Harley, destruction of property—except we got the hog running again so that wouldn't stick. One of them has some legal training, he was going to sue your ass for civil-rights violations, too."

"*They* were the victims? I was set up and ambushed."

"They didn't steal *your* Harley. They didn't hit *you* with a club."

"Cornstalk."

Kunkel shrugged. "They're city boys. What do they know?"

"So what were city-boy, legally trained, Hell's Angels doing in a cornfield at night, besides chasing me and having a good laugh?"

"You got me there, Bill. Whatever it is those people do at night. They weren't bothering anyone, that's all I'm interested in."

"They were bothering me."

"Or the other way around, to hear them tell it. The county paid for the tow of your car, by the way. It's on me . . . this time."

"Thanks, and there won't be a next time. What did you do to them?"

"Do to them? I moved them on. That's half of what this job is, Billy. Keep 'em moving, don't let trouble squat in your territory, but don't cause trouble yourself, either."

"So you had a word with them, did you, Pat?"

" 'A gentle word turneth away wrath,' according to someone or other. I gave them three or four gentle words and told them to go chase my friends into the river in some other county."

"Just keep them moving? The old hot potato approach to law enforcement."

"They hadn't broken any laws besides riding cycles without a helmet—'course, you were guilty of that yourself—but I don't see any point in keeping them around until they do, either. . . . It's a complicated, job, Billy. You got to get used to that."

"Pat . . . it sounds like you're counting on me for something again. I beg you not to do that. I just demonstrated that I'm not the man for it."

"You give up on yourself too easy, Billy. . . . Go get some sleep. You'll feel better about the whole business when you wake up."

"My memory of humiliation is a bit longer than that, I'm afraid."

Billy stepped out of the car but hesitated by the window.

"Did you find Joan Blanchard's son?"

"I thought you said Duane had him."

"I think he does. I don't know for sure. You said you'd get him for her."

"Billy, I got a few other things on my plate right now, you know? First I got to find Sandy Metzger, I got to get the TV people out of town, I got to assure everybody Falls City isn't a hotbed of teenage assassins and they can sleep peaceful at night without chaining their kids to the bedpost—and then maybe I'll have time to get involved in a child custody case. . . . Why don't you just get the kid for her?"

"I thought you said Duane was too dangerous for me to mess with."

"So, don't mess with him, just get the boy."

Kath stepped onto the porch, her arms crossed over her chest, her face dark with disapproval. She needed only to tap her foot to complete the stereotype of the disapproving housewife.

"What now?" she demanded.

"Good morning, Kath," said Kunkel, smiling.

Her tone softened as she addressed the sheriff. "Good morning, Pat. Do I need to bail him out or anything?"

"Nothing like that. Just having a chat."

"We're all frightened enough without finding a sheriff's car outside our door first thing in the morning."

"No need for anyone to be frightened, now, Kath. We don't want to spread that."

"Spread it? We're not catching it from each other, Pat. We're scared for good reason. And you know it."

"I know nothing of the sort. It was a one-time thing, a freak, everyone's perfectly safe."

"Perfectly? Is Principal Cohan safe? Is Sharon Shattuck safe?"

"You sound angry with me, Kath. It's not my doing. Nobody wants to put this behind us any more than I do. And we will, real soon."

"Everything's fine, Kath," said Billy. "I was just engaging in some water sports. I'll be right in."

Kath kept her eyes on Kunkel as if she did not want to recognize her brother's presence at all. When she finally spoke she still did not look at him.

"She called you three times last night."

"Who?" Billy asked, but Kath had already returned to the house with an ominous abruptness.

"I wouldn't go in that house just now, if I was you," Kunkel said. "Better just crawl straight into the doghouse, save yourself some trouble."

"I'll meet you in there."

"Are you kidding? I'd love to have a doghouse to hide in right about now. There's no place in the county where people won't be looking at me like I'm a worthless asshole for not preventing the damned shooting in the first place. Your sister is mild, Billy, and too much of a lady to really get mad. If I don't get Sandy Metzger behind bars damned quick, people are going to be throwing stones at my car."

"I still don't think it's Sandy."

"You're entitled to your opinion—barely." Kunkel grinned wickedly. "And who's the woman's been calling you all night?"

"How would I know?"

"You got that many of them already, and you just back in town? Ah, the ladies. What is your appeal, Bill?"

"Sure, it's me dev'lish charm, now, isn't it?"

"Next time you run into some of those big old boys on their choppers, try the charm, Bill. You don't drive real good."

Kunkel drove off with his grin still burning in Billy's vision. And now I'm the town clown, he thought.

But Kath was not laughing. She was close to tears and she kept her arms laced across her body as if they were the only things holding her together.

"I've had Pat Kunkel bring my father home, I've had him bring my husband home. He's a fine, sweet man, but Billy, I don't want him bringing you home, too. I've had enough of it."

"I haven't been drinking, Kath."

"They towed the car. Look at you . . ."

"I know. I'm sorry. I don't want to scare you."

"With all the rest of this going on, Curtis Metzger in my house, you getting into fights, kids shooting people—Billy, of course I'm scared."

He reached out to comfort her but she pulled away, face twisted in disgust.

"Go take a shower. You smell like low tide. . . . And then call that woman so she'll stop calling here."

"You mean Joan?"

"Where are your shoes?"

"Why do you call her 'that woman'?"

"I don't want any more of it, Billy. I mean it. There's a limit to how much I can take."

She walked into the kitchen before Billy could say anything more. He heard her release her tears in there but told himself it would only embarrass her if he offered comfort. When he emerged from the shower and Kath was fine again, he told himself he had been right after all— but he knew he was wrong.

CHAPTER SIXTEEN

The morning began with reporters at Joan's door, smiling and persistent, keen to interview a victim. They came in a pack, all of them at once, as if by prearrangement or in observance of some tacit journalistic credo that thou shalt not seek answers before first light. It took her several minutes to hobble to the door, still groggy from the drugs they had given her to sleep, and the extra time gave her a chance to prepare her mind before she faced them. As much as one could be prepared for the energy and insistence of the media.

"Do you know who shot you?" they asked in a variety of ways as soon as she opened the door. Implicit in each question was the deeper inquiry, "Do you know why you were shot?" Deeper still was the query Joan asked of herself. What did you do to deserve this?

She looked at them and blinked and opened her mouth in reaction and their voices fell away as one so they could hear her response, to be replaced by an amazing susurration of cameras clicking, automatic rewind motors humming, tiny tape recorders spinning. It was like a lull in a twilight conversation when all the cicadas and crickets reasserted themselves. But she did not speak and the manic surge of voices, frustrated by her hesitation, repeated themselves, each a little louder, faster, more frenzied than the one before, trying to climb atop and over the others so that it was *their* question she addressed, *their* camera she faced when she spoke, when she finally broke down and addressed them. And they were fully confident that she would, *must* address them, answer them, appease them, for did they not represent the People? And did not the People have the sovereign right to know, to be informed, with a claim superior to all others, to be let in on the secret of what it felt like to be shot?

She wanted to answer, she wanted to oblige. They seemed so keen to know, they hung so eagerly upon the expectation of her words. They were seductive in their attentiveness, but they were also frightening. Joan thought again of a swarm of insects, buzzing at her ears, her eyes, her nose, waiting for any opening she offered.

It was hard being rude and they depended on that instinct toward courtesy, the impulse of the average citizen to answer when spoken to. But speaking at all would provide the opening for them to swarm into, Joan realized. Even a polite invitation to go away would seem to them like the beginning of a conversation. Joan stepped back and closed the door without a word.

They increased their volume for a moment, then fell into consternated silence. They were unaccustomed to being shut out. Even hardened policemen and manipulative lawyers were unable to remain mute before them. Everyone, *everyone* wanted to speak to the media, or to break down and weep for the cameras, or take an infuriated swipe at them. *Something.* It took them several minutes to realize that she would not respond to the doorbell or the knocking on the door. They couldn't know that Joan had taken to the shower to let the water drown the sound of their importunings.

The phone calls started almost immediately, and after hanging up on the first two reporters Joan took the telephone off the hook.

By noon it seemed safe and she stepped on to her porch and eased herself into the plastic chair that served as her outdoor furniture. There was a good breeze and in the shade of her porch roof it was cool, or at least as cool as it was going to get unless she made her way to the Hinky Dinky Supermarket and wandered the air-conditioned aisles. The humidity was dangerously high as it always was at this time of year, the level of humidity that led to thunderstorms and tornadoes as nature lashed out in fury to be rid of such discomfort. Joan was wet with perspiration just from the effort of living, but it was a sweat she had learned to appreciate for it cooled, especially in a breeze. The body heat that built up before sweat finally beaded on her skin to afford some relief was far worse.

High school had been scheduled to open in four days but that was very much in doubt now. Counselors would be on their way from Omaha, specialists in dealing with communal trauma, and they would probably spend several days working with the children and the teaching staff of the high school. Perhaps they would offer to work with Joan as well. She knew she would refuse their help. Her trauma was not like that of the others. She did not suffer survivor guilt, she did not agonize over why she was spared and others were killed. Not now, not after her telephone conversation of the previous evening. She was certain that she had survived simply because the shooter had failed to hit a vital spot. And her guilt was not over surviving, but from *causing* the killings.

She saw Billy walking toward her in a T-shirt and shorts and sneakers, appearing, from a distance at least, all of eighteen years old. He wasn't looking at her and for a moment she thought he had not seen her, that she still had a chance to slip into her house and change clothes, wash away the perspiration, do something fast and transformative to make herself look eighteen again, too. She laughed at herself. And just what would that be, what magical lotion did she have that would turn her youthful and virginal again? . . . Well, at eighteen, almost virginal. Certainly inexperienced if not actually un-experienced. Knowledge is power, so they said, and if so, just what power had she gained from her rather dismal and disappointing knowledge in that department over the years? There was nothing she could do in the next two decades, much less the next two minutes, to change what time had done to her.

Billy stopped on the sidewalk in front of her house and held his arms out as if stunned by the sight of her.

"They said it couldn't be done," he said. "But they were wrong. You've gotten even prettier."

"Fooled you then, didn't I?"

"How do you do it? What is the source of this radiance?"

"I feel like wilted rhubarb," said Joan. "The heat's gone to your brain. . . . Are you going to stand there like that until everyone else in town knows you're an idiot?"

"They already know," he said, but he dropped his arms and joined her on the porch.

She saw that he was dripping with sweat just from the exertion of walking in the sun and the blue of his T-shirt had turned almost black with moisture.

"It would be a good day for an air-conditioned car," she said.

"I am temporarily without transport," said Billy. "Grounded, you know." He stood over her, smiling and flicking away the beads of sweat that accumulated on the tip of his nose. "Shall we stay on the porch and have everyone wonder what we're talking about? Or shall we go inside and have them all wonder what we're doing?"

"Those are some pretty poor options. . . . Thank you for the flowers. They're lovely."

"You knew they were from me?"

She laughed, scoffing. "Who else?"

"A secret admirer, perhaps?"

Joan's face darkened. "Don't even suggest it."

"I tried to call. Your phone's off the hook. Or did you call me just to thank me for the flowers?"

"No."

"No word from Will, yet?"

Joan struggled to her feet but brushed off Billy's attempts to help her.

"Let's go inside, where it's really uncomfortable," she said.

His flowers were in a vase on the coffee table, looking bright and unaffected by the heat. A fan purred in the corner of the room, sweeping back and forth, and every few seconds some of the flower petals would stir in response to the artificial breeze.

"The only air conditioner is in my bedroom," Joan said. She made no motion to go there, so Billy sat on the sofa where the fan hit him intermittently. After some shuffling and shifting of crutches, Joan sat beside him, keeping a space between their bodies.

"How's the leg?"

"The least of my worries."

She wore a tank top that showed a clear outline of her breasts as she maneuvered to prop her injured leg on the edge of the coffee table. She was slouched down, half reclining, and the picture might have been inviting except that there was nothing playful in her manner today. The edge of flirtation was gone and Billy thought she looked as if she had been crying.

"What is it?"

She wiggled her foot until the shower clog fell off and onto the table.

"I got a phone call yesterday," she said.

She studied her toes instead of looking at Billy.

"And?"

"It was Duane." She spoke flatly, trying to stick to the facts and keep the emotion at bay. "He has Will with him."

"Well . . . good."

She looked at him for the first time since entering the house.

"So we know where he is," Billy continued.

"He says he's going to keep him."

"He can't . . ."

She spoke forcefully, impatient with the interruption.

"He can do what he wants, unless somebody stops him. He says I'm an unfit mother, he says . . . he says a lot of things. All of them nasty."

"He's always been an asshole . . ."

She dismissed his contribution with a wave of her hand.

"I can deal with an asshole. This time he's . . . he's different."

"In what way?"

"He sounds . . . I don't know how to describe it. The things he says about me . . . it makes me shiver."

"Is he threatening you?"

"Not that way. He doesn't need to. I've seen his work up close, remember. I know what Duane can do . . . this time he's threatening to really keep Will."

"No chance. That's already been resolved in court."

"No chance? Billy, you've been away too long. Duane always gets another chance. *Always.* He should have been in jail ten times over by now but he's still walking around, still doing whatever he wants. . . . He walked right into your sister's house and scared her silly, didn't he?"

"She chose not to press charges. It was really only trespass and that's hardly worth pursuing—legally, I mean."

"Nothing is ever worth pursuing when it comes to Duane. He knows just how far he can push things and get away with it. He knows just how much people will take because it's not worth the effort or because it would cost too much or because they're afraid of him or because they just know it wouldn't do any good, he'd still be here, they'd still have to live in the same community and they'd see him on the street, smirking at them, hating them with his eyes and they'd never know when he'd pop out of the darkness and . . ."

"I'll get Will. I'll get him today."

"No."

"I don't have to live in the same town with Duane. I'll take care of it."

"I'll call Pat," she said wearily. "Maybe he can do something."

"Pat already told me to do it if I want to. He's too busy now."

"You don't understand . . ."

"Help me out, then."

"He says he'll take me to court this time."

"I doubt it. Technically, he's guilty of kidnaping right now."

"He'll take me to court because . . ."

Joan stopped and closed her eyes. Billy touched her shoulder, felt the heat and clamminess of her skin. She pulled away from him.

"He says he's been keeping notes," she continued, her eyes still closed. "He calls it a 'book.'"

"What kind of notes?"

She glared at Billy suddenly, as if he were to blame for her problems.

"Why, my sordid activities, of course," she said sarcastically. "He has the date and place of practically every time I've been alone with a man since we got divorced."

"You're kidding."

"I don't have that good a sense of humor. I don't find it funny."

". . . Just being alone with a man?"

"That's enough for Duane. There's only one reason he'd be alone with a woman, he assumes it works both ways. You're on the list, Billy."

"Me?"

"You were seen carrying me into my house. How many neighbors would testify to that, do you suppose? Half a dozen?"

"That was perfectly innocent."

"Not perfectly."

Billy paused. "Why not perfectly? Refresh my memory."

"Because my mind was not pure. Was yours?"

"Of course not, but my mind hasn't been pure since I was ten. What's that got to do with it?"

"I'm glad I wasn't the only one, at least."

"So there was some flirtation, or a few happy thoughts, so what?"

"To any rational person, nothing. But he knows how I think, you see. . . . He knows some of those incidents in his 'book' were a lot less innocent than ours. He probably doesn't even care which, he knows he's right some of the time."

"You're a single woman."

Joan paused. "They weren't *all* before we were divorced. . . . Do you think I'm terrible?"

"Of course not. He was cheating on you right and left . . ."

He had offered her the easy way out, but she would not take it.

"Some of his jealousy is justified, you see. So if he accuses me of everything, part of the time he's right."

"Joan, it's just speculation and it's probably not even relevant. It would never stand up in court if he can't prove anything."

"How many would he have to prove?" she asked. He knew it was a challenge more than a question.

They were silent for a moment as the fan purred and struggled against the hot, humid air. How many *could* he prove? Billy wondered. And did it matter? . . . Did it matter to Billy? He was surprised to realize that he felt some of Duane's jealousy for a woman to whom he had no claim at all. He avoided her eyes until he could safely look at her again.

"I don't think the judge would even allow that kind of material."

"Who wants to take that chance? Do I want to risk defending my honor in court? And how do I do that? Deny everything? Deny just those that are true? Does it matter? If I'm accused, I lose. Joan Blanchard, school nurse and town slut. You know what they say about nurses, don't you? They're all easy, girls with the round heels, mattress backs."

"It's all bullshit, Joanie. Nobody cares."

"And *that's* bullshit. *I* care, even if nobody else does, and they do. And so do you."

"No, I don't," he said, angry with himself at the weakness of his denial. "In the first place, it's none of my business, and in the second place, so what? Do you think I'm a Christian missionary myself?"

There was more he could have said about the hypocrisy of conventional morality, the need of humans for warmth and affection, the injustice of the double standard and any number of other well-practiced justifications and rationalizations to make her feel better . . . and maybe sometime he would, but now he knew that by hesitating he had already failed her. He wished her past was something other than it was, he wished her reputation were better, he wished that Pat Kunkel's "possible" did not sound so tawdry in his ears.

If she read any of Billy's ambivalence, she gave no sign of it. "Now he's back in control," she said. "I have to come to him, and play it by his rules."

"What does he want? Does he really want custody?"

"No, of course not. Having Will around would cramp his style. He just wants to get at me, to watch me crawl, to have another turn at me. He wants to show he's still in charge."

"He must have given some conditions, something specific he wants in exchange . . ."

"He wants me to come get Will in person. He wants me to come to his place, to sit and 'talk' and convince him that I'm 'worthy' of being the mother to my son. But it won't be talk, of course."

Billy waited. Joan became interested in the workings of the fan.

"What will it really be?" he said finally.

"First he'll push me around, then work me over a bit. But carefully, so nothing shows, no bruises on the face. Then he'll rape me a few times," she said matter-of-factly. "He won't consider it rape, of course. In his mind I'm still his property. Forever. To do with as he sees fit. And of course I won't be allowed to just lie there and take it. God knows I've done that with him often enough in the marriage bed. He'll make me struggle, he'll find some way to make it so bad, so distasteful, that I'll have to fight back—and then he can defeat me. It's no good to him unless there's some kind of sick victory involved. I will have to scream and curse and try to hurt him. I will have to get *emotionally* involved so he can break me and make me remember it. It only hurts if you care and he'll manage to make me care before he's through."

"What a sick son of a bitch."

"Not so different from a lot of others," she said disdainfully. "Just more so."

Did she believe that? Billy wondered. If men were so bad, why did she seem to like them so much. Why was she so "possible"? And if they all mistreated her to some degree, how much had she participated in that behavior? How much had she sought it? Was she just a victim of male aggression, repeatedly, helplessly—yet voluntarily? Or did she solicit it in some way? Did she want it? Require it? It seemed to Billy that the more he learned about her the less he knew.

"I'll get your son back for you," he said.

"No, Billy . . . I'll do it. It's my job."

"You're incapacitated."

"Not for what Duane wants," she said. "He won't care if I'm on crutches or in a wheelchair. As long as I can crawl."

"I'll need to borrow your car," Billy said.

She paused again. He sensed her reluctance to speak.

"What is it, Joanie?"

"Billy, are you sure Sandy Metzger shot us, the way they're saying?"

"No, I'm not sure of it at all. I don't think he did. . . . Why?"

Joan shook her head.

"Do you have some idea who did it, Joan?"

"Just a feeling."

She inhaled deeply, glanced at him, held his eyes for a moment, then looked away, exhaling loudly. Again she shook her head.

"It's not as if you're making a judgment. Nothing will happen unless the facts support your feeling," he said, knowing it wasn't true. A feeling was all that was required to set a powerful chain of events in action. Once started, even if only because of a feeling, an investigation was potent, determined and nearly irreversible and it automatically carried a bias of guilt against its object, popular fictions about presumption of innocence notwithstanding.

"I'm biased. I don't want to say this just because I hate him so much . . ."

"Duane."

"He sounds different. He's always been close to the edge. . . . He sounds like he's gone over."

"Where are the keys?" he asked.

"I don't know that I'm right . . ."

"I'll get Will away from him, then we can worry about the rest of it."

"Why are you doing this, Billy?"

Billy paused. It was a question he had not yet asked himself but he knew the answer would be complicated.

"Haven't you heard? I'm the good guy."

"You really are, aren't you?"

Billy grinned. "As long as I'm not required to do too much."

"I don't believe you," she said.

"No one does. It's me charm," he said.

As he opened the door she said, "Don't go straight at him, Billy. Be sly."

"I took a course in it," he said.

There were no reporters and no cameras in sight as he got into her car and drove away.

CHAPTER SEVENTEEN

B illy drove home and changed from shorts to a pair of khakis, the coolest long pants he owned. They were nowhere near cool enough and he felt the clamminess under the cloth as soon as he returned to the car. But they would serve another purpose, or so he hoped.

His uncle Tim Wittrock, the honorary Irishman, owned a farm just outside of Rulo and Billy drove past the high school on his way to Route 159. The cameras and television reporters were back there again, looking a bit lost and bewildered, Billy thought, as they used the high school for a backdrop to follow-up stories without any new information. Judging by the report he heard on the car radio, Sheriff Kunkel had managed to stonewall very effectively and the media were stuck with a murder story without any leads or suspects. The whole town might have already convicted Sandy Metzger in their minds, but either they had not passed the word on to the media, or the media was exercising some restraint in naming him for fear of lawsuits. The case of Richard Jewell, the security guard falsely accused of the Atlanta Olympic Games bombing, apparently had a lingering, dampening effect on the rush to judgment. The reporters looked at Billy wistfully as he drove by, perhaps hoping that any passing car might drop a new witness into their lap to enliven their flagging stories.

Joan's car was not air-conditioned and Billy was drenched in sweat before he hit the town limits. The breeze generated by his greater speed on the highway felt as if it came from a furnace and offered scant relief, but still he drove with one arm out the window, directing the moving air onto his face. He had forgotten the simple pleasure of using his hand as an airfoil and letting it rise and fall in the wind.

The dust cloud over the silo complex seemed to hover just above the ground, weighted down by the same heat and humidity that oppressed the humans. As Billy approached and the man-made mist of grain chaff enveloped his car, he thought working in the silos must be like laboring in the mines of hell. Both Duane Blanchard and Curtis Metzger spent their days toiling in the complex. Had it made them into the hate-filled creatures they were? Might it not do the same to anyone who had the misfortune to spend a lifetime in such a place?

His speculation was broken by a car pulling abruptly onto the highway in front of him, appearing out of the haze like a giant mechanized carrot. The Chevy accelerated quickly, tires squealing, racing deeper into the mist until its flat orange color was gone entirely.

Billy sped up until he could see the Impala again. It was unlikely that he had been wrong in what he saw, but he wanted to be certain. They were halfway to the Rulo bridge over the Missouri before the two cars emerged completely from the dust cloud. There was no mistaking the car, it was the same one Pat had stopped on the day he expected Billy to be his shotgun-toting backup. The day I let him down, Billy thought ruefully.

There were only two black teenagers this time, but the car still rode so low to the road that it appeared to be weighted down by several tons of extra baggage. The youth with the blue bandanna knotted on his head was swiveled in the front seat to keep an eye on Billy. They locked eyes for a moment until a slow grin spread over the teenager's face. He turned his head toward the driver and spoke. Both of them laughed.

It seems I'm remembered, Billy thought. And once more the source of inn-o-cent merr-i-ment. The Chevy slowed and its hazard lights flashed in distress. The bandanna boy gestured for Billy to pull to the side.

What are we up to now? Billy wondered as the Chevy slowed still further and he slowed in response. He advised himself to let it go, whatever it was, just let it go. Not his business, not anything he wanted to get involved in. But the boy in the bandanna continued to gesture and to flash that big, malicious, mocking grin, and when the Chevy pulled off the road entirely, Billy followed it onto the shoulder, following the challenge of the grin.

Both cars stopped, engines idling, the Chevy shivering like an excited horse with the power under its hood. The boy with the bandanna beckoned with his finger, still grinning, still mocking. Just drive on past, Billy told himself. Don't be an idiot, don't get out of the car, don't get involved, you've already made a fool of yourself by responding to his taunting, that's enough, just drive on and if they follow turn onto a local road, their car is too low slung to keep up with you on a rutted, dirt road, they'll scrape with every bump.

The driver with the shaven head turned in his seat and stared at Billy, his expression dead flat and all the more menacing because of it. The grinner started talking to the driver, pointing at Billy and laughing. The driver slowly nodded his head in agreement as if they had sized Billy to the inch. Proven a coward already during the run-in with the sheriff, and now betraying himself as a half-wit as well. Point to the side of the road and he pulls over. What other tricks could he do? Beckon with your finger and see if he comes to you?

You got me pegged, me boyos, Billy said to himself. He opened his door and got out of the car. A dead sucker for an invitation. Give the lad a wink and a pat on his head and he'll follow you home. Starved for company, I am. Bikers, gangbangers, I'm such a social animal I'll befriend them all.

He kept the derisive monologue in his head turned up to full volume as he walked to the Chevy so he couldn't stop to think about what he was doing. Or why. Sure, 'twas the Irish in him, was it not?

"You fellas in distress, are ya?" he said, his brogue on full. "I see your lights are flashing. Would you be needing assistance at all, then?"

The driver glared at Billy with a look so hard it had to be phony. Even the glare could not disguise his youth. They're just boys, Billy thought. Not innocents, most likely, but young and full of youthful posturing.

The grinner did the talking, his head bent and craning sideways across the driver so he could see Billy.

"What up? We thinkin' *you* be los'," he said in an inner-city accent that Billy suspected was as bogus as his own. Ebonics was not a reality in the Midwest, just a fashion.

"I'm not lost," Billy said. "Just befuddled."

The grinner was delighted. "You be fuddle? Why dat?"

"I'm trying to figure out why a couple of kids from Kansas City keep showing up at this grain elevator. You must eat a lot of corn."

"Das it," the grinner offered. "Cain't *get* enough."

The driver broke his silence. "Da fuck's dat *yo* bidness?" he demanded. "You a cop?"

"Not a bit of it, lad. Nothing like."

"Why you be pullin' us over? Every cracker in this state think he get to stop and talk to the brothers?"

"You pulled me over, as I recall."

"He be Kunk' fren," the grinner interceded.

"Would that be *Sheriff* Kunk' you're referring to?" Billy inquired.

The grinner continued to explain. "He be Kunk' backup. Badass wif a shotgun." The details of their previous encounter amused the grinner enormously. "Bad ass wi'out no shotgun!"

"Happy to amuse."

"Amuse dis, mothafucka," the driver said. He pulled his unbuttoned shirt to the side, revealing a .45 pistol tucked into his belt.

Billy took an involuntary step backward.

"He be amuse'," the grinner said delightedly. "He be fuddle' and amuse' by dat. Ain't you, my man? He gettin' all white-face he so damn amuse'. Yo, I never see a white man get whiter like dat. How you do dat? Where all dat blood go? Tyquane, looka dat, all his bloods go to his feet or somewhere."

"I'm lookin'," said the driver.

"What could scare a man like dat? Tyquane, you show him you' dick?"

"He faint, I be showin' him my dick."

"Yo, yo, Fuddle', looka dis." The grinner produced a snub-nosed .38 and held it by the tip of the handle, pinched between thumb and forefinger. He waggled it back and forth distastefully, like a dead mouse. "Lookat I foun' in *my* pans."

"Cracker gon' be have a heart attack, Defone," said Tyquane.

"Pale as a ghos'."

"Kunk' got him a badass backup, yo."

The grinner's gun disappeared back under his T-shirt. "You keep breathin' now, Fuddle. Don' want Kunk' sayin' I scare' his man to death."

"Don' be followin' us and shit," said Tyquane, suddenly bored with the business. He eased the Chevy onto the highway and drove away with leisurely insolence, leaving Billy to stand there ashen and motion-less and contemplating how his reputation had spread so far and fast.

That was the worst yet, thought Billy. Toyed with by children. Laughed at and mocked by a couple of louts with iron in their belts as I stood there shaking like a cottonwood leaf in a high wind and fighting a terrible battle to control my various sphincters. Time to give it up entirely, me boyo. Rent a padded room somewhere and just lock yourself in and jibber at shadows. Congratulations, Avi Posner, you murderous son of a bitch, you've done a very thorough job of it. . . . He looked for the demon's laughing mouth and dragon teeth, but found him nowhere, not leering in the windshield, not dancing gleefully in the mirror, not even chuckling in his head. . . . Perfect, thought Billy. I did this all by myself, no help from the local demon necessary at all, a'tall. I'm a graduate, totally on me own.

And why did he follow the gangbangers in the first place, great gobshite that he was? The driver had it right, what bidness was it of his? Was it some atavistic cop/snoop gene that kept him poking his nose where it wasn't wanted and wasn't safe and was liable to get busted, or worse? Just old habits that he had not yet unlearned? Or was he a flaming eedjit, which seemed the most likely explanation? A refined masochist who reveled in disgrace and humiliation. But not pain. Take a pass on the pain, please. Just tear me pants off and make me walk naked around the town square while sniveling and sniffing, trying to hide my shame. The odd bit of self-degradation was just the ticket, just the t'ing for the local hero. . . . And if I keep going, keep asking for trouble and getting it and backing down and then keep at it anyway, like a monumentally stupid bulldog—well, blame it on the Irish in me.

And speaking of Irish, he had come to the right place. Tim Wittrock's farm was not so much run-down as passed over, as outdated as Tim's generation itself. At 160 acres it was too small to be efficient in an age of agribusiness, too poorly located to be a target for acquisition by one of the conglomerates. Tim worked it part-time, making his real income from a job at the hardware store and his wife's position at the library, and when he retired, which would be soon enough, he would keep it as an antiquated hobby until he died. After that he could not muster enough interest to worry about its disposition at all. The family farm, at least Tim Wittrock's family farm, was of as much use to him as a cowboy's saddle in the city. It still worked, the land still produced, but what good was a saddle without a horse, or a farm that could not support itself?

Billy found Tim in the shade thrown by the barn, working on a Case tractor that had been new during the Korean conflict but looked to Billy as if it came straight from a newsreel of the Great Depression. It, too, was as much hobby as useful tool, but Tim kept it clean and working with a hobbyist's zeal. As he did increasingly these days, Billy's uncle Sean kept Tim company, yammering away with news and advice—each given to spurious inclusions of Sean's invention—a bottle of something by his hand. The older he became, the more he grew to resemble Lord Jimmy, his older brother and absolute superior when it came to drinking, charming, and passing out. Sean was improving with age. Although his charm tended toward the bellicose and his drinking fell on the sloppy side, his passing out was edging toward the sterling category.

Sean was the first to spot him. He raised his beer bottle in greeting. "Billy boy!"

As Tim straightened from his labors to look, Sean was already clawing at the cooler to secure a beer for his nephew. He carried the cooler with him now as a matter of course.

Reserved and formal, even when reeling from an early-afternoon high, Tim wiped away the grease and offered his hand. Sean offered a beer.

"How's the lad?"

"Top of me form, Sean, sure now. Couldn't be better, hale and flush with honors." If Sean ever detected the note of satire and irony in Billy's brogue, he never let on. That it was in direct reaction to the Irish-tough-guy heritage that had been slathered on the young Billy like the grease on Tim's tractor was a subtlety that would never have occurred to him or any of the uncles. Billy was not as certain about the aunts. They seemed always less beery, less boisterous and, in their quiet ways, much sharper.

"Flush with honors! Ah, Billy, your dad would have been so proud to see how you turned out." Instantly sentimental, Sean appeared to be already only a blink away from tears.

"Congratulations," said Tim, forestalling him.

"What for?"

"For pounding the shit out of Curt Metzger," Sean said.

They knew already. Faster than the Internet.

"Not that much, really. The hog did most of the work."

"The hog was a good touch," said Tim. His eyes looked slightly glazed from Sean's beer, but the man was so short and squat and stable it was impossible to imagine him toppling over from alcohol alone. Sean was another matter entirely. Billy noted that his bleary-eyed uncle never moved from his secure position against the rear wheel of the tractor. The cooler was within an arm's reach.

"The hog was a great touch," echoed Sean. "And if ever a man needed a good stomping and hog chewing, it was Curtis Metzger. Don't know why I didn't do it myself years ago."

"You've got an enemy now, of course," Tim said.

"They say you can tell a man by his enemies," said Billy.

"They do say that, they do," agreed Sean. He seemed slightly baffled by the meaning.

"I wonder if I can borrow a tool from you, Uncle Tim."

"Sure."

"Sure he can. Give him what he wants, Tim."

"I said sure."

"Tight as a virgin's asshole, your uncle Tim. Give him whatever he wants, for Christ's sake. He deserves it."

Tim led Billy into the cool of the barn. The tools were lined up neatly on a Peg-Board, their outlines traced in black. It was the array of a man who knew the value of his tools, not to mention their location. Billy selected a prising tool, half the length of a full-scale crowbar but otherwise identical.

"Got a job to do," Tim said, the question implied but not asked.

"A bit of prying," said Billy. He inserted the crowbar down the inside of the back of his trouser leg. The curved end fit neatly over his belt, securing it within quick and easy reach.

When he had pulled his T-shirt so that it fell outside his belt, he turned slowly for Tim's inspection.

"See anything?" he asked.

Tim pursed his lips as if detection took an extraordinary effort of concentration.

"Not really."

"Good enough," said Billy.

"Going to be hard sitting like that."

"That'll keep me on my toes."

Tim nodded dimly. Billy wondered how many beers the two of them had finished so far, and how many more they would manage before quitting or collapsing. Was this it, was this the fate of all the men in his family, to spend their declining years drinking too much while looking for shade, their bodies sweating out the booze as quickly as they sucked it in? Not a great deal to look forward to, he thought. But a better fate than some.

"Be needing any help?" Tim asked.

"No, thanks, Uncle Tim. I think I better do this alone."

"You can count on Sean and me, you know. Whatever kind of job you got, you can count on your uncles."

Billy could just imagine his two half-loaded uncles, wading into trouble face first, shouting Erin Go Bragh, upholding the honor of the Irish to the last drop of alcohol in their veins. . . . Or maybe he did them an injustice, maybe they were all as tough and courageous as they claimed for each other. Maybe it was only Billy Tree, son of the late lamented Lord Jimmy, who showed the feather and let down the side and shit his pants and turned into a quivering ghost at the sight of two teenagers toting guns. . . . And if so, why was he shoving a crowbar down his pant leg? Why wasn't he at home, hiding under the bed where he belonged?

"Thanks, Uncle Tim. I know I can count on you guys. I just don't think I need any help for this job. But I appreciate the offer."

"Sean will be disappointed."

"Let's not tell him, then," said Billy.

Tim held a finger to his lips and exhaled a shhh that Sean could probably hear in the feedlot.

Billy drank a beer with them and asked the de rigueur questions about the crops and heard the predictable answers—the crops were never good enough these days, or else the prices were too low because the crops were *too* good. Farmers seemed to prosper in inverse proportion to their success as farmers. In the land of plenty, the providers of that plenty had very little. It made as much intuitive sense as quantum physics and farmers of Tim Wittrock's age and size, squeezed out and going down, no longer tried to figure it out.

Billy listened to them complain until they were bored with it before inquiring about Thom Cohan.

"Who would shoot such a man?" Sean demanded, then immediately answered his own question. "The sniveling little coward."

"Who's that?"

Sean sought for the proper name, waving his beer bottle in frustration. "What's his name, the little bastard?"

"What did people think of Cohan? Did he have any enemies, any vendettas going?"

"A fine man, a fine, fine man. Terrible tragedy. The sneaky little shit. What's the matter with kids today?"

Billy addressed his questions to Tim. Sean had slid into the blurry, loose-tongued world of free-floating sentiment.

"Anything out of the ordinary, any rumors about him?"

Tim shook his head sagely. "He was a straight shooter."

"Straight shooter, straightest damned shooter. You don't know, Billy, you got no idea," Sean confirmed.

"How about women? Was he seeing anybody?"

"Ah, the women." Sean's eyes drifted upward and he smiled in a vague, all-encompassing way. "Lord love 'em."

"Uncle Tim?"

Tim hesitated. "It's hard to say, Billy. You hear things. You don't want to spread gossip."

"Fucking gossip. You got no idea, Billy."

"A little gossip might help me right now, Uncle Tim."

"I don't like to mess with people's reputations, Billy."

"One of them's dead, Tim. What did you hear?"

"Just talk, you know, Billy. That don't make it true."

"I understand."

"Don't get upset."

"Why would I get upset?"

"I always liked her, myself."

"Who?"

"Always liked her," Sean agreed.

"Who, Uncle Tim?"

"Joan Blanchard," Tim said.

"Always liked her."

"There was something going on between Joan Blanchard and Thom Cohan? Is that what you're saying?"

"Don't get angry now."

"I'm not angry," Billy said. He was not sure what he was, but anger didn't seem to describe it.

"Don't get angry, Bill," Sean said.

"It was just one night, far as I know. They were doing some blow . . . things happen."

"Doing some blow?" The word sounded as out of place coming from Tim Wittrock as a spate of classical French. "Cocaine? Are you saying Thom Cohan and Joan Blanchard were doing cocaine together?"

"Don't get angry, Bill," Sean said. He seemed to be losing his grip on the tractor tire and he would jerk himself erect periodically like a man fighting off sleep.

"I'm not angry, Uncle Sean. I just want to be clear. You saw this, Uncle Tim?"

Tim shrugged. "Looked like it. Maybe I'm wrong."

"Do you know what it looks like?"

"See it on television all the time," said Tim. "Dickheads snorting, shooting up, you name it. Everybody knows what it looks like."

Sean gave up the battle against gravity and slid to the dirt, resting his back against the tire. He didn't spill a drop. "Fucking disgrace," he offered, although Billy wasn't certain if he referred to himself or the portrayal of drug use on television.

Tim expanded upon his explanation. "Plus I did some of it myself that night."

"You did—*what*, exactly, Uncle Tim?"

"Some blow."

"You snorted cocaine?"

"A few lines. This was a while back." Tim shrugged. "Everybody else was. No big deal."

Billy felt like a child being told the truth about sex. Not *his* uncle. Squat, stolid Tim Wittrock would never . . . not in Falls City . . . not his family.

"I don't do it anymore, Bill. This was back a ways."

"Filthy habit," said Sean.

"I was depressed for a while there," Tim offered.

"Never touched it," Sean said. He was addressing the dirt between his feet, intent on convincing it of his innocence. "Never touched it."

"Where was this?"

"Elks Club, I think. A dance, charity thing, something. I don't remember."

Billy decide to concentrate on the one portion of Tim's recital that he could actually conceive of.

"And Joan and Cohan went there and did some coke and . . . what?"

"They didn't go together, they didn't leave together. They just kind of, you know, seemed to *be* together while they were there. You know how Joanie can look at a man."

"No, how can she look at a man?"

"Don't get upset."

"Why does everyone keep telling me not to get upset? I'm not upset. What would I be upset about?"

Tim smiled as if enjoying a private memory.

"Jesus Christ, this fucking town. Everyone thinks they know more about me than I know myself—and before it happens."

"Have a drink," Sean offered.

"Where did they get it, Uncle Tim? Where'd they get the cocaine?"

"I don't know. Cohan usually had some. Maybe Joan had some. I don't know."

"Cohan usually had some? Was he known for this?"

"No more than anybody else. Somebody usually has some. It's not hard to find."

Billy bade his uncles good-bye and walked to the car, trying not to limp because of the crowbar. He marveled at his own naïveté. Privately, he had scoffed at Kunkel's mention of drug problems in the town, chalking it up to a lawman's preoccupation. But his uncle's blasé account of its prevalence was impossible to ignore. As for Joan's involvement with Cohan, if that's what it was . . . He tried to analyze what he was feeling and found he could not put a name to it but it was decidedly unpleasant.

There were nearly three hours before Duane Blanchard's shift at the elevator was over. Billy was still not entirely certain of his strategy for dealing with Duane, but he knew he was not going to confront him at his place of work. Whatever was done was best done without witnesses and on ground of Billy's choosing.

First he drove to Blanchard's house on the old Bedwell farm again, hoping to get lucky and find Will sitting on the porch, just waiting for a ride home. It was no surprise that no one was there.

Billy tried the key that he had stolen during his last visit, jiggling it unsuccessfully in the lock for a minute before concluding it was the wrong key. Perplexed, he put it back in his pocket, drove the car to the side of the house, and launched himself from its roof onto the roof of the house and into the second-story window again.

Duane's room was unchanged and uninteresting to Billy, but the bedclothes in the guest bedroom had been rearranged and an empty soda can sat on the windowsill. Two places had been set for breakfast, if *setting* was not too formal a concept for a cereal bowl with residual milk by one chair and a glass that had once held orange juice by another.

On an impulse Billy went into the small downstairs room he thought of as Duane's office. This time he examined the room carefully, kneeling to see if anything was taped underneath the card table or chair, tapping the walls for hollow sounds, checking the floorboards. In the closet where he had found the guns, he shoved the coats to one side and felt along the shelf until his fingers touched the boxes of ammunition for the weapons. As Billy stood on his toes to feel the length of the shelf, the floor groaned enticingly. When he could not prise up the creaking floorboard with his fingers he used the tool he had borrowed from his uncle.

On close examination, Billy saw nicks and depressions in the wood where knives or screwdrivers had been inserted for the necessary leverage. The nails had been bent over on the bottom side so that the board came up with no resistance whatsoever. It was a sloppy job, one that might avoid detection by the casual observer, but certainly nothing intended to fool a trained inspector, or even a diligent amateur. Either Duane wasn't hiding anything he cared much about, or he wasn't worried about the likelihood that anyone would be looking for it.

Billy pulled up the floorboard half-expecting to find Duane Blanchard's stash of pornography. Instead, he found an opened box of baking powder, a tea strainer, and a box of sealable sandwich bags. There was enough room in the space between joists to accommodate two or three full-sized freezer bags but Billy found nothing more. He probed and tested the other floorboards in the closet but discovered no more secret spaces. Whatever went in with the baking powder to make it worth hiding was not there now. Judging by the state of Duane's kitchen, the baking powder was not used for cooking, nor the tea strainer for tea unless Duane was literally a closet chef. It seemed unlikely.

As he was about to exit the house, Billy stopped abruptly and returned to the office. He had remembered what he had *not* seen. Duane's hitting gloves were gone from the desk.

CHAPTER EIGHTEEN

———❧———

As he walked out of the farmhouse the flash of light he had seen during his last visit stuck him again like a splinter in the corner of his eye. He crossed the feedlot to the excitement and disappointment of the chickens, scaled the fence, and stepped into the field of alfalfa that lay between the farmhouse and the slash of trees. Some of the leaves of the scrub oaks intervened with his line of sight and the light winked and blinked seductively with every step.

The trees were gnarled and stunted, their bottom branches lying close to the ground, and Billy had to pick his way through them in an elaborate weave. A trickle of water seeped and spread itself through the center of the tiny copse, barely wetting the bottom of the streambed.

The trees seemed wilted from thirst, and the merry winking of the sun's reflection from the bicycle mirror mocked the etiolated surroundings. The bike appeared to be in good condition. Billy checked the alignment of the wheels, the air pressure in the tires, the smooth functioning of gears and chain. The seat was not torn, there was no rust, no serious dents or dings.

Billy investigated the streambed for footprints or tire marks, then looked at the tires again for any accumulations of mud or dirt still adhering to the treads. He looked under the seat for egg cases or other signs that insects had been making a home there. Finally he returned to the field of alfalfa and tried to imagine a scenario in which someone would ride the bike through the field, park it in the trees, unscratched, fully functioning, then walk off and forget it. It seemed improbable in the extreme.

He had two hours to kill before the end of the shift at the elevator complex, and more than enough to think about so he let the car steer itself north and west along the country roads while he tried to make sense out of his confusion. Two bicycles on the old Bedwell farm, one in the barn—presumably Will Blanchard's—and one tucked away in trees where somebody must have carried it. Was it Sandy Metzger's bike? Had the two boys pedaled out to the farm and hidden Sandy's bike? And then hidden Sandy as well? Or had Duane Blanchard brought both bikes and both boys in the back of a truck and dumped Sandy's bike himself. Duane was admitting that he had Will, but no mention had been made of Sandy. Had he dumped Sandy along with the bike? Billy wondered if he should go back and walk the Bedwell farm in search of a shallow grave. He had no good reason to jump to such a conclusion except for a very biased view of Duane. It was not even an intuition—he placed some qualified trust in his intuitions—it was closer to a wish. Perhaps a desire for the local villains to be guilty of all local villainy. Things seldom worked out that efficiently in life, he knew, because villainy did not come in discrete particles, it smeared itself across the fabric of society like an ineradicable stain.

He arrived at the section corner and turned north on Highway 73, driving parallel to the route he had trudged through the cornfields the night before. When he reached the bridge he reversed the car and backed into the rutted path so that the nose of the car was a few yards off the highway, far enough back from the road to be screened by the corn, but close enough to be able to get out in a hurry. He wanted no repeat of yesterday's fiasco.

As he had assumed would be the case, the bikers were gone. He walked the length of the path, pausing where he had taken his ass-over-elbows plunge into the river, feeling even more ashamed of his behavior than he had the previous night. A single wide-wheeled motorcycle track led to the edge of the bank and ended in midair. A few feet away part of the edge had been gouged away where they had pulled the motor-cycle out of the water. Billy scuffed at the bike track, trying to eradicate the traces of his recent disgrace.

Have to shift a lot of dirt to cover up all your messes, boyo. You need a bulldozer just to take care of the past twenty-four hours.

A chorus of crows erupted behind his back as he walked farther along the path. He turned to see them in the distance on the far side of the bridge, a swirling cloud of black scolds, twisting around each other like an ebony whirlwind. Everyone's entitled to their opinions, he thought, even the birds. It was one of the oddities of the American outlook.

At the end of the path the bare dirt expanded like a balloon on a string, opening into a clearing in the corn that had been created by the cycles. He could see their tracks going round and round in a circle tangent to the bank, like movie Indians circling the covered wagons.

The birds caught his attention again as the volume of their dis-turbance increased. He turned to see them wheeling in the sky in a flurry of anger, some of them seeming to swoop at others, wings spread suddenly as brakes, then flapping again, talons extended as if to snatch their prey from the sky. Territorial dispute, thought Billy. Gang warfare in the sky.

He turned back to the traces of a gang on the ground. The bikers had left their mark, but it was as banal as the trash from a family picnic. Food wrappers littered the circle—Billy thought he recognized the stick and greasy paper from a corn dog—along with empty beer cans, cig-arette butts, and one discarded pint whiskey bottle, only its open mouth showing above the soil where a foot or tire had all but buried it. There were flecks of oil and carbon marks on a few standing cornstalks that had absorbed hot exhaust fumes at very close range, but nothing to indicate any activity that couldn't have been perpetrated by a handful of teenagers in half the time.

So what had Billy stumbled into that merited the systematic pursuit of half a dozen bikers? A late-evening meal alfresco in the cornfield? A simple country get-together? Had they swarmed after him like bees in defense of their nest because he had disturbed their digestion?

The crows sounded a still more strident note of outrage and Billy looked to see one of them drop from the midst of the turmoil like a black handkerchief, wings fluttering ineffectively. Others broke off the engagement in the sky and swooped down after it, swift as avian arrows as they disappeared from his sight below the level of the corn.

Billy returned to the spot where he had abandoned his sister's car the night before and looked for his footprints leading into the corn. They were not hard to find and the site of his encounter with the two bikers was trampled down like a message from aliens in a British wheat field. He examined the spot where he had knocked the second cyclist from his machine and saw the imprint of the cycle, the depression made by the biker's body, even the impressions of the chains on the biker's leather jacket. Moving to the spot where he had commandeered the motorcycle of the first biker and begun his inept joyride, Billy knelt in the dirt beside a small mound of dirt that had been formed by spinning wheels. It was the kind of detail that would have gone unnoticed in the night, but it stood out boldly in the brilliant sun, a lump of something under the soil, its contour accentuated by the mix of shade and sun.

Brushing the dirt aside, he revealed a plastic bag the size of a manila folder. The top was heat sealed, the plastic thicker than a home freezer bag. Inside glistened a shower of diamond slivers, corruscating in the sunlight. Billy shook the bag gently and blew off the remainder of the dirt. Hefting the bag in his hand he immediately ruled out diamonds and water ice, even assuming ice could survive in the baking heat. He isolated a single crystal and pinched the bag hard between his thumb and forefinger as if squashing a bug. The crystal shattered into powder.

The sound of a tractor approaching on the highway made him stand and listen intently. The tractor passed the turnoff and slowly receded and Billy realized that he had been holding his breath. He was frightened with good reason. He held enough crystal meth in his hand to keep several dozen addicts supplied for weeks. Billy knew little about the street value of a drug like "ice," but he knew enough to understand that what he was holding was not one biker's stash, it was an industrial-sized, professionally packaged bag that would be broken down into individual servings and sold—whether on the streets of a city or the sleepy sidewalks of Falls City—for serious money. Enough money to justify considerable mayhem. People killed for a good deal less and they were not apt to abandon it without very good reason. Some of the sweat that drenched his body was not from the heat and not from the beer he had shared with his uncles. When the bikers realized that the "ice" was missing, they would return for it, and he didn't want to be chased by them a second time.

But why had they not returned already? Many hours had passed since they had decamped in the middle of the night, they must have discovered their loss by now and figured out how it had happened. Why were they not here by now? Why not long before this? If Billy had found the "ice" without even knowing what he was looking for, surely the half-dozen bikers could have found it and been long gone by now. There were no additional footprints around the area where the first biker had been knocked from his machine, no signs of any search. Could Sheriff Kunkel have put such a scare into them that they would not risk returning, even for such a valuable prize? It hardly seemed Pat's style. He would talk them away, negotiate their absence—not terrify them.

Then what? They had not been here and by this time it appeared that they weren't coming because surely if they were looking for something lost they wouldn't come by dark of night.

Billy carried the bag of crystal meth to Joan's car and looked for a place to hide it. It was too big for his pockets and he was not going to stuff it in his belt to complicate matters if he ever had to put the crowbar back down the back of his leg. It couldn't be left on the seat in plain sight so that any passerby could see it. After a few minutes' thought Billy realized he wouldn't be able to keep it from detection by any serious investigator, either. Cars used for smuggling drugs had special compartments built in, but Joan Blanchard's Plymouth was used for transporting no more precious cargo than herself and her son. He slipped the package under the spare tire. Any experienced cop would find it within two minutes, but at least it would be secure from a casual snoop.

The crows had gone berserk. No longer in the sky, their insistent cawing was louder and more incensed as if the energy used to keep them in the air could now be devoted to their full-throated screech. There was nothing unusual about crows in a cornfield, but there was something out of the ordinary here. Billy crossed the highway and followed the river downstream.

The chocolate brown waters of the Little Nemaha flowed like warm mud, sluggishly transporting the runoff of irrigated, fertilized, pesticided fields to their eventual destination in the Missouri River, which was itself nicknamed, for apt and obvious reason, the Big Muddy. It was hard to believe that he had floated to safety last night in that effluvium of water and soil; in the dark the water had seemed like a warm haven, in the light of day it looked impossible for a fish to survive in its opaque embrace. Billy followed the river until he was past the spot where he had run aground on the sandbar. The marks of his clawing ascent up the bank and into the cornfield smirked at him from the loose dirt. A few yards farther he encountered the birds.

The crows were on the other side of the river, on the edge of the soybean field, their bodies not obscured by the low-lying plants. They were gathered in a circle around the fallen bird, their mouths wide open, panting for relief from the heat—Billy tried to imagine the solar radiation absorbed by a pitch-black body in full sunlight on a day like this. It was a miracle they weren't all baked—and screaming, screaming. As he watched, one of the crows hopped forward and pecked at the bird in the center. Another joined it, took a stab at the fallen one with its long beak, then hopped back. The downed crow, its wings splayed to either side as if to prop it up, turned its head toward each tormentor and cawed in protest, but seemed powerless to defend itself. One by one the other crows advanced, screaming and pecking. Emboldened by the waning resistance, they stayed longer, pecked harder and with more effect. In violent parody of an elegant dance, the birds in the circle surged inward, struck at the helpless victim, then hopped back to their place, beaks wide open, screaming hatred, or triumph, or bloodlust.

After several minutes the bird in the circle appeared to resign itself to its fate and it folded its wings next to its body and let its head drop, accepting each blow without protest, its beak still open, panting.

They pecked it, still cawing in raucous chorus, until it fell on its side, pecked it until the only motion in the victim was caused by the force of their blows, pecked it so that its inert body danced sideways in the dirt, recoiling from each blow as if it were a rolled black sock being used by children for a ball, pecked it until it was dead and still pecked it well beyond death.

Billy had never seen anything like it in the natural world and he watched with horrified fascination. He remembered that in the compilation that included a gaggle of geese and an exultation of larks, they were known as a murder of crows.

One by one they seemed to lose interest in their dead fellow and they hopped away, reassembling a few yards further downstream in a squalling black cloud upon the prize that had initiated the territorial war in the first place.

Lying under the heaving raven blanket of squawking birds was a lump of something that twitched with each peck and tug. At first Billy thought it was a hog, squirming to be free of the torment, but the color was wrong. There was only one living animal he knew of that had the pale sickly hue of hairless flesh never exposed to the elements.

Billy hesitated. Why did he have to be the one who discovered Sandy Metzger's body? He did not want to look at it, he had seen enough corpses to last him forever. Why not drive away, let the farmer stumble on it eventually? What concern, ultimately, was it of his?

He slid down the bank and into the muck on the river bottom. He was not going to repeat last night's performance and lose another pair of shoes, so he tugged them free of the mud and tossed them onto the bank before wading deeper into the chocolate water. Closer to his eye the river lost its opacity and the surface water became clear even though he could not see his feet on the bottom. When the river lapped at his chest he began to swim in a sedate breaststroke, keeping his head up. On the far bank he could see the trail where Sandy had dragged himself out of the water. There were no footprints, just a prolonged smear of soil and weeds, occasionally a deeper depression where his fingers had dug for a handhold. Sandy had come out of the water on his belly like a lizard and made it only a few yards into the bean field before collapsing for good.

He smelled the body before he reached the top of the bank. It was the odor of excrement, not decay, which meant the body had voided itself on dying, but not long enough ago for the reek to dissipate. In this heat, in another day, it would be the nauseatingly sweet stench of rotting flesh, not the more familiar stink of shit.

The birds scattered begrudgingly from the body at Billy's approach, reluctant to give up their feast, and they hopped only a few yards away, scolding and watching him, their maws open to pant, regarding him with obsidian eyes. The body was on its back and the crows had gone after the soft parts first. The eyes were gone, the tongue was in tatters, and the cheeks were torn open. The rest of the body showed signs of their work, but the early birds, or the dominant ones, had concentrated on the face.

Billy closed his eyes and exhaled forcibly, fighting a wave of nausea. He had seen worse in his time, but that did not make this sight any easier. Irrationally, he threw clods of dirt at the crows until they took to wing, surprised and indignant. They had been prepared to share their find, if necessary, but not to give it up entirely.

Not much could be told by looking at the face, but one thing was certain. It was not Sandy Metzger. The body was that of an older man, the hair thinning and gray, the musculature loose and frail. The abdomen, already swollen with gas, was soft, unmuscled. This was not a body that had spent hours and months lifting weights.

The corpse was completely naked, partly covered in dried mud acquired during the crawl up the riverbank, but the mud was not sufficient to hide the enormous welts and bruises that ran from its shoulders to its feet. Someone or something had pummeled the body when it was still a man, when it still felt every one of those blows. It looked as if something had run over the living body again and again—Billy could not help but think of motorcycles. The odd angle of one of the legs made it clear that at least one bone was broken, but with the mass of injuries, it was probably many. The man had crawled from the river on his belly because that was the only way he could move.

They had stripped him bare, probably to humiliate him, maybe to search him as well, and then inexpertly, brutishly tortured him by the simplest possible way—beating him. Billy was no expert in forensic medicine, but it was not hard to imagine that some of the bruises came from something broad and blunt, like a fist. The longer, narrower marks, some of which had broken the skin, looked as if they could have been administered with chains. Whatever they had sought from him, pleasure or information or punishment, they had tried to get it by simply pounding it out of him.

Ultimately, he had eluded them, as was evident by the trail of his passage from the river. Either they had beaten him and discarded him, perhaps left him for dead, or they had been distracted in some way and he had escaped even though barely able to move. Had Billy been the distraction? Had he blundered into the torturing of this poor soul last night? While the bikers were chasing Billy, had this man taken the same route Billy would take minutes later and dragged himself into the river and let its sluggish current transport him away from the killing ground?

He returned to what remained of the face. Despite the desecration of the crows, there was something familiar about the ears, the hairline, the shape of the skull. The jaw was askew, broken where something had struck it a fracturing blow. Another blow had pushed the nose to one side. Much of the blood had been washed away in the river, but he had continued to bleed some after crawling to his final resting place. The last of his blood was dried and crusted on his upper lip and a trail of ants ran from it down to the ground in a shifting black thread.

There was something he needed to remember, an image trying to force its way into his mind. Billy turned away from the body for a moment, his eyes on the crows but his mind struggling to find the memory. He stood still long enough that the boldest of the crows hopped tentatively forward, hoping to resume the banquet. Seeing the crow's awkward, tentative motion, Billy suddenly recalled the sight of Huford Peck hurrying away from the bikers like a frightened bird, arms flapping like broken wings. He could not recognize the corpse from its face, but Billy knew with a sudden certainty that he was standing over Huford.

The bikers wanted his "shiny," whatever that was. But he had said something else. "They want what I know." What could Huford know that anyone else would want badly enough to beat him to death for? Did they find it, Huford? Did you tell them what you know? Did they get your shiny?

Billy had to alert the sheriff, but he didn't want to leave Huford's body to the further ministrations of the crows. Unless he wished to stand guard until someone wandered by, however, he had no choice. He removed his shirt to drape it over Huford's face. It was not likely that the crows would be deterred more than a moment or two, but he could think of nothing else to offer. As he bent to spread the shirt, Billy noticed a glint of light from Huford's open mouth. While the crows tightened their ring, closing in on the body, Billy knelt on hands and knees in the dirt and fought his revulsion as he peered past the tattered tongue and deep into Huford's throat.

When his shadow covered the corpse's face he saw nothing but darkness but when he straightened to his knees, the sun covered Huford's face and was reflected back as if from an internal mirror. Billy had seen the state police at work gathering evidence from Sandy Metzger's room. If that was their standard, Billy would feel no qualms about interfering with the evidence in situ.

Billy probed gently into the recesses of Huford's throat, trying to avoid glancing at the hollows that had once held his eyes. Adjusting his position on the ground to get a better angle, he nudged his knee against Huford's abdomen. With a rumble a bubble burst in the stomach and a gust of mephitic gas issued from Huford's open mouth accompanied by a faint whistling sound. Billy turned away, gagging back the nausea.

His fingernail worked under the edge of the object and Billy was able to prise it up enough that he could grasp it with his fingers. Pulling it out, he turned it in the sunlight and watched the cartridge case sparkle and flash.

It was a .22 shell, brass, the poor man's gold. Was this your shiny, Huford? Is this what they wanted from you? Did you try to swallow it to hide it from them? Or did they push it down your throat as a malicious metaphor?

Billy held the casing gingerly between his thumb and forefinger, touching only the firing rim. He had no idea whether fingerprints would survive the inside of a man's throat, but he had a healthy respect for the modern crime lab—if not always for the policemen who provided it with evidence. Searching for a few moments, waving his arms at the encroaching crows as he walked, he found a twig and inserted it into the shell casing. With the twig holding the casing aloft and safe from any further contamination by his hands, Billy eased himself into the water and slowly swam across with a one-armed backstroke.

He placed the shell casing on the front seat of the car before retrieving an old blanket from the trunk and returning to cover Huford's body. The crows had taken quick advantage of his absence and were feasting again. Billy yelled and whirled the blanket over his head and chased the whole circle until every one of the birds had taken flight. The more fainthearted flew away but the majority simply withdrew to a safe distance and settled to the ground like a shower of black rags, where they watched with the patience of born scavengers that knew that men grew weary and lost interest in crows soon enough. Furious, disgusted, and frustrated by their persistence, Billy charged after them, screaming and twirling the blanket like a deranged cowboy trying to turn a stampeding herd, chasing them still farther away only to find that some had slipped in behind him and settled on the abandoned body again, as unavoidable as falling ash.

He slumped into the dirt beside the body, sweat pouring from him and making pockmarks in the soil. He opened his mouth, panting from the exertion of chasing the birds, but the air outside seemed hotter than his breath. It was like gasping inside a furnace; what comfort could it give the crows?

As he sat in the sun, trying to calm himself, Billy realized that he had grown used to the stench of the corpse and the horror of its appearance had faded as well. It was like sitting beside a comrade wounded in war and Billy felt oddly attached to Huford, as if they had suffered some great ordeal together. He waved a solicitous hand over Huford's face, dispersing a swarm of insects that had gathered while he was doing futile battle with the crows. Doubting that it would thwart the birds for long—or the insects at all—Billy draped the corpse with the blanket and weighted the edges with dirt before crossing the river a final time. After the heat of the field, the water felt as cool and refreshing as a mountain stream and Billy yearned to stay there, but when he looked back he saw the crows already tugging at the blanket. A toe, pale and swollen as a maggot, popped out from under the cover and a bird was instantly upon it. Billy scrambled up the bank and back to the car.

CHAPTER NINETEEN

It seemed to take an interminable time for the sheriff to arrive following the phone call and Billy sat with the body until he did, ringed by crows that never tired of screeching at him. It occurred to him, in an excess of self-consciousness, that there was something timeless and Sophoclean about his vigil, as if he were an ancient Greek grieving the loss of a loved one, standing guard against the carrion eaters. Tibetans buried their dead this way, he reflected. Cut them up and left them to the vultures, recycling the bodies and at the same time—so they believed—taking part in the divine. Maybe it was the majesty of the Himalayas that made the difference, he thought. Or maybe the birds. It was hard to find anything celestial in the gaping, protesting mouths of squawking crows. More likely there was nothing noble or tragic about his sentinel duty at all. Perhaps he was more like a loyal dog than a grieving Greek, standing by the fallen master for a while before wandering off in search of another, more stupefied by the sudden loss of animation than emotionally bereft. What was Huford Peck to Billy Tree, after all? A few moments of imagined solidarity as paired town freaks, the gargoyle and the walker, inspired by Billy's blatant indulgence in self-pity. A handful of exchanged sentences that made little sense to Billy and perhaps none to Huford, either. And yet he felt his battle with the crows was the best thing he had done in years, ennobling to both himself and Huford in some way he did not understand, or at any rate did not wish to diminish by examination. He knew that he felt he was doing good, sitting in the dirt, broiling in the sun, waving his arms threateningly at the crows, and it had been a very long time since he had felt he was doing good about anything.

When Kunkel and Lapolla finally arrived with an ambulance, Billy resented their intrusion. For a moment he felt like the snarling dog that refuses to let anyone approach his fallen master. Like the dog, he quickly got over it.

Kunkel studied the scene for a long, silent moment, glancing now and then at Billy while the ambulance driver and Lapolla kept their distance. He tracked the scene much as Billy had, noting the trail leading from the river, the traces of Huford's tortured progress. When he removed the blanket from the body, the crows hopped in expectation. Kunkel knelt where Billy had knelt and studied the corpse with his face wrinkled against the smell. Every so often he would look away from the body and study Billy with the same curious, detached gaze, as if trying to find the connection between the dead body and the live one.

Kunkel rose, a hand in the middle of his back as he stretched. "Lapolla!"

The deputy hurried forward, trying not to look directly at the body. "Yes, Sheriff."

"Can't you do something about those birds?"

While Lapolla chased the birds, Kunkel addressed Billy for the first time since his arrival. "The son of a bitch," he said.

"Who?"

"What would he want to do this to Huford for?"

"It wasn't one man. It was half a dozen bikers."

"You think?"

"Christ, look at him."

"Well, I've done that, Bill."

"You think one man did all that?"

Kunkel shrugged and indicated Huford's legs with the toe of his boot. "Not that. Cycles might have done that, I won't argue with you there. But his arms, his face, his chest, even here on his ribs—that's not from a bike, Bill."

Billy rose and studied Huford again.

Kunkel continued. "I don't want to pull rank on you, but how many dead bodies have you looked at?"

"Not many," Billy admitted.

"But any is too many, right?"

Billy nodded. "Too many. I don't much care for it."

"I've seen a whole lot too many," Kunkel said. "As coroner I get just about everybody who doesn't die in his sleep."

"As coroner?"

"The county sheriff is also the county coroner in Nebraska," Kunkel explained. "Oh, I use Doc Lippold if I need an autopsy. He's the medical examiner. But I get to—I got to—look at them first. Not the favorite part of my job."

Kunkel squatted heavily again, gasping unabashedly as he lowered his weight to his hams. "Look at that mark, and that one there." He indicated bruises on each cheekbone. "That's from a fist. Those on the jaw, too."

The sheriff balled his fingers and held them close to each of the bruises, then traced them down the body, from the temple to the rib cage. Billy could see that the marks below the waist were all made differently from those above.

"So they beat him with their fists until he fell, then they ran the bikes over him," Billy said.

Kunkel shook his head. "Ever see a man get beaten up really bad by more than one person?"

"Other than Rodney King?"

"Well, he's a good example. Most of the time the man was lying down when they were wailing on him with their sticks. Same deal when a bunch of guys beat up on somebody. It doesn't take much to get him on the ground and then they kick him. That's usually what does the damage, the kicking. And he's usually rolled into a protective ball, so most of the kicks land on his legs, his back, the backs of his forearms, where here most of this was done straight on. Most men don't hit another man in the face more than once, Billy. Forget that shit you see in the movies. You hit someone on the cheekbone or the forehead or the eyebrow like this, you're gonna break your own hand. Most men aren't going to do that more than once."

"But somebody obviously did."

"That's right, somebody did. Somebody hit him hard, and a lot, and straight on, like he was a punching bag."

"Why didn't he fall like you said?"

Kunkel took a deep breath, then exhaled furiously. "Christ, that stinks."

Lapolla ran in the same fruitless semicircle Billy had tried, waving his nightstick at the crows as they hopped twice, took to the air, then settled in again behind him.

Kunkel rose once more. Billy heard his joints creak.

"I'm sure he did fall, Billy. And then he was helped to his feet again so he could be hit some more."

Billy looked at Kunkel incredulously, trying to take in the scenario. "So one after one they go in and break their knuckles, is that what you're saying?"

"No. Look again at the pattern of the blows. Head, ribs, head, chest, head, ribs. Some high on the shoulders, some on the biceps when the poor old guy managed to deflect a few. . . . He was *boxed*, Billy, if that's the word for it when you can't fight back."

"By somebody who didn't break his hands."

"In my opinion as county coroner, yeah."

Billy winced at the vision of someone hitting Huford, dragging him to his feet, hitting him again as the baffled and helpless man stood there stupidly, absorbing punishment, probably never fully comprehending what was happening.

"The son of a bitch," he muttered.

"If I'm right," said Kunkel. "I've been wrong before. I'll have Doc Lippold take a look, but what I don't get is what the hell it was all about. Why bring poor old Huford Peck out in the country like this just to wail on him?"

"I think I can help with that. Or maybe confuse things a bit more . . ."

At the sound of a shot Kunkel turned to see Lapolla with his pistol out, firing again at the crows.

"Lapolla!"

Lapolla looked wild-eyed with frustration, his entire shirt front dark with sweat, his hat long since lost in the chase.

"Well!" he sputtered in justification.

"Christ in knickers, put the gun up. Go sit in the car and cool off." Kunkel shook his head in despair over the help he was forced to hire, then turned to see Billy facedown in the dirt, his hands covering his head.

Kunkel sank to one knee beside him and put a hand on his back. The heat coming through his shirt seemed enough to sear flesh.

"It's all right, Bill," he said comfortingly.

Billy sat and brushed dirt from his face. He spoke in his thick brogue.

"It's all right, is it? Right as rain?"

"Lapolla was shooting at the crows . . ."

"Just looking for worms myself."

Lapolla stood gawking at Billy, half-afraid he had somehow shot him. The sheriff waved the deputy away with a motion and a snarl, then helped Billy to his feet although he needed no assistance.

"One of those flashback things," the sheriff offered solicitously. "Post delayed stress syndrome or whatever. The Vietnam vet deal."

"No, Patrick, nothing of the sort. Kind of you to give me an out, but I didn't have time to flash back to anything at all."

Kunkel brushed at the dirt on Billy's shirt, then gently removed some soil from his chin with a big finger.

"It's okay, Bill," he said softly. "Nobody here but me."

"And me," Billy said. And that, of course, was the problem.

Kath was folding laundry when Billy walked into the house. His sweat-soaked jeans and T-shirt had absorbed the dirt of the field like a blotter and he was soiled from neck to knee. Kath glanced at him and then away.

"Sorry, Kath. Two days in a row, I know."

She snapped imaginary wrinkles from a towel before creasing it precisely.

"Twice in less than twenty-four hours, actually," Billy corrected himself. "I'm going to stop this, I promise."

Kath snapped another towel with a resounding pop.

"Or I could do my own laundry, if you like."

"Might as well put those straight into the machine," she said, not looking at him.

Billy removed his shirt and trousers and dropped them into the washing machine, standing in the kitchen in only his briefs.

"Now wash yourself," she said, still not looking at him. "I'll have some things ironed for you by the time you get out of the shower."

"You don't need to iron anything for me. I don't want to put you to the trouble . . ."

"You may not care," she said, "but I do. You won't walk out of this house like a scarecrow."

She sounded remarkably like their mother, Billy thought. His little sister had turned into another beautiful Annie Keefe, angel of the Tree household. He resisted the urge to embrace her, knowing that his near-nudity would only embarrass them both, but he stood in the center of the room, smiling at her until she finally looked at him.

His grin broadened, showing off his teeth, and he thrust his arms out in display. " 'Tis a wonder you are, to be sure," he said in his accent. "A beautiful human being and a fierce washerwoman."

She laughed despite herself.

"Clean yourself."

"You're more than I deserve, entirely."

"Use soap," she said, struggling to sound stern. "And stop talking like that. It makes you sound like an idiot."

"She calls me an eedjit, and still I love the woman."

She picked up one of the folded towels to throw at him, then changed her mind and hurled an unfolded one across the room.

He could still make his sister laugh, Billy thought while showering, but it was laughter of exasperation, the kind reserved for an exuberant child whose spirited belief in his own charm outstrips his comedic talent. My welcome is wearing thin, he thought. Not a thing to be proud of, to wear out a saint. She puts up with Stuart Sime, the itinerant husband, for years and years but Billy had just about exhausted her patience in a few days. It was only because she was frightened for him; he knew that. Well, he couldn't blame her; he was frightened for himself and was pretty well fed up with Billy Tree as well.

Thoughts of Stuart Sime made him reflect on his sister's life, something he realized to his shame he had done little of for years. What sort of existence could it be, acting the part of wife with no husband, the part of widow when her man was very much alive? Billy was hit with a surge of remorse over Kath's lonely and neglected state.

He emerged from the shower wrapped in the towel and got dressed in the kitchen with the fan blowing directly on his still damp skin and chilling him just enough that the newly washed clothes, fresh from the dryer, felt luxuriously warm.

"It's good of you to take me in," Billy said.

Kath looked up from rolling his socks. "What are you on about?"

"We haven't really talked about it. I want you to know how grateful I am, Kath."

"Don't be silly. You're my brother."

"Not a very good one, I'm afraid. You must have been lonely with Stuart gone most of the time."

She was very still for a moment, assessing the size of the gap between them.

"Not always."

He regarded her carefully; something about her face seemed suddenly fragile. To his amazement, her eyes filled abruptly with tears.

"It's none of my business," he said.

"I know that better than you."

"I'm happy you found someone. I'm glad for you."

She lifted her chin defiantly, accepting no patronizing approval from him. The tears began to fall unheeded down her cheeks.

"I didn't say I'd had other men, you know. I didn't say that."

"It's all right. Why shouldn't you? You've been abandoned."

"Only two," she said. "In fifteen years, only two men."

"I'm not judging you."

"You're not qualified to judge me."

"I know. I admit that."

"I'm not ashamed. We cared for each other. It's not like you're thinking."

"Kath, I'm on your side."

"I don't want you to think I'm one of those women like . . ."

"Like who?"

"Never mind."

A tear dropped from her cheek and she reacted, startled, as if it were a living thing. She snatched at it, trying to catch it in midair, then wiped her cheek with her fingers.

"I shouldn't have said anything," he said.

"That's not it."

"What, then?"

"They were good men, both of them. I want you to know that."

"You don't have to explain."

"We had—relationships. It wasn't casual."

"Kath, you don't need to explain."

"You seem to need to know."

"No, I don't."

"I needed each of them. They needed me, I think. We were there for each other at the right times."

"I'm glad someone was here for you. I should have been."

"You?" she snorted. "What good would you have been? Billy, I was depressed, I needed a man. . . . Nobody was hurt by it. Nobody else, anyway. We were very careful, very discreet."

What would constitute discretion in Falls City? Billy wondered. They would have had to have been moles, conducting their clandestine affair underground, judging by the high profile he seemed to have in his innocent visits to Joan Blanchard.

"Kansas City," she said, seeming to read his mind. "We would meet in Kansas City. Once in Omaha." Each city was a two-hour drive one-way. Passion required mileage in the hinterlands.

In a holdover from his childhood, Billy did not like imagining his sister sleeping with anyone at all. He had classified her sexuality as taboo from an early age and as a preadolescent he had fought more than one battle to defend her honor from the usual schoolyard speculation—but he was deeply curious to know who her lovers were. He could think of no tactful way to ask.

She blew her nose on a paper napkin and returned to the laundry. He remembered her as a teenager, the kid sister, never a tomboy, never less than feminine, but determined to join in her brother's games. Tackled too hard, tripped by surprise, shoved, bullied, she would cry, openly, freely, with no pretense of hiding it. Billy and the others would stand by, temporarily abashed at having hurt the girl, but she would always recover before their patience wore out and step back to resume her place in the game, face still wet with tears. She never apologized for weeping and never let it stop her from continuing. Billy had secretly envied her that quick, gratifying release. Later in the day she would help her mother with the evening meal and the household chores, folding napkins and arranging silverware, the natural rose in her cheeks not quite covering the fresh bruises from the afternoon's melee. Still later the three of them would watch television, mother and daughter happily tearing up at programs Billy found too mawkishly sentimental to tolerate. He never knew if it was the same quality of tear she produced for an elbow to the stomach or a tale of a child reunited with his lost dog, but after all these years Kath's tears still had the power to make him feel shamed and inadequate.

"The funeral's tomorrow," she said. "Will you go with me?"

He hesitated, trying to put the question in context.

She continued. "I don't think I have the strength to go by myself."

"I didn't know you were friends with her."

"Who?"

"Sharon Shattuck."

Something about his remark amused her fleetingly.

"I barely knew Sharon. It's not her funeral."

"Oh," he said, feeling stupid for not realizing that she meant Cohan.

"I warn you. I'll probably be pretty wet." She tried to laugh self-deprecatingly, but the remark triggered her tears again instead.

"Kath, I'm sorry. I had no idea."

"Nobody did. Nobody there will know why I'm crying like the widow. Will you come with me?"

"Of course I'll come."

"Don't worry, I won't embarrass you too much. I've gotten pretty good at doing this silently."

"Do you want to talk about it?"

"Of course I want to talk about it. What do you think? But I'm not going to. Not to you. I need to tell another woman, someone who would understand, but there's no woman in this town I could trust. I wish Mother were alive."

"Mom? She'd never understand."

Kath regarded him silently and in that moment Billy felt the life-long certitude of a saint fall away. Of course his mother would understand. How else had she survived drunken Lord Jimmy Tree for four decades? Why had it never occurred to him before this—and how long had his sister known? Probably since she was old enough to comprehend, Billy thought ruefully. Why were men always so late to learn?

"How did you get involved with Cohan?" he asked finally, putting off the troubling speculation about his mother for another time. Or, better yet, hoping to forget it entirely.

She looked at him sharply. "You really are persistent, aren't you? You just can't let a thing go."

"I'm concerned, Kath."

"Concerned? Or nosy?"

"You're my sister."

"When it's convenient."

"I suppose I deserve that."

"Oh, I don't really blame you. You were leading an exciting life. Why should you care about what was going on in Falls City?"

"I cared."

"Oh."

"I just didn't ask."

She laughed. He grinned at her.

"Didn't want to pry, you know," he continued in his accent.

"Unlike now." She shook her head and her short brown hair bounced and resumed its place. Kath had taken to wearing her hair in the kind of cut that Billy thought of as voluntarily asexual. Not quite short enough to be boyish, not quite long enough to be feminine. It was the kind of coif that said "don't notice me." Men lost their hair with age, women retained theirs, but stopped using it.

"I was depressed, there was no great secret about that, everyone could tell, I suppose. Thom had some business with our office, we got to talking...he told me I didn't have to feel so sad. I thought, yeah, here's a come-on. I was surprised, him being the high school principal—but that wasn't what he meant at all. He was just a friend. He was concerned, like you, only really. And he asked. It was just a little talk. I could see he was a very decent, sensitive man. About a week later we ran into each other at the Lions Club pancake breakfast. I'd been crying, I guess, or looked like I was going to—I did that a lot then—and he gave me something that made me feel better. I was grateful. He was the first man who had really seemed to care about me since . . . for a long time. We saw each other a few more times, just sort of ran into each other, you know, the way you can't avoid in this town. He helped me those times, too."

She offered her empty palms to the ceiling, powerless to describe the transformation from friendly concern to powerful attraction.

"I realized I needed him in my life," she continued. "He felt the same way."

"What did he give you to make you feel better?"

"I don't know exactly."

"A pill? A powder? What?"

"Don't take that tone. There was nothing evil here. It was a pill."

"Was it Prozac? Was it speed?"

"No! It was just like a lot of caffeine or something."

"Christ, Kath, do you just pop whatever somebody hands you?"

"I didn't *pop* anything. He gave me a couple of pills a couple of times, and it helped, and I was very grateful. Don't make him into a drug pusher. He was the high school principal. He wasn't going to poison me."

"Did he keep giving you these pills?"

"No, not after a while. I didn't need them and to tell the truth, I was a little scared of them, I thought maybe I'd get to like them too much. Besides, I wasn't unhappy anymore. . . . I had him."

"Did you pay him for these magic pills?"

"He wouldn't let me."

"Did he say where he got them?"

"I didn't ask."

"Did you tell Pat about them?"

"Why would I tell Pat?"

"Somebody was giving you an illegal substance."

"I don't know that it was illegal, and even so . . . Billy, this is not a big thing. Everybody takes something now and then. Sometimes you just need something."

"Christ."

"And stop saying that. You took pills when you were in pain, didn't you? I was in pain. I took something."

"I didn't take something somebody else pulled out of his pocket."

"Well, maybe you should have and you wouldn't be so judgmental."

"I'm sorry, Kath. I'm overreacting. I guess I'm feeling protective . . . a bit late, I know. . . . Was he good to you? Was he a good man?"

Her face grew soft. "Yes. He was a very good man."

"Were you . . . was it over?" he asked.

"It ended three years ago. If these things really ever end. With the way things were then, we really had no choice."

Billy tried vainly to recall what had happened three years ago in his sister's life.

"Stuart came home," she said. "It made us both realize what we were doing, what we were risking."

"Stuart left again," Billy said. It was the refrain of her married life, she did not need to be reminded.

"It was over. It gave us both a chance to think. We came to our senses."

"If Stuart was gone again . . ."

"Oh, Billy, it's too complicated," she said, annoyed. "Do you think you can just walk into the kitchen and have me bring you up to date on the past fifteen years in thirty seconds? Do you think you could possibly begin to understand things that quickly? Do you even think you deserve it?"

"No, I suppose not."

"It's just like this town. Do you think you can possibly understand it after all this time? You knew it as a child, but most of us live in it as adults. Those are two different worlds. Do you think it's just cornfields and a deranged boy with a gun? There are lives being lived here, Billy. We're all in a mare's nest of lives, everybody's is caught up in everybody else's. What makes you think you can just grab one strand and pull it free?"

"Is that what it looks like I'm trying to do?"

"I don't know what you're trying to do. Whatever it is, you seem to be making a dangerous mess of it."

"You're right there." He sat and unrolled a pair of socks that she had just rolled and put them on. "I don't seem to have a clue what's going on."

"I shouldn't have asked Pat Kunkel to come talk to you," she said.

"I wanted him to bring you out of your self. You were just sulking in your room. . . . I think it was a mistake. You would have come out of it eventually on your own."

"I don't know that I would have. You did the right thing for me. I'm the one who's screwed it up ever since. But that's not your fault."

"Why not just quit it?"

"I want to help," he said, realizing as he said it that it was true. "Pat could use some assistance. . . . I like being involved—in a frightening, confusing way. . . ."

She had stopped listening to him. Kath sat at the kitchen table and pulled the laundry basket onto her lap as if for comfort. The tears continued unabated and she wiped them away with a knuckle.

After a moment Billy left her alone.

CHAPTER TWENTY

Joan met him at the door, leaning on a single crutch that stretched her T-shirt provocatively across her breasts. Billy wondered if she knew how good she looked, how instantly desirable. He concluded that she did not, that women could not appreciate how closely they were scrutinized by men in every costume and every pose, or how easily men were titillated. Had he had time to think about it, he might well have concluded otherwise, but he did not because she was moving impatiently toward him, unable to hide her look of disappointment. She swiveled her head to either side, hoping to see someone following behind him.

"It's all right," she said, excusing him without explanation. "I shouldn't have let you try to get Will in the first place."

"I didn't try."

"Oh."

"I mean, I didn't find him, he wasn't at Duane's. I was going to check later, when he got off work, but things got involved."

"I see."

"It's complicated."

"I'll do it," she said. "I'll go out there tonight. If Will's there, maybe he won't do anything. Maybe he won't demand his payment."

"I said I'd do it, and I will. I don't want you going out there, Joan."

"It'll be all right. There's no reason you should have anything to do with this at all. It's my problem."

"I'm going to get him tonight," Billy said. "But I thought we'd do something first. How are you feeling?"

"I feel fine."

"Are you up to a little drive?"

"A drive? . . . With you?"

"That's part of the deal, I'm afraid," he said.

"Shall I change?"

"Joan, if you looked any better, we'd get arrested."

She smiled.

"Is that a compliment?"

"It is."

She arched her back slightly, thrusting her breasts forward, an action that pulled the T-shirt up to reveal a patch of bronzed skin on her stomach. She glanced down at herself. Billy felt a strong urge to fall to his knees and kiss the smooth, taut flesh of her belly.

A knowing smile suffused her face. "You're a tit man, aren't you?" she asked,

"I'm a man," Billy corrected. "I like the whole female package. Of which you seem to be possessed, in full, magnificent splendor, by the way."

"That's much better than 'nice tits.' "

"Well, you deserve better," he said. "You deserve a speech, an oration, an aria of praise for looking like that."

"I'll wait if you need to take a deep breath before you start."

"Alas, I am no singer. A great appreciator but no Pavarotti."

"A great bullshitter, which is fine by me, right at the moment. You lay it on with such a heavy hand no one could ever take you seriously."

"Hum. I'm not sure how to take that."

"Not seriously," she said.

"There's one slight hitch in all this gaiety," he said, smiling broadly. "Do you mind if we take your car? I'm on foot."

Joan paused. "How were you planning to get my son if you didn't have a car?"

"I planned to use yours," he said, smiling even wider.

He helped her into her car, shoving the passenger seat back so she could stretch her leg. With his arm around her back, one hand touching the smooth brown flesh of her uninjured leg, he eased her onto the seat. Her face was inches from his, her breasts no farther away, and her perfume, a subtle suggestion of lilacs, seemed to envelop him with an invitation to stay where he was, bent over her like a supplicant, the warmth of her body radiating a heat he could feel beyond that of the sultry air. Billy straightened abruptly, narrowly avoiding the top of the car with his head, causing her to gasp a warning, then to chuckle at his obvious discomfiture. As he walked around to the driver's side of the car, he reminded himself of Joan's reputation as a "possible" woman, of her alleged alliance with Cohan.

"Dangerous territory, Billy lad," he muttered to himself. "Not to be entered into by the bumbling likes of you, me boyo. Not with your inclinations towards slippery slopes."

"What?" she said.

"Did I say something?"

"Something about slopes."

"So I'm talking aloud now, is it? It's come to that. All those little screws are coming loose and popping right out of my head."

"You need a good screwdriver," she said.

He drove for a full block pondering her possible meanings.

They motored south to the end of Harlan, then back north on Stone Street, making the great circle loop of his teenaged years.

"What are you doing?" she asked, as they reached the elementary school that delimited the northern reach of Stone.

"Remember when we all did this on dates?" He drove to Harlan, one block away, then turned south once more.

"Is this a date?"

"No. This is a joyride."

She laughed. "If this is joy, what do you do for fun?"

"I don't remember," he said. "It's been so long."

"It will come back to you," she said. He glanced at her, but she was looking straight ahead and her face gave away nothing.

"How well did you know Thom Cohan?" he asked. He had not planned on bringing up the topic but it was itching at him furiously and her flirtation—if that's what it was—only exacerbated it. Had she really had an affair with the high school principal? And if she had, what difference did it make? Had she done so during the time that Billy's sister was also sleeping with the man? And, again, what difference did it make? Billy understood himself well enough to know that he could assess the difference only when he knew the answer. At that point, his emotions would tell him what his brain refused to calculate.

"We had a . . . complicated . . . relationship," she said, choosing her words carefully. "He was my boss—sort of. I worked for him and with him for several years. He was my friend."

"Sort of?"

"No, no qualifications. He was my friend. But it wasn't always a smooth friendship. Thom was a moody man. He had a lot of things to deal with in his life and when his mood was down, he wasn't someone you wanted to be around. When he was up . . ."

"When he was up?"

"He was great," she said with finality.

Billy felt the need to denigrate the man. He didn't like the idea of his being great with her.

"Was he manic-depressive?"

"Just moody, I think. A lot of us are. I'm not much fun when I'm in a bad mood, either." She turned to face him. "You probably ought to know that."

"Okay," he said. "I've been known to have my off moments as well."

"Really? I wouldn't have guessed."

"You wouldn't be having me on, would you now?" he asked in his brogue.

"Would this be an off moment?" she asked.

"Actually, I'm in fine spirits," he said, dropping the accent. "Don't let the accent fool you. It sounds like I'm in pain, but I'm really not. Feeling rather fine, matter of fact. Cruising up and down with the prettiest girl in town by my side. Who could ask for more?"

"Charming Billy."

The phrase sounded dismissive. "Did he ever offer any help in one of those moods?"

"Like what?"

"Moral support? Back massage? Drugs?"

"All three, as required. Do I detect a sudden change in tone?"

"It's my Secret Service training. I ask direct questions. It makes for poor conversation."

"I thought you were supposed to be a great observer. That's what Pat says."

"But a real clumsy questioner. If somebody's written a death threat to the President, you don't have to be terribly subtle in the interview."

"And why am I being interviewed now?"

Billy sighed, disappointed with himself. "I'm sorry. Bad habits."

"If you're going to come at me like that, I might as well talk to the television people."

"Are they still around?"

"Only one came by this morning. Guess they're losing interest."

"I do want to talk to you about him sometime, though."

"Why?"

Billy paused.

"That's what everybody's asking me."

"You don't really want to root around in my past, do you? . . .'Cause if you do . . ."

He drove, avoiding her eyes while she looked at him.

She considered and rejected several possible conclusions to her statement. "I'd just rather you didn't," she said finally.

"Me, or anybody?"

"Anybody," she said. ". . . *and* you."

They drove past her house again and she turned to look at it as if studying it for the first time.

"This is just as big a treat as it was in high school," she announced.

"Some fascinations never fade."

"He's found you," she said.

"What?"

"I saw his truck about two blocks back. He's driving parallel to us on Harlan. . . . It's what you wanted, wasn't it?"

Billy could see no point in lying about it. He had been trolling for shark, with Joan as the irresistible bait, and Duane Blanchard had caught the scent in the water. Had someone in town seen them together and called him, or was he simply always there, waiting to be activated, like a latent virus in the blood?

"I didn't see the truck."

"You're not as used to looking for him as I am," she said. "I don't even have to see him anymore, I can feel him."

"How do you live with that?"

"Do I have a choice?"

"Is it that red pickup?"

"Curt Metzger's? No, it's his own, dull green, with all the sheen worn off. Duane likes new things, new toys, new women—but he's no good at taking care of them. So he borrows them, uses other people's, puts a few dings in them, then gets rid of them." She made no attempt to hide her bitterness.

At the next cross street Billy looked to his right to see if he could spy Duane's pickup, but saw nothing.

"He's there. Trust me," she said.

It occurred to Billy that he did trust her, but he was not sure that he should. Gossip and rumor had worked their corrupting effects, eroding his original feelings for her. Her refusal to talk about her relationship with Cohan did not help, either, although he could interpret that as commendable discretion—if he chose to. Choosing to think the best of her was difficult with so much innuendo to the contrary.

Billy continued to drive south on Harlan as it left town and changed its name back to Route 73. He drove slowly, giving Duane ample opportunity to come into view before the highway eased itself from one swell to the next. Within a mile he caught sight of a dull green pickup in the rearview mirror.

"Believe me now?" Joan asked.

"I believed you right away."

"Do you mind telling me what we're doing?"

"I thought I'd buy you a beer."

"If Duane catches you with me you'll be drinking it through a straw," she said. "Let's just turn around and go home. You don't want to be caught out in the country."

"We're going to get your son."

"Not this way, whatever you have in mind. I'll get Will myself."

"I said I'd get him, and I intend to. All you have to do is sit and drink a beer and look lovely. You've already got the lovely part down pat, and that's the hard bit for most people."

"You don't have to prove anything to me, Billy. I know you're not afraid of him."

Billy laughed. "Ah, but I am. What I have to prove is that I can get your son back for you."

Scotty's Southside was optimistically listed in the Yellow Pages as a restaurant but would have been more accurately described as a roadhouse. With none of the rowdy flair of the artificial bulls and caged musicians of its Texas cousins, nor the bluesy soul of the Southern variety, Southside was a place to eat a chicken-fried steak, get drunk, engage in some angry words and cheap sentimentality, and possibly take a swing or two at another drunk in the parking lot. Billy's car crunched over the gravel-strewn lot and came to a stop close to the rear of the building. Joan gave him a curious look for parking so far from the entrance, but said nothing.

Before they reached the door, she asked,

"Are you mocking me?"

"What do you mean?"

"You're limping. Are you making fun of me and my crutch, or did you hurt yourself?"

Billy adjusted the pry bar in the back of his trousers. "I've got something in my shoe," he said.

She tipped her head and regarded him speculatively. "I'll ask you again. What are we doing?"

Billy glanced toward the highway, then steered Joan inside with a hand on her elbow.

"Getting Will," he said. "It's a time-honored law enforcement technique. Just play along with me and do what I say for the next few minutes, just as if I knew what I was doing."

"*Do* you know what you're doing?"

Billy grinned with what he hoped was a charming display of self-confidence. He knew what he was doing; he didn't know if it would work. There was no reason to confuse Joan with the distinction, however. Having one of them shaky and uncertain was enough.

Half a dozen Mexican workers had crowded themselves into a booth together in a form of self-imposed ethnic segregation and were speaking rapidly in Spanish, their normally lustrous black hair still coated with grain dust from the elevator. Two farmers sat at the bar, gazing without interest at the television that had the sound permanently turned off. They wore their caps indoors and out and certainly while drinking beer, making only the slight concession of pushing the bills up from their foreheads to accommodate raised bottles, revealing a strip of untanned flesh as wan and bloodless as day-old fish. The backs of their necks were as brown as the faces of the Mexicans.

"Very nice," said Joan, surveying the place with a quick glance.

"Atmosphere. Besides, we're not staying."

He ordered two beers and slapped several bills on the counter as the jukebox segued from an early 1950s rock and roll song to a maudlin country-western ballad that had known some popularity two decades earlier. Billy looked out a begrimed window as Duane's pickup pulled into the gravel and dirt parking lot.

"He coming?" Joan asked.

Billy nodded. "Yep, and we're going."

Steering her by an elbow again, he led her through the kitchen and out the back door. Kath drove Joan's car forward and glided to a stop beside them.

"Kath will take you home," Billy said. "I'll bring Will to you there."

"What is this?"

He opened the car door, lifted Joan in his arms, and slid her onto the seat. "Deception."

To Kath he said, "Count to twenty, slowly, then leave."

Kath handed him the keys to her own car where she had been sitting, awaiting their arrival. The look in his sister's eyes was disapproving and he turned away quickly, softly closing the door.

"It's a brilliant idea. Really," he said, expecting neither of them to believe him. In fact, it was not much of an idea, scarcely a plan at all, but lacking the manpower and electronics of the Service, he had chosen the simplest low-tech solution he could think of.

Drawing the pry bar from his pants, he jogged around the back of the building, staying below the windows. Duane had backed his pickup into the parking space, its nose pointing out as if ready for a quick getaway. Or pursuit.

Billy watched the women pull onto the highway in Joan's car and drive away then he hurried toward Duane's truck. The undrunk beers and money Billy had left on the counter should keep Duane in place for several minutes expecting Billy and Joan to return from wherever they went, maybe the restrooms. Duane would give it a little time before he became suspicious, and a little time should be all that Billy needed. He crouched beside the rear tire of Duane's pickup, keeping the body of the truck between himself and the view from the window. Wriggling the sharp end of the pry bar beneath the rim of the tire, he positioned it just past the air valve and stomped on it with his foot. When he was greeted with a gratifying sound of escaping air he prised further with the bar, increasing the tear to an unsealable hole.

"A classic maneuver," he thought to himself. "Known to tire-slashers, delinquents, and cowards everywhere."

When he drove Kath's car out of the parking lot there was still no sign of Duane but his truck canted to one side at a very slight but gratifying angle. "Bless you for a patient man, Duane Blanchard. Sit there and wait for my return."

It was dark by the time he reached Duane's house on the old Bedwell farm, the sky heavily overcast with angry clouds storing the rising heat and damp of the day, and lights from the farmhouse stood out like a beacon far at sea. Someone in the house was combating the blackness of the outdoors with every light in every room. Billy tried to remember himself at fifteen. Still afraid of the dark but ashamed to admit it? Would he have lighted up the house like a Christmas tree at that age? Probably. Bravado started early in the Tree family, but true conviction took a while longer. He had been puffed full of false courage when he was fifteen but he had not been fool enough to believe in it until several years later. The full-swagger, cocky-underdog oppressed-by-history-and-circumstance-but-hard-as-nails, tougher-than-leather, snapping-turtle-tenacious, cut-his-head-off-and-he-still-won't-let-go Irish didn't come until he turned twenty-one, when he stepped into it up to his follicles like a man donning a family suit of armor. Another son of Erin claiming his rightful legacy.

There was no verbal response to his knock on the door, but he heard the familiar sudden scrambling from within the house. How many times had he heard it in the Service as the mildly mad, the deranged, the paranoid, and the delusional whom he had come to interview stirred in a mix of dread and glee at the rap of knuckles they had come to yearn for and fear? They were not people who got many visitors. A knock on the door or a ring of the bell meant unwanted company, excitement, an occasion for panic. Billy recognized the profound difference between the behind-the-door rustlings of normal people putting on shirts, straightening up the most proximate mess, adjusting a greeting face, and the frantic scrabblings of those who genuinely had something to hide. Over the years he had learned to gauge the level of anxiety within a home just by the sounds of the movements within—and the silences. The silences were the most telling. He could picture the guilty men and women on the other side of the door freezing like hunted animals hunkered under a bush, their bodies immobile as their hearts threatened to burst through their chests—or moving stealthily to hide the incriminating document, close the revealing drawer . . . or get the weapon.

There was a different quality in the inaudible movement of a stalking animal and the hush of the cowering one. Or so he told himself, so he had come to think through years of experience. He had based his own actions on this perception, on being able to judge whether the creature on the other side of the door was a frightened bunny, or a bear. And of course he had been spectacularly wrong in the case of Avi Posner, he reminded himself. Fatally wrong. All the more reason to err on the side of caution—read cowardice.

The noise within the house had stopped and Billy felt the hairs on his neck stiffen in warning. It was the wrong silence. He flattened himself against the wall next to the door, struggling to maintain his breathing as it threatened to stop on him all together. Every centimeter of his skin prickled with fear and sweat poured from beneath his arms.

Beejayus, he thought. "Just look at you. Nothing has happened. Stand up, quit your cowering. It's not Avi Posner on the other side of the door. It's a fifteen-year-old boy who's still afraid of the dark . . . but, ah, Christ, so am I, afraid of the dark and everything that's in it."

A bolt snicked out and in, feeding a shell into a rifle chamber. The motion was oiled and smooth but it roared in Billy's ears like thunder.

Billy ran for the car, hurling himself to the ground with the protective bulk of the engine between his body and the house. Crushed into a ball, he awaited the first bullet, remembering with vivid horror how it hit him like a hammer blow, how it stunned before it hurt, how the kicks would come, one after the other, inevitable, unavoidable, and how he would howl and beg and cry and still he'd be shot again and again. . . .

Only silence from the house, no snap of shots, no whining of bullets, no noise from impact on the dirt, the car, the body. Billy rose carefully to his knees. He put one hand over his mouth to muffle his panting breath; he couldn't hear the house, couldn't hear the gun, couldn't hear himself think, he was making so much noise just breathing.

The light falling across the hood of the car and onto the hardened dirt of the driveway dimmed, then dimmed still more as Will snapped off the lights in the living room. He could not have clearly seen Billy outside the house before because of all the light in the room—but he had realized it before Billy had.

I'm slipping fast, he thought. A fifteen-year-old is ahead of me. Will was now in the dark with the rifle and Billy was in the remaining light spilling outside from the other rooms of the house. If not a sitting duck, a currently kneeling one, sheltered by the car, but only until the rifleman moved. Or Billy did. His brain screamed at him to creep into the car and drive away, or failing that, to just turn tail and run into the deeper darkness and keep on running out of town, out of the state, out of the situation. They were both murderous, father and son, and it was none of his business in the first place. None of his *business*! Let Joan secure her child herself. Joan Blanchard meant nothing to him, and her son even less, so why was he risking his life for either of them? To rescue a boy who was pointing a rifle at him from somewhere in the dark? What kind of rescuing was that? Who had he stumbled across in Duane Blanchard's home in the middle of nowhere in the middle of the night? What hornet's nest had he just accidentally stepped into now?

The disturbing thought joined the chorus of messages his brain screamed at him, but Billy's body refused to move. Getting into the car would make noise, give his position away, and leave him exposed for perilous seconds as he backed up, turned around . . . running was even less of an alternative. Expose his back? He was afraid, but he wasn't crazy, or so his body insisted. It refused to budge, preferring real temporary safety to the faint possibility of permanent security. Another minute without lead slugs tearing through him was better than vulner-able, hazardous flight.

The recalcitrance of his limbs led his mind to believe that all was well. It was a simple chain of logic. He was not shot, no one was shooting, therefore he never would be shot. He was like a man on a raft, drifting through a sluggish section of the river and thinking it would always be thus, even as time and current propelled him toward the maelstrom of the rapids.

The brief irenic moment was shattered by the first shot as it smashed through the windows of the car and showered his head and neck with glass. Reflexively, he flattened himself, but when he heard the front door slap open, he responded to a different reflex, one he had thought long dead. Staying low, Billy opened the driver's door, turned on the car's ignition and snapped on the headlights. The beams illuminated the porch, temporarily blinding the gunman, and Billy took his momentary advantage and sprinted around the back of the car and toward the side of the house. Another shot rang out and the bullet ripped into the metal of the car as Billy dived for cover around the corner of the building. The next shot took out one headlight—Billy could tell by the lessened light—and by the time he had made his way to the back door of the house the other light was gone.

Billy waited until he heard movement from the shooter before he slipped through the back door, using the other's noise to cover his own. He crouched in the darkness of the house, waiting for a move from his adversary before he budged, matching him step for step and praying to place his foot on no loose floorboards, no cat's tail, nothing to betray his advance as anything more than an echo.

The rifleman was on the driveway now and Billy could picture him in his mind, warily approaching the car, firing once and then again at nothing, hoping to keep whoever he thought was in the car pinned down. And when he found no one in the car, what then? Would he walk into the darkness, pursuing a wraith, exposing himself with every step? Not likely. He would pull back into the house, make his adversary come to him and save the hunting for daylight. He would not be expecting to find Billy in the house, waiting for him. Or so Billy fervently hoped.

Flattened against the wall, Billy crept across a hallway and toward the front door. He could hear Will moving in the driveway, still un-certainly circling the car, trying to figure things out. By the time Will made his way back to the porch, Billy was behind the open door, concealed and waiting.

Will hesitated just beyond the door, scanning the vast darkness of the drive, the feedlot, the fields beyond. He kept the rifle barrel pointed toward the darkness, more in warning that anticipation. The boy did not expect the driver of the car suddenly to leap up and wave at him—but he wanted the driver to know (for he was sure he was out there watching) that he was still armed, still vigilant, and far too dangerous to meddle with.

He backed through the doorway, reaching for the sill with his heel, never turning his back on whoever waited in the dark. The door hit him like a swinging two-hundred-pound weight and threw him forward. He sank to one knee, breaking his fall with a hand and the butt of the rifle. He tried to turn but he was shoved forward again, this time by a foot on his butt, and he slid onto the porch face first. The rifle was wrenched from him but Will's finger jerked a final shot before releasing its grip.

He squeezed his eyes shut, expecting to die immediately.

"Don't!" he begged.

"Why not? You tried to kill me."

Will rolled over and opened his eyes.

"You're not Sandy," he said.

"Very good. My guess is you aren't either. So you must be Will Blanchard."

Will stared at Billy. His features were hard to make out in the darkness.

"I didn't mean to shoot at you," he continued.

"Five or six shots by accident, was it? That's very careless."

Will started to sit but the rifle barrel swung quickly to point at his chest.

"Stay put until we get to know each other a little better," said Billy. "Right now I'm still shaking so hard I might shoot you just out of excitement."

"I wasn't shooting at *you*."

"No, it seemed to be mostly at my sister's car, but since you thought I was in it, I still take it as an unfriendly act."

"I thought you were someone else."

Will started to say more but Billy cut him off.

"Just shut up a minute, kid. Right now it's all I can do to keep from beating you over the head with this thing."

Billy leaned against the side of the house, the rifle jumping slightly with each heave of his chest. Sweat popped out on his forehead as fast as he wiped it away.

"Damn it, boy," he said after a minute.

"I'm sorry."

"That doesn't begin to cover it."

"Are you all right?"

"Do I *look* all right?"

"I didn't hit you, did I?" Will asked.

"There's more than one way to kill a coward.... The only thing good I can say for this is it's better to be shot at and missed than shot at and hit.... That's no reason to go around being shot at."

"I really didn't mean it."

"Another good argument for gun control. You thought I was someone else. We covered that. Who did you think I was?"

"Sandy."

"You're supposed to be Sandy's friend. Why were you shooting at him?"

"I thought he wanted to kill me."

"Why would he?"

"Who are you?"

"Now you need an introduction? Somebody told you not to talk to strangers—but it's all right to shoot at them? I'm Billy Tree."

"Oh. You're *him.*"

"You put a lot of weight in that *him,* and it didn't sound all that respectful. What *him* am I?"

"You're the guy who's . . ."

"Who's what?"

"You and my mom."

"No, Will. Not me and your mom. I'm your mother's friend. That's all. You don't mind if she has friends, do you?"

"No, but . . ."

"No buts. We're friends."

"My dad says . . ."

"Ah, now we get to it. Come inside."

"Are you going to shoot me?"

"No."

"Okay . . .'cause you're still pointing the gun at me."

"I feel more comfortable with it that way than the other way around. You understand."

Will preceded Billy into the house and turned on a lamp in the living room.

"Sit on the floor," Billy instructed. "Excellent. Now tie your shoe-laces together. Tie them tight."

"Is this so I don't run away?"

"It's so you don't run at *me*. I don't know how fast you are, but I don't think you can out-hop me."

"Why would I run at you when you've got the gun?"

"Fortunately I'm not required to supply you with a motive. Now cross your arms and put each hand under the opposite heel. . . . The *opposite* heel. Very good."

"Like this?"

Billy turned a straight-back chair to face the boy and sat, the rifle across his knees, one hand on the stock, close to the trigger.

"Well, unless you're a circus performer, or I fall asleep, that should do it."

"I really scared you, huh?"

"You don't look all that frightening right now. Maybe it had to do with the gun."

"My dad said . . ."

"What?"

"Never mind."

"Now is the time for intimacies, boy. What did Duane say about me?"

"He said you're chickenshit."

"He's a fine judge of character, your dad. But then I'm a rather famous chickenshit around here, so it wasn't much of a call. . . . Hold still, quit squirming. You make me nervous."

"This isn't comfortable like this."

"You teenagers have a very short memory. You were shooting at me three minutes ago. Why should I make you comfortable? Don't you think some slight punishment is called for?"

"Were you really in the FBI?"

"Secret Service."

"What's that?"

"Where have you been, Will? I've been here a couple of times looking for you and you weren't around. At least you didn't shoot at me, so I assume you weren't here. So where've you been during the day?"

"With my dad."

"At work?"

Will nodded.

"You've been at that giant elevator during the day for the past three days?"

"Yeah."

"Why?"

"Dad said I'd be safe there. I go up to the very top of the silos and shoot rats. They pay me a dollar a rat."

"You shoot rats with this?" Billy patted the rifle.

"No, that'd be too much, it'd ricochet around and hit us. They give us a pellet gun. It'll kill a rat, but it won't go ricocheting around like a bullet."

"Us? You said they give *us* a pellet gun."

"Me and Sandy. We spent a lot of weekends up there. You can make pretty good money."

"Who was your dad keeping you safe from up in the top of the grain elevator?

"Sandy."

"He's hiding you at the top of a silo where you and Sandy work, thinking Sandy won't look there?"

"Yeah, I guess."

"Why did you think Sandy was going to kill you?"

"My dad said he might try. That's why he's keeping me with him, so he can protect me."

"What reason would Sandy have to kill you?"

"What reason did he have to kill all those teachers and shoot my mom?"

"I don't know. Why do you think he would do it? You were his friend. Did he ever talk about doing something like that?"

"Not really . . . he said he was going to do something big someday, something that would show his father up, or something. I don't know, it was hard to tell with Sandy what he really meant."

"Did he have anything against Sharon Shattuck?"

"Did he shoot her? I didn't know. He didn't have anything against her, everybody liked Mrs. Shattuck. Aw, God, that's too bad. That really sucks. . . . He might have hated some of the others, but not Mrs. Shattuck."

"He only shot three people, Will. Shattuck, Thom Cohan, and your mother."

"I thought he killed lots of them."

"Is that what your father told you?"

"I guess. I don't know, I just thought it was lots of them."

"No. Just three. He could have shot more, he had more targets, he had more time, I'm pretty sure he had more bullets. He just shot three. And you don't think he could have intended to shoot Sharon Shattuck. . . . Could he have intended to shoot your mother?"

"Dad said maybe he wanted to kill all three of us."

"All three of . . . the Blanchards? You were his friend, about his only friend, as I hear it. Your father is his father's friend. Why would he want to wipe out the Blanchards?"

"I don't know."

"Did he ever shoot at you?"

"No."

"Did he ever threaten you?"

". . . He used to say he'd rip my head off for me, that kind of thing, but he never said he'd kill me."

"Did he ever shoot at your father?"

Will snorted contemptuously at the idea of anyone daring to threaten his father. "Are you kidding? He's not that stupid. My dad would kill him if he ever tried that. He'd break every bone in his body."

A well-conditioned lad, thought Billy. His old man has him thinking exactly what he wants.

"So if he's never shot at you or your dad, and never threatened to, the idea that he's going to wipe out the whole family is stretching things a bit, isn't it?"

"He shot my mom."

"Someone did. Your mom was shot, that's for sure. . . . Okay, Will, time to go. My heart's pumping normally again."

"You were really scared, weren't you? You should have seen yourself."

"I think we covered that. . . . Can I count on you not to attack me again?"

"Sure."

"Sure, is it?"

"I promise."

"Okay, on your feet and into the car."

"Where are we going?"

"Home to your mother. She's been very worried about you."

"Dad said it was all right to stay with him."

"I'm sure he did."

"Can I untie my shoelaces now?"

"No. Hop."

Billy followed as the boy hopped to the car but paused before closing the door. He put the rifle atop the car roof, then elaborately removed the remaining bullets and put them into his pocket.

"I'm not taking you at gunpoint, you know. I'm just driving you to your mother's. Assuming the car still drives."

"I know."

"You want to see your mother, don't you?"

"Sure."

"Why didn't you call her?"

"We don't have a phone."

"You're kidding."

"My dad has a cell phone. He doesn't see any good reason to pay for both."

"Why didn't you jump on your bike and pedal home?"

"Dad said Mom felt safer with me here."

"Oh, he did, huh? Well, now she feels safer with you with her. Okay?"

"You don't like my dad. I can tell."

"I haven't talked to your dad in twenty years."

"You still don't like him, though, do you? . . . People are afraid of my dad—that's why they don't like him."

"He told you that, too?"

"Yeah. So?"

"Did he tell you why they're afraid of him?"

"Because he could rip their heads off if he wanted to."

"Like Sandy?"

"What?"

"Would he rip their heads off the way Sandy threatened to do to you?"

"I don't know what you mean. He wouldn't kill anybody. He'd just really jack them up."

"And you like that idea, don't you?"

"You got to be able to take care of yourself."

Billy shook his head in disgust. "Christ, boyo, and you're not even Irish. . . . Get in the car."

Billy got behind the wheel and jammed the gun between his left side and the door. "I'm not forcing you to go with me. Is that clear?"

"Sure . . . but why?"

"Kidnapping. I don't want anybody coming around claiming I took you away at gunpoint."

"Who'd do that?"

"In this day and age? And also, I don't think it would help anyone if you told your mother I kicked you in the ass on the porch."

"Okay. And you don't tell her I shot at you, okay?"

"Will, unless we continue to operate in the dark of night, she might notice a few bullet holes. I still haven't figured out how I'm going to explain it to my sister."

With both headlights gone and only one parking light to illuminate their way, Billy drove very slowly back to town, half-expecting at any minute Duane Blanchard's pickup to materialize in front of them from the roiling black clouds that fell all the way to the horizon.

He parked in the alleyway behind Joan's house, where the car was not exactly hidden, but at least not visible to a cursory drive by.

"You can untie yourself now," he said.

Will stood outside the car, waiting for something more from Billy.

"Is that it?" Will asked.

"You want me to walk you in? Go see your mother."

"You're not going to . . . ?"

"What?"

"Nothing. I thought you'd . . . nothing, great."

"So go on. Tell her I'll talk to her tomorrow. Dealing with you ought to keep her busy the rest of the night."

Will hesitated. "Can I have my gun back?"

"No."

"What if I need it?"

"You expecting an attack by a squirrel or something?"

"What if Sandy . . . ?"

"When was the last time you saw Sandy, Will? Before or after the shootings at the school?"

"About a day before, I guess."

"Did you ride your bikes to your dad's place together?"

"No. My dad picked me up when I was on my bike and drove me out there."

"Then don't worry about Sandy. He's not going to bother you."

"How do you know?"

"Good night, Will. Be nice to your mother."

Billy drove home via the darkened alleys when possible. He was halfway there when the storm that had been threatening since dusk hit with thunderous force and within seconds he was driving into a vertical sheet of water that came through the shattered windows as if someone had aimed a hose at him. His feeble parking light became useless and he tried to navigate by the light that spilled from the houses into the alleys. Creeping along, squinting against the rain that hit him from the front and both sides simultaneously, he maneuvered nearly blind, hoping that each shadow that darkened, then disappeared into the surrounding blackness, was just that, shape without substance.

Home at last, he parked the car in the garage and walked to the house. There was no point in trying to sprint through the pelting rain, he was already wet to the skin. As he reached the porch, a bolt of lightning ripped from the sky and for a second everything was lighted in a frieze of frozen motion. Billy saw a pickup truck parked half a block away, facing toward him. Was it a human figure he saw seated behind the steering wheel, or a trick of the lightning?

The lighting was chased by an enormous thunderclap that seemed to shake the house itself, and then the rain filled the universe again, even harder and louder than before. Billy stood on his porch, staring in the direction of the truck. Light from the Linscotts' window caught some reflective edge of the truck's metal surface and it blinked periodically as some intervening branch of waving tree or bush alternately obscured and revealed, obscured and revealed, as if mocking Billy's surveillance.

Standing in the darkness, Billy removed his shirt and shoes and pants, thinking about burdening his sister with yet another load of laundry. The car was beyond worrying about. There would be no way to assuage her wrath and disappointment and fear over finding the vehicle with windows smashed, riddled with bullet holes, and as sodden as if he had driven it through a river. He wondered if insurance covered such mistreatment but could think of no good reason that it should. At the moment, Billy himself seemed a dangerously vulnerable and uninsurable risk.

He stood a while longer, still watching the pickup blink at him. It was too easy to conjure a face to go with that batting eye. Avi Posner's features materialized out of the darkness, shaping themselves around the twinkling light, taunting him with his dragon-toothed grin, and Billy thought he could hear the sound of his laughter over the pelting rain.

A pair of headlights moved slowly in his direction along Harlan, coming from the south, the only vehicle still moving during the deluge. Billy instinctively squatted and pressed his back against the wall of the house as the lights came closer. With punctilious correctness, the driver signaled a turn although there was no other traffic visible anywhere, and slowly swung onto Twenty-third Street to pass next to the side porch where Billy crouched in the darkness. The car slowed even further as it came abreast of the porch and Billy saw in the wash of the headlights that the driver was looking in his direction. The beams picked out the pickup on the corner and the brake lights flashed once as the driver nearly came to a halt, then inched past the pickup. This time Billy was certain he saw a figure behind the steering wheel of the truck.

The sheriff's car turned onto Lane Street and disappeared from sight. Ah, Pat, my friend, you can't protect me always, he thought. I take the trouble with me wherever I go and no amount of mother-henning on your part will secure me from all of it.

Billy removed his socks, wrung them out, then did the same for the rest of his clothing before stepping quietly into the house. He put the clothes in the washing machine, then returned to stand by the living room window, where he could still see the pickup. The angle was different here and the waving branches did not interfere with the light, so the eye had ceased to blink. Instead it shone dully through the storm like a squinting, monitory reminder of his inadequacy. If any features came from the storm to surround the eye now, they were those of Walter Matuzak, scowling disapproval.

What would Walter have done in these circumstances? Stand naked in the darkened safety of his house and peer out at trouble? Not in his short, irascible life. He would sprint to the truck, rip the door open if not off its hinges, and drag Duane Blanchard into the street, where he would proceed to stomp on him. And what would I have done in the past? Billy asked himself. Something subtler, something more carefully thought through. But *something*. I would not have cringed in the darkness, hoping trouble would go away. Or praying that Sheriff Kunkel would drive it away from me.... But then Walter was dead and that earlier Billy Tree was no longer in existence. All that's left is me, Billy thought. This limp, moist thing, the current issue of Billy. Not much to say for him, but at least he's alive.

The sheriff's car made a circuit of the block and returned from the north, then turned left onto Twenty-third Street again. This time it stopped abreast of the pickup and Billy could make out the shape behind the wheel of the truck as it shifted to the passenger side, the better to hear the sheriff. The sheriff's car moved off, then stopped a few yards away, waiting for the lights of the pickup to snap on and for the truck to drive slowly away. The truck's lights swept past Billy's window and too late Billy stepped back into the shadows of the house. Did he see me? he wondered. And the answer was, of course he did. He knows you're there, he knows you're afraid.

A few minutes later the sheriff's car made a third pass by Billy's house. It stopped at the alleyways and sent its spotlight searching both ways before driving on. Billy sighed. If only all his demons could be flushed so easily, sent to their homes with a firm but conciliatory word and a flash of light.

CHAPTER TWENTY-ONE

Kath quit speaking to him when she saw her car. Billy had expected tears or recriminations, but she simply turned on her heel and walked back to the house without a word, leaving his explanations and apologies to curdle unsaid. He spoke them anyway, trying with glibness and charm and sincere regret to gain, if not her forgiveness, at least a response. She answered with prolonged sighs, as if his insistent voice were enough to tax her to the limit, all by itself. It seemed to Billy that she did nothing but exhale all morning, mixing her slump-shouldered sighs with random puffs and openmouthed pants, as if the only thing holding her together were breath control. A particularly large gust of venting issued from the laundry room when she discovered his latest deposit of abused clothing, but when he volunteered to do the laundry himself she closed the door in his face with no more malice or deference than if she were trying to exclude the cat.

They walked to the funeral. The Presbyterian church squatted on a corner of Harlan like the truncated top of a battlement, presenting a curved brick turret of an entrance to the street and a longer exposed flank to the funeral home that sat on the opposite corner. The jokes concerning the juxtaposition of church and mortuary were endless and unvarying, as if the combination excited comment but no particular creativity. Worshipers ascended an exterior staircase behind a low screen of brick and could stand for a moment looking down at the sidewalk from an elevation of half a story as if their spiritual superiority were made physically manifest and they towered—or semi-towered—above those who had not yet risen to the entry to salvation. It was the most elevated entryway of any church in town—a small but real difference to its congregation, the sort of distinction that one did not speak about but took a small measure of vindication from.

Billy and Kath had to turn the corner and backtrack several yards in their approach to the stairway, forcing them to pass under the observation deck for a prolonged period and from two different angles, and it seemed to Billy that every eye in town was on him from above, judging him with the censorious vision of the Old Testament God and finding him seriously lacking. He felt as conspicuous as if he were still bedecked in last night's outfit, covered with dirt from his roll in the Blanchard driveway and as soaked and bedraggled as a wet rat, squishing with every step. There was an expectancy in the community with regard to Billy, a standard that he had always surpassed, and was expected to surpass again. Pat Kunkel made assumptions about his abilities and character; Kath's hopes could be measured by the degree of her disappointments; and Joan, who discreetly left her expectations unspoken, was also waiting for something from him. Even Duane Blanchard seemed to think of Billy as a rival worth worrying about. They and the whole town had known him as a standout, one of the few who left Falls City to gain distinction in the larger world, a recognized hero. And now they were beginning to see him as he was, a spectacular disappointment as a hero, a failure as a man. Billy felt a profound urge to fall to his knees before the elevated jury of his peers and cry out his surrender. "Don't look to me for anything and that's what I'll give you."

The entire population of the town seemed to be at the church. When Kath pointedly moved away from him to find a seat elsewhere, Billy stood against the wall behind the last pew, where he was soon joined by Pat Kunkel who habitually attended all church affairs as close to the door and an early exit as possible. To many in the congregation, Pat's appearances in church seemed to be little more than a quick glimpse, as if he were making a head count for official purposes while keeping the door propped open with one foot.

"I get calls," he would say cryptically, tapping the radio on his belt, hinting at awesome and mysterious emergencies even as his eyes twinkled mischievously. The sheriff had about him in all but his most serious moments the air of a boy who was getting away with something just naughty enough to be rewarding. Billy imagined Tom Sawyer attending a church service with the same repressed glee, knowing he was going to slip away before anyone noticed.

"You look bad," Kunkel said as he sidled up to Billy.

"Thanks. Kind of you to say so."

"Look like you been soaked and wrung out and shrank when you dried."

"That's approximately it."

"Boys will be boys. I know how it is. But that's about enough now, Billy Boy. You're going to get yourself hurt if you keep it up."

"I'm a believer, Patrick. You're preaching to the converted."

"So you say, but you just keep sticking your foot into things. I want you around to help me out, Billy. That doesn't mean do my job for me. I was going to get the kid back to his mother when I had the time."

"I know you would. What can I say, I'm impulsive and headstrong."

"You better hope you're headstrong because now you got Duane ready to pull your head clean off your shoulders."

"Duane has an aggressive streak. You ever noticed?"

"I can't always be around to pull him off. Best brace yourself 'cause you're either going to get a licking or give one."

"I have a few contingency plans."

"I hope you do."

"They're not any good, but I got them."

"I'm serious about this, Billy. Remember what he did to the druggist from Auburn. And who knows if he would have stopped if I hadn't gotten there?"

"Perhaps you'll have a stern word with him."

"I did have a stern word with him. And I'm having a stern word with you, now. Watch your ass."

Kunkel looked around to see if he had given offense to anyone, but no one seemed to have noticed. He poked Billy's shoulder with a finger.

"And I want to see you in my office after this," he said. "I got lab reports back on that shell casing and the drugs you found."

Billy was about to inquire further but the music began and Kunkel stepped slightly away and straightened, assuming a respectful, serious demeanor. Billy surveyed the congregation, looking for Joan, and when he turned again, the sheriff was gone. And grinning when he hit the sidewalk, I'll bet, Billy thought. Off to smoke corn silk behind the barn while his less fortunate schoolmates stay and get uplifted.

The previous night's storm had cooled things only temporarily and by the time the church was packed with bodies, the heat returned in full, late-summer force, wilting the parishioners, the minister, and even the music so that the hymns seemed to issue from the mourners' mouths, then, instead of rising, slump limply to the ground. By service's end Billy was drenched with sweat from no greater exertion than standing and watching as others lamented the passing of a man he'd never met.

The television crews were waiting outside the church to film the bereaved community, hoping to fill a last few minutes of news time with interviews of citizens saying what a good and kind man the deceased had been, before driving their cameras back to Omaha and Kansas City and forgetting the story for good. It occurred to Billy that the sheriff might have slipped out early in anticipation of the news vultures, deftly avoiding yet one more interview about the fact that he still had not made an arrest in the killing of two of his constituents. Billy had not seen or heard anything at all about Huford's death and suspected that Kunkel, in his capacity as country coroner, had managed to avoid any suggestion that the deaths were related, or, indeed, that therewas anything unusual in the passing of a mentally handicapped homeless man.

But then Huford wasn't really homeless after all, Billy realized. He seemed like a nomad because he was always on the move, but he *did* have a place where he slept at night. A place where presumably he kept his extra clothing, the treasures he garnered in his travels, whatever he possessed that he considered worth saving. It was normal procedure to search a victim's home for links to his possible murderers. Had anyone looked in the space Huford called home?

Joan touched his elbow as he started down the external stairs of the church. He turned to face her and she fell quickly in step with him, her arm linked with his.

"Hi."

Billy looked behind them and saw Will dragging his feet several paces back. He glanced at Billy, then looked away sheepishly.

"Thank you," she said. She didn't look Billy in the face, but kept nodding politely to the other mourners. She wore a dark blue suit that was too warm for the day—but then any clothing at all was too warm for the day—and a thin line of moisture covered the tiny ridge of her upper lip. Billy had a strong urge to lick it off.

"Don't look at me like that in public," she said, still not turning her eyes to him.

Billy smiled.

"I'm weak willed," he said.

"You didn't give me a chance to thank you for bringing Will back to me," she said.

"I thought my presence there would just make it harder to have the reunion you needed."

"That was very considerate of you."

"I know when I'm not wanted."

"Do you know when you *are* wanted?"

"I've been wrong about that more than once in my career. I like to tread softly."

"Are you saying you need a sign?"

Billy chuckled. "Well, not exactly a vision. A strong hint might do."

"You didn't give me a chance to thank you properly," she said, without any change in tone. "I would like to thank you properly. . . . Is that good enough?"

"Lacking voices from the sky or handwriting on the wall, I suppose it will have to do."

"Do you know the stand of cottonwoods just north of the section corner?"

"The ones along the Muddy? I used to shoot tin cans off of that bridge."

"Bring some wine," she said as she slipped her arm from his.

"When?"

"After dusk. Maybe it will cool off by then."

"What kind of wine?"

She was moving away from him, sliding into the crowd.

"The wet, expensive kind," she said.

Duane Blanchard had not been at the funeral and Billy saw no sign of his truck as he walked the length of the town toward the old power plant. Just before the train station he turned east, traversing a weed-ridden asphalt road that had baked and frozen unattended for so long that its surface had as many fissures as cracked leather. The effects of time and the weather made it look as if it had been shattered by a gigantic blow. After following the road on its steep, short climb Billy ascended to the top of a rise and came upon a large brick building dating from the 1930s that lay in the middle of a depression it seemed to cause by its own weight. The old power plant looked like an illustration of Einstein's concept of warped space-time, the massive bulk of the plant forcing the surrounding land to form a concavity around it.

In Billy's youth the plant had never rested, its giant diesel generators whining without cease. On quiet nights, without the noises of human life to distract him, he could hear the throb of the diesels as he lay in his bed by the open window. The pulse was so low, so regular, so insistent, that it was almost as if he felt it, as if it traveled through the ground and into the foundation of the house and up through the beams to his bed and to his body. The whole town seemed to quiver ever so slightly in sympathetic resonation with its source of power, a rhythm so regular and subtle that it would force its way into their full consciousness only when it stopped, like the beating of a heart. The diesels had been shut down several years ago when the town was finally hooked up to the regional grid and the thrum that permeated the senses of the community like the distant sound of locusts was silenced at last.

It was not until he looked at the site that Billy remembered the old, haunting sound and realized that it was gone.

The building was now a ruin. Stones had long since taken out the few, high windows and someone had used the brick wall for target practice, plugging away at a crude bull's-eye that was still faintly outlined by red surveyor's chalk and deeply dented where the bullets had hit. Where the ricochets had ended up after impact with the hard brick surface, Billy could only imagine.

The huge front doors, large enough to accommodate the entrance of the giant diesel turbines, were locked with a heavy chain, although to prevent what theft it was hard to say. No one was going to back a pickup or tractor to the doors and haul away an outdated fifty-ton generator. Or at least he could hardly do so unnoticed. In any event, a small side door permitted all the access any thief would need. The wood on the door frame had been recently shattered, as if kicked in. Whatever sort of lock Huford had been able to apply had been of no use.

The inside was cavernous, dank, and surprisingly dark. Coming from the bright sunshine, Billy was temporarily blinded as he stepped into the interior. Beams of startlingly bright light pierced the broken windows, but seemed to shed illumination nowhere but where they landed, carving quadrangles from the darkness. He stumbled once as he advanced over the door sill and his momentum carried him forward several steps before he seemed to walk into air made solid. For a brief frantic moment he felt as if he had stepped into a grave and he recoiled in disgust. Billy opened the door as far as it would go, propped it there with a rock, took a deep breath of the outdoor air, then returned. It was hard to know which was more oppressive, the stench or the humidity. The building reeked of unventilated humanity, folded, twisted, and compacted atop itself for years and years until the scent filled the space like a noxious solid. The stink of old socks, wet leather, dried sweat, unwashed male, spent semen, urine, rotted food, wet ash, halitosis, rodent feces, mildew, fear, despair, loneliness, and any number of other unidentified odors, all mixed and brewed and stewed and steeped in perpetual darkness and unrelenting humidity. Things might enter from the windows that lay just under the ceiling, but it was certain that nothing—scent or moisture—ever went out.

His eyes, nearly stinging from the smell, became accustomed to the dark and gradually the landscape of a city dump took shape from the gloom. The floor was concrete but it seemed everywhere overladen with dirt, sediment, or whatever form of algae could establish itself in such a place. Footing was slick and treacherous, as slippery as a cavern. Central to the room was a circle of stones that served to contain the ashes of many fires. Huford's winter heat source. Fuel, most of it twigs and sticks, lay scattered about nearby. It was the closest thing to order in the building; everything else was scattered and tossed as if a hurricane had swept through the place. A torn mattress—retrieved at what cost in dragging it here Billy could only guess—had been sliced on both sides and across the middle so the stuffing fell out. Huford's clothes were tossed to the four corners, the pockets of all the pants and jackets ripped open or entirely off the leg.

His discovered treasures, the bounty of Huford's daily walks, were everywhere: hubcaps, bottles, tools, tires, mirrors, pocket knives, water pistols, rings with stones, rings without stones, brooches with clasps, earrings, empty wallets, wallets with pictures and cards and driver's licenses, purses, backpacks, schoolbooks, magazines, forks, spoons, glasses, plates, even oddly shaped sticks and rocks that had caught his eye, all the debris and detritus that had been cast away or lost or forgotten along the roads and streets that Huford patrolled, anything and everything that caught his fancy and could be carried in his bags or on his back. There were condoms still in the packets, drug paraphernalia, contact lenses, sporting trophies, combs, barrettes, scarves, neckties, brassieres. Anything discarded by others in haste or guilt or disgust had found its way into Huford's cave. And it had all been recently and uncaringly inspected, rejected, and tossed away haphazardly so it lay without rhyme, reason, or order throughout the giant room.

Billy examined the two giant diesel generators. The valuable copper wiring had been stripped, rendering the machines useless, but Billy was certain that action had nothing to do with the tossing of Huford's belongings. Theft of valuable property was understandable, even predictable, but the fine, if frantic, sifting of a junk heap was something else, and caused by a motive other than greed or avarice or simple sustenance. And in a place as repellant as Huford's cavern, mere vandalism would not begin to inspire the deed. Somebody wanted something very badly to take the time to cause so much havoc.

He heard the sound of someone stepping back in distaste, a fumbling, reluctant footfall at the doorway. Billy held his position, shielded from line of sight by the bulk of the generator.

"Keer—rist. What did you do, shit in here, Huford?" The voice was loud but directed to no one. So far, the speaker was speaking to himself.

Billy did not move, although he knew it was not the kind of open door one encountered by accident. Whoever was there was there for him.

"Come on out of there, Tree, you shitstick. I know you're in there . . . it smells just like you."

Billy stayed behind the generator, pressing against its iron bulk for further cover. Its surface was cold and moist within the surrounding heat.

"Where are you, asshole?"

Billy could imagine Metzger squinting into the darkness, his eyes not yet adjusted. He briefly considered rushing at him while the big man was still half blind, but he didn't know if Metzger was alone. Or armed.

"Come out where I can see you, chickenshit."

There was a lack of certainty in Metzger's voice, as if he were slightly embarrassed about yelling into a void. He was not positive that Billy was there in the darkness. It might be possible to stay quietly in place until Metzger got tired and convinced himself that Billy had gone. It was a confrontation that could be avoided.

"Tree!" Metzger bellowed.

Echoes reverberated throughout the vast, empty space, reinforcing the sense of being in a cavern. Billy half-expected to hear a rush of bat wings.

What urge to suicide or defiance motivated him, Billy could not tell. Hiding was a tactic, but not a possibility. Maybe it's my blustering uncle Sean in me after all, he thought ruefully. Whatever moved him, it would not allow him to remain silent under these circumstances, not cowering in a hole, not from Curtis Metzger.

He leaned his head back against the generator, aiming his voice upward.

"How you doing then, Curtis? How's life treating you?"

Billy could hear the relief and triumph in Metzger's tone as he congratulated himself on being right after all.

"Come out where I can see you," Metzger demanded.

"How's the leg?"

"Come out here and I'll put my boot up your ass. We'll see how my leg is."

Silence was no option for Billy, but caution still was. He eased himself to his stomach on the floor and inched forward enough to see around the generator. He could not remember when he had put his hands on anything that felt so unclean. Unpleasant visions came to mind of celery left too long in the refrigerator, slowly liquefying in the back of a cool, dark bin. He wished whatever was under his palms now were something as innocuous as celery.

"I can wait," Metzger called. He was moving his head back and forth as he spoke, directing his voice to all quarters, hoping to give the impression that he knew where Billy was. "I got the air."

The big man was planted firmly in the doorway, his bulk nearly filling the space, the light shining from behind him so that he seemed to be without face or feature, just an undifferentiated threatening mass with arms and legs. If he had a weapon, it lay within the mass, because it was not in either hand.

"I got the air," Metzger repeated, pleased with himself for staking out the advantageous spot.

You also have the light, Billy thought, which in this case was a disadvantage. As long as he stood half in the light, his eyes would never adjust.

"What can I do for you, Curtis?" He made no effort to hide himself. While standing in the light, Metzger would only perceive Billy's head as one more shape on the floor—if he could see him at all. As long as Billy did not move, as long as he did not present a shadow taller than all the others, Metzger would never see him.

"We got a score to settle."

"I believe we've already done this, Curtis lad."

"You got your special sock with you this time?"

"I got better than that," Billy bluffed.

"What? . . . Whadda you got?"

Billy allowed Metzger to worry about the possibilities while he himself scanned the debris in search of a suitable weapon. Most of Huford's treasures were small, or soft, or unwieldy.

"You did a pretty good job of tossing this place, Curt. But then you had help, didn't you? Who was it, those bikers?"

"I don't know what you're talking about. As usual."

"Yeah, it was the bikers. You didn't find what you were looking for, though, did you?"

Billy stood and moved toward the other side of the generator as he spoke. He would have to come out from behind its mass eventually, and when he did, he wanted to be able to move very quickly toward whatever weapon he located before Metzger was upon him.

"Come on out and I'll tell you all about it," Metzger said. His voice was still fixed in the doorway.

"It looks like an awful lot of trouble for a shipment of meth. Who was Huford going to tell? Who would believe him when he said he saw such fine, upstanding local citizens as you and Duane out in the cornfield, buying drugs from the Angels?"

"You don't know shit. You think you do, but you don't know shit about shit."

"Who sent you here, Curt? Your pal, Duane?"

"Nobody sent me, I could follow you myself. You *walked* through town, you stupid asshole."

"Funny, I didn't see you following me."

"Hah-hah."

"Didn't see you at the funeral, either."

"Cohan was an asshole."

"Where's your son, Curt?"

Metzger was silent. Billy could hear him breathing deeply through his broken nose, the air whistling loudly like a defective wind instrument.

Billy affected a sympathetic tone.

"They've killed him, haven't they, Curt? The sons of bitches have killed your boy."

Metzger continued to wheeze, his rage building. He sounded to Billy like a bull preparing to charge.

The firewood was too thin, too brittle, it would snap after the first blow was struck. The remaining stump would serve to stab with, but Billy did not want to seriously injure Metzger, he wanted to evade him.

What he needed was something hard and wieldy that would stun the big man with a single hit. Billy realized that he knew more ways to demobilize or kill than he did to stupefy. His training, like his instincts, had been for survival, which meant immediate and devastating attack. He could think of half a dozen ways to kill Metzger with the trash on the floor, but none to simply—but temporarily—immobilize him. He scanned the room again, searching for something specific. He did not see it, and realized that the pillagers had told him everything by the one thing they had taken.

"You did know Sandy was dead, didn't you, Curt? Or were you hoping he was really hiding out somewhere? No, you must have believed that. You must have swallowed that shit everyone was saying, or you would have killed Duane by now."

Even Metzger's whistling breath went silent. Billy made sure he was listening, not moving, before he spoke again.

"Of course you didn't know Duane killed your boy. That would make you a party to it, and even I can't believe that about you. Money's not worth that."

"You don't know what you're talking about," Metzger said without conviction.

"But you know, don't you, Curtis? Duane didn't tell you, but you know what happened anyway, don't you? Sandy didn't shoot those teachers and he didn't run away."

"I know what you're up to, and it's not going to work."

"It's true, isn't, Curt? You didn't know it at the time—you may not have even thought about it till now—but you know in your heart that it's true, don't you?"

Billy abandoned his shelter behind the generator and stepped into the open. He watched as Metzger responded to the motion and leaned his massive head forward, peering into the gloom. As Billy had hoped, the big man was all but blind as long as he stood in the doorway. He had learned nothing from his previous encounter with Billy. That, after all, was what it meant to be stupid. Billy moved several steps to the side, noting Metzger's slightly befuddled reaction and response time. Due respect to Metzger's brute strength did not include fear. Billy had never been afraid of Metzger and he realized there was no need to be so now. He took a step forward.

"The question is, why did Duane send you here now? What does he hope to gain by this? What is he hoping for, Curt? That you'll beat the shit out of me? I would have thought that was something he'd want to do himself, since he takes such pleasure out of pounding on people. Or does he hope that I'll hurt you again? . . . That's possible, isn't it, Curt? He's your friend, but if he's willing to kill your son, he won't hesitate to see you get messed up again."

"You ain't about to mess me up," Metzger said dully.

Billy walked toward the door with exaggerated slowness. He wanted Metzger to get used to movements that were molasses slow. When the sudden strike came, he would be even less prepared to deal with it.

"No, I'm not. I'm not your enemy, Curt. We had our disagreement, but that's over, that's behind us. I wish you no harm. If I did, I'd come after you, wouldn't I? You know I'll leave you alone if you leave me alone, but you can't say the same for Duane, can you? Sandy never did him any harm, did he? You've never done him any harm, either . . ."

"What you got this time?" Metzger asked, peering at Billy's hands. "A baseball bat or something?"

Billy measured the distance between them carefully. He stopped just far enough away that one quick lunge by Metzger would not put him in his grasp.

Billy held his hands palm up.

"I don't have a weapon, Curt, because I'm not going to fight with you. And you're not going to fight with me."

"I'll just stomp you."

"I offer you my hand," Billy said, extending his arm. If Metzger reached for it, the big man would be off balance. If he lunged, Billy would already have his arm in position to stave him off.

Metzger had neither response. He stared at Billy's open hand as if trying to fathom a conjuring trick.

"I want you to come with me now, Curtis. We'll go to the sheriff and tell him what we know about Duane . . ."

"What you think you know."

"What we both know. Just tell Pat what's going on and let him take it from there."

Billy glanced at Metzger's legs. There was a decided bulge where the bandage covered the hog bite.

"You are one dumb son of a bitch," Metzger said contemptuously.

Billy kicked him squarely in the bulge on his leg. Metzger roared in pain and reached for his wound, dropping his hands and lowering his head. Billy chopped him on the back of the neck and as Metzger staggered forward Billy kicked his bad leg again. Metzger went down heavily on his face with a wet, slapping sound. Billy paused, briefly, to see if he sprang up. Instead, he rolled over, groaning.

"Curtis, this is not your sport."

Metzger made a choking sound and spat. The blood from his nose was streaming into his mouth.

"Stop making me do this to you," Billy said.

Metzger struggled to a sitting position, cupping his hand over his nose as if to protect it from further abuse. When Billy moved a step toward him, he raised a big hand in submission.

"Tell Duane he'll have to do it himself," Billy said.

Metzger gargled something.

"What?"

Metzger spat again.

"He will."

"Now as far as I'm concerned, this business is finished between us. I don't bear you any grudge, it's done with. . . . If you don't agree, get up and I'll hurt you some more. Otherwise I'm going to walk out of here and forget we ever had any troubles at all. Next time we meet we'll be starting fresh. Okay, Curtis? . . . Clear? . . . Get up and I'll hurt you some more. Stay there and it's all over, you don't have to go through it again."

Billy braced himself to deliver the next blow to Metzger's bad leg. He did not intend to wait for the big man to rise but would attack him at his first motion, hitting him when he was off balance and defenseless.

After a lengthy pause, Metzger nodded his massive head.

"Good on you, Curtis," Billy said in his accent. "Good man you are. . . . Are you going to be able to get out of here and make it to your truck all right."

"Yeah."

"Right then. I'll see you."

Billy left him there and walked into the sunlight.

CHAPTER TWENTY-TWO

Lapolla made a sweeping U-turn when he encountered Billy and pulled his squad car alongside him, pointing his vehicle into traffic—except there was no traffic.

"Hey," he said, leaning his head out the window.

"How you doing? Got everything under control?"

"Aw, you know. Not a whole lot going on today."

Billy grinned. "It's all a matter of being in the right place at the right time, I suppose. It seems to me the joint is jumping."

Lapolla made the mistake of leaning his forearm on the outside of the car. The heat of the metal made him retrieve it with a small yelp.

"It's a scorcher," he offered. "I don't see how you can walk so much in this heat."

"I have trouble with cars," Billy said.

"Sheriff said to give you a ride. He said you've got an appointment."

Billy kept walking. Lapolla kept pace, glancing nervously ahead, aware he was in the wrong lane.

"Thought I'd clean up first," Billy said.

Lapolla seemed to notice Billy's appearance for the first time. "Geez."

"You said it."

"Looks like you been . . . what?"

"Crawling on my belly like a reptile."

"Well, yeah."

"Just trying it out, wanted to see how the reptile role fit. I used my arms and legs, though. More like a lizard or newt than a snake."

"I getcha," Lapolla said, although he obviously did not.

The deputy gasped in alarm as a horn blared uncomfortably close. A car filled with teenagers swerved around him, one of the boys offering a finger for Lapolla to inspect.

"Little shits," the deputy said without heat. "I guess I am in the wrong lane, though."

"Technically. But then again, you are the law."

Lapolla chuckled sheepishly at the presumption of such a lofty title.

"No, but really, Sheriff said to drive you over."

Billy slid into the seat next to Lapolla. The deputy closed his window to preserve the air-conditioning, took one breath, then surreptitiously opened the window again. He glanced at Billy from the corner of his eye.

"I know. I'm sorry, I forgot, I've gotten used to the stink by now," Billy said. "It was your idea to give me a ride. I'm happy to walk if you want."

"We're almost there."

"Let's see how long you can hold your breath," Billy joked. Lapolla took it as sound advice and Billy noticed that the deputy didn't speak again until they reached the office of the sheriff's department.

Kunkel entered his office from the restroom, still drying his hands on a paper towel, and stopped abruptly on seeing Billy.

"What is it with you, Billy? I see plenty of farmers who get dirty, but you're something else. I don't think I want to know what that shit is, some of it looks like it's still moving."

Billy told him briefly of his visit to the power plant and his encounter with Metzger. When Billy was finished, Kunkel shrugged.

"Curtis was stupid and violent to begin with. Now with this thing with his son, he's probably so torn up by guilt and all that and doesn't know how to deal with it. . . . I guess it just made him a little more violent and stupid than ever. But I'm not going to worry too much about Curt's broken nose. What the hell were you doing there in the first place?"

"I wanted to know what those bikers were looking for when they stripped Huford naked. I thought it might be the shell we found in his throat. His 'shiny.' Which made me think he tried to swallow it rather than give it to them, because if they were looking that hard for it, they wouldn't have given it back to him, even by ramming it down his throat."

"So you thought they'd go looking for it where he slept?"

"Wouldn't you? And they didn't find the shell, and maybe that wasn't what they were looking for in the first place. Because they found something they wanted, and they took it."

"What?"

"His footwear. There was everything in the world in there except a pair of shoes or boots. Huford lived his life on his feet, he walked nonstop. He had to have something for his feet where he lived because he sure as hell had extras of everything else."

"Maybe he just had the pair he was wearing when the bikers got him. We haven't found any of those clothes."

"And why do you suppose that is, Pat? Do you think the bikers were planning to wear anything Huford had on? He was no fashion plate, even by their standards. They took his clothes and got rid of them a long way from here because if they threw the clothes away where you'd find them, you'd wonder where the shoes were, why they hadn't tossed them aside too."

"And why hadn't they?"

"Think about it."

"Don't do that, you make me feel stupid. Just tell me."

"Remember the footprint we found in the ditch where the shooter left his bike? The print that wasn't the shooter's? I think it was Huford's.

It makes sense, that was part of his route, he went by there every day. The shooter picked up his shells and put them in Sandy's room for us to find, but he must have dropped one when he got onto the bike. Huford came by on his regular rounds, saw the shiny shell glistening at him. . . . How soon after the shooting did he come by? We were there within, what, an hour, hour and a half? So he was there before that, but how much? Soon enough to see the shooter? Maybe. Maybe the shooter saw Huford and knew that he could identify him . . ."

Kunkel held up a hand to stop Billy and punched a button on his radio.

"Lapolla? Come in."

"Lapolla here, Sheriff," the deputy's voice responded.

"Where are you?"

"Just past the section corner. Nothing going on."

"Christ, I know that. Go to the old power plant, take your flashlight, and search the place for shoes, boots, anything that somebody would wear on his feet. Got it?"

"You bet."

"And Lapolla, don't call back complaining about how bad it smells. I'm in the room here with Billy. I know how bad it is."

Kunkel clicked off the radio.

"I'm trying to follow you on this, Billy, so slow down and help me out. You think Sandy saw Huford seeing him when he got on his bike so he got the bikers to kill him . . ."

"Not Sandy. Even if the kid did do the shooting, and I don't think he did, he's not going to be capable of manipulating the bikers or having the presence of mind to search Huford's things or take the shoes . . ."

"I don't quite get why anyone would want the shoes in the first place."

"So you wouldn't find out whose print it was, who might have been a witness. Huford wasn't likely to volunteer the information— although by the time they tossed Huford's place he had gotten away from them, thanks to my distraction. They had to remove Huford as a witness and the shell as evidence. . . . They were half successful. . . ."

Kunkel opened his desk drawer and removed a .22 shell in a plastic bag. He tossed the bag to Billy.

"Maybe completely successful. It came back from the state crime lab. No prints. They couldn't tell if they'd been deliberately wiped or cleaned by contact with Huford's throat and saliva, or if there were ever any there to begin with."

"Shit."

"Me too. I was hoping we'd get lucky."

"Well, the shooter didn't know it was clean. Or he couldn't take that chance. Just as he couldn't take the chance that Huford would talk to somebody and tell him what he saw . . ."

"Who would Huford talk to?" Kunkel asked.

"Who knows. Anybody who talked to him first. Me, for instance. Or worse, you. You spoke to him sometimes, didn't you?"

"When I saw him on my rounds, sometimes, sure. He wasn't exactly a conversationalist."

"The shooter couldn't take that chance, could he? He couldn't even take the chance that Huford said something strange to somebody—just like he told me about his "shiny"—something that wouldn't make sense until later. But if you found out that the print in the ditch was Huford's, if you started asking questions about anyone who had spoken to Huford after the shooting and they offered anything that led you to the shooter—but the only thing that the shooter *knew* linked Huford to the shooting was his footprint—thus the importance of the shoes."

"Christ, when do you think all this shit up, Billy? It seems to me you spend all your time being chased or roughed up or shot at . . ."

"I don't sleep much. And it makes sense."

"I suppose. You're going to have to diagram it for me, but I guess I believe you."

"And you know what else it means," Billy said, leaving the statement to hang in the air.

"I asked you not to do that. It makes me feel really dumb. Just tell me what else I'm supposed to know, don't tease me with it."

"Let me tell you a story, Pat, and you tell me where I'm wrong."

"That's the same thing. Just tell me the story, then explain it to me. Don't make me volunteer my ignorance."

"There's nothing ignorant about you, Pat. We're just seeing things from different perspectives. Yours is a fine overview and mine comes from spending half my time crawling around on my belly for one reason or another. Maybe I see some things from down there that you miss from up above."

"Okay, you spared my feelings. It's not just that I'm missing every-thing, it's because I'm on a loftier plane. Now give me the worm's-eye view. And I certainly hope you're right, because, Billy, I'll tell you the truth, I don't know what the hell is going on around here, and I've been here all my life . . . and if you tell that to anybody else I'll have to arrest you for slander."

"I don't know if I understand it completely, either, and I certainly don't have all the details, but try this. Start with Duane Blanchard. First, the man is dangerously jealous of his ex-wife. That much you have on record. Next, I think he was involved in bringing drugs into town. There was a connection with the bikers. That bag of meth was intended for Falls City and we don't know what else they may have passed on to Duane before I stumbled into them. I think he was fun-neling the drugs into the high school through Sandy Metzger, and maybe Thom Cohan, too."

"Thom Cohan? Come on, Billy."

"The man was a pharmacopeia, Pat. He was passing out pills to everybody. It wouldn't be the first time a school official was involved. It takes somebody on the inside to make drug transactions possible in a school setting. It could have been the janitors, or any of the teachers, but Cohan was walking around with his pockets full of goodies all the time."

"You're straining, if you ask me."

"I think the druggist in Auburn is part of the ring, too. I suspect that the meth and who knows what else came from Scott Falter, through the bikers, and into the hands of Duane and probably Curt Metzger, too. That's why Duane didn't finish the job when he had already beaten him half to death."

"Funny, I thought I was the one who stopped that fight."

"Didn't you ever wonder why Falter didn't press charges after an assault like that?"

"We tend to take care of our own problems around here, Billy. This isn't New York, where you call for the cops if someone sneezes on you."

"And you don't call the cops if your partner's in an illegal drug business, either. That sounds like a better reason for Falter to lick his wounds than good old Midwestern restraint. . . . You want me to go on?"

"I'm having fun. If I weren't listening to you I'd have to go over to Huford's mess and poke around myself. Talk away."

"So we have a man who's dangerously jealous, maybe insanely jealous. Criminally jealous at the very least. His ex-wife has a . . . flirtation . . . with the high school principal. Let's say the principal is giving him a hard time about something else, too. Maybe he wants a larger cut of the drug deal, I don't know, something. So he wants to get rid of Cohan but naturally doesn't want to get caught. No problem, he's got a perfect scapegoat, a kid who's known to be a little tipped away from center to begin with, the kind of kid people would believe might go crazy, and the kid's got a built-in grudge with the principal, too, since he was kicked out of school. Plus, Duane has permanent access to the kid's house, he knows the kid's habits and routines because he's a friend of the boy's father. . . . He takes a pair of sneakers from the boy's room, takes the gun from his closet, the rug from the living room, takes the boy's bike, pedals over to the field, plants a couple of footprints using the boy's shoes, does the shooting, picks up the cartridges, backs out dragging the blanket to clear his own tracks, but being sure to leave the one from the sneaker, hops on the bike and is gone."

"You don't think you're carrying this thing with Duane just a little bit too far, do you, Bill? Letting it maybe cloud your perceptions, as they say?"

"It makes sense, Pat."

"Does it? What about Sandy? Why does he let himself be framed? Why doesn't he come out and say he's innocent?"

"Would you believe him if he did?"

"No. But a jury might, if you were his attorney."

"I don't think Sandy is still alive. Duane would have had to get rid of him before he did the shooting. His bike is in a little grove of trees on Duane's place. Do you think Sandy rode to Duane's, ditched his bike, and walked to Kansas City?"

"So why did he shoot Sharon Shattuck? Is she a drug dealer, too? Or is she up to something funny with his wife?"

"He had to make it look like it was a kid killing teachers. Kill Cohan and it's a murder. Kill two teachers and shoot up the place and it's a massacre. She had the misfortune of being the closest to Cohan."

"And why'd he shoot his wife if that's why he's doing all this?"

"Either he wanted to kill her too, and did a bad job, or she was an accident. I don't know."

"Well, if you don't know, I sure don't. And it's a pity, because you seem to know everything else.... Now tell me the truth, Billy. If you weren't having a thing with Joan, would you be after Duane this hard?"

"I'm not having a thing with Joan."

"Billy."

"I'm not."

"Everybody thinks you are. Including your sister."

"Kath told you I was?"

Kunkel tossed a paper clip toward a distant wastebasket and missed badly.

"It slipped," he said, belying the small ring of paper clips circling the basket.

"Why would Kath tell you I was having a 'thing' with Joan?"

"Maybe because it's the only way to explain your behavior. She seems to think you're acting just a little bit erratically. 'Course she might be influenced by the bullet holes in her car."

"It's the laundry that bothers her."

"You haven't done much to help there today. What *is* that on your clothes? . . . Never mind, I don't want to think about it. And to be fair, Bill, it's *you* that bothers her. It's you that bothers me, too. I asked you to work with me, meaning I wanted you to work *with* me, not go running all over the county getting in trouble."

"I'm just following my instincts."

Kunkel heaved himself from his chair and bent with a grunt to pick up the paper clips that had missed the wastebasket.

"Why not try following *my* instincts, instead?" he said. "Let me give you just a little bit of direction. I do have some experience, for what it's worth."

"I don't *want* to behave like this, you know."

"Well, nobody else is urging you to do it."

"I can't seem to help myself. I get a thought and I just go, I don't know why."

"Well, you don't have to be a genius to figure it out."

"Meaning?"

Kunkel paused, debating with himself whether to continue. "Well,

I'm not Freud, Bill, but don't you think there's some compensating going on here?"

"For what?"

"You don't have to prove anything to me, Billy. You did what you had to do in an impossible situation. You survived, you got through it. I can see, anybody can see what it cost you. You don't have to keep paying. You don't have to convince anybody around here. You'll always be a hero here, no matter what."

"You think that's what I'm doing? Proving something?"

"Not for me to say, I guess."

"But you just did."

"Well, fuck, Billy, why do you think you're doing it? Why do you think every other day you got your head on some chopping block or another? Being a law enforcement officer in this county is just not that tough. So how come it's life-threatening for you if you don't make it that way yourself?"

"I don't know. Bad timing?"

"You're a smart cookie, a lot smarter than I am. I can't think you're fooling yourself or that you can't see something as obvious as this."

Billy rose to leave, then sat down again. He studied his feet for a moment, clenching and unclenching his fists.

"You going to hit me?" Kunkel asked.

"No, Pat."

"You going to abuse my office furniture or anything?"

"It's a hard thing when your motives are so obvious to everybody else. . . . The worst thing about being attacked by the truth is that there isn't any good defense."

"I'm not attacking you. I'm just trying to figure out why you're doing all this."

"Well, compensation aside, do you think there's any value in my conclusions? Or don't you buy any of this?"

"I'm not *not* buying it, I can't reject anything as wrong until I know what's right . . . but I don't have a whole lot of enthusiasm for it, either. Maybe you should talk to the staters. They're running most of the investigation now, anyway."

"They took it away from you?"

Kunkel tossed a paper clip with more vigor than usual.

"We're *co-operating,* according to them. . . . They wear you out,

Bill. There's so many of them, and they're so fucking *eager*. I'm just me."

"You have your deputies."

"Please. Crack sleuths, every one of them. . . . I didn't mean that, they're nice fellas. They mean well. . . . I don't know, Bill, I'm just getting along in years. I'm getting tired of swimming upstream. Ten years ago I would have wrapped this mess up by now and put a boot up the ass of the staters, just for fun. Now . . . I could really use some help. Your help, Billy. Not cowboying. Help. Not just in this case, either. But all the time. I won't be in office that much longer. Just help me till then, or take the whole thing over, if that appeals to you . . . run for sheriff yourself . . . and in case you're wondering, that's not easy for me to say."

"I know, Pat, and I'm flattered. . . . I'm also not the man for the job. For that matter, I don't believe you're running out of steam, you're just getting your second wind."

"Sucking wind is what you mean."

"I don't believe it."

"It's not a question of belief, Billy, just a matter of fact. It wears you out, all of it. You spend your lifetime trying to help a community, you think you know the people—and then, Bam! You find out you been living in a different world than everybody else all along. . . . It's a goddamned mystery."

They both fell into a silence, muted by the indisputable reality of life's unfairness. Kunkel tossed a few more paper clips, missing the wastebasket with every try, and Billy watched as if something important rode on every shot. He did not agree with Kunkel that life was a mystery, because the term mystery implied an eventual revelation, however long delayed, as if the natural order of life were temporarily suspended or obscured by some outside agency. Pull away the curtain of confusion and the natural order would be restored, ticking away, clock-like and preordained. To Billy, there was no mystery in life because there was no natural order to begin with. Only muddle. Disorder was the normal state of things. Some of the muddle might prove to have a discernible proximate cause and some might not, but it was still all just muddle, thicker in some places than others. It was probably not the ideal philosophy for a man involved with enforcing the law, but then Billy did not think of himself as the ideal man for that job, either.

"What do you want me to do?" Billy asked as another paper clip caromed off the wall, embarrassingly off-line.

"I'll tell you what." Kunkel lowered the front legs of his chair to the floor and faced the desk like a man preparing to work. "I'm going to call Meisner, that state asshole, and I want you to tell him everything you told me about your Duane theory. He won't have any biases about it one way or the other and that way you're on the record and you'll get a fair shake on it. I'll look into your ideas about Duane, too. Maybe you're right. Who knows? If he is involved I don't think he'll be able to lie to me convincingly for too long. . . . If I do that, will you find Sandy Metzger for me? Or if you think he's dead, find his body. Fair swap?"

"Fair enough."

"Nothing else, though, Bill. No more fights, no more chases . . . and stay away from Duane. You'll only get your head knocked off."

"Okay."

Kunkel tossed a final paper clip. It rattled into the basket with a satisfying metallic sound. Both men smiled, as if something fine had been accomplished.

"You don't mind walking home, do you?" Kunkel asked. "I don't want you on the upholstery."

CHAPTER TWENTY-THREE

B illy walked past his sister's house to the liquor store that perched on the edge of town, where it seemed to suggest that strong spirits were advised for all who entered. He bought a bottle of red wine and one of white, selecting by price because he was no student of labels or châteaux. Which begged the interesting question of how much seduction was worth to him in dollars and cents. He assumed seduction was what Joan had in mind for their tryst in the cottonwoods, although if "seduction" implied any resistance, it was not the right word. Would too cheap a wine imply that he did not value the prize it was intended to win? For that matter, would the quality of the wine make any difference at all to either of them in the long run? Or the short? Would a bottle of what had been known in his youth with impolitic brevity as dago red cancel the whole enterprise? Billy could not imagine that he had been invited to a wine-tasting session. In his mind they would open the wine of her choice, more for the sake of formality than anything else, a few sips would be taken, an excuse for a brief pause to quell the nerves, then wine would become the least of their interests for the next hour or so. Or so he intensely wished.

He found a bottle of each in the twenty-dollar range and also bought a corkscrew and two plastic wineglasses, putting it all in a large shopping bag with the name of the establishment emblazoned on both sides lest anyone doubt that he was walking through the streets of town with fuel for an assignation. The look on the clerk's face, one of slight recoil accompanied by rapid blinking as if his eyes were stinging, reminded Billy that he stunk. He hurried home to cleanse himself.

There was no official parking by the bridge over the Muddy, but decades of lovers had flattened and compacted the ground where they left their cars on a corner of the field to such an obstinacy that the farmer, trained by his profession to recognize a force of nature when he encountered one, no longer tried to cultivate it. Romance took only a small bite from his arable land, but a stubbornly persistent one.

Billy pulled his sister's car alongside Joan's. He was pleased to see that she had preceded him into the woods; he had not misread the signs. He would have had to be blind to do so, he thought, but he also knew that when it came to women he often misinterpreted their semaphores.

The cars pointed their noses partly into the trees and the high corn covered them from behind, but they could scarcely be considered hidden. If no one was looking for them, or if no passerby was curious about who had staked out the trysting ground that night, they would go unnoted, but Billy had no great faith that local curiosity would take a vacation on this particular night. He wondered briefly if Joan understood the risk she was taking, but quickly realized that she must certainly comprehend it far better than he. She had lived her adult life within the strictures of small-town secrecy—and had not managed very well, judging by the taint of rumor that accompanied her. And what were her options, after all? In such a town adult romance had no better refuge than the teenaged variety. Checking into the lone hotel, where the desk clerk and maid most likely knew one from church, was not to be considered. Billy had discovered what happened with even a social call to Joan's house. Lovers would have to don balaclavas and dark clothes and slink through the night like ninjas to avoid detection in each other's homes. Did that leave only the cornfields, the riverbanks, the cottonwoods, the haunts of horny adolescents? Apparently.

Billy reached for the shopping bag on the front seat and heard a clink of glass against metal as he dragged it toward him. The prise bar was still on the front seat, where he had left it two days ago, wedged into the crack. Billy fingered it for a moment, considering. He was about to make love to Duane's ex-wife. Surely it would make sense to have a weapon with him. On the other hand, if he removed his pants—as he strongly hoped he would—how was he going to explain the prise bar down the back of his leg? Did one take a metal rod to a late-night assignation? Was there not something squelchingly antiromantic about it? How would Joan react to his bringing a weapon to make love to her? Could a reminder of the danger of her ex-husband possibly be helpful to the proceedings? In a way, it was a philosophical decision, he thought. Which did he value more, his hide or his heart? Billy hesitated; he had a healthy respect for both. Finally he left the prise bar on the seat. I'm just a fool for love, he thought, approvingly. But a quieter, less celebratory voice insisted that he was just a fool.

The grove of cottonwoods quivered above the surrounding farmland like the bleached bristles of a shaving brush held in a palsied hand. Always more sensitive to breeze than those of other deciduous trees, the cottonwood leaves seemed permanently atremble even at times of dead calm. With the sun down, the earth released some of the heat of the day and the rising warmth was enough to keep them rustling. Billy heard the trees as he approached, sizzling softly in their motions, like something frightened moving quickly through dry grass. It was after dark, as Joan had requested, but the moon was full and hugging the ground and the blanched bark of the cottonwood trunks shone with a ghostly light. For the moment the grove was like a fairy wood, or at least as close to it as could be found in farm country.

Joan had spread a blanket and was reclining, propped on an elbow, one knee up, her eyes on the river in a posture so reminiscent of a painting that Billy suspected it was posed. He did not mind the artifice.

She wore khaki shorts and a plain white T-shirt, such an anomaly in an era when every such garment advertised a product or a slogan that he wondered where she had acquired it. As he drew closer he noticed a small pocket applied above one breast and it occurred to him that the shirt might have once belonged to her husband.

She looked at him as he approached with a slight turn of her head, a movement so isolated and restrained that he knew for certain that she had affected the posture for his benefit. Which meant that she was as fully aware of how desirable she looked as he was.

He eased onto the blanket, propping himself on an elbow to face her. It surprised him at first that she had given no greeting, but then he realized that he had not done so either, they had both assumed and required the other's presence—there would be no need for formalities or wasted words.

They were eye to eye, a foot apart, and he could feel her breath on his face, smelling faintly of mint and wine. She had begun on her own, not waiting for his bottle. Billy started to speak, she arched her eyebrows slightly in expectation, but there seemed no reason to break the silence. Instead he let his eyes search her face, absorbing all the details hungrily. He did not know how to describe her face. He had no terms with which to characterize, even in his own mind, the details of her beauty. It was simply a face that he had always thought lovely, a shape and set to the eyes that suggested warmhearted mischief and a willingness to play, a slight overbite that parted her lips and made her seem to be perpetually expectant, a fullness and softness to her mouth that compelled him to kiss her. It astounded him that he had fought that compulsion so successfully and so long. He put a finger to the tiny crow's feet beginning to entrench themselves beside her eye and trailed it slowly to the point on the bridge of her nose where it stretched against her skin as if trying to burst through, then traced the finger further down, following the contour of her nose, caressing the nostril, and onto the ample upper lip. She closed her eyes as he allowed his finger to caress her mouth and then conclude its journey of discovery at her chin. Although he had done it many times, it now seemed to Billy that he had never really touched a woman's face before. Never treasured it so much, never felt it so completely. Something huge and complex and stubbornly adamantine in his chest had suddenly melted, sending a relaxing warmth through him.

He ran his fingers slowly across her temple and into her hair, as soft and thick as young grass, and up to the shell of her ear. She moaned slightly, or he thought she did; it was hard to be certain against the background of the whispering leaves. He ran his finger along the rim of her ear from top to bottom, then back again, following the whorls, touching her as gently as if she were everywhere bruised. Her eyes closed again, and her lips, and she exhaled heavily through her nose; he could feel the small breeze against his skin.

Billy continued to explore her face in wonder, amazed that such a treasure was at his fingertips, careful lest he damage it, astounded at his good luck. He had wanted this woman since he was old enough to know what wanting one meant, and now he realized how deeply his desire went. Wanting her was not only part of his past and part of his present, but a deep and formative part of himself. It had always been there, covered, disowned, disguised, ignored, growing with every year and every further instance of denial until he lay facing her in a fairy wood of shivering leaves, and it suddenly demanded acknowledgment and release. He was shaking as if he had a fever. If he had been standing, he didn't think his legs could have held him upright.

"You know . . ." he started to say. His throat was dry and his voice cracked. He had no idea what he was going to say.

Her lips moved but he heard no sound, though he strained to hear. Her eyes were still closed and Billy's fingers continued to move, caressing her flesh as if operating on their own. They moved to the soft, vulnerable skin of her neck and she leaned her head toward his hand, trying to trap it there.

Her lips moved again and Billy moved still closer to her.

"What?" he whispered.

His hand was on her upper arm and it seemed to have gone there without his direction. She gasped and he felt gooseflesh spring up under his touch. A troubled, surprised look on her face turned immediately to a tiny smile. Peeking discreetly from between her lips, her teeth were almost startlingly white against her bronzed skin in the moonlight.

His fingers crept under the sleeve of her T-shirt and felt the roundness of the globe of her shoulder, then moved to the back of her shoulder blade. He trailed his fingernails as lightly as a breath along the flesh of her back and she shivered and arched her back and sighed with a tremulous "ahh."

She spoke again, a protracted suspiration of sound, no louder than the leaves, and he heard his name.

"What?" he whispered again. "What did you say?"

She ran the tip of her tongue along her upper lip, moistening it as if her mouth were as parched as his throat.

His hand, unguided, moved to the very top of her breast, where the flesh began to fill and rise from her chest. His fingers crept across the swelling mound as slowly as if limning something holy. She was breathing in short sighs, thrilling and waiting. As his fingers moved across the cotton of her shirt, lingeringly ascending, she rolled her head slowly side to side, eyes squeezed tightly shut, willing him on. When they brushed across the firm apex of her breast she moaned loudly.

"Come on, Billie," she whispered.

"What?"

"Come on, Billie." Half pleading, half demanding, and, as always with Joan, with just a suggestion in her tone that she was ahead of him, waiting impatiently for him to catch up.

He lowered his lips to hers and held them there as gently as he could. They were both quivering with nerves but soon their lips seemed to meld together, to blend with a soft completeness that made anything else, any motion, any grinding or thrusting of tongues unnecessary. With his mouth against hers, Billy felt as if he shared with her all that mattered and that they were floating together on a zephyr as light as the one that stirred the leaves. They held the kiss, just their lips in embrace, for a very long time as if they feared that to break it off would be to lose something magical.

Finally they moved apart, sharing their sense of amazement with wide-eyed grins, then kissed once more, only to discover that the magic could be found again at will.

Of course it didn't stay that way. They made love to the same languorous pace, each exploring the other's body with hesitant caution, as if handling a baby bird, until the slow build of tension had both of them throbbing with expectation.

"Come on, Billy," she whispered again. "You're making me crazy."

He didn't need another invitation and once he entered her they both sighed loudly, struck with the same wonder that had assailed them with the first kiss. Joan was a versatile lover, passive when he needed to be in control, demandingly active when her time came, and irrepressibly vocal as her excitement increased. They came together, both of them howling enough to wake the night.

Afterward she sat atop him, panting, her eyes half closed, her lips split in a wide smile. The moonlight reflected off the sweat on her chest and breast and she shined like silver.

"Like a flying fish, breaching the water," he said.

She didn't ask him what he meant and didn't care. She slumped forward, holding her weight on her arms. He stretched his own arms upward and she collapsed into his embrace. They began to laugh simultaneously, dazzled by each other, stunned by their performance.

Sometime in the midst of their preoccupation a truck with its headlights off had crept to a stop on the roadside. Billy had not heard the soft tread of someone approaching across the packed dirt. He had not heard the sound of fingers sliding into leather gloves nor of Velcro closing upon itself. Without warning, without the monitory sound of snapping branch or rustling grass, the man was suddenly there, beside them.

Billy saw the boot pull back preparatory to a kick. He rolled away with Joan in his arms so the blow hit him between the shoulder blades and not on her head, then scrambled to his feet in time to see Duane Blanchard grab his ex-wife by the hair and pull her to her feet.

Joan screamed and Duane hit her once, very hard, in the solar plexus. She folded upon herself, gasping for breath, and sunk to her knees.

"Just won't learn, will you?" Duane asked. His eyes never left Billy, who was circling to his left, moving closer to the shopping bag that held the wine bottles, the corkscrew, any possible weapon.

Duane stepped in front of the bag.

"What's it take with you?" Duane asked.

Billy was still semi-erect and he held one hand in front of himself, embarrassed in front of another man even though embarrassment seemed the least pressing problem at the moment.

"I mean, what the hell does it take for you to get the message?"

"Oh, sure, I'm a slow learner, me," Billy answered in his brogue.

"Poor stupid useless Curt. Twice. A visit to your sister. The boys on the bikes, the jungle bunnies with their guns, even my son taking a shot at you . . . man, I'd think anybody with half a brain would figure it out. You're not welcome around my wife."

"You keep well informed about my travels, Duane."

"You're not welcome in town."

Duane wore blue jeans and a long-sleeved denim shirt despite the heat. The boots completed the image of a cowboy. Lean, rawboned, and mean as a snake. The gloves were the only incongruity. Billy recognized them from his visits to Duane's house, the driver's gloves with the fingers cut off, foam padding inside to protect the user's hand from impact, lead tape just under the leather to give the fist the power of brass knuckles.

Billy glanced at Joan, who was on her hands and knees, still gasping for breath. There was nothing he could do for her now except to survive himself. He backed until he felt the water against his heel.

"Well now, don't go away, Billy. I been looking forward to this."

"Sure, now, Duane, lad, I'm sure everyone has. A good time had by all?"

"You babbling? What is that?"

"A touch of the Irish, lad. Gives me that bit of luck, don't you know."

Billy continued to back into the water. He felt it lap at his knees, warm as a bath after soaking in the summer's heat all day long.

Duane shook his head in disgust. " 'Charming Billy.' I never got that. What's so charming about you?"

Billy backed in further. The water was waist high, the sluggish current tugged at him without conviction.

"It's me boyish ways. I don't beat up on women, for instance. Funny, but they like that. I don't lie in ambush and shoot people. I don't deal in drugs and funnel them into school."

"You don't do much of anything but run, do you?" Duane stopped at the river's edge, looking distastefully at the water flashing silver in the moonlight.

"I don't kill teenagers, either. Where's Sandy, Duane?"

"I give up. Where's Sandy?"

"Did you bury him? That wouldn't be too hard with a few million acres of cultivated ground all around you . . . but then dogs might find him. A farmer might plow him up. Frost heave might bring him up in the spring. . . . So where'd you hide the body?"

Duane continued to study the water as if contemplating whether or not he was willing to get wet.

"Women like that mouth that just keeps yapping, don't they? That's what's so charming about Charming Billy. He won't shut up, just like a woman."

"Of course when I find Sandy, they'll know he didn't do the shooting, and they can start looking for who really did it. And that would be you, Duane."

"I think I'm going to shut your mouth, because, you know what? It's annoying." Duane stepped into the water, his face registering displeasure as the liquid filled his boots.

"I just want to warn you, Duane. I'm not going to box you."

Billy backed in further, hoping the water would reach to his chin, but it rose no higher than his chest. High enough to drastically impede Duane's mobility, but not deep enough to eliminate his fists as weapons.

"That's all right. I'll do the boxing."

"I may drown you, though."

Duane hesitated for a step, contemplating a possibility that did not ordinarily arise, then moved forward.

"You may shit, too," he offered.

Billy took his eyes off Duane just long enough to take in Joan, who was sitting on the blanket, still dazed by the blow but breathing normally again.

Duane extended his left arm and the glove grazed Billy's forehead. It was a probing blow intended only to help Duane determine his range, but Billy was surprised by its neat efficiency. As he had feared, there would be no off-balance lunges, no wild flailings. He was not facing the huge but hapless Metzger. And the power from a mere tap was awesome. The depth of the water may have greatly reduced Duane's ability to maneuver, but it had done the same to Billy and he still had to avoid getting hit. Two or three blows at full power would render him defenseless.

He threw a jab of his own, keeping it sharp and straight from the shoulder, and recovered quickly. Duane blocked it easily with his right hand and when Billy threw a second jab, faster and harder, Duane tucked his head into his shoulders, his hands up defensively in front of his face. Billy's fist struck him on the forehead.

Billy recovered and moved backward, turning against the current, which was now attempting to push him toward his opponent. His hand smarted from contact with Duane's head and Duane was grinning at him. Without gloves, how many such blows would it take to break a hand? Not many.

Still grinning, Duane flicked a jab, then another and another, all of them deliberately a few inches short and a few fractions of a second slow so that Billy could catch them on his hands and forearms. Every one of them felt like being tapped with a hammer.

"You're doing really good," Duane said. "This ain't going to be easy for me, is it?"

"You're a sadistic bastard, aren't you?"

Duane shot a full jab, followed by a right cross. Billy saw it coming and pulled his head back from the jab while throwing his left arm up in defense. Duane's right-hand fist hit him flush on the bone, keeping the blow from Billy's head. A few more of those, Billy thought, and I won't be able to raise my arm.

"Look at you, you're boxing! You're boxing!" Duane crowed. "And you said you couldn't."

"I said I wouldn't," Billy said. He ducked under the surface and propelled himself toward Duane's body, remembering to keep driving with his legs to overcome the resistance of the water. Duane stepped back, but too slowly, and Billy wrapped his arms around the man's legs. Duane struck down savagely, alternating blows with either hand. Any one of the punches would have driven Billy to his knees if they were on land, but the water cushioned and arrested them and they landed harmlessly on his shoulders.

Squeezing Duane's legs together, Billy rose. As Billy's head returned to the air, Duane's hit the water. Billy shifted his grip on the legs, lifting them higher, and Duane was forced underwater, his hands flailing. He struggled violently and one leg slipped from Billy's grasp. Thrashing desperately, Duane managed to place one leg under himself and brought his head to the surface, arms swinging wildly. His leaden gloves struck Billy on the elbow and forearm as he hopped frantically to maintain his balance. Billy lifted Duane's leg higher and the other man's head was forced beneath the surface again.

Joan waded into the river, still nude, holding a wine bottle by the neck.

"No," Billy yelled. "Stay out."

She struggled against the weight of the water, striding purposefully but in slow motion toward the men. The moonlight coruscated off the water on her breasts as they bounced in and out of the river with each stride like Billy's earlier vision of flying fish.

"Too deep for you," he tried to say, but Duane thrashed his way to the surface again, twisting and torqueing his leg in Billy's grasp, loosening his grip with every motion. This time Duane struck out purposefully, landing two heavy blows in succession against the hands that held him. His fists landed like rocks against Billy's fingers and his grip gave way as Duane fell backward into the water again, but this time with both legs free. Billy lunged forward to renew his grip on Duane, any part of Duane, to keep him close enough to neutralize his striking power.

Joan was within a few steps of Duane's back. The water was nearly to her chin and she strained against it, head tilted forward like a ship's figurehead. The current spread around her neck in a lacy collar of bubbles and foam.

Duane rose with a triumphant roar as Billy reached for him, grappling with his arms. The first blow caught Billy on the ear, driving him to the side. He clung to Duane's left arm, but the right was still free and Duane hooked it like a scythe against Billy's temple. Billy sagged and the leaded fist hit him again, bouncing off the side of his skull. He went under the water, still clinging to Duane's arm. His mind already fogged by the blows to the head, Billy groped for Duane's leg again. When he rose he tried to keep behind Duane's left shoulder to shelter his head from the blows, but Duane had anticipated him and he pivoted as Billy came up. The fist landed on Billy's chest and for a moment he felt as if his heart had stopped.

Joan struck from behind as Duane moved to the side, the wine bottle glancing ineffectually off of his back. Roaring with anger he back-handed his ex-wife across the face. Billy saw her eyes roll back in her head as she slipped below the surface. He sank himself, clawing across the riverbed, feeling for her in the turbid water. She was limp in his grasp, making no effort to help as he put his arms across her chest and rose to the surface. Duane struck him in the back of the head, driving Billy's face forward onto Joan's skull. Her head hung limply, her mouth and nose just inches above the water. If he released her, she would drown.

He threw up his forearm, turning to face Duane obliquely, like a fencer, his other arm keeping Joan above the water. Duane hit him on the leading elbow and pain shot through his whole arm. When he lowered the arm in reaction, Duane swung the right again in a sweeping hook that bounced off of Billy's shoulder and against his jaw. Even as a glancing blow the fist felt like falling against a rock.

"One hand tied behind you, huh?" Duane said. He seemed incongruously merry for one engaged in a murderous attack. And Billy had no doubts that the intent was murderous. "You're not good enough to try that."

In control again, Duane was the boxer once more, toying with a weak and helpless opponent. He jabbed with his left, hitting Billy high on the cheekbone. Billy grabbed at the fist in vain with his free hand. As if to demonstrate the hopelessness of the tactic, Duane hit him with another jab over Billy's outstretched arm, bouncing the heavy glove off his nose and cheek. Blood poured from Billy's nose, staining his face and chest dark in the pale light.

Joan stirred against his arm and Billy turned his head toward her as Duane swung two rapid blows in succession into his face and the back of his head. There was an explosion of light behind Billy's eyes and he slumped into the water. Gasping, he surfaced again, barely aware of where he was. Joan's face was in the water and he pulled her head up again. Duane drove a fist into his shoulder blade and Billy stumbled forward, falling on Joan, forcing her back into the water. When he tried to straighten, Duane hit him where his head met his neck and Billy crumbled, sliding into the water like a muskrat gliding home.

He came to his senses aware that something was prodding him with increasing desperation. Joan was trapped under him on the riverbed and pushing frantically to get out from under. They broke the surface together, breathing stertorously.

Duane stood in front of them, his teeth shining in the moonlight as he smiled. He bobbed up and down in the water, his boxer's bounce turned playful in the buoyancy of the river.

"Well, there's my girl," he said. "There's my traitorous bitch wife."

"Duane . . ."

"I'm glad you're up, darling. I want you to watch this last bit."

He jabbed at Billy and Billy's head snapped backward as the blood flew in a dark spray.

Joan stepped forward but stopped when Duane pointed a finger at her.

"If I hit you again, you won't come up," Duane said to her.

Billy lifted a hand from the water and swung weakly at Duane, who moved his head and laughed at the attempt.

"You just don't know when to quit, do you?"

"Like a turtle," Billy muttered.

Duane hit him again and Billy wobbled, too spent to move, too sapped by the blows to defend himself. Just staying up was his only triumph. And also his only way to stay alive.

"He's a charmer, Joan, no doubt about it."

Duane feinted with his shoulder and Billy's head sagged back as if hit, then slumped forward again, eyes blinking.

"You're done," Duane said. "You're all through, boy."

Billy tried unsuccessfully to spit and blood and saliva clung to his lip in a stringy chain.

Duane struck with a fast combination and Joan screamed and Billy heard a noise as he sunk beneath the water. He was dimly aware that he knew the sound but he had no context for it and couldn't remember what it was. He collapsed to his knees on the riverbed, his head a foot beneath the surface, and the current kept him from falling forward. He rocked gently back and forth with the force of the water, knowing he had to get up again to breathe, doubting that he could. Joan screamed again, her voice sounding mute and far away, and Billy struggled to rise. He flapped his hands futilely like a child learning to dog-paddle, but it was not enough to lift him and his legs refused to assist. He did not think he could rise a foot higher; he was not sure it mattered.

He was aware of noise and activity above him as his lungs finally prevailed and forced him to his feet. As he broke the surface, he lashed out with his arms, hoping to catch Duane with a lucky blow, a scratch, a bite, anything that would at least make a mark on him so that he had not been beaten to death while giving nothing in return.

"Whoa, Bill."

Billy lashed feebly once more at the shape in front of him, then his hands were grasped and he felt himself being lifted out of the water and planted unceremoniously on the broad shoulder of Pat Kunkel.

"Hold still now," Kunkel said.

Joan's face appeared in front of him. Her eyes were wide and frightened.

"Hold still," she said. "Hold still. It's all right, it's all right." Her expression did nothing to assure him that anything was all right at all.

They were moving slowly toward the shore, backward. Joan walked beside him, steadying him on the sheriff's shoulder. Kunkel's other hand was towing Duane Blanchard's body by the shirt collar. Duane's face lolled gently from side to side in the current, into the water, out of the water, into the water, like a mockery of a living swimmer. Duane's feet slid downstream and bumped against Joan's legs. She gasped and jerked away.

In the shallows Kunkel dumped Billy heavily into the water again. The strain of dealing with two bodies was evident on his face.

"Let me get him to shore," Kunkel said. To Joan he added, "Just keep his head up."

Joan knelt beside Billy, her arms wrapped around his body, her naked flesh pressed against his. He tried to follow Kunkel with his eyes, but Joan's face was in his way. She mistook his movement and pressed her cheek against his.

"It's okay, it's okay, it's okay," she repeated desperately, trying to convince herself.

Billy tried to say that he was all right, but he heard the words emerge as a mumble unintelligible even to himself.

"Shhh," she said, "shhh, shhh." She put her hand to his face and drew him to her breast, offering instinctual comfort. He stayed there, his aching face pressed against the softness of her flesh, knowing that all was not well, despite her words, but allowing himself to just give up and give in at last. He clung to her, marveling at the curative powers of a woman's breast, the water tugging and pulling gently at his body, until Kunkel returned, wading in to his knees, to pull him to his feet.

This time he lifted Billy in his arms, carrying him as gently as a baby, slipping once as he emerged onto the muddy bank, but righting himself and depositing Billy on his feet, where he clung to a tree while the sheriff returned for Joan, who was still on her knees in the water, her face in her hands, her body wracked with sobs.

Billy's head swam dizzily now that he was upright again and he slid to the ground with his back against the cottonwood trunk and put his head between his knees as a wave of nausea swept over him. It took him a moment to make sense of what lay at his feet but as the wooziness faded he realized his toe was touching one of the weighted gloves that had nearly killed him. Duane's body was stretched before him, a gaping hole in his chest looked black in the moonlight.

Kunkel lifted Joan easily into his arms and she buried her face against him, still sobbing. When he placed her on her feet she continued to cling to him and Kunkel embraced her with such tenderness, such unself-conscious compassion that Billy could not help but wonder if the sheriff had held her glistening, naked body before.

Billy crawled to the blanket and retrieved his clothes. He dressed himself while sitting on the blanket, suddenly eager to cloak his nudity.

"He was going to kill you, Billy," Kunkel said.

"Pretty near did," Billy admitted. He could not tell if the words emerging from his swollen mouth made any sense.

Joan disengaged from Kunkel's embrace, shaking her head, wiping a forearm across her face as if annoyed with herself. Kunkel's hands stayed on her shoulders a fraction of a second too long, Billy thought. She was too slow to turn her back to him to dress herself. He found their comfort in the situation shocking.

"Christ, I warned you to stay away from him, didn't I? What made you mess with him?"

"He came at me."

"Run away. Just run away. I told you, you didn't have a chance against him in a fight. . . ." Kunkel looked down at Duane's corpse, then again at Billy, who was struggling with his jeans. "You just don't know how to run away, do you, Bill? It's just not in you."

"I had a plan," Billy said. "There's not much you can do when you're naked and don't have a weapon but I thought if I got him into the water . . ."

"This was so unnecessary," Kunkel said sadly. "Dumb son of a bitch." He shook his head side to side. Billy was not certain if he was referring to Duane's behavior, Billy's, or his own. The sheriff trudged wearily toward the road and in a few moments Billy heard the crackle of the radio and a response of electronic sound.

Joan shrugged her clothes on indifferently, her eyes on Duane's body the whole time.

"Were we worth it?" she asked.

Billy did not know how to process the question. It did not seem to be directed at him particularly. Was she speaking of Billy and Joan? Or Joan and Duane? Or some other grouping that Billy did not have the strength to contemplate at that moment?

Despite the temperature Billy began to shiver and realized for the first time that he was cold.

CHAPTER TWENTY-FOUR

ecuperation required a high price in depressing familiarity as Billy lay on his bed and once more contemplated the wallpaper and the ephemeral figures dancing through the design. This time, however, the phantoms did not bear Avi Posner's leering face. They bore no face at all, but merely twisted and writhed their way through the lattice of design like a nest of worms held in the hand, twining through the fingers, sending a message of chaos without resolution. There was no meaning to be found in the wriggling mass, no head to be severed that would put the body to rest. There were a hundred heads and the severed parts would only regenerate new ones.

His body mended quickly; there were no fractures, no punctures, no organs assaulted or imperiled. He ached badly for two days as he lay and watched the worms of his fantasy animate the walls. On the third day of silent nursing, Kath sat on the edge of his bed when she came with his lunch tray. Her face was lined with care. She looked weary and resentful of the cause.

"I can come to the table," Billy said.

She nodded. "Good." She stayed on his bed, not looking at him, her face drawn.

"I know," he said, touching her hand.

She looked at him questioningly,

"I know how hard this is for you," he said.

"You'll have to go, Billy," she said quietly.

Billy patted her.

"I know. I knew it. I don't blame you."

"I can't sleep, waiting for you to come home, not knowing if Pat is here to say hello or to tell me you're . . ."

"Shhh. Shhh. You're right, you shouldn't have to put up with me and all of this."

"That's right," she said with sudden assertiveness. "I shouldn't have to. I don't have to. I won't."

"Give me a couple of days to find a place."

"You're staying in town?"

Billy realized that he was as surprised as she was.

"You're staying in Falls City?"

"I guess so," he said wonderingly. "I guess I am."

"What's here for you?"

Billy hesitated. He was not certain how to answer, even less certain that he knew the reason himself.

"Is it *her*?" she demanded. "Are you staying for *her*?"

"Why do you hate her so much?"

Kath dismissed the question with a snort and a wave of the hand. "I don't hate her."

Billy had expected no answer, but believed that he had divined it for himself. If his understanding of the timing was correct, Cohan had gone from Kath to Joan, and in much the same way, initiating the relationship with something from his seemingly inexhaustible pockets to make the lady feel better. Billy wondered if the ill-timed return of Stuart Sime had anything to do with Cohan's departure after all, or simply provided a convenient screen to mask the reality of his switching to another woman.

Kath was on her way back downstairs when he swung his legs out of bed.

"Kath, you told me you'd known two men. Thom Cohan was one . . ."

She paused, waiting for the question even though she must have known how it would hurt her.

". . . It's none of my business, but was Pat Kunkel the other?"

She stared at him for a long time and he could see the battle going on within her mind reflected on her face.

"You don't know what it's like to be alone," she said finally.

He did not think it necessary to remind her that of course he did know what it was like.

To a town already stunned by sudden deaths, the funeral for Duane Blanchard was yet another straw upon a growing burden of inexplicable sorrows. The assembled congregation did not mourn so much as suffer through it, doing the right thing even for the wrong person, shouldering this further assault on their sense of security as mutely as they carried the coffin to the hearse. Although a man of few friends and many enemies, Duane Blanchard mustered a full house in death.

Billy stood behind the last pew again and watched the sheriff deal with those entering the church. Many of the mourners stopped for a word with him, offering condolences as if Kunkel were a close relative rather than the man who had killed the deceased. Kunkel acknowledged them somberly with a nod of the head and a shrug of his large shoulders. No one seemed to hold his duty against him; they commiserated with him for being forced to perform it. And when they saw Billy they looked at him appraisingly as if, echoing Joan's question at the time, they wondered if he was in any way worth it. They regarded his battered face, but none of them caught his eye. If anyone was to blame for Duane Blanchard's death, they seemed to be saying, it was not the man who pulled the trigger, not the deceased himself, but Billy Tree, the battered survivor.

*   *   *

oan watched from her bedroom window as Billy approached her house. He seemed different after Duane's death, she thought. At the funeral he had hung back, regarding her from a distance. She had felt his gaze upon her, but when she turned in his direction he was always looking away, or studying the ground. Chief mourner by default, she had left the church first and passed close by him, but when she caught his eye, he merely nodded, his face the same impervious mask of studied sobriety worn by everybody else.

He hesitated now as he came toward her house and his body language was diffident and reluctant, like that of a boy sent on an errand of duty he could not avoid. She pulled away and hid behind the curtain when he looked toward her bedroom window, embarrassed to see his discomfiture. Had she become an obligation so quickly?

Will opened the door and stepped back, unable to hide his surprise at seeing Billy's face.

"Wow."

"I look better if you squint," Billy said.

Will studied him a moment longer. "Huh," he concluded.

"Will, I want you to know I'm sorry about your father."

The boy nodded and looked away, uncertain still how to deal with the expressions of sympathy. "Thank you" seemed an odd response.

"I need to talk to you," Billy continued.

"What for?"

"Sandy. I'm sorry, but we're still not finished with Sandy."

"I don't know where he is. Everybody's asking me. I don't know."

"I believe you. But you might know more than you realize."

Joan entered from the bedroom. She had changed from her funereal black to jeans and a man's blue work shirt with the sleeves rolled up to her elbows.

"You pick a bad time for questions," she said.

"My timing is always off."

She dismissed Will with a twist of her head and he left them gratefully. They stood looking at each other for a moment, neither making any movement toward the other.

"You look bad," she said.

"I know."

She sat on the arm of the sofa, then stood again immediately, repelled by the casualness of the posture. She wrapped her arms across her chest. As she looked at him her anxiety registered as anger.

They each seemed about to speak and stopped; each made a tentative move toward the other, a slight shifting of weight, a motion short of a real step, but their uncertainties kept them in place and silent until the silence felt too oppressive to bear a moment longer.

"For Christ's sake," Joan erupted. "This is awful."

"Isn't it?"

"Where do we stand, Billy? . . . Just tell me where we stand."

"I don't know."

"I should have waited," she said, shaking her head. "It was too soon to sleep with you."

"That was the only timing that's been right."

"No. It was too important. I should have waited."

"No, Joan . . ."

"I trivialized it for you, somehow. . . . You think it was just . . ."

"No."

"You think . . . I know what you think of me . . ."

"I think you're wonderful." She waggled her head, refusing to take his remark seriously. ". . . but I have to ask you a question. I don't want to, but I think I have to know."

She dropped her head in disappointment as if she already knew the question.

"You and Pat Kunkel . . ." His voice trailed off. He did not want to formulate the sentence.

"Does it matter, Billy?" she asked wearily. "Does it really make any difference?"

He could not answer.

"Does anything matter that we did before we knew each other?" she continued.

He wanted to say no. He wanted to say that their lives began three nights ago in a cottonwood glade on a blanket by the river when the moon was full and the leaves rustled like fairy wings. But he knew it wasn't true. Some things mattered, different things for different people, but one couldn't dismiss thirty-seven years as if they had no meaning or had not formed the characters they possessed.

She took his silence as insistence.

"Do you want me to list everybody for you?"

"No."

"Do you want to tell me about all of yours?"

"No."

"You just want to know about Pat? Is it that important to you?"

It was, although he didn't know why. Nor could he admit to her that it mattered. He stood mutely before her, feeling stupid and childish in his need to know.

"Is a yes or no enough?" She sounded so tired and sad, he sensed that if she told him it might be the last thing she ever said.

"I don't want to know," he said abruptly. "You're right, it doesn't matter. Don't tell me."

"I will if you insist."

"I don't. Forget it."

She looked at him for a long time without speaking.

"I'd do my life over for you, if I could," she said. "Except for Will, I'd change whatever you wanted."

He put his finger to her lips. Her mouth was still swollen where Duane had hit her.

"If you did that, who would you be?" he asked.

"Who you wanted."

"Why would you think I know what I want? Just be Joan."

"Is that good enough, Billy?"

He put his hands under her arms and pulled her toward him. She tilted her head backward, resisting a little, insisting that he look at her.

"Is it? Is that good enough? Tell me now, when you don't want sex and you're not trying to charm me."

She put her hands on his chest and gently pushed him away, still watching his face closely.

"It's good enough," he said. "It's more than good enough, it's more than I deserve, it's . . ."

"No charm, Billy. No flattery. Good enough is good enough."

He saw hints of green in her eyes that he had not recognized before, flecks and splinters like the remnants of shattered emeralds. As at the moment of their first kiss on the riverbank, Billy felt something tight and hard loosen in his chest and suffuse his body with warmth. Suddenly he wanted nothing more from life than to hold her and feel the warmth forever.

"Someday I'll tell you whatever you want to know," she said. "If you still want to know it. But I've lived a life, you know that. So have you. I thought in a way that would help. I thought we'd appreciate each other all the more. Maybe."

Billy sagged onto the sofa. He felt as if he had struggled through a great battle and lost. "I must be an idiot," he said, but he was smiling with relief. Somehow losing the battle was the way to win.

"Yes. Part of the time. . . . I don't think I'd feel so comfortable with you otherwise."

She sat beside him and after a moment they found themselves holding hands.

"I was so terribly frightened," she said.

At first Billy thought that she meant because of him, because of the prospect of losing him.

"We're so lucky," she said. Her voice quavered and he realized that she was holding back tears.

"Yes," he agreed.

"I mean to even be here. I thought we both would die. . . . It was so close, for a moment I thought I was shot, too."

"I know," he said.

"How would you know, you were barely conscious—or underwater. Did you even hear it?"

Billy struggled to catch up. She had gone somewhere in her mind without him.

"Hear what?"

"The shot. It was so loud because it was right next to me. And I didn't see it coming. I thought Pat was going to calm him down, the way he usually did. He was always able to control him. I saw the gun, I knew he was wading towards us with the gun in his hand, but he was holding it up—keeping it out of the water, I thought. I didn't think he was going to shoot him. I thought he might hit him, but that was the worst—and then he was so close when he did it."

"He couldn't have done it from a distance, he might have hit you."

"I know. . . . It was just so close. Duane didn't have a chance . . ."

"Duane was killing me, then maybe you . . ."

"I mean he didn't have a warning. I'm not sure he even knew Pat was coming . . ."

"Joan, we can't blame Pat. I'm the reason Duane was killed. Pat did it to save me. I'm responsible. Me. No one blames Pat. I *knew* I was asking for trouble, I *knew* he would come after me. You warned me, Pat warned me, even Curt Metzger warned me. I did it anyway."

"Why did you?"

"I wanted you so bad . . . I *want* you so bad."

He knew it was only part of the answer and realized that she might know it as well, but it served to bring her into his arms and against his chest. From there it was not difficult to convince himself that it was the whole answer.

CHAPTER TWENTY-FIVE

illy left the house at midnight, pausing first to listen to his sister's breathing. She was awake, silent in the darkness of her bedroom, listening to Billy outside her door listening to her. He wondered if he had awakened her when he rose from his bed or if she had lain there the whole time, waiting for the creak of the floorboard, dreading the hushed closing of the outside door as her wayward brother crept quietly into more trouble. Had she ever slept before he came to stay, he wondered, or had she been like this since her marriage to Peripatetic Stuart Sime, holding her breath and waiting forever for the other shoe to fall? Kath was right, he had to go. She would never sleep, never take a carefree breath until he did. Just as he would not be able to stop, it

269

seemed, until the worms on his wall were linked head to tail in a line, all confusions straightened, all questions answered.

He carried the prise bar in his hand because he had a long way to go and did not want to limp the whole distance. The elevator was eight miles from his house, a distance he could walk in three hours if he stayed on the roads. Via the fields, staying out of sight, it would take him closer to five and he wanted to be there, and hidden, before sunrise.

Three hundred yards from the house he was in a cornfield and the difficulty of concealment resolved itself. Following the rows he was hidden by their height and gave no more sign of his passing than an errant breeze. He skirted the town, staying parallel to it but far enough away from the houses to avoid arousing the dogs. When he hit the railway tracks he turned east and followed them, walking on the ties or the roadbed when they traversed fields and the only possible observer would have to be hiding in the corn himself. It was at the road junctions that he feared detection and he slipped into the fields well before them and sprinted across the clearings low and fast like a fox.

There were stretches where the fields on his line were planted in soy beans, ground-hugging plants that offered cover only to a snake, and he gave them a wide berth, sticking to the corn and milo even when it cost him time and distance.

The night was overcast again with distant rumblings promising more rain and Billy made his way with little visibility, relying on gross and massive features to tell him where a field ended and a road began. The rest was easy and required more trust than vision because the corn rows were as straight as a man on a tractor could drive. The railroad tracks, too, had been laid down with scant interference by an unyielding topography. Straight was the most efficient way to go and straight they had gone.

As he approached the elevator, there was light in the sky, the reflection from the clouds and the elevator's own permanent nimbus of grain dust in the lights of the granary complex. From a distance the elevator seemed to rise from the soil like a giant's castle, something from a Wagnerian nightmare, huge and somber and menacing, its very top in the clouds, lightning crackling in the distance. Billy stood in the shelter of the field and listened. A low grumble emanated from the silos like the moan of souls in torment as the structures complained of the endless stress of supporting their massive load of constantly shifting grain. The noise seemed almost below the level of human hearing, as if he were feeling it as much as hearing it, taking in the vibrations through his feet. As if the earth itself were in restive grievance.

What a place to work, he thought. No wonder Metzger and Blanchard seemed half mad with violence. It would be like spending their lives in the paws of a beast, hearing its stomach rumble incessantly, waiting to be devoured.

He was in position by sunup, sitting in the field of corn speckled with dust that extended right up to the graveled lot of the complex. With every breeze some of the dust sifted off the leaves of the plants and settled on Billy so that he was rimed like a baker by the time Curt Metzger's cherry red pickup pulled into the lot and disappeared around the silos. The rest of the morning shift followed soon, a mix of Anglos and Mexicans, the beef-and-milk-fed locals standing half a foot taller than the others.

He pulled his shirt over his nose to keep from breathing the dust but he might as well have tried to stop inhaling the air itself. His mouth tasted of flour and he yearned for a cold, acrid beer to cut the taste and clean his tongue. Work here all day, every day, and how many beers would it take? Work here a lifetime . . .

It was not until midmorning that the Impala with the Kansas City plates made its incongruous appearance, scraping against the highway as it made the minimal dip into the parking surround. There were two riders and Billy recognized them both. The bald-headed one pulled the car to a stop, facing away from the highway. Not exactly the action of someone anxious about a quick getaway. Tyquane, the driver, got out of the car, followed by the one with the bandanna on his head. Billy struggled to remember his name, then gave up the effort. He remembered only that it was one of a kind, nothing he had ever heard before and nothing that he would recall by running through the alphabet. This time the youth wore a red bandanna. Not ideal for camouflage.

Billy scrambled through the corn to get a better angle as the gangbangers approached the elevator on foot. Bandanna boy carried a battered briefcase that he put between his feet when he stopped and removed his bandanna from his head and tied it over his mouth and nose. He looked like an outlaw but Billy knew this was no robbery; the gangbanger was merely protecting himself from breathing the ubiquitous dust. Tyquane waited impatiently, obviously contemptuous of the other youth's attempt at prophylaxis.

Still in cover of the corn Billy returned to their car and opened the hood. The gangbangers reemerged within a few minutes, Tyquane punching numbers on a cell phone, glowering at the silos for their interference, then trying again as he approached his car.

"Top of the morning to you, lads," Billy said as he stepped from the concealment of the corn. The prise bar was tucked in his belt behind his back.

"Yo, it Kunk fren'." Detaching his bandanna and replacing it on his head, the gangbanger smiled broadly. " 'Sup, Kunk fren'? I almost didn' recognize you wid dat face. You even uglier than last time. Somebody whup you real good."

"You should see the other guy, as the saying goes."

"I forgets yo name. Fud . . . fud . . . Fuddle, that it, ain't it?"

"Fuddle will do fine, sure, 'tis an improvement."

"Fuck off," said Tyquane. "We doin' bidness."

"Or trying to. Your contact man wasn't there today, was he?"

"What you know about it?"

"Oh, only speculation and surmise," said Billy. "You seem to show up on a regular basis."

"Only surmise? Sheee. He only got surmise, Tyquane." His smile broadened. "Surmise ain't worth shit, Fuddle."

"That's about the proper value, all right. And since it's so cheap, let me throw some more at you. The first time I saw you guys there were four of you and you looked an awful lot like a war party. Today you're about as casual as drug dealers can get. From that I surmise that your competition is gone."

"Who that be, Fuddle?"

"Stop talking to him, Defone. Get in the car."

"That would be a motorcycle gang, a bunch of white supremacists, among other things. They won't be back for a while because they're wanted for murdering a harmless local character."

"Dat right?"

"Just a surmise, Defone."

Tyquane was behind the wheel of his car, still punching numbers on the phone. "Get in the car."

"I be *talkin'*, Ty. My man Fuddle and me having a conversation."

"Yeah, Ty, join in. Don't be antisocial. This is a friendly sort of place. You can correct me when I go wrong. . . . Besides, you're not going anywhere in your car, anyway."

Tyquane turned on the ignition and was greeted by silence.

"Why won't the man listen to me, Defone? Would I lie to him?"

"You always good for a laugh, ain't you? You a very comical white man."

"Okay, asshole, 'sup wid dat?"

Tyquane emerged from the car and stalked menacingly toward Billy.

"Nice of you to join us, Tyquane. Defone and I are having a good time."

" 'Bout to get even better."

"Right you are. So here's the deal, guys. I took some vital working parts from your engine. Not big but crucial, you know what I mean? All the fuses. That's why you get that curious lack of reaction when you turn the key. And I buried them in that field behind me. Big field. Little fuses. You'd be digging for a long time trying to find them if I don't tell you where to look. Certainly long enough for the state police and the sheriff and the national guard to get here and take a look at what's in your briefcase. And of course the drugs are still in there because Duane wasn't here to take them off your hands."

"What you want?" growled Tyquane.

"I got what he want, don' I, Fuddle. Got what you want right here." Defone lifted his shirt to reveal his .38 protruding from his belt. "This what you want, ain't it, Fuddle? Some of dis right in the face."

"Very kind of you to offer. I really must get myself one of those someday, but that's not what I'm after."

"That's what you gon' get you don't start digging for what ever you took."

"Shut up, Defone," said Tyquane.

"Amo shut him up. Put a cap through his mouth."

"Well, you might do that, Defone, but then it would be hard to get your car working and you'd not only have to explain your drugs, you'd have to explain my body."

"Explain shit."

"What you want?" asked Tyquane.

"I'd like your cell phone."

"My cell phone."

"That's it. That's all. You keep the drugs."

Defone reached for his pistol and Billy hit him on the wrist with the prise bar. The gun clattered to the ground as Defone yelled and grabbed his arm.

"And we were getting along so well," said Billy.

"Shoot his ass," Defone implored. Tyquane made no move toward his weapon.

"What you want with my cell phone?"

"I just want to make a call, Ty."

"Shoot the motherfucker!"

Defone cradled his wrist against his body.

"I be talking to the man, Defone. You tole me talk to him, I talking to him."

"He try to kill me!"

"He try to kill you, he still be whaling on you. He still whaling on you?"

"I admire your logic, Tyquane. So, do you want to give me your cell phone and I'll give you what you need to take your briefcase and get out of here?"

Defone reached for his gun with his uninjured hand. Billy hit him on the elbow with the steel bar. Defone screamed and rolled on the gravel.

Tyquane regarded his fallen comrade with detached curiosity.

"What? First time didn't hurt enough?"

"Slow learner," Billy offered. He dragged Defone's gun closer to himself with the end of the prise bar.

"Why I don't shoot you in the knee, make you tell where it is?"

"Shoot his knee!" Defone offered.

"It's a thought," Billy agreed. "But how do you know I won't faint from the pain? How do you know you won't sever an artery and I'll die from loss of blood? How are your first-aid skills, Ty? Up to speed?"

Tyquane ran a hand over his shaven head and looked at the dust that had accumulated there during his brief visit to the elevator.

"Think you're a smart son bitch, don't you?"

"No, Tyquane, I think *you're* a smart son of a bitch. You got nothing to lose except a cell phone. On the other hand, you fuck with me, you end up like your pal."

Tyquane wiped his head again and slapped his hands together to create a small cloud.

"How come you so fucking brave, all of a sudden? Last I see you, you be shitting yourself."

"Ah, well, last time you showed me your great big old gun. And I didn't have a weapon."

"That be you weapon? You call that a weapon?"

"I do. What do you call it, Defone?"

"Motherfucker," said Defone. He levered himself into a sitting position, cradling both arms as if holding a baby.

"There you go. It's a motherfucker."

"Maybe I show you my gun anyway."

"Do that and I'll have to break your arm. . . . Then who's going to drive your car? . . . It's just a cell phone, Tyquane."

Tyquane shook his head in derision, unimpressed, indeed unimpressible, then turned back toward his car.

"I'll get you the phone," he said.

Billy matched him step for step, maintaining the gap between them, and when Tyquane reached for the back of his belt and started to turn, Billy hit him on the arm then quickly just behind the ear. His knees buckled and Billy helped him to fall with a blow to the hamstring. He scooped the gun from Tyquane's belt with the curved end of the bar.

"It's only a phone," said Billy as he retrieved the cell phone from the front seat of the car. He tucked the phone into his pocket and stood in front of Defone. Tyquane writhed close by.

Defone winced, his eyes on the crowbar swinging easily in Billy's hand.

"How old are you, Defone?"

"Say what?"

"How old are you?"

"Nineteen."

"Don't you think that's a little young to be sitting in the middle of the sticks with a broken elbow and a sneaky white man standing over you with a crowbar? Most people would want to postpone that situation till later in life. See, the problem is you're the wrong age for this kind of work. If you'd been a couple years younger, you'd have been scared enough to give me the phone. If you'd been older, you'd have been experienced enough to know it didn't matter. But at your age, you had to prove something, both of you had to prove you're smarter and badder than I am."

"You going to hit me again?"

"Do you need it?"

"Shit no."

"My advice to you is get out of the business, Defone. But I surmise that you won't. . . . You'll find the fuses under your right front wheel. Just stick them back in there and I think you'll be okay."

"You didn't hide them in that shit?"

"In the cornfield? Hell, why would I do that? I'd never find them again."

"You gon' call me a doctor?"

"Okay, you're a doctor." Billy stepped into the cornfield. "Hang on there, Defone, and I'll let you make the call yourself in a minute. I just want to get a clear signal." He vanished into the field and reemerged in a moment. Billy dropped the cell phone at Defone's feet.

"Give some thought to that career change," Billy said.

Defone watched him walk toward the elevator. He did not make a move toward the telephone until he saw Billy step into the maw of the building.

CHAPTER TWENTY-SIX

They labored as though in a sandstorm, more than a dozen men
with goggles and white face masks making them look like smog
victims in Tokyo, their shirtless bodies slick with sweat in the
oppressive heat, the grain dust clinging to the perspiration as they shov-
eled and scooped the mix of grain and chaff that had escaped the giant
hoppers and accumulated within the base of the giant structure. Electric
lights, partially obscured in the haze, offered what little light there was
to work by, but the wattage was low by design. Brighter light would
have been reflected from the suspended particles in a glare, no more
useful than high headlight beams in a blizzard. Billy had heard of ex-
plosions in the basal tunnels of smaller silos when the dust-laden air

277

had been exposed to an open flame. What kind of blast could this enormous assembly provide?

Most of the men were Mexican, short, squat, with jet black hair that shone through their dust caps with every toss of their heads. Curt Metzger towered over them, more than a full head taller, looking like a giant amid a team of dwarves in some subterranean myth of the European imagination. He stopped working for a moment and turned his massive head in Billy's direction. Billy could not tell if he was recognized from that distance through the gloom, but Metzger continued to stare toward him, his shovel held in both hands across his body like a rifle. A few of the men closest to Metzger turned to see what the giant gringo was looking at but saw nothing to merit the interest. Only Metzger continued to stare through the haze, his eyes invisible behind the plastic goggles.

Billy found the internal elevator where Will had said it would be and he rode it to the top of the complex. Stepping out of the shaft he found himself on a metal catwalk that extended for close to a quarter of a mile into the distance, its terminus shrouded in haze. The open grid of the catwalk ran parallel to the open tops of the silos, each as wide as a house, butted one next to the other, and each filled ten stories high with grain. Far below him, faintly visible through the iron skein of metal on which he trod, were the workers he had seen earlier, even Metzger dwarfed now by the distance, all of them laboring like trolls in a mine.

As Billy looked down, fighting vertigo, a growling began in the distance, followed almost immediately by the roar of a landslide of grain, an avalanche rising *up* the mountain and spewing forth suddenly from the exterior chute and into one of the silos. The noise of the machinery and the flying grain was deafening. Kernels aimed at the center of the silo rebounded crazily off of each other and some flew from the open mouth of the silo and through the fretwork of the catwalk and showered down onto the workers below who had covered their heads with their shovels at the first roar. They waited patiently for the shower of golden grain to cease, then turned their umbrellas into shovels once more and bent again to their labors.

Even as the din continued Billy became aware of motion, a general convulsion at his feet as if the catwalk were suddenly alive, but it took him a moment to realize that it was not the catwalk that was moving, but the rodents on it. They raced towards the newly spilled grain from both directions, their dark coats well camouflaged against the matte black of the metal walk. A sudden swirl of rats, seemingly materialized from nowhere, sucked toward the grain like iron filings to a magnet. Not many grains were caught or balanced on the lattice of the catwalk, but it appeared to be enough to sustain a sizeable population of animals and they flowed around Billy's feet like furred liquid. As the roar died away he could hear the scrabbling of their claws on the metal, their squeals of greed and aggression.

Leaving the rats to their feast in the distance, Billy peered over the side into the nearest silo. To his surprise, the ten-story-high column of wheat was not still but constantly roiling, like barely simmering water, but in reverse. Here the water did not rise to fall back upon itself, but sank ever deeper with glacial slowness as tiny pockets appeared on the surface, only to be filled with the surrounding grain sinking quickly into them. The individual grains were neither square nor round and they would never settle into a perfect equilibrium as the pressure of the surrounding mass twisted and turned them, slipped them against each other, seeking always the least stressful configuration. Billy could understand why the rats did not simply leap onto the tops of the mounded grain; they would be sucked under as soon as they exhausted themselves trying to scale the sheer walls to get out again. The bold ones who made the leap would die fat and slowly for there was no way out for a rat, once in. A metal ladder was built into the wall, but the vertical risers were too far apart for the rodents. The rats he saw now were the timid ones, or the wiser ones, the survivors who had not made the leap into the treacherous banquet.

As he watched, the silo in front of him began to recede with an accompanying shusshh, the noise of many skiers he had heard a week ago from the outside. A load was being extracted into a railroad car and its rapid descent caused a vortex to form in the field of wheat, a whirlpool of grain. Falling and spinning at the same time, any rat atop the wheat would be sucked under by an irresistible pull. The level stopped its descent a quarter of the way down the silo. If anything had survived being sucked under it would be buried by the next load cascading in from above.

Amazing that boys would be allowed on the catwalk for any reason, Billy thought. It would take no more than a misstep, a playful push, and the unlucky child would be on his way to a slow death by suffocation. Could help arrive from below before the quicksand of grain devoured the victim? The place should be equipped with lifelines like a ship at sea. He wondered if the insurance company knew that teenagers roamed this catwalk killing rats. It seemed a Dickensian job and a peril more in keeping with a third world nation than the planet's most litigious society.

The elevator had arrived during the uproar of the maelstrom in the silo and Billy sensed the presence of another person before he could hear him. He looked at the end of the catwalk and saw a large bulk, backlighted by the light rising from the shaft, features indistinguishable. The man's shadow stretched before him, darkening the catwalk further, and seemed to extend his mass indefinitely.

"That was quick," Billy said.

"I was already close by when I got the call. I figured you were around here somewhere . . ."

"I think I've found Sandy's body," Billy said.

"Oh, yeah? Where?"

The shadow stretched toward Billy.

"In one of these silos, moving up and down beneath the grain like a waterlogged tree trunk in the ocean. Just the way you told me about it."

"I never said anything about that."

"Sure you did, Pat. The first time you showed me the elevator itself. Sounded like something you wanted me to know about."

"You have a good memory."

"I observe things, Pat. That's what you wanted me to help you with, remember?"

"Was that what I wanted?"

"You said something else I thought was interesting."

"I hope I was entertaining."

"Your approach to crime solving, remember? Everybody will tell you everything they don't want you to know, if you talk to them long enough. As if they wanted to give themselves up but just didn't know how to do it."

The shadow lengthened, reaching Billy's feet, as the sheriff walked slowly toward him. He moved carefully, like a man uncertain of his balance, his head bent to accommodate the slope of the domed ceiling.

The catwalk was not that narrow, the ceiling not that low, Billy noted. Kunkel was uncomfortable, maybe a little afraid.

"Vertigo's a bitch, isn't it, Pat? Not as bad as losing your night vision, though. Although that doesn't really trouble you, does it? You drive at night all the time."

"Part of the job."

"The first lie you told me. How you were getting too old for the job. Man, they couldn't get you out of this job with a forklift. You *are* the sheriff. Not just the current office holder. You *are* the sheriff. Like a birthright."

"Nobody does it better. This county would be chaos without me. Who else should do it? Lapolla? Any of the other weakfish?"

"Funny, I thought you wanted me to do it."

"You're kind of losing favor in my eyes, Billy."

Behind him, another silo gasped and gave up some of its grain in a whoosh and startled Kunkel. He moved toward Billy in response.

"That's close enough, Pat." Billy backed up, keeping the distance between them too much to cover in a single lunge.

"What did you want the phone for, Billy? What was so important you'd risk your neck with those two black-assed cowboys just for their cell phone? Who'd you call?"

"I pressed the redial button, Pat. Just wanted to see who they called once they learned that Duane wasn't there to buy their drugs anymore. I thought I knew who it was. I wanted to make sure."

Kunkel gave a slight movement of his head as if he had already known a sad but undeniable fact. "I always liked you, Billy."

"I know, Pat. I believed that part. I liked you, too. That's probably what took me so long to figure it out. . . . What was it, a power play? Did Cohan want more money, a bigger share?"

"Billy, what did you do with the guns you took from those KC boys?"

"I have them tucked in my belt behind my back."

"And the thing you hit them with?"

"That's there, too."

Kunkel sighed audibly. "Oh, Billy, you really are a glutton for punishment, aren't you?"

"I figure I have some coming. For my sins, don't you know, me boyo. For me sins."

"I never cared for that Irish crap."

"It wears on you, doesn't it? Imagine how *I* feel. . . . So why did you have to kill Duane, Pat? You had Sandy Metzger all trussed up as Cohan's shooter. No one's ever going to find him in here and prove you wrong . . . and if they do, I'll bet the county coroner will decide it was suicide, won't you, Pat?"

"I shot Duane to save your life, Billy boy."

"All you had to do was pull me out of the water. You shot him in the back from point-blank range. . . . Is that what I was for, Pat? Did you know that Duane and I would come to the point where you'd have to kill him to save me? Or were you hoping I'd kill him for you? That would have been tidier for you."

"No, I never thought you'd kill anybody. You don't have it in you, you've lost the stuff. . . . Those KC boys want to press assault charges against you. I'm afraid I'm going to have to take you in until we get this straightened out."

"And then I'd resist arrest and you'd have to shoot me, too?"

"I'd never shoot a friend, Billy."

"Tell you what. Why don't I take *you* in? I'll make a kind of citizen's arrest, Pat. Take you in, get your confession signed, get you in jail. Then I'll be a character witness for you at your trial."

"See, that's what I always liked about you. You have such an active sense of humor. You don't tell jokes, but you have a humorous way of looking at things."

"What did you do it for, Pat? You don't live like a man who wants money."

"Never cared about money. You know, I'm a little surprised you even picked up those guns. I thought you were scared of them."

"I ask myself, why would a heavy man wear long sleeves even in this weather? What would people see if you showed your arms, Pat?"

Kunkel paused for a long moment. Another silo at the far end disgorged a load of grain and the shush of a thousand skiers reverberated along a quarter mile of concrete.

"You don't miss too much, do you?" Kunkel said at last. His tone was darker now, but more certain, as if he had made a decision.

"I figure the black gang wanted to be your new supplier. Cheaper, were they? The old supply line was the bikers through Duane and Curt—or was Curt too stupid to trust?—plus some supplementary supplies from the pharmacist in Auburn and then to Cohan. But Duane and Metzger had *issues* with Cohan, as they say these days. So it was easier to just get rid of the entire chain. Besides, you didn't want to risk a war between the bikers and the blacks, did you? You might not be able to control that. And you are very much in control of everything, aren't you?"

"There's no way to keep the drugs out, you know. None. People want 'em, they'll pay someone to get them and the harder it is for them to get them, the more it costs, but they still want it. You can't stop them. All you can do is control them. A good sheriff does what he can, not what's impossible."

"And you're a good one."

"You know I am. You got to do things you don't like in this job. Like right now. I don't want to have to arrest you, so just come on with me and we'll make it informal as long as we can."

"No, I don't think so, Pat."

"I don't think you're going to use those guns, Bill. You might end up shooting a friend like you did before."

"I didn't just shoot a friend, Pat. I also shot a bad guy. This time I could do both at once."

Kunkel hesitated, trying to read Billy's determination.

"Your word's still good by me," Kunkel said finally. "Right now this is just between us. If you tell me you're going to forget about it, I'll walk out of here and let you be. We can both forget about it. Anyway, it's over. Nothing else is going to happen. Sandy's gone, let the Feds look for him. Duane's gone and I saved your life in the process. Nobody's going to mourn him much."

"How about Huford?"

"Huford." Kunkel chuckled. "Who's going to miss Huford?"

"I will."

". . . Billy, I like you too much, I don't want to have to shoot you."

"We're in agreement there. Tell you what, Pat. How about neither one of us shoots anybody, we just leave together."

"That's what I'm suggesting."

No chance, Billy thought. If I relax for a second, I'm dead. If I let him behind me, I'm dead. Draw the gun now, he implored himself. Draw the gun *now*.

Kunkel gestured with his left hand. His right stayed close to the butt of his gun. He smiled. "Let's go, then. I'll buy you a beer."

Billy was covered with a clammy sweat that had nothing to do with the heat.

"After *you*," said Billy.

Kunkel's smile broadened. "Sure thing. . . . You're not going to shoot me in the back, are you, Billy?"

"I hope not, Pat . . . but my nerves aren't good."

"I see that. You don't look real healthy."

"Tough week."

"You look scared. You scared, Billy?"

"I've been scared since I got home."

"Glad to hear you think of it as home, anyway. We're all real pleased to have you back. . . . So what are you more scared of, me or just pulling your own gun? You know I couldn't hurt you . . . or is this one of your windshield things?"

Billy's thoughts screamed in his head, shoot the son of a bitch before he kills you! Do it now! Shoot him! His arms hung at his side as if paralyzed. None of his muscles would obey him, only his tongue seemed to work.

"You don't have me quite assessed to your satisfaction, do you, Pat? You're still not quite sure of me."

Kunkel's eyelids flickered down, seemed almost to close.

"I'm sure of you, Billy. I've got you figured out. I know I can trust you. Just to prove it, I'm going to turn and walk out of here."

"Not yet!" Not yet because when he showed him his back it would be over. Not yet because he knew Kunkel would draw his weapon and turn back to shoot. Billy was too far to reach Pat with a couple of quick steps, he himself had set that distance.

"What?"

Billy could see it in his mind already, see it as if it had already happened, see himself frozen, helpless as Pat's pistol swung onto him, unable to make himself move. Not yet, not yet.

"What about Joan?"

"What about her?"

"Why did you keep trying to warn me away from her? Duane wouldn't have come after me if I'd left her alone. None of it would have worked."

Kunkel smiled, but his eyes never left Billy's hands. "Because I knew you were a stubborn Mick. I warned you every step of the way about everything, didn't I? It didn't stop you from doing a damned thing. All I had to do was tell you not to do something, and you'd do it, sure as shit."

"So you controlled me, too."

"Until this. You went too far, as usual. . . . Now we can't go back. Let's go, Billy."

"Not yet. I know about you and my sister, Pat."

"Really? Your sister's a fine woman."

"I know it."

"She means a lot to me. It seems to me you're mistreating her."

"You're probably right. How about Joan? Was there ever anything between you and Joan, too?"

Kunkel smiled broadly. "You're even dumber than I thought, Billy. Why would a sane man ever want to know a thing like that? . . . Time to go."

Kunkel turned to his right so that his bulk shielded the movement of his hand. Billy knew that he would draw his weapon, knew it with every fiber of his being. He sank to one knee to reduce himself as a target, at the same time groping behind his back for one of the guns.

Firing a gun is not an instantaneous action. The safety must be inactivated, the action cocked. Kunkel's weapon had barely cleared the holster when the roar of incoming grain began. The rats heard it before the men and were already streaming toward them as Kunkel fumbled with the safety. He saw them coming like a moving floor at the same time that he realized Billy was kneeling before him. As he chambered a shell they surged past Billy in a torrent, squealing, claws clattering on metal, and swept against his feet and legs like the surf. He yelled involuntarily, appalled at the tide of rats skittering around him, bouncing off his shoes and pants, and fired wildly into the air over Billy's head. The roar of rising grain exploded behind him as the great shower of grain burst from its pipe. Kunkel swiveled, startled, and stepped backward. His foot descended on a rat that screamed in alarm and he jerked his foot away in horror, losing his balance. Grain caromed and ricocheted off itself and onto the catwalk, catching in the gaps of the fretted ironwork, and the rats scurried under and over Kunkel's shoes to get at it, pushing his uncertain balance to the limit. He flapped his arms and yelled again, Billy forgotten, the gun forgotten, everything forgone in an effort to maintain his equilibrium. Sawing the air, with no more hope of flying than an ostrich, he teetered back on his heel, brought his other foot down on a rat, and fell backward into the silo behind him.

Billy stayed on his knees for a moment, his unfired gun in his hand, frozen there by the startling picture of the sheriff launching himself into the void. Recovering, he hurried to the rim of the silo and looked down. Kunkel lay on his back, fifteen feet below the catwalk, still stunned from the fall.

"Don't move, Pat."

Kunkel blinked, coming to himself.

"Lie flat," Billy called.

Kunkel looked to his side, where his gun had fallen muzzle first into the grain. Only the butt was visible. Kunkel rolled onto his side and up on his knees to reach for it—and sank to his thighs. Startled, not yet grasping his situation, he grabbed the gun and tried to stand.

"Hold still," Billy yelled.

Kunkel managed to get his feet underneath himself—and sank to his waist.

"Jesus," he said, as the enormity of his situation struck him for the first time.

"Lie down, Pat, lie down."

Kunkel looked toward Billy, becoming aware that he had been yelling at him for some time.

"I'm stuck," Kunkel said.

"Lie down. You'll spread your weight like a snowshoe. I'll come help you."

But Kunkel was caught in panic as deep as the grain. He tried to walk toward the ladder, increasing the rate at which he sank.

"Billy!" he cried.

"Flatten out!" But it was too late, the sheriff had already sunk beyond the point where he had any options. All that was left was the inexorable slow-motion fall. His motions could only accelerate it, they could not arrest it.

Billy climbed down the ladder, hooked his knee over the last rung above the surface and reached out along the grain like a rescuer trying to advance over thin ice. Kunkel reached toward him but even that movement sent him deeper. The grain was at his chest and his arm was a full foot away from Billy's hand.

"Bill . . ."

"Don't move, don't move at all. Let me do it."

"Bill . . ."

Billy stretched out still further, moving his arms in a breaststroke to advance across the grain, dust filling his lungs, his nose just inches above the surface. At the very limit of his reach, his legs quivering with the effort, he touched Kunkel's arm with his fingertips.

"Pat, drop the gun."

Kunkel stared at him, his eyes huge and imploring.

"You have to drop the gun so you can use your hand."

Kunkel's normally ruddy complexion was pasty white and drenched in perspiration. Billy recognized the symptoms of shock. He was a man no longer in control of himself.

Billy grappled for a grip on Kunkel's shirt and pulled until the material tore off in his hand. He had budged the sheriff not an inch, but Kunkel was now up to his neck, his eyes wide and staring but seeing nothing. Kunkel's lips were moving soundlessly. Billy could see him mouthing "Bill . . . Bill . . ." over and over again, a useless mantra.

"I'm going for help," Billy said. "Don't move. Don't move at all. We'll get you out."

Billy felt a tug on his arm and for a moment thought Kunkel had managed a grip of some kind, but then he became aware of the sound of skis and saw the level of the corn seethe. The falling grain pulled at him, gripping him with a thousand tiny hands, threatening to tug him off the ladder. The strain on his knee, the rung cutting against the tendon, made him cry out in pain and as he dipped his head in reaction the falling grain clutched at his head as well, yanking him under. Thousands of tiny impulses propelled him downward, relentless as gravity itself, and he felt his grip on the ladder weaken. His open mouth was filled with corn, his nostrils clogged; grains scraped and clawed across his face and eyelids, rasping his skin, each adding one more tiny impetus to sink.

And then it stopped, the maelstrom had sunk below him, and Billy was left hanging from the side of the silo by his knee. He pulled himself back to the ladder and watched the roiling surface subside another foot before it became calm again. Yards away, out of his reach, the surface was still in turmoil, a singularity within the hole, as Pat Kunkel continued to struggle frantically. Like a grave with a living corpse, the grain heaved and thrashed and settled ever lower. All was still for a moment, then a hand suddenly thrust toward the air and within the hand a gun. The gun fired once, wavered, then slowly withdrew into the encompassing gold.

CHAPTER TWENTY-SEVEN

Winter seized the plains like a spasm, freezing the streams, icing the roads, fortifying the stubble on the fields into shafts of ice. There was snow, but seldom enough to render the gray and barren landscape picturesque; or there were blizzards, a different kind of flood, isolating the town even further by blocking highways and downing power lines. Those on the farms labored to save the livestock in an annually recurring crisis. Those in town curtailed activities, stayed inside, shut themselves down. Through it all, with neither trees nor landscape to impede it, an icy wind swept down from the north, passing through as fast as it could like everything else that approached the town, creating a low whistle from the poles and chimneys

289

and high-tension wires, a gelid keening that was so insistent that they noticed it only when it stopped. With the same mute persistence of their ancestors who first put the plow to the land, and of the restless Sioux and Pawnee and Omaha who preceded them, they hunkered down and endured.

But not all days froze the nostrils and brought tears to the eye. There were days when the sun shone, days when the snow was ideal for sledding and snowballs and front-yard designs. Moments of beauty and calm when the endurance made sense and reminded the inhabitants of the reason they did not follow the wind south and leave a land that tested them so.

On such a day Joan had Billy drive her to the cottonwood grove along the Muddy. They walked through the trees that stood thin and leafless and vulnerable now as if all that timorous shivering of summer had been in anticipation of just such a winter. The water had turned to opaque ice except for a slender trickle in the center of the riverbed where a dark stream bounced and heaved beneath the thinnest glass-clear film.

Joan stared at the trapped, tormented water with her eyes out of focus while Billy watched her, trying to divine her thoughts. The community's great seismic heave of tumult and dying was long since over, the last of the funerals attended, the town not only out of the media attention but already completely forgotten by the rest of the country, replaced again and yet again by other outrages. All that remained was this, he thought. Some private mourning, some emotional scars where affections and assumptions had been ripped away from the spirit.

She crossed her arms over her chest, hugging herself, but not against the cold. Billy slipped an arm around her shoulders.

"Losing anything that's been a part of your life for so many years has to be painful," he said, probing for her thoughts.

She uttered something, a negative sound, and continued to stare toward the futile dance of the imprisoned trickle of black water.

"He was with you one way or another for twenty years," Billy continued. "I understand."

"You don't," she said, turning to face him. Her cheeks glowed from the cold. "You don't get it. The scary thing is that I barely remember him at all. I have to make an effort to think about him. To be so easily forgotten—isn't that frightening?"

She pulled a poinsettia blossom from her pocket, a hasty clipping from a Christmas leftover, and tossed it onto the ice.

"What's that for?"

"For Will," she said. "For the one good thing he ever did, giving me my son."

The scarlet flower looked shockingly out of place in the winter landscape, brilliant and doomed.

They heard the grinding of compacting snow as a car pulled to a halt alongside their own. A flash of sunlight reflected through the trees from the white door. After a moment Lapolla stepped into the tiny clearing. He looked sheepish, tugging at his equipment-laden belt, avoiding their eyes as if he had intruded at a delicate moment.

"How you doing?" he asked.

"Just standing around in the cold," Billy said.

"I gotcha . . ." He tugged at his belt again. The outfit was designed for a bigger body, Billy thought. No amount of adjustment would ever make it fit Lapolla.

"What is it, Bert?" Joan asked.

"I know you probably don't want to do this," he said to Billy. "But we got a little trouble. I wonder if you'd mind giving me some advice."

The deputy hitched, then spit for no apparent reason while waiting for a response.

THE END